W9-CEJ-066

WHERE THE TRUTH LIES

WHERE THE TRUTH LIES

A NOVEL

RUPERT
HOLMES

RANDOM HOUSE
NEW YORK

This is a work of fiction. All incidents and dialogue, and all characters with the exception of some well-known historical and public figures, are products of the author's imagination and are not to be construed as real. Where real-life historical and public figures appear, the situations, incidents, and dialogues concerning those persons are entirely fictional and are not intended to depict actual events or to change the entirely fictional nature of the work. In all other respects, any resemblance to persons living or dead is entirely coincidental.

 Published in the United States by Random House, an imprint of The Random House Publishing Group, a division of Random House, Inc., New York, and simultaneously in Canada by Random House of Canada Limited, Toronto.

Library of Congress Cataloging-in-Publication Data
Holmes, Rupert.
Where the truth lies / Rupert Holmes.
p. cm.
ISBN 0-679-45220-6 (acid-free paper)
1. Women journalists—Fiction. 2. Los Angeles (Calif.)—Fiction. 3. New York (N.Y.)—Fiction. 4. Entertainers—Fiction. 5. Comedians—Fiction. 6. Singers—Fiction. I. Title.
PS3558.O367 W48 2003
813'.54—dc21 2002037054

Printed in the United States of America on acid-free paper

Random House website address: www.atrandom.com

2 4 6 8 9 7 5 3

First Edition

For Liza

Boys are capital fellows in their own way, among their mates;
but they are unwholesome companions for grown people.

Charles Lamb

AUTHOR'S NOTE

As a twenty-six-year-old woman, I had an undepleted girlish energy that allowed me the capability of living a life and writing about it at the same time. Astounding. Thus a majority of what follows was scrawled by this scrivener as it occurred in the 1970s, often within hours of the events described, the alphabetic characters and my own character being formed in the same moment and the same manner: recklessly, hastily, often indecipherably. However, I eventually came to realize that I could not publish any of what I'd written until at least one person who figures in this narrative had died. *(It's nice to have something to look forward to, don't you think?)* It was not, in fact, until this year that these pages could be printed, along with certain other writings that bear closely upon a story I've wished to tell for so very long.

I must admit I'm somewhat alarmed by the naïveté I display in some of these pages, as well as the chauvinism of not only others but myself. Things were simply very different then.

I will also confess outright that I have occasionally touched up what I wrote (though perhaps you will think I have not touched up enough). Having admitted this, let me rush to add that most of what follows is actually worded as I first inscribed it, with only some proper names and present tenses changed. My Prose Nouveau (being of a vintage frequently purple, with a tart finish) remains largely as it was, to my immense mortification and, hopefully, your mild amusement.

The writings of Lanny Morris and related material derived from my conversations with Vince Collins are reproduced here by express agreement and may not be used without written permission.

K. O'Connor
Kiawah Island, S.C.

WHERE THE TRUTH LIES

ONE

In the seventies, I had three unrelated lunches with three different men, each of whom might have done A Terrible Thing. The nature of their varying "things" ranged from obscene to unspeakable to unutterable, and you will surely understand if, as a writer, I was rather hoping that each had. (Done their particular Terrible Thing.)

In the case of my lunch with the first man, I knew by the time he rested his gold Carte Blanche card upon the meal's sizable check that my hopes were abundantly justified.

In the case of the second lunch, even while a busboy filled our water tumblers, I realized that my dining companion was as innocent (and inevitably tedious) as a playful pup. But neither of these men need concern us here.

As for Man the Third (whom you shall meet in but a few paragraphs), I left our first repast feeling much the way I feel after a dinner of *chirashi* and green tea . . . full but starving. To paraphrase Mark Twain regarding a literary puzzle, it seemed my studies had already thrown considerable darkness on the subject, and if my research continued, I would soon know nothing about the matter at all.

He had agreed to meet me for lunch at the restaurant of his choosing,

Le Carillon, which is gone now but which was, for that particular month of the mid-seventies, the restaurant of choice for the Hollywood community. Lots of brass, both hanging on the walls and seated at the tables, was the look of the period. Heaps and heaps of flowers everywhere. I was greeted (if a full military dress inspection can be called a greeting) by a searingly stunning young girl who had almost as many inches on me as I had years on her. This is my way of saying that I was a jaded twenty-six when all this took place, and if you picture me at all, you might picture me five-five in height and fairly trim from a steady diet of Tab, menthol Virginia Slims, and encroaching deadlines for slick publications. I apparently was also fairly "cute," or so lots of married men had taken the time to tell me.

I gave the hostess my name and she went searching for it in her reservation book, almost certainly the only book she had ever read through to the very end.

"O'Connor, O'Connor," she murmured, pleased to have learned a new word.

"I'm meeting with Mr. Collins," I added.

The Gossamer Girl (not just her hair—even her exposed navel was somehow gossamer) nodded in recognition and said, "Oh yes, he's just finishing his first lunch." She indicated the restaurant's small bar. "If you'll take a seat, Mizz O'Connor"—the use of "Ms." was still quite new at the time, and she buzzed charmingly on the letter *s*—"I'll let you know when he's ready."

So it seemed I was taking a seat at the bar, which was tended by another fair Ophelia, who was just as uselessly lovely as the hostess. She stood on endless legs capped by a blank, beauteous face with the big, empty eyes of a murder victim. "Ophie" (as I'd now named her) asked me, with the delivery of an actress trying to give importance to a perfunctory part, what I'd like to drink.

"Dry vermouth on the rocks, twist. Noilly Prat if you have it," I pronounced perfectly. This was my good-behavior drink. Vermouth on the rocks at lunch was the seventies equivalent of mineral water. We all drank at lunch in the seventies. How any competent work was done after three in the afternoon during that decade is, for me, as mysterious a question as the one I had for Mr. Collins, upon whose pleasure I was waiting.

There was a brass-framed mirror behind the bar, hung on the bottle-green velvet wall between an ornamental brass coal scuttle and an ornamental brass footbath. In the mirror, I could see the back of Vince Collins's head. He was seated with a female who was dressed in a women's business outfit of the time—pin-striped jacket, vest, extremely tight skirt riding high on her thighs. I couldn't see Vince's face, but the female's alternated between an earnest *"Does what I'm saying make any sense?"* expression and an occasional giddy laugh, apparently more at something he had said than at something she had said. I couldn't hear his voice as more than a low, burry murmur.

My vermouth was set before me by the Oph. I had the thought that when Vince finally allowed me to sit at the grown-ups' table, I would not want to be making my business pitch while contending with food that required advanced cutlery skills. I had once tried to promote a series of essays on "high infidelity" to an editor at *Viva Magazine* while simultaneously attempting to disassemble the near covey of quails that littered my plate. Never again. We were now, in the seventies, well into the Age of Egg-Based Skillet Cuisine, and I wondered if a ratatouille crepe or Gruyère omelette was on the bill of fare. I certainly wasn't going to order anything that couldn't be cut with the side of my fork.

"Might I see a menu?" I asked of the Oph.

"Oh, don't worry, they'll be giving you one when you sit down at your table," she reassured me in her most affable Braniff Airlines stewardess manner and moved to the other end of the bar.

In the mirror, Vince's table companion laughed again, displaying several sets of teeth. Vince laughed as well, low and lovely, as one might expect from a pop recording artist who'd been heavily influenced by Crosby and Como.

In a magnificent manifestation of the Totally Disproportionate Reaction, I was now beginning to feel . . . rejected. Yes. Hurt, jilted by this man who had never met me. My ears were toasting with embarrassment and jealousy. His pin-striped lady friend in the mirror had become the embodiment of girls I'd loathed in high school—hurtful girls whose names I'd long ago forgotten, Janet Maitlin, Ann Rakowsky, Lisa Robb, Sarah Connelly, and Barbara Tozer. The goblet of vermouth before me was the humiliating punch bowl of the Sadie Hawkins dance where Kevin McMahon had arrived with me but danced the evening thereafter with another. And Vince—

"Mr. Collins is ready for you to join him at his new table," said my perishable hostess.

I got down from my seat at the bar feeling, yes, a bit absurd about my wounded heart. My left eye saw Vince's dining companion departing the restaurant. She had stopped to laugh with a table of men. One slid his hand onto her pin-striped rear end. She laughed at this as if her left buttock were the Algonquin Round Table and his flattened palm George S. Kaufman. The hostess led me like a sedated calf to a spanking-brand-new table where Vince was waiting upon my arrival. The restaurant's lead busboy rushed around Vince, transferring his half-finished bourbon on the rocks and chaser from his prior table to our new table, wiping the glasses clean of condensation as he set them down.

"Sorry to keep you waiting," said Vince in an absurdly familiar baritone.

People think to themselves all sorts of things that would be embarrassing or humiliating if heard aloud, and thank God, they rarely voice them. As a writer, however, I've always felt it's precisely my job to voice exactly such things and for you to enjoy hearing them and for me simply not to mind my embarrassment and humiliation . . . as a diabetic doesn't *mind* a hypodermic injection, as a boxer doesn't *mind* a sharp blow to the head. This is nothing more than the shamanlike obligation clearly stated in the job description when I first applied to the Famous Writers' School for Famous Writing.

So I will voice that, in the moment when I first met Vince Collins, my rush of thoughts ran: *My God he is truly gorgeous* (*gorgeous* not being a word I can recall ever using previously), *He's a little shorter than I thought he'd be, That cashmere turtleneck and camel's hair jacket must have cost a fortune,* and *I wonder if he's circumcised.*

Please understand I was not thinking this last thought because there was anything visibly bulging in the vicinity of his crotch. I just had this premonition that I would have a definitive answer before I was done with him, or he with me.

It was, however, a very nicely trousered crotch.

"Not at all," I said, which was a bit of a mismatch to his "Sorry to keep you waiting." I sat, but as I attempted to segue into the clever opening I'd formulated over the course of several days and practiced to a state of careless perfection, Gossamer Girl intruded herself, bearing my half-finished vermouth from the bar. As she set the goblet down before me, its oversized straw fell out of the glass and onto the carpet.

"Oh, your straw," she said, as if I were the one who'd dropped it. Reflexively, I reached to pick it up, but she corrected me. "Don't do that," she said. "We have more." She gave a look at the busboy, pointing at the straw so that he and everyone else in the restaurant would see it. I looked back at Vince. My lemon wedge was sitting stupidly in the middle of my glass before me and I was sitting stupidly in the middle of my chair behind me. There we all were: my chair, my lemon, my straw, my self. "I've never been here before," I said unfathomably.

"Have you had something to eat?" he asked.

"Oh sure, while cooling my heels at the bar I consumed a bowl of lobster bisque, Chateaubriand for two, potatoes lyonnaise, petit pois with pearl onions, scarfed up a half carafe of pallid claret, and concluded with a large Dairy Queen dipped in rainbow sprinkles. You made a lunch appointment with me, I've been seated at your table all of forty seconds, and you want to know if I've eaten. Of course I haven't eaten."

Of course I didn't say this. I opted instead for a chipper "No, but actually I had a late breakfast. I'm not really very hungry."

A waiter appeared. Vince looked at him and said, "Nope." The waiter understood and turned to me. Vince counseled, "If you're hungry, the soft-shell crabs here are out of this world."

"Soft-shell crabs it is," I intoned smoothly with a small-mouthed smile, handing the waiter my menu while suppressing a tidal wave of absolute panic. I've avoided soft-shell crabs my entire life. I'm not comfortable with any mode of consuming them. I've actually seen people hold them in both hands, biting away at an entire dead animal as if it were a foul gray sandwich. I hate soft-shell crabs.

"Good choice," nodded Vince.

"Yum," I concurred.

He took a small pull at his bourbon on the rocks. I could detect its aroma from across the table, caramel and chocolate and grown-up. Vince was a grown-up. A lot of guys my age sported hair twice the length of mine, wore chokers of faux jade and faux teak, and favored bracelets carved from rhinoceros bone. Vince wore a watch. A thick, heavy, expensive watch. If he were ever kidnapped, he could turn that watch over to his captors and walk free, and they'd probably give him twenty dollars for cab fare home.

"So my manager sent me over some of your work," he said. "You have a pretty interesting angle on things." A slight frown. "What you said about the Rolling Stones wasn't very nice."

I searched my memory. "The only reference I've ever made to the Rolling Stones was to compare them to Orpheus, Liszt, and Frank Sinatra."

"I know. That wasn't very nice. I don't care what you say about the other two guys, but Frank is a friend of mine." He turned his drink clockwise as if he were fine-tuning a radio station. "The thing about Ben Gazzara was pretty good, what I read of it."

"Thank you."

"And the one about Godfrey Cambridge." He stopped rotating his drink and eyed me. "Funny, you were really *in* them a lot."

I hoped I wasn't sure what he meant. "Into the people I was interviewing?"

He took the most infinitesimal sip of his bourbon, as if it were merely a reminder to himself to have a drink sometime in the future. "No, I mean you were *in* the interviews a lot. All over the place, almost every sentence. They were as much about you as about them."

I winced and fumbled, "Well, that's a new journalistic style and sort of what magazine editors currently seem to want—"

"I mean, Godfrey Cambridge does a great stand-up and Oskar Werner's a nice enough actor, so I understand why someone would want to read about them, but whenever I read one of these interviews where the interviewer says, *'This is how I felt the morning I woke up to meet the Pope and this is how I felt when the Pope greeted me and, you know, the Pope reminded me so much of my very best friend Mike,'* I always think, 'Who the fuck is Mike? Who are you? You don't do a stand-up, you've never been in a movie, why am I supposed to be interested in you? I'm interested in the Pope, tell me about *him.*' "

Add me to the list of today's specials, I thought, skewered and flambéed. He must have seen me withering and wilting because he rushed to add, rather kindly, "But fortunately for you, you come off as interesting. So you can kind of get away with it."

Joy. He seemed to be liking me. He took a normal sip on his bourbon, which my research said was Jack Daniel's.

Vince continued, "Okay, so: a million dollars is a lot of money. I can get that for acting in a picture or two, but for a book that you would write *for* me? Who do I have to sleep with?"

I started to reply but he added, "Incidentally, if the answer is you, I might do this deal for nine hundred thousand."

I loved it. *(I know, I know, but Vince Collins had just told me he found me desirable to the tune of a hundred grand. I loved it. Leave me alone.)* Filing the compliment under "Mornings When I Hate Myself: Remedies," I tried to get us back to business. "You've heard of Neuman and Newberry?"

"Your publisher."

"*Your* publisher, if you go along with this. They're launching a new men's magazine, it's going to be called *Master**—like *Playboy, Penthouse,* but with a heavier emphasis on journalism. For men who used to read the original version of the *L.A. Free Press* or *Rolling Stone* but have grown to enjoy the feel of slick paper. The photo layouts will be slicker, too. Mock Scavullo with a tinge of S and M. The whole image of the magazine will be very hip, very trendy."

As I pitched this, Vince reached for a straw that stood in a glass of neat club soda next to his bourbon. He put his finger atop the straw, sealing off one end, and lifted the straw over to his drink. The straw remained full of club soda; none spilled out as he lifted it. I remembered seeing an experiment like this in seventh-grade science, something to do with air pressure or water tension. Vince's hand and straw poised over his bourbon on the rocks like a casual bombardier. He lifted his fingertip away from the top of the straw, and the club soda flumed down into his drink. Vince was to repeat this action throughout our conversation, topping off his bourbon with little dashes of club soda. That and his extremely small sips might account for why Vince was never seen not drinking in public but was never seen publicly drunk.

"Okay. Put me down for a year's subscription," said Vince.

"What Neuman and Newberry want from me is a book about you. Not a puff piece—but let me rush to add," I rushed to add, "that it would also not be a hatchet job. If you look through my work, you'll see I try to present a balanced view of my subjects. I leave all conclusions to the reader."

Vince took a sip on his drink and chewed a piece of ice he'd found within it. "But . . . I don't think we *like* 'balanced,'" he smiled in all seriousness. "We *like* puff pieces. We don't really want the reader arriving at their own conclusion, do we? I'm not running for public office. I don't

*The magazine was ultimately named *Pulse* and lasted only five issues.

affect your taxes or a housing project in Schenectady or decide whether or not we go to war. I'm a goddamn Guinea crooner doing the occasional impersonation of a movie actor. I get publicized, not analyzed."

It wasn't as if I hadn't expected this response. I'd come prepared with a Plan A through Plan H. I wanted this deal. I wanted the check attached to this deal. They would put the book in the window, and wherever the cover photo and the name Vince Collins were displayed, my name would be right beneath them. I jumped to Plan G. "It would be only your words," I offered.

Another minuscule sip. "How would that work?" he asked.

"I will only quote you. We'd publish the book as a transcript. I won't twist your words around, paraphrase you, or quote you out of context. It would be up to me to get what I need out of you. You'd be responsible, however, for anything you said. We'd tape the interviews—I'll need several weeks of your time, maybe months, although I can work around your schedule. If you say it, I can use it. If you don't, I can't."

He looked around the room for the first time since I'd sat down. A man with distinguished silver hair was sporting distinguished silver muttonchops, a gleaming silver choker, and a blue tank top that allowed all of us to see that his underarm hair was similarly distinguished. I'd have estimated that his breasts, nicely outlined behind his tank top, were at least a B-cup. The man saw Vince, hoisted his drink in a *salut.* Vince did nothing and looked back at me. "What if I were just to talk about the weather?"

"No, you'd have to answer all my questions. There would be no *'no comment'*—we'd put that in the contract. You'll have to trust that you can answer in the way that you want, and I'll have to trust that I can get from you what I need. My publishers are confident that I can." This last part may not have been true, but Vince didn't need to know that. I think I was feeling the vermouth a little.

Another plop of club soda from the straw, like a police lab technician examining a bloodstain under a microscope and adding a drop of some chemical reagent from a long pipette. "So I don't understand how this book connects up with this magazine they're starting."

"They want to amortize their investment in you. They're looking for some very strong stories for the magazine's debut. A prepublication excerpt from your book would be a great addition to the premiere issue."

He knew where this was leading. "Any thoughts on what the excerpt would be about?"

There was no way to finesse it. "Sure. It'll be about the Girl in New Jersey. I'll want you to tell as much as I can get out of you on the subject. That would be the focus of the magazine piece. The book will cover your entire life."

Vince thought about this. He reached for a cigarette from a pack of Viceroys. I liked that he didn't have an expensive case for them, although he could well have afforded it. He offered me one.

"I have my own," I said, reaching for my pocketbook. "I'll join you."

He did have an expensive lighter, a stick, as solid as gold can get. As he lit my Virginia Slims menthol, he asked, "And would Lanny be putting his two cents into this as well?"

I thought of the folded-up letter from Lanny's attorney that was resting deep within my bag. "Lanny says he's writing his own book about it."

Vince laughed one laugh. "That's rich." He downed his bourbon in something more than a sip. "We like that," he said, meaning he didn't like that.

TWO

Dear Miss O'Connor:

I am a partner in the law firm of Weisner, Hillman and Dumont, which currently represents Mr. Lanny Morris on a wide range of business affairs. We are in receipt of your letter of July 19, which was in response to a letter from my senior partner Mr. John Hillman dated July 11, which was in turn a reply to your initial letter of June 28 regarding a proposed book about our client, to be written by you for Neuman and Newberry Publishing, Inc.

Mr. Hillman has asked me to relay to you that he has indeed spoken again personally with Mr. Morris regarding both of your letters, and can reconfirm for you that our client has *no* interest at this time in assisting any biographical efforts regarding his life or career, or the life or career of his former partner, Mr. Vince Collins. The monetary terms and royalties you proposed on Neuman and Newberry's behalf, while both considerable and appropriate for an artist of Mr. Morris's stature in the entertainment industry, do not enter into this decision. Money is not an issue here. With all due respect, our client is simply not interested in the project you propose.

We are not, as your second letter seems to suggest, unaware of your own credentials, which are quite impressive for someone to have accrued in only, as you state, "the five years since [your] first published article." Actually, Mr. Hillman informs me he read and enjoyed a piece you wrote about the jazz musician Miles Davis for Esquire Magazine last year. Our client's decision is not a personal or professional rejection of either you or the generous offer proposed by you on behalf of Neuman and Newberry.

In point of fact, it is my understanding that Mr. Morris is well under way with the writing of his memoirs, and therefore would clearly not wish to undercut his own autobiographical efforts by lending support or assistance to a third-party effort, since his own recollections will provide the public with the most accurate and personal account of his memorable career.

Please be advised that we are prepared to exercise all our client's rights and options to prevent any unauthorized or unlicensed works trading upon the life, name, or likeness of Mr. Morris, and will pursue all legal remedies at our disposal to discourage same.

Very truly yours,

Warren Richter, Esq.

WR:ah

cc: Mr. John Hillman, Esq.
Mr. Lanny Morris

THREE

Like all single women transplanted to L.A., almost immediately upon arrival I became the ecstatically proud owner of a clunker of a used convertible. Mine was canary yellow. A nice thing about being a woman in southern California was that you felt no shame claiming a deadbeat car from a parking valet. For a woman, a beat-up convertible was thought to be a personality trait, and in L.A., a little personality went a long, long way—so much so that Hollywood imported people like me from the East who still had one (a personality, not a convertible). On the other hand, a man in L.A. shrank from acknowledging ownership of a rusted Chevy Caprice like a rock-star father of a groupie's baby in a paternity suit.

I believe there was a regulation that such cars had to have either one door that wouldn't open (or if it could, it could not then be closed again) or one window that wouldn't roll down (or if it could, it could not then be rolled up again). I had selected the more exclusive "nonfunctional door *and* window" option package from Cal Worthington at Worthington Ford, along with a fully functional AM radio.

At the moment, a recent oldie was playing on said radio in the full glory of monophonic sound, a breezy rendering of "Fool on the Hill"—not the Beatles version but a 1968 remake by Sergio Mendes and Brasil

'66. Continued success had caught the group totally by surprise and they'd recently had to scramble and rename themselves Brasil '77. In only a few more years they'd have to raise their integers again, and logically this process would continue into the new millennium, when they'd become Brasil '11, which struck me as sounding like a partial volleyball score. To its light-headed arpeggiation, I wheeled my sassy way into the Hollywood Way gate of what was now being billed as the Burbank Studios.

It had once been the private property of Warner Bros., but the studios were coping with harder times, and back lots were being converted into profitable tract housing. MGM's acreage was now supplying middle-class shelter for those who had once sought shelter in an MGM picture. *Sic transit Gloria Swanson.* Paramount was down to nothing. Whenever their *Mission: Impossible* TV series needed a generic Iron Curtain city street, they'd hang a generically foreign sign such as FUMEN NET outside the studio cafeteria, whose exterior had been cunningly designed decades ago in a Bavarian Tudor style to serve just such a purpose. This was pretty much the extent of their back lot. Twentieth Century–Fox still had the elevated train set from *Hello, Dolly!* but little else. Universal was a theme park where, from your tram, you might catch a glimpse of Darren McGavin and Jo Ann Pflug lensing a Tuesday Night Movie of the Week.

Only Warners' Burbank Studio still had those gloriously overlapping structures that could one morning be a hotel courtyard on the Île de la Cité with a curlicued Métro entrance just beyond its wrought-iron gates and the next day be the Russian embassy in midtown Manhattan. Not to mention a slew of western streets from the days when Warners cranked out *Cheyenne, Bronco, Sugarfoot, Maverick,* et al.

Vince had been given office space in one of the two-story structures recently assembled not far from the ersatz New York streets that demarcated the northern fringe of the lot, a no doubt intentional distance from the main administration building. These structures looked like nothing more than a respectable motel, which was appropriate, as the rooms had a fast check-in and checkout rate. They generally served as cubbyholes for new talent, who were being rewarded with their own little production office to match their own little production deal, or as a morgue for stale talent, this final relocation the equivalent of being asked to vacate the premises.

Vince was neither of these commodities. While he was no longer the box-office champ he'd once been, his name alone could carry a movie to the break-even mark, and coupled with a popular actress and a script that suited his intentionally offhand style, he could still rake in a few shekels. The fourth entry in the series of films featuring his soldier-of-fortune character Colt Carrera had actually been well received by the critics, at least for the kind of mindless escapist fare that it was. *Death Is Cold* with Angel Tompkins and Victor Buono had not netted as much as *Death Is Warm* or *Death Is Green,* but no one had yet voiced the notion that Vince was slipping. His most recent film, *Casa Grande,* was still in production. It was a Warners project, and while Vince was shooting interiors and a few street scenes on the western sets nearby, the company had given him the suite of offices as a home away from the well-appointed Winnebago that awaited him on any outdoor shoot.

I parked my Caprice and walked up a flight of concrete steps to the second level. Midway along was a door bearing the discreet lettering PAUS & ANTER. I had researched my prey well enough to know that this was the name of Vince's production company, and not a badly spelled invitation. The company was really named after his three children, Paul, Sandi, and Terri. The ampersand was just Vince's little joke. He had another production company created solely to keep a few pennies out of the hands of his ex-wife. That company was called "FTC Productions." When someone asked what the letters stood for, Vince said the T was for *That.*

I paused and entered. There was a compact woman in her thirties behind a desk talking down to someone on the phone. She looked up and through me. "Yes?"

"I'm here to see Vince Collins. My name's O'Connor."

She got up from her desk and took me back onto the walkway outside the office. She pointed toward the buttressed backs of some standing street sets. "He should be on Maple Street. See that curving street with the old-fashioned houses? He should be at the end of it. Walk on over, he's expecting you."

I'd been in L.A. for a while now and I'd forgotten about walking. I passed a firehouse that was a town hall on its north face and a bank on its south face. I was curious enough to saunter around to its fourth side. A movie theater. I turned onto a gracefully curving street that had to be Maple. It could have been a background cel for *Lady and the Tramp.* Every house was painted white, and trees were plentiful along the street, although some of them had clearly been rented rather than rooted, and nary a one of them was actually a maple.

I was relieved to see there was no movie crew. In point of fact, there was no one on the street at all. Narration by Rod Serling would have been appropriate. It was as if I had turned a corner and found the way back to my childhood, an immaculate, shaded street in a small midwestern town, orderly and respectable and caringly maintained. Only that hadn't been my childhood, not in the slightest.

I heard a pleasant, light *ponk* and saw Vince. He was on the front lawn of the last house on the street, its thick grass mowed low and even, stroking a neat row of golf balls into what apparently was a hole in the ground—yes, it was a perfect putting green. He was wearing a cardigan the shade of Gulden's mustard over a smooth white turtleneck, with nice trim pants in a herringbone pattern. His socks were tan and his loafers were brown and tasseled.

"Hi again," he said without taking his eye off the ball. He stroked a slow, assured putt into the cup. "Thanks for walking over. Nice street, huh?"

"Very Thornton Wilder," I murmured. Remembering that Vince hadn't finished high school, I added, "He wrote a play called *Our Town.*"

He was focused on another ball. "That's right, and *The Matchmaker* and *The Skin of Our Teeth.*" He looked up at me for the first time with a strange smile on his face. "What, you think I've never heard of Thornton Wilder? Gee, you must really take me for a greaseball." He gave a little shiver, which looked odd on a warm day. "Jesus."

I tendered my apology. "I'm sorry if at our first meeting I forgot to mention that I'm frequently a total idiot." I was pleased to see him smile back, so I tried to change the subject with the incisive observation: "It's so quiet here."

Vince lined himself up behind a golf ball. "Well, this is a *real* back lot, you know, not like that fireman's carnival over at Universal. You're only supposed to be here if you're making a movie or preparing the set for one. Just so happens no one's making a movie right now."

"No TV?"

"*The Waltons,* but their house is way over by the lagoon."

"They shoot *The Waltons* here?"

"That's Walton's Mountain behind you."

I turned back and tried to mentally crop out the high-tension wires on the brown scrubby hillside rising directly behind the lot. "My God. That *is* Walton's Mountain. I always assumed they shot that on location."

"They did. This is the location."

I shook my head. "I've driven by that hill a thousand times. Forest Lawn is off to the right, isn't it? My God, Walton's Mountain. Burbank."

Vince collected up the golf balls and dropped them into a wooden box, which he set down on the front porch of the house. "If you like this part of Burbank," he said, taking off his cardigan and draping it over his arm, "let me show you somewhere even better."

I was apparently to get the tour. We hooked around the end of Maple and headed up a western street. It was the end of the afternoon on a Friday, a day viewed by most of the L.A. workforce as purely optional. With the studio successfully evacuated until Monday, we were completely alone, strolling the streets of a ghost town.

There were perhaps better times to reflect that some people in my trade believed Vince Collins might once have been involved in the murder of a young woman. Personally, I found this impossible to believe, not only because Vince was so attractive but also because he had made so many successful movies since then. (I realize there's an underlying flaw in this line of reasoning, but wouldn't our world be so much better if we all tried harder to put our trust in people who dress really well and purchase superior colognes? Or do you find me a tad shallow?)

A saloon bore the painted sign PARIS, TEXAS, apparently one of the locales of his latest Western, a genre that was gradually exceeding musicals, comedies, and adventure films in his repertoire. I asked him idly what accounted for his recent emphasis on sagebrush and saddles.

"Italian Westerns are big right now." He smiled. "Who's more Italian, me or Clint Eastwood? My next film is *The Dago Red River Valley.*"

We rounded a turn into another long western boulevard, this one slightly uphill and coated with a black siltlike powder.

"You see this dirt?" he asked, kicking up a smoky cloud of dust. "So, this is Laramie Street—they use it mainly for the more civilized western towns after the Civil War. Dodge City, Tombstone, Laredo. But it can also double for 1890s San Francisco. And if you want to use it for a 1920s or '30s setting, all you have to do is put in some old electric streetlamps, make the saloons into general stores and emporiums, and you have yourself your perfect midwestern Depression town. But the dirt road is a dead giveaway. It should be a paved street, and sure they could pave it, but then they wouldn't be able to use it as a western set the next day. So what they do is . . ."

He bent down, picked up some of the inky dirt of the street.

". . . they spray-paint the dirt black."

I squinted at the well-rutted street, and sure enough, the jet-black dirt *would* read as paving, certainly in long shot. "They're probably doing this for a *Waltons* episode. You know, *'John Boy goes into town to buy compost and cornpone'*?" Vince stood up, smacking the dirt off his hands. "The first time I saw them doing this, I thought, 'Yup, that's what Hollywood is. A place where they give dirt a paint job.'" He smiled disarmingly. "Did you bring that letter?"

"Yes, I've got it here." He watched me as I reached into my bag and produced the letter from Lanny's attorney. It had been with me on Wednesday at Le Carillon, but I hadn't wanted to show it to Vince until I was sure I wasn't committing some kind of legal or ethical breach. "It's a letter to you," I'd been told by Bernard Besser, senior attorney for Neuman and Newberry. "From a junior partner in a law firm. He doesn't characterize anything as being privileged information. You can show it to anyone you like." I was liking Vince, so I showed it to him.

He read it as we crossed the street. I looked both ways, which was absurd since there wasn't a car on the lot. He folded it up and handed it back. "I guess if Lanny is going to talk about things, I can too, huh?"

We were now flanked by two rows of venerable New York brownstones. I asked casually, "So, have you and Lanny talked since the split-up?"

"Never," he said quickly.

"Why?"

He took my arm so gently that it was impossible to take offense. "Off the record? Lanny can be a bit of a monster. A cruel one." He waved away the thought by gesturing at the brownstones. "This is my favorite street because it looks exactly like my old neighborhood. If we had a broomstick and a Spaldeen—that's what we called those pink rubber balls that Spalding used to make—you and I could have ourselves a nice game of highsie-lowsie."

I looked at a street sign. "Euclid Avenue."

"That's what *they* call it. For me, it's Forbes Avenue and Hooper."

"We had a Euclid Avenue where I grew up."

Vince conceded, "Yeah, I've never understood this 'Euclid' thing. Most every town I've ever played has a Euclid Avenue. How do you figure that? I understand a Maple Street, Oak, Elm, Washington or Jefferson, Broadway or Main. But . . . *Euclid?* When did a Greek mathematician become beloved to the people of this nation? Does every town have an Archimedes Avenue? A Pythagoras Plaza?"

He was much smarter than I'd anticipated. There was also something strangely familiar about his riff. It wasn't until later that I realized he was to some degree aping the delivery of Lanny Morris. Maybe when you work so long with somebody, you don't even notice you're doing it.

As I laughed, I leaned against a brownstone wall and a piece of its plaster broke off behind me. He reached out to steady me and ushered me to where Euclid Avenue made a T-shaped intersection with French Street.

"And, uhhh, 'you must remember this,'" Vince murmured, gesturing to a lovely brownish-gray boulevard that revealed itself as we turned the corner. It was a location from *Casablanca,* one that had been etched into my retinas years ago. The current moniker of "the Burbank Studios" had made me forget that this was still *that* Warner Bros., and this corner was where Rick and Ilsa had first been in love, in flashback, within a few steps of the Arc de Triomphe.

"I'm in the same French street where Bogart and Bergman were," I murmured.

"It's just plaster of Paris." He smiled. Oh, what a clever lad was he, who had displayed in several of his films the same gruff masculine hurt that Bogart had patented a generation earlier. It made me remember that Vince was a movie star. When I was nine, I'd seen this same man embrace Lizabeth Scott and Martha Hyer on corners exactly like this. I'd stared at the screen, twenty-five-cent bag of popcorn in my hands, my eyes and palms growing damp.

I looked now at Vince, his shoulders wide beneath his turtleneck, his breath so charming, his hair so nicely tousled. What were we up to? I wondered.

I was not yet acclimated to dusk on the West Coast. The sun hung around much longer, shining at unusual low angles that I wasn't used to seeing. The clouds were a livid violet wall, assembled in the south end of the sky like an Apache nation preparing to descend upon the cavalry.

Now Vince led me past a cosmopolitan row of buildings verging on what could have passed for Central Park South and Fifth Avenue and up a hillock through a Bohemian village designed in early Gepetto. Paris had yielded to Germany as easily as Alsace-Lorraine had to Hitler. There was a rounded doorway set in brick between a cobbler's shop and a tobacconist's. Vince swung open the door, revealing the beginning of a long flight of slate steps down an overgrown hillside. I don't mean ten or twenty steps. I mean Cinderella Running from the Palace at Ten Seconds to Midnight steps, down and down the side of a ravine.

"Okay, so what you have to do is not look back until I say so," instructed Vince. "Just look straight down at your feet and the steps and don't turn around until I tell you."

I said okay, and he led the way, walking sideways like a crab. Vince was literally leading me down the garden path, for I perceived vegetation on either side of me, thick moss and ivy, and beds of tall plum-colored flowers matching the damson sky.

"Okay," he said at last. "Turn around."

I did. Delirium. Rising high above me, as if pressed into the side of a soaring cliff, were the almost Gothic towers and turrets of an immense Asian castle. Mad spires and ominous gates were cloaked in writhing tendrils of overgrowth. Every now and then the cliff was broken up into little plateaus, with a stone bench here, an incense burner there, and flat rocks that might have been altars for strange rituals.

Dumbstruck, I looked to Vince for elucidation.

"Shangri-La," he explained. "The main exterior for that *Lost Horizon* musical. With those great crooners Peter Finch and Liv Ullmann. A big bomb."

"The set alone must have broken their budget," I said.

He straightened a small statue of a dragon. "They've amortized their losses a little by using it on the TV series *Kung Fu*. They never show the entire set, but they do tight two-shots and it reads as Asia."

Burbank again. Who knew.

"You want to have a drink?" he asked.

"When?"

"Now."

"Where?"

"There." He indicated a Winnebago resting on concrete blocks at the foot of the hillside. "Warners keeps this for me when I'm filming here." The trailer was long and wide, no doubt long enough for a well-stocked bar, certainly wide enough for a queen-sized bed.

Ah. Aha. So we had gone through the Lollipop Woods, around the Rainbow Trail and up the Gumdrop Pass, evaded the Molasses Swamp, and now we had finally arrived by an exact throw of the dice at Candyland, where I was to be the bonbon bonanza with the creamy filling, the fornicated fondant, the all-day sucker to cap off Vince's afternoon of stroking golf balls into a vacant receptacle on his personal putting green. This was why I'd been taken on my VIP backstage Burbank tour, at the culmination of which our guests are respectfully reminded that it is traditional for the tour guide to receive gratuitous sex if you were pleased with his services. And I'd been gawking and geeking my hayseed way through the whole thing like a breathless heroine in a Harlequin novel. I wouldn't have been surprised if there were a painting in Vince's trailer of his most recent ex-wife, guarded by the compact woman from his office, whose name would turn out to be Danvers. *"This was the* previous *Mrs. Collins. They found her shattered body at the foot of the castle's highest turret."*

I felt foolish and disappointed and insulted. (Did I mention I felt foolish as well?) Quickly, I also felt the fear that Vince's interest in collaboration would extend no further than the stubbing out of our postcoital cigarettes. I wanted the book deal badly. I also found Vince attractive. I had to handle both of us very carefully.

I looked down the last few steps and toward his trailer. "So this is what I've descended to?" I said this lightly, as if it were merely a play on words.

He smiled affably. "You don't have to join me if you don't want to. I'm just a little thirsty." He started toward the steps leading into the Winnebago. I stayed put. He fumbled apologetically, "I, uh, I really have to have something. When I was fifteen, me and the guys went out and tied one on. I got home around midnight. My mother took one look at me and said, 'Vince, you *must* be drunk.'" He paused. "And I've been following her orders ever since." It was clearly one of his stock lines. "So . . . I'm having a drink."

"Do you want to sleep with me?" I asked him.

He replied, in a nice manner rather than a leering one, "Well, I'm sure

I'm not the first man who wanted to. You're interesting, smart, and attractive. Yes, I'd like to sleep with you very much. But, actually, I'm just asking you inside to have a drink."

I knew that if we both went inside, and if we both had the drink, we'd both be having sex before the low California sun had set. I think he knew it too. I said, not mean-spiritedly, "I think I need to know about the proposition I put to you yesterday before we discuss any proposition you might have for me today."

He sat down on a step and looked at me as if disillusioned. I couldn't tell if this was fake or not. Vince had starred in some bad scripts, but he was not a bad actor. "Are you saying you'll say yes to my proposal if I say yes to yours?"

"No. I won't sleep with you if I'm working on the book with you."

He laughed. "But then if I say I won't do the deal, you *will* sleep with me?"

"No, I won't sleep with you if you turn down the deal." Now I could have used the drink he had offered me. "But I'll sleep with you when the book is done."

I think I almost surprised him.

I added, "Hell, I might even sleep with you twice. I find you 'interesting, smart, and attractive.' On top of which you're Vince Collins. It would be fun to be watching a movie on TV with a friend and suddenly you come on the screen and I say casually, 'I've slept with him.'"

"What if, in the course of interviewing me, you hear things that make you decide you don't like me? You'll still sleep with me?"

Could I marry someone I didn't like? I don't think so. Could I sleep with them, once, if they were physically attractive? Puh-leez. "Everyone has character flaws," I shrugged. "As you're already learning about me. I wouldn't be doing this book if I didn't believe there's something controversial or sordid I can learn about you. I'd be shocked if I didn't turn up something unseemly, and my employers would be outright angry. So when I threw myself into the offer, it wasn't with the illusion that you're a saint. The deal is the deal."

He moved toward me and held out his hand. I took it. It felt long and dry. "Okay, you give me your word and I'll give you my words."

"I give you my word."

He walked up the steps to his trailer. "My attorney is Harold Cohen;

Lucille in my office will give you his number." He motioned to the door. "The offer still goes, for the drink." I thought it was better not to and said as much. He apologized, "Well, forgive me if I don't walk you back, but I'm going to have one. By the way, you don't have to go back up the steps." He pointed out a route around the bottom of the hill that would lead me to the parking lot and my Caprice. I watched him open the trailer door and some perverse imp made me ask, with my head slightly perched, "So was *I* what clinched the deal?" It was despicable fishing on my part.

He moved down a step. "If I had planned to say no to the book, that would mean I think you're pretty hot stuff, wouldn't it? On the other hand, if I'd been planning to sign all along, I may have just gotten a piece of your sweet tush for free. You're the brains in this outfit. You tell me." He stepped into his trailer, leaving me with a last smile, his warmest of the day, but like the low sun of dusk in Los Angeles, its appearance and its angle looked a bit odd, all the same.

An hour later, at my apartment complex in Studio City, I passed the fragrant, sticky blossoms that surrounded a small fountain outside my window. Their fumes were a fine marriage with the scent of Jungle Gardenia I always wore. I stopped to open my mailbox in the sheltered area outside my door and instantly saw that one of the letters was from Weisner, Hillman and Dumont, the law firm that represented Lanny Morris.

FOUR

Dear Miss O'Connor:

My associate Warren Richter has kept me apprised of your continued dialogue with our office. I apologize for "dropping out" temporarily from our correspondence and hope you'll agree that all our communications have been cordial in tone and respectful of the artistic accomplishments of both yourself and our client Mr. Lanny Morris.

Since Mr. Richter's last letter to you, I have again personally spoken with Mr. Morris regarding your interest in his career. I will be candid and tell you that he initiated this particular phone call, in which he informed me he had read more of the work samples your agent has made available, and that he continues to be impressed with your talents.

While my client is still not interested in creating or endorsing the project you proposed in your first letter to our firm (a book to be underwritten and eventually published by a division of Neuman and Newberry), he also does not wish to impede or obstruct any efforts on your part to create a work about his life and career. In fact, he has expressed to me a desire to, in a small way, assist you in this endeavor. (I say this, of course, without prejudice to my client's legal rights.)

Toward this end, I am wondering if you would be willing to present yourself to this office Tuesday, August 12, at noon. If that is not convenient, please call so we may arrange an alternative date. We are advising you in advance that you will not be allowed to make use of any kind of tape recording or transcription device on our premises, nor will you be allowed to make any written notes. We hope you will understand that this is a regrettable necessity in order to protect Mr. Morris's interests, and is unfortunately a prerequisite of your acceptance of the appointment. Likewise, your person and any property you bring with you may be examined by a security woman we will engage for such purposes, so you may wish to dress and accessorize yourself so as to most easily facilitate and simplify such an examination. Again, we assure you that these stern-sounding dictums are precautionary measures and are not, of course, intended to cast any personal aspersions upon you.

I very much look forward to meeting you in person. Please contact us upon receipt of this letter to confirm or reschedule.

Very truly yours,

John Hillman

John Hillman, Esq.

JH:rv

cc: Mr. Warren Richter, Esq.
Mr. Lanny Morris

FIVE

The receptionist was on the phone with a new boyfriend and smoking a new brand of cigarettes being test-marketed on the West Coast. Tramps, they were called, an attractive tan-colored cigarette bearing the licensed image of Charlie Chaplin on every pack. "Buy 'em or bum 'em" was their slogan, cute cigarettes marketed to give cute cancer to women. Weisner, Hillman and Dumont occupied an entire floor of 7760 Sunset, the last outpost of business real estate before Sunset Strip segued into Sunset Boulevard and directly across from the nicest of the Hamburger Hamlets (the one with the open Danish modern fireplace in the middle of the room, where your waiter would roast you marshmallows for dessert if you asked nicely).

The reception area could not have been more respectable if there'd been a baptismal font and a brace of acolytes. Pecan paneling outlined cream-and-gray-striped walls, upon which hung framed lithographs of sailing ships. There was no way one would have suspected that this firm was in any way connected to show business.

I got the receptionist to put her boyfriend on hold for a moment and explained that I was there to see Mr. Lanny Morris. "Not here," she said tartly and, while apologizing profusely to her boyfriend, waved me toward the seat she'd allow me to take.

Hillman's secretary came out to greet me. She was a pert British blonde named Gillian (standard issue for that rank of attorney), who was smoking a St. Moritz, an expensive menthol cigarette that came with a glossy gold band wrapped around its filter. "So you're here, t'riffic!" she gushed. She turned to the receptionist. "Leslie, could you tend to the Mr. Coffee machine, it's getting a bit like paint in there, I'm afraid. If you'll come this way, Ms. O'Connor."

She led me down several hallways filled with desks upon which Selectric typewriters were manned by middle-aged secretaries who did most of the firm's real work. Gillian was pretty giggly about things. "So you know that we have a lady who's here to frisk you, I'm afraid. Sor-ry! Are you all right about that then? T'riffic! We did warn you about that in the letter, didn't we? Although I can't think where you might hide anything in that outfit," she confided.

I'd purposely worn something clingy and see-through, a knit macramé over a body stocking, purportedly to show that I had nothing to hide but also, I suspected, to make a strong first impression on Lanny Morris. Who was not on the premises.

Gillian showed me into a small windowless law library. Before leaving, she introduced me to Naomi, a big woman who amply filled her navy blue outfit, which vaguely resembled a policewoman's uniform without actually being such.

Naomi ambled over to me and recited, "Please raise your hands above your head and move your legs as far apart as possible." In the dress I was wearing, the latter wasn't very far. Naomi then felt me up. Every part of me. I don't care what anyone else would have called it, Naomi felt me up.

The door opened. A tall, too thin fellow entered, wearing his age (mid-sixties) on his Harris tweed sleeve. His suit was crowned with what was, for the time, a defiantly conservative maroon bow tie.

"Miss O'Connor! John Hillman, very glad to have you here. I'm terribly sorry about the, uhm, you know"—he nodded toward Naomi—"but such is the situation. Now I'll need you to sign these releases where you see the X . . ."

I signed wherever he said. "I thought I was going to meet with Lanny Morris."

He nodded. "Well, in a sense you'll be doing just that." He placed a black ring binder on the library table. "This is a selection from my client's writings. He wanted you to have the opportunity to read it."

"Why?" I asked.

"My understanding is that he believed it might assist you in some way." He looked inquisitively at my gal-pal Naomi. "Miss . . . ?"

"Schall," Naomi elucidated. She was thumbing through a copy of *Seventeen* with fervid interest.

"Miss Schall will remain here to make sure you don't memorialize or take away anything you read. This material is offered as what I believe is called 'deep background.' Meaning you may not quote from or paraphrase *any* of it. You understand?"

Hillman left the room and there was this silly *Citizen Kane* moment, me seated at the room's sole mahogany library table, about to read the late Great Man's private memoirs . . . only the Great Man was very much alive and kicking. I remembered that when I'd asked Vince a few days earlier why he and Lanny had not spoken since their breakup, he'd confided, *"Because Lanny can be a bit of a monster."*

Okay. I have all the pluck of every heroine who ever idiotically blundered her way down the stone stairs of Dracula's castle to investigate a strange noise in the crypt. Besides, I had Naomi here at my side to protect me.

I touched the cover of the ring binder. "You King Kong," I thought. "Me Fay Wray. Let's meet the monster."

SIX

This is not going to be like any of my other books you've read, *Laugh Clown Laugh* by Lanny Morris with Dick Schaap, *24 Frames a Second* by Lanny Morris as told to Rex Reed, et cetera. This one I am writing all by myself, for reasons you don't want to know.

If you bought this book—and if you didn't, *"Police! Shoplifter!!"* (joke)—then you know all about me. Of course you do. They've got a street in downtown Barcelona and a movie theater in Taiwan named after me, so if you're sitting there reading this in Plainfield, New Jersey, sure, you know me.

About my life prior to the summer of 1959, anything you'd want to know is in my other books. Some of it is funnier than it is true, but after a while, the stuff that isn't true has been retold so many times that it's become true, even for me. Maybe I wasn't born quite so poor *("We was so poor that . . .")* but I definitely wasn't born rich. And maybe Vince and I actually *had* worked together once or twice before the night when my bio says we first met and invented a comedy act for ourselves in the kitchen of the Café Arcadia five minutes before we had to go on. But listen to me: what I'm going to be telling you now is as truthful as I know how to make it, even if sometimes the truth is not my best profile.

Where this accounting needs to begin is in the suite that Vince and I would share at the Miami Versailles Hotel whenever we worked there. It's their best suite, gorgeous, the presidential suite as it happens, though Eisenhower didn't stay there. It would have been a big waste if he did, because in 1959, Ike would never have been able to accommodate the procession of broads that paraded into and out of the place.

For me, back then, the world is divided up into four types of girls: sluts that I boff; nice girls who in bed turn into sluts (these girls I boff with pleasure); nice girls who remain nice in bed (these I generally leave for the working stiffs, because civilians need to get laid, too); and my mother. Her I don't boff, despite the name my manager calls me in moments of anger. I have no desire to boff my mother. I sort of have that in common with my father. (Joke.)

It's about five in the afternoon and I'm in my bedroom, just starting in on this girl. Denise is her name, she handles P.R. for the hotel. I've been marinating her for three days, very gentlemanly, very courteous and *galant,* as they say, and now I've got her dress off and she's half under the top sheet. She's wearing one of those low-cut black bras that turns into a kind of demi-corset (not that this girl needs a corset because she is really pretty skinny). The bra goes down to the end of her ribs for support and lets her breasts float like they're on a platform, which in a low-cut dress makes them seem a lot bigger than they end up being. Sort of a cheat. Her panties don't match—they're light blue, the bra is black. Why do women think this is all right?

I'm about ready to pull off the annoying panties, and she's doing nothing to stop me, when there's a knock at the door of the living room. I sigh that sigh of annoyance. "Don't go anywhere," I warn her. (Like I'm worried!) I take my black-and-maroon Dunhill robe, silk, from the dresser where Reuben, my Filipino valet, always leaves it neatly folded, and I walk to the door of the suite. It's a room-service boy, with the champagne Denise had wanted (the price of admission, from my point of view).

I usher the room-service boy into the bedroom. You can tell a lot about a woman by the way she acts when she's in bed and a room-service boy enters the room. Sometimes a girl will sit up, light a cigarette, like there's nothing in the world funny about her being naked under a sheet, me being in a robe; it's obvious that we're in the process of screwing, so why not let a stranger wearing a red uniform with gold braid into the room? Then there's the kind that pull the sheet over their head and act like they're asleep—or, even better, the ones who scrunch real flat, thinking the bed will look empty. Shyness. I like that.

This time (as happens quite frequently to Vince and myself) the room-service boy is a girl. Gorgeous, gorgeous redhead, hair flowing down like sparkling burgundy onto her gold braids. The uniform fit real nice (meaning tightly) and she had some build on her, I'll tell you. I wished then and there I could trade Denise in for her.

I'd ordered "a bottle of the bubbly, Versailles label." The bottle shows up in a nest of crushed ice, and the name Versailles makes it look like it's French, but it's really Great Western, from the Finger Lakes in upper New York State. The hotel marks it up from three to nine dollars, but it's still a lot less than the Mumm's Cordon Rouge at twenty bucks. So everyone wins: the hotel turns a fat profit, the girl thinks she's special, and I get to pop my cork. Half the time it ends up getting poured on her breasts or stomach anyway, and I defy anyone to tell imported from domestic when they're slurping it from between two D-cups that've already been soaked in an overdose of Arpège from Lanvin. (I'm not really a guy who needs to mix sex with honey, whipped cream, chopped pecans, or champagne, but some women expect these things from a celebrity and I hate to disappoint them. I'm pretty thoughtful that way.)

The gorgeous room-service girl takes the ice bucket off

the cart. "Over there by the flowers," I tell her. I see that in the bed Denise is lighting a Salem.

"Can I have your autograph, Mr. Morris?" says the room-service girl. People are amazing, aren't they? Here I am, *flagrante delicto,* mid-bofferino as it were, and she wants my autograph. But I'm very nice about these things. Never bite the hand that applauds you, my agent says.

"Certainly," I say. I step over to the stack of eight-by-tens that Reuben leaves out on the dressing table, on top of which rests a Scripto Admiral, one of the few pens that writes on a gloss finish without smearing. You learn these things. "What's your name, sweetheart?"

"No, I meant I need your signature, Mr. Morris. On the bill?" she says, handing me the leatherette billfold containing the check for the champagne.

In the bed, Denise issues a sharp-edged little snort of a laugh. I notice this. Yeah. Go mention my name to her tomorrow, see if she laughs.

I look back at the room-service girl. She has an award-winning rack, a C-cup at least, and her pants are tightly wrapped around a rear end like two independently owned and operated honeydew melons. With that out of the way, I look at her face. She's got that Irish thing. Maureen, I bet her name is. (It is, I learn; I'm incredible.) She smiles. Short teeth, wide tongue. We like that. She adds in a hurry, "I mean, believe me, I'd love to have your autograph, but we're under orders not to ask."

I smile over at Denise in the bed as I sign the check for the room-service girl and add below the tip and total the words "Ring me in this room in one hour." I fold up the billfold, she takes it from me and says, "Thanks so much. And if there's anything else you need, Mr. Morris, please just ask for Maureen in room service."

She hasn't looked in the billfold, so I walk her out of the bedroom to the door of the living room.

"I left a little tip for you in there," I say, indicating the billfold. "You should look at it after you leave. I don't think it will disappoint you."

She thanks me as I pat her ass lightly twice and close the door behind her. I look across the living room at the door to Vince's bedroom, which is shut. I go over to the door, knock two times, then once, then twice again. Our code knock. There's no answer. I then move quickly back to Denise, who is stumping out the last of her Salem. I toss off the robe.

"Who was that knocking now?" she asks, annoyed.

"Me. On Vince's door. Making sure he wasn't in his room."

She looks cautious. "He said he was driving up to Palm Beach."

"Sure. I just thought better safe than sorry." I reach below the sheets and slide the panties off her. "Which reminds me. Talking about safety . . ."

"No, not inside me," says Denise. "My period ended two weeks ago."

"I'll use a Trojan."

"I once got pregnant from a jerk who used a Trojan."

"Beware Greeks bearing gifts," I say, which I thought was witty. Some people are very surprised when I do intellectual humor like that.

Not her. She says, "The operation cost my father five hundred dollars. The doctor who did it was younger than I am. Probably a student aborting his way through medical school. I don't think he did a great job. I still feel a little funny whenever I pee."

At this point, the ice bucket seems a more inviting place to park myself than in this bony maroney. These P.R. ladies, every hotel has at least one. I swear there's a conveyor belt in Detroit that turns them out when there's no demand for Studebakers. Cold metal, glossy paint job, hard on impact. (For Vince, a hotel's P.R. ladies are the equivalent of the basket of fruit we get when we check in. "Compliments of the Management.")

I down a fast glass of champagne to loosen up my libido, pour one for her and a second for me. "Here's to us," I say. I drink half the second glass and undo the demi-corset while she sips. It is just as I had thought: the bra had made them look as big as they were ever going to look. The only interest I have now is whether her oral skills go beyond talking a blue streak to the Miami columnists about the Versailles's current headliners. I'm hopeful. Vince has very high standards in that department.

"'To us,'" she sniggers. "You and I aren't what one would call an 'us' kind of thing, are we?"

"Like you and Vince are?"

"I don't know. It's been feeling like Vince and I might be something more than"—she looks around the room—"this."

"Then why are you doing—this?" I say.

She smiles. "Well, you're pretty hard to say no to. You don't really give someone a chance. That's kind of appealing. And it's exciting to be the object of Lanny Morris's interest, even if only for the twenty-four hours his partner is out of town. I didn't even know you were interested until yesterday, since lunch you haven't stopped talking, and now I'm naked in your bedroom."

"You don't have to do this," I offer.

"Oh, it's the kind of thing I do." She lights another cigarette, which I don't think is very cordial of her, considering what I had planned for her next. "I was spoiled growing up, so now I always make certain to spoil things for myself. I'm liking Vince. I'm wondering if we might have some kind of future beyond your three-week booking here. So, therefore, according to the way my psyche functions, it must now be time for me to do Vince's partner while he's out of town." She moves her legs apart. "Don't you think?"

I'm thinking to myself, I know this girl from every college town we've ever played. They're called graduate students, teaching assistants, and in a major city, if they're over twenty-two, they're "career girls." The absolute easiest lays in this great nation of ours. At a party, they stand there scowling all night while you're trying to charm some curvy blonde. And they'll be there in a straight black dress, severe black hair: your basic neurotic, Seven Sisters, folk music, "I must sleep with a black man before I die or I am not a true liberal" type. Around three in the morning, you've lost the blonde so you offer to drive the neurotic brunette home, which you do with long stretches of silence. You pull up to the apartment building or student housing where she lives, you ask if she would like to screw in the back of the car, she mumbles, "Yeah, all right," and you ball each other's brains out. When it's over, she won't give you her phone number. "It was what it was," she says. She walks to the front door and you notice she has no ass at all.

I'm noticing that lack of ass now as I'm proceeding to boff Denise. She's making noise and I'm making noise but not so much noise that I don't hear the door to the bedroom open.

In walks Vince.

He's saying, "Lanny, I decided not to go to Palm—" and I feel Denise turn into a sleek salamander beneath me, her skin instantly clammy. She goes from sixty to zero in under two seconds. She's looking at Vince. I get up off her, which leaves her looking really naked, not sexy-naked but more like on-an-operating-table naked. Now she's looking at me and I can see she thinks somehow I'm so smart and such a celebrity that there's something I can think of to say that will make all this just fine.

"Sorry, Vince," I mutter.

I love Vince. Vince is such absolute class. He goes to the champagne bucket and pours himself a glass, sips at it. He scowls. "Jesus, they call anything 'champagne' these days. What vintage is this, nineteen past noon?" He empties his glass into the bucket, withdraws a pack of Cavalier cigarettes, and flames one with a single pass of his solid-gold stick lighter. He takes a nice long drag, exhales, flicks the ash into the bucket. "So?"

I look at him. "So?"

He indicates Denise. "I hope you love her, Lanny. Because if you love her, I say, Well, hey. Love and all that. But if you don't, this means you care more about a quick piece of ass than our partnership."

"Vince . . ." says Denise.

He looks at her, puzzled that she would even speak. He has an expression on like *I'm actually curious what it is you might possibly think you have to say.* "Was my partner raping you?" he asks and looks around the room. "I see no signs of a struggle. A small stain on the sheet there, but it wouldn't appear to be blood."

She reaches for a Salem and lights it. "Forget it," she says. There's a little mascara smeared below her right eye. It looks like a smudge of chocolate cupcake frosting around a kid's mouth. I guess she had more feelings for Vince than I thought.

Vince turns to me. "Did you know she was something more to me than the usual thing, Lanny? Because if you did, that would make this enemy action." He turns to Denise. "You should leave now. This is private between me and my partner."

We watch her put on her dress over her naked body and slip into her shoes. Then she somehow shoves the rest—panties, nylons—into this little clutch bag. I feel sorry for her, but what's happened has happened. She says, "Vince, there's something you ought to know about me. When I—"

"Denise. You were screwing my partner. That's it."

She nods her head slightly a couple of times, like a defendant who agrees with the judge when he says a stiff sentence is in order. She looks toward me. "Lanny?"

I say nothing. Vince tosses his Cavalier in the ice bucket. It makes a little *pssst* noise. Then Vince says to her (and me): "If my partner ever talks to you again, there won't be any more Collins and Morris. When we cancel the booking, you can be the one to tell your bosses why. Maybe you'll also explain that to the polio research people . . . and all the folks who count on us to lighten the burden of their day."

I can't look Denise or Vince in the eye.

We watch her walk out of the bedroom and we listen to the door to the suite close behind her.

Vince lights another cigarette. I allow myself to voice the scorn for him I'm feeling: *"'. . . and all the folks who count on us to lighten the burden of their day?'* " I roll my eyes. "Jesus, Vince. Thank God you don't write our material."

Vince nods agreement and gives me that slow wink of his. "Thanks, pal."

I move toward the bathroom, complaining. "You could've at least let me shoot my wad, for God's sake. I'm gonna be walking funny all night." Then I remember the gorgeous redhead from room service named Maureen and my mood starts to pick up. I turn on the shower and wait for the water to get like it's from a kettle.

Vince follows me to the doorway. He checks his watch. "Sorry, I thought I was supposed to barge in at twenty after."

"No, you were right," I admit. "Room service took a little longer than I thought it would."

Vince tries to console me. "You didn't really miss out on anything, pal. She was kind of like what's-her-name, the actress we fired. The one who was incredible at her audition and then got slightly worse each day of rehearsals. What was her name?"

"Sheila."

"Sheila, that's it. Every day Denise was trying to make things feel a little more like love and a little less like sex. Another week and she'd have been a virgin."

I drop the robe, step into the shower. I call out, "Sure, I had a hooker who fell in love with me once. When she did, she decided she shouldn't do anything with me that she'd ever done with a trick. She said, 'That's for the trade. You and I are different.' I said, 'You and I are over.'"

Vince sits down on the toilet-seat lid. "Thanks for getting her off my hands so nice and clean. We may have to work here again someday."

"Nothing you wouldn't do for me, right?" I half-grunt. Reuben had laid in some Camay soap for me, but the Miami tap water was still hard. Rinsing was a real chore.

Vince asks, "You doing anything tonight?"

"I'm going to be busy for a while with an Irish girl, a redhead named Maureen from room service. You're not doing her, right?"

You can see how very close Vince and I were. Give you another an example. The very next night, we're clowning around with the audience at the second show. You have to understand that at this point in our careers if you took the part of our act that was formally structured, it would probably not fill two pages, double-spaced. And the jokes, God help us, would read something like:

VINCE: Listen, pal, I didn't come here to be insulted!
ME: Oh, where do you usually go? *(Mug for audience.)*
VINCE: I've half a mind to leave the stage.
ME: Come back when you find the other half. *(Prance around piano.)*
VINCE: That does it. I'm not singing another song.
ME: Always give the public what it wants! *(Walk on inside of ankles.)*

But three-quarters of our stage time was ad-lib, just clowning around with the audience. With the movies going great for us and the TV specials right through the roof, the only reason for playing nightclubs anymore was because of a certain contract certain people had with us that if we didn't take them seriously they'd take a contract out on us, seriously. So we viewed the weeks at the Versailles in Miami, the Biarritz in Vegas, and the Casino del Mar in northern New Jersey as a working vacation.

And when we worked the audience, we were like advance men scouting a location. What we were scouting was who we'd be boffing later that night. It didn't matter if the girls came to the show with dates. They'd come back without them. That was the main reason we didn't mind doing a second show every night; Reuben, my valet, would get word to them after the first show that we wanted them to be our special guests for the second show. How they got rid of their dates I never knew, but they always did.

This particular night, I've got Maureen the redhead ready to room-service me later, so for a change I'm not scouting, just mingling with the crowd, and this fat guy starts heckling me. "You stink, Morris!" he yells at me. Every joke I make he yells, "You're not funny!" It's coming off pretty personal. He's even going out of his way to laugh at Vince's straight lines. Vince is looking at the back of the room for the captain to step in, but we don't see him anywhere.

Now, I don't like to let a heckler take control of the show, but unfortunately this guy is really loud and there's no way I cannot acknowledge him. "Sir," I say, "when you go to the movies, do you talk to the screen?"

"Go back where you came from, you bastard!" Great comeback on his part. I'm also wondering where he thinks I came from. I have a standard repertoire of zingers, but what the guy is feeding me is hard to riff on. What makes it tougher is he's not heckling Vince; it's just me. Vince is sensitive to this and tries the "politely shame them" angle. "Excuse me, sir. Clearly you don't like our act, but you're spoiling the evening for the rest of this nice audience. The management will refund your cover charge if we've failed to amuse you. Now can we please continue the show?" Some decent applause comes from the rest of the patrons, which is, of course, the whole point of Vince saying what he said. The heckler shouts, "No, we all love *you,* Vince. I just think the monkey is a jerk." Meaning me.

Vince hears the word "jerk" and plunges straight into quoting a lyric I wrote for him in our first motion picture, *Smithereens.* The song was called "Just My Pal and My Gal." Vince recites, "Mister: *'I'm honored to work with this jerk,'*" indicating me and walking his hand-mike down to the heckler. Russ Cummings has the piano player noodle behind him as he croons, *"I never frown with this clown. I love to joke with this bloke. I feel real cool with this fool."*

The heckler grabs Vince's mike and says into it, "Fine, but don't give the mike to this kike!"

The crowd can't help but laugh.

Vince starts breaking up too. He says, a bit sheepishly, "Ladies and gentlemen, it's not often my partner and I get topped by a member of our audience, but this gentleman has just done the near impossible, and we're wondering, sir, if you'd be a great sport and help us out onstage. What do you say, folks?"

The folks say hooray. Vince explains, "You see, Lanny and I keep an old routine called 'School Daze,' that's D-a-z-e, in our hip pocket for whenever a celebrity friend of ours might drop by. But don't you think this gentleman—what's your name, sir? Phil? Don't you folks think Phil here is as funny as, say, Red Buttons or Red Skelton or Red China even? How about it?"

The crowd loves this, they're all cheering Phil as he downs the rest of his drink. Vince waves everybody quiet one more time and says, "Now, in this routine, our friend Phil here is going to play a crazy professor who's giving Lanny and me our final high school exam . . . so if you'll excuse us while we help Phil change into a ca-raaaaay-zy professor outfit—Russ, a little costume-changing music, if you please!" He looks at our musical director, Russ Cummings, who quickly calls out a title and cues the band into "There'll Be Some Changes Made."

Well, I don't know what the hell Vince is going on about, but he walks this heckler named Phil offstage, leaving me alone. So I start doing the bit where I ask the trombone player from the house band if I can play along—I make a few noises on the bone and then the slide comes off in my hand and as I try to put things back together, I "accidentally" knock over all the music stands—so now the stage is a shambles and I look into the wings and what I can see is Vince slamming the guy face-first into a radiator by a brick wall just before the dressing rooms. The guy bounces up off the radiator and lands on the floor. I would tell you that the guy has a broken nose, but that wouldn't be true. The guy now has no nose. There's just this black-and-purple mess above his mouth and below his eyes. Someday he might have a nose again, but not this year.

The audience can't see or hear anything, but from where I am, I see plenty. The guy is groaning, weakly. Vince stands over him and says, "You call any goddamn Jew on this planet anything you like, I don't care, but nobody calls my partner a kike, you hear me?" And he kicks him and would have kicked him again if Reuben hadn't stepped in. He pulls Vince away, straightens his tux (somehow not a drop of blood has gotten on Vince's shirtfront, but that was Vince, I'll tell you), and Vince walks back out onstage, suave as ever.

Now the audience is wondering where Phil is. So I ask Vince, for the audience's benefit, "Hey, where's our friend Phil?"

Vince says, "Oh, he developed a sudden case of the jitters."

"Would that be like a virus?" I ask. I give Vince the little hand signal we have that means "Feed the line back to me," and Vince lobs it perfectly.

"Lanny, why do you want to know if his jitters might be like a virus?" he says for the audience's benefit.

"I thought it might be a jitterbug!" I squeal and go into my "I'm so simultaneously ashamed and thrilled with myself" dance. The band starts playing one of those rock-and-roll vamps and I'm good for five minutes, right up through my trademark death-pratfall.

Of everyone in the club, Phil's table is laughing the hardest. They weren't laughing so hard a month later when Vince told the judge that Phil had tripped over a folding chair in the wings. Reuben and the lighting operator and the wardrobe mistress and the showgirls all verified this. The club's captain said so too, and he was particularly emphatic, considering he was in the changing room getting his doorknob polished by one of the showgirls at the time. The judge gave Phil's attorney a little lecture about people who bring unfounded lawsuits against celebrities. Later we signed some eight-by-ten glossies for the judge, one to go in his chambers and one for the window of his nephew's dairy restaurant. (I wrote, "You've *glatt* to be kidding!" Cute.)

Boffing ladies and bashing gentlemen. I tell you, there was nothing under the sun Vince and I wouldn't do for each other.

SEVEN

In Hillman's law library, I slowly closed the ring binder as if irrevocably shutting the door behind a departing dinner guest who'd stayed until one A.M. when everyone else had been decent enough to leave by eleven.*

Very well. I'd faced the Beast, my hands tied to the sacrificial stake of a legal stipulation, and lived. Lanny wasn't King Kong or Dracula, neither as warmhearted as the mammal nor as cold-blooded as the undead. Now there was one overwhelming question in my mind, and as John Hillman reentered the room without knocking, I realized he was the person on the premises most likely to have the answer.

"Miss O'Connor, your time is up. You'll forgive me if I . . ." He moved to the binder and quickly leafed through the pages, making sure none was missing. He then nodded toward Naomi, who indicated that I should put my hands above my head as before. I saw Hillman unconsciously lick his lips. It was one thing to tolerate the liberties Naomi was apparently at liberty to take with me, but I did not want to supply Hillman

*It would indeed be an impressive feat if I'd been able to memorize the pages by Lanny Morris from which I've just quoted in full. Obviously, since I first read these pages in Hillman's office, I've had access to and have acquired the rights to quote from them here.

with any images to carry home to his master bathroom for masturbatory purposes. I asked if he'd mind turning his back. He humored me with a patronizing shrug.

In addition to Naomi's laying on of hands, a second disquieting sensation was creeping over me, and it concerned what I'd just read. It was not merely the sense that "something was wrong with this picture." No, it was more as if I'd been asked to detect what was wrong with this picture and suddenly noticed that this picture was tattooed on the back of a corpse.

As Naomi lumbered out of the library, Hillman must have noticed the dazed expression on my face and asked if something was the matter.

I sat down again and responded, "I think I don't know why Lanny Morris let me read what I've just read. As self-portraits go, he doesn't exactly come off as— I mean, have you read this?" I asked, gesturing to the binder.

He nodded. "It's pretty pungent, I concede. Lacking in pretense, to say the very least."

I sputtered, "Why would he ever want anyone to see this side of him?"

He took a Sobranie cigarette from a teakwood box on the library table. "I have my own theories, but of course I'd only be guessing." I gave Hillman the same eager and attentive look that had signaled my availability to male professors in college. He ventured professorially, "I think it was Jack Kerouac who once said that every person had within himself one great book."

I shrugged. "Trouble is, Jack Kerouac went and wrote more than one book."

He smiled. "I may have meant Jack London. I myself . . ." He lit the black paper tube of Balkan tobacco. "Suffice it to say that while many people announce their intention to write their memoirs, few get beyond typing the dedication. I suspect my client wanted you to understand, firsthand, that he *is* in fact completing a book that will serve not only as his autobiography but also as the definitive account of the shared careers of Collins and Morris. You've now 'heard' Lanny's writing voice, to use your own profession's jargon. Call it what you will—"

"Deplorably narcissistic, obscenely chauvinistic?"

He waved my words away, leaving behind a wraith of blue smoke.

"Such a book, this raw, this honest, would make your own attempted effort . . . Well, there've been some very nice translations of the Bible over the centuries, but they'd run a poor second in public interest to, say, the discovery of the actual stone tablets upon which God inscribed the Ten Commandments. Don't you think?"

I told him that from what I'd just read, the only thing Lanny's chapter had in common with the Ten Commandments was that the latter could not be found anywhere within the former.

He picked up the ring binder in a protective, motherly way and commented indignantly, "As it happens, I think my client is thoughtfully trying to save you a lot of work and grief in aid of a doomed cause." As he walked me to the door, toward which I hadn't been heading, he asked, "Ever hear of a man named Roald Amundsen?"

I knew the name but couldn't remember how, and I admitted as much.

He nodded me out of the library and into the hall. "In 1911, a British explorer named Robert Falcon Scott set out with a small expedition intending to be the first man to reach the South Pole. He and his team faced unimaginable hardship. When they finally reached their goal, they discovered that a Norwegian explorer named Amundsen had gotten there five weeks earlier. All their sacrifice and suffering had been made meaningless. On their return journey, Scott and all his companions died." Hillman smiled. "I think—this is nothing but conjecture on my part—I think my client wanted you to understand that he is, in effect, Amundsen. That he's already reached the South Pole in both the living and the telling of his own story. I think he wanted to spare you an effort as pointless as Scott's, one that staggered its way toward a cold and lonely death."

EIGHT

A driving August rain in Los Angeles. Like February 29, it does actually occur every now and then, and when it does, what a lark! The drains in the street go mad and start frothing at the mouth, and the culverts run over worse than the budget of *Cleopatra.* Half the native Los Angeles drivers, never having seen a heavy rain before, continue to drive at seventy-five miles an hour, unaware of the undertow. The other half, never having seen a heavy rain before, instantly turn around, drive home at five miles per hour, and don't venture out again for days. This mass sequestering is the Southern California version of snowbound and has been known to cause the citizens to "read for pleasure"—but as I say, it doesn't rain in Los Angeles very often.

My cabdriver stared in awe as the view framed by his windshield turned into an impressionist painting in the furious downpour. So stunned was he as the daylight colors bled together on the glass that, momentarily disoriented, he spoke in English.

"Fucking rain," he grunted and glared at me in his mirror as if there were something I could do about it, such as walk. But my bags were already in the trunk, next to the spilled puddle of motor oil that is mandatory in the trunks of all Southern California taxicabs.

We arrived at Los Angeles International Airport, with its theme building designed by Frank Lloyd Jetson, and reached the segment of the white zone designated for the loading and unloading of American Airlines passengers only. My editors at Neuman and Newberry had decided it was urgent that I meet with them in New York to explain the deal I'd put forward to Vince. A phone call like the one I'd already made to their business-affairs department would have sufficed, but for the money they were going to be shelling out, my editors wanted to have me summarize the terms of the agreement yet again in person. Pointless but unavoidable.

My garment bag swept the terminal floor clean as I dragged it over to the long lines at the American Airlines ticket counter. I saw with elation that there was a separate check-in for first-class passengers, and thanks to the good graces of Neuman and Newberry (and my agent, who'd negotiated my deal with them), that meant me.

Although there were only two classes of travel at that time, economy was definitely third class. First class meant a wider seat with a much better view, that view on most flights consisting of the economy passengers trudging by on their way to the rear of the plane, looking at us with a searing envy, wondering who we might be, wishing they were us, noticing the glasses of champagne in our hands. All alcoholic beverages would be premium brands poured from full-size bottles into full-fisted glassware. The caviar cart would be ushered down the aisle by the stewardesses (all blond) named Kim or the lone steward (blond, all gay) named Karl. With caviar ("Would you like diced hard-boiled egg? Capers? Chopped raw onion? A squeeze of lemon? Toast?") would be served tall ampules of Stolichnaya nested in crushed ice. With the fish entrée (possibly seafood Newburg or Irish smoked salmon) we'd be asked to indulge a *premier cru* Chablis. While we were yielding to the tiresome filet mignon *au poivre vert* (I know, I know!), a serviceable Gevrey-Chambertin would be tolerated. At the end of the meal would come the sweet trolley (as the English called it) or *le chariot* (as the affected English called it). Swing low, sweet chariot. On American Airlines, this usually resulted in a made-to-order ice-cream sundae oozing hot caramel and bittersweet chocolate. Next would materialize the liqueur cart, a score of bottles clanking away against one another like a steel-drum band, and then coffee would be served, but even so, a spike of Irish whiskey or a snifter of cognac or Armagnac was always advised. Frankly, it's a wonder the planes didn't simply fly on booze. There was enough fuel in the first-class cabin to keep a Boeing (and oneself) in a holding pattern over the Great Lakes for a fortnight.

For this level of extraordinary (although, I felt, totally appropriate) service, my publishers were being charged an additional seven hundred dollars. Against that, however, you must remember that my headphones were free.

I stepped up to the woman behind the ticket counter. "O'Connor?" I beamed. "Flight 570 to JFK."

"First class?" she asked, looking up at the sign that said FIRST CLASS CHECK-IN. Insulted, I murmured, "Of course," and wanting to show her that I had not just wandered in by accident, I asked, "The plane *is* a jumbo jet, correct? I only fly jumbos." She told me it certainly was and printed out a boarding pass for me.

I wasn't kidding about preferring jumbo jets to all others. What I loved most about flying a 747 first-class to and from New York was its upstairs lounge. Ascending a spiral staircase from your seat, you found yourself in a parlor car lined on three sides with orange-and-red banquettes. There was a slim, well-stocked bar and, in its earliest rendition, a Fender Rhodes electric piano. Once dinner or lunch was out of the way, I tended to antigravitate to the lounge, skipping the in-flight movie (which by FAA regulations was required to star Michael Caine), opting instead for a glance at some book, with a longer glance out the lounge windows at the continent of clouds directly below us.

As it happens, I'm not a great flier. Beejay, my roommate in college, had told me before my first flight that I was in more danger of having a fatal accident in our bathroom than on an airplane . . . from which I reasoned that one should never, *ever* use the bathroom on a plane, as this is clearly the most dangerous place in the world. One of the reasons I most liked the upstairs lounge was that I'd convinced myself that, were the plane to crash, I'd have all the passengers below me to break my fall.

Perhaps Kim and Karl would let me sit up there for takeoff. I stepped down the telescoping gangway that all the airlines were now employing, and crossing the threshold into the jumbo jet, I decided to head straightaway up the spiral staircase for a glass or two of predeparture champagne—

But there was no spiral staircase. It had clearly been stolen. I asked a stewardess, named Kim, about this with some urgency. Her answers were unsatisfactory. Yes, the plane was a wide-body. Yes, it was a jumbo jet. No, it had no spiral staircase. Yes, like a 747, its first class compartment was to the left of the boarding door. No, it was not a 747. Not all jumbo jets are 747s.

Ohmigod. It was a DC-10.

Kim handed me a glass of champagne to steady my shaken nerves and I almost forgot to thank her, so disoriented was I trying to find my seat. The seating configuration up front on a DC-10 was unusual: two-two-two. I was in the middle pair in the last row of first class. Miles away from a window. I did have a well-centered view of the movie screen where Michael Caine would shortly appear. But gone for the journey would be any view of that cumulusian continent of which I was so fond.

"How booked up are you?" I asked Kim. "Any chance of switching to a window seat?"

Kim turned to an older stewardess who was helping a gentleman off with his sports jacket. "Helen, do we have a window seat available?"

Helen shook her head unhappily. "No, doggone it, I'm afraid first is all full—I was just checking that for Marge at the gate." She looked down at me apologetically. "They're almost as jammed up in economy as we are, so I can't even offer you a window back there." She stepped away.

"Would you like a little more champagne?" asked Kim. I sat down and accepted her offer as she tried to sell me on the virtues of the DC-10.

"These center seats are really wonderful. See, if you push here—can I show you . . . ?" She used her foot to depress a button at the base of my seat. "The seat swivels to the left and right, something the side seats can't do." She moved me forty-five degrees one way and forty-five the other. Whee. This was even better than the mechanical pony outside of Woolworth's, and only seven hundred dollars a ride.

Kim then indicated a low circular table to my right. "And this converts into a full-sized circular dining table during our American Admiral service, with damask linen and silverware by Fornari, so you don't have to eat off a tray. Again, that's *only* for these center seats. And today we'll be serving you prime rib carved as you like it at tableside from our American Admiral serving trolley." She was on autopilot now. I shrugged and leaned back, resigned to my fate.

By now first class had pretty much filled up. In the seat to my left was a youngish British executive in a pinch-waisted Cardin blazer and dove-gray trousers that were narrower than the knot in his tie. He was accompanied by a stunning skeletal Nordic model in a white sleeveless top whose pinstripes coordinated nicely with the track marks on her left arm. In the seats in front of them were two Hindus, both in double-knits, one a pale blue LEEsure suit from Lee Jeans, the other a rich brown Trevira polyester with a jaunty yellow acetate scarf at his throat. The two seats in front of me had not yet been filled. The single seat directly to my right was also vacant (maybe I wouldn't have a neighbor on this flight, which would almost compensate for the lack of an upstairs lounge). In the pair of seats on my far right was a couple whose matching convex bellies probably removed the missionary position from any list of their erotic options. In the seats in front of them were two businessmen who did not seem to know each other, one absorbed in *The Terminal Man* by Michael Crichton, the other absorbed in paperwork.

Although the plane was still moored to the gate, a sleepy stupor had settled over first class, as if the staff had done everything it was supposed to do and now we were all waiting for . . . what?

Helen was speaking on the aircraft's wall phone in a suppressed tone. As she was situated by the still-open boarding door, just behind where I was seated in the last row of first class, I could hear bits of what she was saying. "Well, we've been set for ten minutes, Marge, the captain's waiting on you now. . . . Definitely just the three, right? Because I have nothing else other than my own seat. . . . Okay." She spotted me looking at her and flashed me a professional smile, hung up the phone, and called to Kim: "Kim, we're doing an LMA, if you could help." Suddenly all the stewardesses seemed to gracefully converge on the doorway. Entering the plane was a sharp-faced employee in short sleeves. "Fine, we're boarding now," he told someone on a walkie-talkie. "This way, gentlemen," he added to three men who followed him into the plane.

Soft murmurs of greeting went up from Helen and all of the Kims. The three men entered wearing the sober expressions people adopt when they're being allowed to bypass a queue. Two of them moved toward the two empty seats directly in front of mine. The third appeared on my immediate right, taking the seat next to mine with an apologetic smile. He had dark golden skin like an autumnal wax pear, with a gentle face and eyes the color of his skin. Eurasian, perhaps a little Spanish, in his late fifties or robust sixties. He wore a spotless but dated black suit. There were droplets of rain beaded on his hair, which would have gleamed with or without the condensation. He folded his hands, looked straight forward, and smiled at the air.

Fidgeting in front of him was a short man, his little shoulders lost somewhere in a navy blazer. He must have been married to a woman he feared, for he was wearing a flowered shirt that he would never have purchased for himself. He summoned Helen with a crook of his finger. "A Smirnoff vodka on the rocks? And a pillow?"

Helen only half-smiled. "I'll bring that to you shortly but we're running a bit late, as you may well understand, and we have certain procedures required by federal law."

The older man nodded his understanding but added, "The Smirnoff is for him," indicating the man on his left, who looked far too sober to ever want a vodka on the rocks. This other man was tall, trim, and dressed in colors that might have been too bright were they not muted by the fine quality of their fabric and design. He gave me a quick glance of such focus and strength that my eyes were caught completely off guard, allowing him to penetrate the first veil of defense I normally wear in public. The smile he tossed me brought a silly, reflexive smirk to my lips, which I quickly tried to convert into a demure expression. But by then he'd slid smoothly into his seat.

I was to learn shortly that the Eurasian man on my right was named Reuben and that the older man in front of him was a powerful Hollywood agent named Irv Fleischmann.

I did not have to wait a moment more than the very first instant I saw him to know that the man seated directly in front of me was Lanny Morris.

NINE

In point of fact, it wasn't as remarkable as it might at first seem that I now found myself seated one row behind the gentleman whose intimate memoirs I'd been perusing only two days earlier. The almost unjustifiable expense of a first-class ticket (there being no discounts or deals to be had for such a luxury) and the limited number of wide-bodies in service made those twelve to twenty seats on a jumbo jet quite the exclusive club, one where mere moneyed mortals frequently found themselves mingling with the Gods.

Whenever anyone flew first-class to the opposite coast, friends would ask upon their arrival, "Well, did you see anyone famous?" The answer would invariably be something along the lines of "As a matter of fact, both Ann Jillian and that nice Larry Blyden were on our flight and they couldn't have been nicer. They chatted with us while we waited to get off the plane." Since only American, TWA, and United flew nonstop between New York and L.A. (and not all of those flights were the preferred luxury liners), the mathematical odds that a celebrity would be in your midst if you flew first-class transcontinental on a jumbo jet were in fact quite good. Thus it was perhaps not quite so incredibly miraculous that Lanny, his manager Irv Fleischmann, and his valet Reuben were currently positioned at twelve, one, and three o'clock respectively to me.

I was now dimly recalling an interview in which much credit was given to Lanny for insisting that his Filipino butler travel in the same class and stay in the same hotels as he did. It had occurred to me even when I read the tidbit that this also kept Reuben on call and close at (Lanny's) hand all hours of the day. No hiding out with some Mindinao Minnie back in row 23 of economy for good old Reuby Baby, nosiree. Lanny's attendant's attentiveness was quickly verified for me when the captain turned off the NO SMOKING sign some twenty seconds after the wheels left the ground, as was the general policy of most airlines. In almost the same instant, Reuben leaned forward and proffered a cigarette case and gunmetal Zippo lighter to Lanny, who reached behind him for the case without looking back. He simply knew the items would be there. I also recalled reading that the reason Lanny often had Reuben carry his cigarette case and lighter for him was that he couldn't abide having any bulges in his pants that did not originate with him—joke. His pants had no pockets and were, like Reuben himself, made to order. To be fair, I must assert there was nothing haughty or imperious about Lanny's manner. He didn't snap his fingers. He said, "Thanks" in a nice voice as he handed the lighter and case back to Reuben. This was, I guess, simply how they operated, and I'd read that Reuben was extremely well paid for his dedication to the maintenance of Mr. Morris, who was now seated a tantalizing forty-one inches in front of me.

Could you tell a great deal about a man simply by staring at the back of his chair for forty-five minutes? No, not really. The seats had high backs, so not even the nape of Lanny's neck or his ears offered themselves up for any Conan Doyle ratiocination. I *could* see that he quickly received the requested Smirnoff on the rocks, because Helen (who'd bravely volunteered to become his personal stewardess) brought it immediately after takeoff, on a small tray along with a porcelain nut dish filled with almonds. I can visually verify that his left arm looked nice taking the tray from her. She leaned forward to hear something he was saying or requesting. Helen laughed a giddy laugh and stepped away, returning moments later with an American Airlines sleeping mask, even though it was only around four in the afternoon. His left arm took it from her, his seat reclined, and I assume he took a nap.

I wondered whether he'd asked for the mask in order to reduce visibility from *his* side of it or to reduce his own visibility to the surrounding passengers. He was certainly lucky in that those seated in the two rows ahead of him hadn't seemed to have noticed his entrance just prior to takeoff. The two Hindustani gentlemen on his left didn't show any signs of recognition, perhaps because *Two Flatfoots from Flatbush* had never played at the Raita Rialto in downtown Vindaloo. The Brit and his Nordic model citizen were seemingly far more interested in themselves than anyone else, and it looked like a trip for the two to the loo to do the dirty deed was all but inevitable. For the moment, everyone in first class was by design or by ignorance playing it very cool about Lanny's presence in their midst.

Stewardess Kim gifted me with my complimentary headphones, which were simply hollow plastic tubes that sent sound stethoscopically to one's ears. I put them on, heard the thrilling strains of Paul Mauriat and His Orchestra performing "Love Is Blue," and wondered what, if anything, I should do about this unusual situation.

Introducing myself was an option, but it was hard to know where I ranked on Lanny's hit list, based on our asymmetrical correspondence. Was I enemy, nuisance, rival? Did he really know of me or had this all been the doings of John Hillman, Esquire? I had never actually received a letter signed "Lanny Morris," but surely I wouldn't have been given access to his memoirs without his knowledge and consent.

For an instant, I entertained the narcissistic notion that Lanny was following me: that he'd pulled a few strings easily accessible to someone of his status, learned when I was flying back to New York, and booked these seats specifically to observe me—but if he wanted to have me shadowed, he could have hired someone to do it. I suddenly had a disconcerting thought accompanied by a chill, which I at first took to be the overhead air vent blowing directly upon me. I half-reached to adjust it before I realized that the frisson I felt was internal.

Forget thinking that Lanny Morris was following me. Much more likely he'll think I'm following *him.* Like an obsessed fan, or the paparazzi, or the "journalist" Moe Cohn, whose Miami-based column had dug up dirt on people like Lanny right up through the late fifties, raking them into the muck with a sharp-edged hoe.

Here I am, having written repeated letters to Lanny and his representatives, pleading my case, sending him excerpts from my published oeuvre, negotiating an agreement with Lanny's ex-partner, poring over Lanny's offered memoirs . . . and now a mere three days later I'm sitting in the midst of his entourage en route to New York. If I were Lanny, wouldn't I be suspicious?

I tried to remember if any of the articles that I'd sent to Lanny's lawyers carried byline photos of me. As best I could remember, they hadn't. There was a piece I'd done for *Viva* in which I'd tried to uncover the secret identity of "J." (the author of the recent best-seller *The Sensuous Woman*). The magazine had made much of "K. O'Connor" (my usual billing) searching for "J."—but I'd been photographed wearing a harlequin's eye mask while supposedly scribbling notes at the bedside of three men who were cavorting with a lanky, identically masked woman—purportedly the aforementioned "J." but in reality a model named Menorah.

I flipped audio channels and detected an anemic rendition of the Grieg Piano Concerto, to which I vaguely listened as I filtered the issues at hand through the wadded cheesecloth I laughingly call my brain.

Midway through the Adagio, senior stewardess Helen came back to Lanny and murmured some words in his ear. His seat back straightened and I saw his hand returning the sleep mask to her. She asked him a question and could not quite hide her simultaneous glance in my direction. Oh, Helen was very professional and the soul of discretion, but it certainly seemed as if she was talking about me. My favorite expression is "Even paranoiacs have enemies," and I was about to be proven at least partially correct.

Helen nodded to whatever Lanny's reply was and stepped back to me as if one thing led to another. "You'll be having dinner with us today?"

I refrained from saying, "No, I'll just go down to the corner and pick up a fried-egg-and-bacon sandwich," and replied that yes, I would be dining in today. Helen recited, "As part of our American Admiral service this afternoon, we're offering our exclusive in-flight table dining, which consists of two center tables seating four each. Will this be all right?" I assumed that Helen's conference with Lanny had been to ask if he minded dining with a civilian (me), and since he apparently was fine about that, who was I to reject dining with Lanny Morris (him)?

"Fine by me," I smiled.

Helen gave a go-ahead nod to steward Karl, who had moved up behind me. He gushed, "Well, then it looks like you're having dinner with Lanny Morris!" as if this were a feature of American Airlines' Admiral service along with carved roast beef. With that, he rotated my chair twenty-three degrees clockwise toward the center of the plane, where it locked in place. Likewise, Reuben's chair was rotated by Kim toward me. Fleischmann was then quickly rotated by Kim in my direction. We were beginning to emulate the Mad Tea Party ride at Disneyland. Helen, of course, saved for herself the final honor of swiveling Lanny into position at our table for four. A large circular tabletop was snapped by Helen and Kim onto the smaller circular table that had been in front of me and on my right, which now served as the base of our dining table. Karl whisked a salmon-colored tablecloth around the table like an artful barber and fastened whatever kept it in place. Immediately a low weighty vase of silk flowers was plonked down in the center of the table, as matching dinner service was laid down . . . and there we were, as precise and compasslike a table for four as you'll ever see.

Lanny turned and spoke to me for the first time. He neither smiled nor frowned.

"Hi."

"Hi," I returned. So far, I was every bit his equal.

He took the tabletop in both of his hands and gently tried to toggle it. It wobbled a bit. "Guess we should get the waiter to slide a matchbook under the airplane," he smiled. He peered under the tablecloth, adjusted something that went *snap,* and reappeared. This time the table was steady. "That should hold. Guess we're dining together. That okay with you?"

"Fine by me." I'm just *so* fucking good in these situations.

Lanny nodded across the table. "This is my friend Reuben." Reuben nodded graciously. "And this is also my friend—technically speaking—and business manager Irv. My name's Lanny." I was surprised to discover that Lanny had a very intelligent face. Quite sensitive, to be honest. Most of the simian expressions for which we'd come to know him, especially in cartoons and on posters, were not in evidence, at least for the moment. He looked a little like a Jewish Danny Kaye, except that of course Danny Kaye *is* Jewish. And of course his hair was not red. Then again, I assume neither was Danny Kaye's. "What's your name?" he asked.

"Bonnie," I lied just as natural as can be. "Bonnie Trout." I listened to my voice lying to him with a keen but detached interest. I hadn't consciously decided to lie until the moment in which I did. There was still time, I thought, to take it back, pretend it was some kind of joke, although one would be hard-pressed to find its punch line.

Ah, but now it really *was* too late to retract it. In the time it took me to remove the napkin ring from the linen at my place and spread the napkin upon my lap, the falsehood had jelled very nicely into an official regulation lie. I felt as if I were standing on the rear platform of a caboose, looking back at a switch in the tracks, and watching one pair of rails curving away from the other, out of sight, behind trees, now gone forever.

"Nice to meet you, Bonnie," said Lanny simply. I thought about all the jokes that anyone named Bonnie Trout has heard from people to whom she's just been introduced. I thought it showed some class that Lanny moved along without comment. I suppose when you've spent your life making and writing jokes, you have too much self-respect to hit lobbed pitches out of the park.

Over my shoulder, Kim inquired, "Would you like wine, a cocktail, or would you prefer to stay with the champagne?" As I was the woman at the table, apparently all questions and service would be directed first to me. Chivalry over Celebrity. I opted for a Sancerre, as did Lanny. Irv asked for a Cutty and soda, which was made for him on the spot. Irv's voice was like his looks: pinched, pointed, New York. Reuben waved away the offer of a drink and replied, "Just ice water, please," in a low, mellow voice that hardly bore an accent.

"What do you do, Bonnie?" asked Lanny as they poured his wine.

"I teach," I said.

"Where?"

"In Manhattan. P.S. 29 on Orchard Street."

"What do you teach?"

"Second grade."

"Really? How old is a second-grader these days?" he asked.

I tasted my wine and calculated. I'd been five in kindergarten, six in first grade . . . "Seven years old. Sometimes six or eight, for part of the year, depending on when they were born."

"Well, we have a lot in common. You teach second grade, I went to second grade. Irv, you went to second grade, didn't you?"

Irv buttered his club roll. "Many times. Tell me, Miss Trout, what do they pay a second-grade teacher these days?"

God, how would I know? Enough to afford a one-bedroom apartment on Thirty-third Street on the East Side. How much would that go for, three seventy-five a month? You should never pay more in rent than one week's salary. Fifty-two times three hundred and seventy-five is . . . "About twenty thousand a year." I sipped some wine. "With tips."

Lanny gave a pleasant single laugh at this. It was not his trademark cackle. As a matter of fact, except for the name, the general timbre of his voice, and certain aspects of his looks, I'm not sure I'd have recognized this man as being Lanny Morris.

Irv shrugged. "I don't mean to be impolite, but I was wondering how a second-grade schoolteacher affords to fly first-class."

Lanny and Reuben both looked at me with interest. I used my knife to spatula one of the three petite medallions of smoked salmon that Kim had set before me and transfer it onto a round of toasted English Hovis bread. "Well, I have a pass that allows me free use of the subway on weekdays . . . and the hot lunches at school, while pretty deplorable, are only fifty cents . . . and I'm the mistress of a wealthy married man, and when he and his wife go on vacation, he treats me to a first-class trip in the opposite direction. But look at me, talking only about myself." I turned to Lanny. "What do *you* do for a living?"

Lanny froze for a moment, then nodded his head, acknowledging my zing. Reuben and Irv both looked confused.

Lanny replied lightly, "I'm a French impressionist painter. Mainly out of Tahiti. But I just do that to pay the bills. My real ambition is to become a stockbroker in Paris."

Irv shook his head disapprovingly. "Don't get it," he said.

I thought it might be politic to show that I did. "Paul Gauguin," I enlightened Irv. "He gave up being a successful stockbroker to become a painter in the South Seas."

Irv frowned at Lanny as if his client had made a bad career move. "You think the average person knows that?"

Lanny looked irritated. "I'm making idle conversation, Irv, I didn't realize the meter was running. Okay, how about: *Good evening, mesdames, messieurs, I'm a French impressionist, and for my first impression, let's hear from my good friend Toulouse-Lautrec.* I could drop to my knees for this, and if my sports jacket is long and thin enough to spread out on the floor, it'll help the gag. Then I say, *Ah l'amour, l'amour, I paint with Benjamin La Moore, usually in a shade of sacré bleu, and if I run out of that I use some Dutch Boy—not the paint, you understand, I mean I like to* use *some poor little Dutch Boy in my strange little Frenchie way*—okay, Irv? You know, sometimes I actually go off duty." This wasn't said bitterly or venomously.

"Sorry," offered Irv. He tasted his Scotch smoked salmon on Hovis and asked Kim if she could find some cream cheese. She went to see what they had in the galley.

I said to Lanny, "I guess people expect you to be funny all the time."

"Not if they get to know me, they don't. I'd much rather do your kind of work."

I shook my head. "We all need a good laugh."

Lanny grimaced. "Yeah, well, that's what I tell my writers, but they keep coming up with the same bad jokes."

Irv hastily explained, "Lanny doesn't have any writers. He writes all his own material. I wish he wouldn't, because it eats up his time, but that's how he is."

Lanny hissed, "Quiet, Irv, I've been blaming my bad jokes on my nonexistent writers for years now." He mock-glared at me. "Don't ever repeat what he just said or I'll have to have you destroyed."

Kim took away our hors d'oeuvres plates and laid down some lovely sea-blue china in the shape of fluted seashells filled with their rendition of coquilles Saint-Jacques.

Lanny continued in the most conversational of tones, "For nearly two hundred million years, the dinosaurs had dominion over this planet. We've been around for, oh how long has it been now, fifty thousand years? So *Homo sapiens* will have to survive until the year 199,950,000 A.D. before we can call ourselves as successful a race as your basic dinosaur. And yet, Bonnie, in all that time, not even once is there the slightest evidence that any dinosaur ever went into show business."

He added gravely, "There is nothing, for example, to suggest that one dinosaur made all the other dinosaurs sit around the fire at night and watch him as he said, *You know, I think if we ever met a stegosaurus, he'd look a little something like this. . . .* No tummling Triassics, no juggling Jurassics—a *Tyrannosaurus rex* was the closest they had to a stand-up act." He reminded me a little of Vince talking about Euclid, which had reminded me a lot of Lanny. "But why second grade, Bonnie?"

"Well, my children don't know how to use drugs or weapons yet. I can still take the kids in a fight, including even the most muscular of the boys. Some of them may be in love with me, but none of them want to have sex with me, including the most muscular of the girls. The disparity between the bright ones and the dumb ones is not so great yet, so the results of my work or lack thereof are not so depressing yet. They have no homework that I have to correct in the evenings. Some of their fathers are only a little older than I am, and some of those fathers are already divorced—those parent-teacher conferences can be an excellent way to meet eligible men in a private setting without having to sit around a bar all night. I get ten weeks' paid vacation, excellent pension and medical plan. In one more year, I'll have such solid tenure that I could molest the winner of a spelling bee with a field hockey stick and they *still* wouldn't be able to fire me. The question isn't why I decided to teach second grade, the question is why everybody else doesn't."

It played rather well. Especially with Lanny, who both laughed and eyed me with interest. I'd heard the above speech virtually word-for-word more than once, which is why I could recite it so well. Imagine it said by a fairly pretty girl in her twenties with nice lips, a really cute haircut, and a knowing way with her eyes. It played rather well.

Down the aisle Helen and Kim wheeled the American Airlines beef trolley. Helen, obviously the Carver, now had on an apron and gloves and looked quite a lot like Sue Ann Nivens. The flight attendants asked us the searching questions they had no choice but to ask: "Rare, medium, well? Horseradish cream or au jus? Chives, sour cream, butter, and would you like any—" The plane bumped a hard bump, like we had gone over a very big log in the road. Only of course there was no road.

Then this huge plane made a collective noise like an old clock shop being hit on its roof by a giant's hard fist. Helen, carving beef for the other center table, now looked down at her left hand. A neat line of blood appeared where the carving knife had sliced along it nicely.

"Shit," said Helen, watching the blood racing out of her hand. "Oh shit. Karl?" The plane bounced (bounced? yes) down and up. The FASTEN SEAT BELT sign went *bing*.

We were rocked suddenly to the hard right, then hard left. If we'd been on a train, I suppose we would only have felt we were rounding two hairpin curves twisting around a mountain. But of course we weren't on a train. A few drinks fell very quietly off the trays of those seated at the windows. We suddenly remembered that we were not in some pleasant Lawry's The Prime Rib on La Cienega Boulevard but in a long metal tube, a javelin being self-hurled at a height nature had never intended any of us to achieve. We lurched again, this time a bit sickeningly to the stomach. Helen, Kim, and Karl raced the beef trolley up the aisle, hitting Reuben with a corner of the cart as they did so, and secured it somewhere near the galley.

The wall phone upon which Helen had been notified of Lanny's arrival rang a series of bell tones. I remember once being told that six bells was the captain's command that every stewardess must take a designated seat, even if it meant throwing a passenger out of it, so that they might be best positioned to save others after the crash. Had I just heard two sets of three tones or one set of six? Helen listened on the phone and nodded. She then spoke over the P.A., using the phone as her mike.

"Ladies and gentlemen, the captain says we are encountering unexpected turbulence and we ask all passengers to return to their seats."

Making matters worse was the fact that the NO SMOKING sign immediately went on with a pleasant *ding.* I only associated "no smoking" with the first moments of takeoff and the last minutes of landing. Surely that couldn't be good. I hated that *ding.* The people who manufactured the device that made that *ding* weren't on the plane with me, damn them. Where was my upstairs lounge now? If anyone could have broken my fall, it would surely have been the overweight couple to my right.

Lanny, Irv, Reuben, and I were seated at a circular table that was turning and shuddering as if at a séance. I would have suggested we join hands and try to contact the dead, but I was afraid we'd have a more direct connection any second now. Reuben was no longer smiling but was doing his best to hold on to the tabletop. Irv just sat with a grim set to his mouth as if his teeth were clenched, which they most likely were. His fist was wrapped tightly around his glass. Most of his Cutty Sark and soda had spilled onto the tablecloth.

I looked at Lanny, feeling panic rising within me. He smiled in a breezy manner. "You really don't have to worry," he said. "I know it feels scary, but try to keep in mind that the engines are lifting and sustaining a two-hundred-ton airplane—that's the ridiculous part. A seventy-mile-an-hour head wind isn't going to make this baby break a sweat."

I guess I didn't look convinced. He cupped my hand with his. "I'm a pilot myself, Bonnie. Believe me, we're fine."

Despite having researched Lanny a bit, I had not known he was a pilot. This I found more reassuring than the part about lifting two hundred tons of metal into the air. After all, for this technological hubris, surely the buffeting we were now receiving was God's version of a good spanking. I was terrified about that last spank, the "one for luck."

I thought about telling him who I really was. It would be nice to share a secret with him. An act of communion. "You know, I'm not a second-grade schoolteacher and my name is not Bonnie. I'm the journalist who wanted to do a book about you and Vince." That's what I would say. But I didn't.

The glorious thing about turbulence is that it rarely ebbs away in incrementally smaller bumps and milder jostling. It usually just stops, like a poltergeist's tantrum. This did just that. Suddenly all was calm, all was bright. The FASTEN SEAT BELT and NO SMOKING signs went out. Reuben immediately proffered Lanny's cigarette case toward me, but I indicated that I had my own. He then offered it to Lanny, who snatched at a cigarette. Reuben slid Lanny's lighter across the table to him and Lanny lit up shakily. "Jesus," he muttered.

"What?" I asked.

"I hate flying," he said.

"Well, how do you pilot a plane if you hate flying?"

He took another drag on his cigarette. "Who pilots a plane? I just said that to make you feel better. Sorry, didn't mean to lie." He put out his cigarette half-finished. "I hate flying."

Irv called out, "Waitress?" to Kim, who was making the rounds. I could see by the galley that Karl was wrapping a bandage around Helen's hand. Helen looked pale. I didn't dislike her as much as I had.

Kim stepped over to us. Irv held his glass out. "Cutty rocks, please? A stiff one."

She nodded acknowledgment of the order, then said in a low tone to Lanny, "Mr. Morris, I know this is a terrible imposition, but we could really use your assistance back in economy."

Irv spoke up. "Mr. Morris is a passenger, miss, and his privacy is—"

"I understand and I'm very sorry, but we are permitted by FAA regulations to request any assistance that a passenger may be able to provide in an emergency. Physicians, technicians, amateur pilots—" She turned to Lanny. "We have a passenger who's hysterical."

"Great, she can be my head writer," said Lanny. He unbuckled his seat belt and slid away from the table. "Fuck," he muttered. He acted as if he'd had to do this before. He turned to me and beseeched, "Keep me company?"

I nodded and rose, somewhat unsteadily, owing to both the wine and the previous few minutes. Reuben also started to rise, but Lanny said, "No, Reuben, you see that Irv gets his drink and find out if the stewardess who cut herself could use some of your first-aid training." (Lanny later explained to me that Reuben had been a combat medic attached to the Philippine Scouts during World War II.)

Kim led us quickly back to the crowded economy section. Toward the rear of the right aisle, a big, middle-aged woman was being pinned down by a stewardess, whose knees were planted on the woman's shoulders. The passenger was disheveled and emitting grunting sounds as she struggled. "You have to calm yourself now," said the stewardess, whose name tag read BARBARA. The passenger cried out, "I can't breathe, my lungs have collapsed!" and tossed Barbara off her. Racing up the aisle, she screamed, "I have to get off the plane!" and rammed into Lanny, who'd placed himself in her way. He winced at the impact but embraced her. "Hey, hey, hey, what's with all the commotion, missy?" he inquired in a fabulous impression of himself.

On the movie screen in front of us was the image of Michael Caine. The in-flight movie had obviously been started before the turbulence had hit. Lanny nodded toward the screen and whined in his trademark adenoidal voice: "Hey, usually I think when you make this much noise at the movies, you get thrown out of the theater, but usually I think the theater isn't at twenty-eight thousand feet, huuuuh?"

The woman froze. "Lanny Morris," she said. Starstruck awe suddenly outranked panic. She searched his face. "You're the *real* Lanny Morris. You're on this flight?" she asked somewhat redundantly.

"If I'm not, missy, the in-flight movie is in three-D, what's your name, sweetheart?"

"Dolores Kreutzer," she said. "You're my biggest fan."

He smiled and said in his singsong voice, "You would be surprised how many nice people say that, although I think they mean it like the whole otherwise, huuuuh?" He did an upward portamento on the "huh." He was no longer the Lanny Morris I'd been dining with.

Dolores clutched at his arm. "I got scared, I was afraid . . ."

"Of the bumping and the not nice with the hurting and bouncing, huuuuh?"

"You wouldn't let me die, would you, Lanny?" she asked like a child.

He switched to his Vegasy, virile voice. "Sweetheart, I haven't died with an audience since the Concord. You think the Lanny-Man would let anything happen to you? I'm your biggest fan, remember? C'mere, hug-

hug. Hug-hug." He embraced her. She trembled in his arms, in a completely different fashion than her thrashing hysteria. He patted her back and soothed, "Okay, Scooter, you gonna let Lanny get you to New York safe and sound now?"

Stewardess Barbara chimed, "There, Dolores, you hear that? Lanny said everything's okay, so everything's okay now, right?"

I thought it was wonderfully absurd that the stewardess voiced such credence in Lanny when he hadn't been given barometric readings, weather updates, or the flight plan even, huuuuuh?

"If I crash with *you,* Lanny, it was worth it," Dolores gushed. "May I have your autograph?" She reached into a nearby seat pouch and pulled out the plastic laminated card showing how to adopt the brace position and where to exit the plane in case of a landing on water. I could see Lanny anticipating a problem. He looked down the aisle and, of course, every eye was on him and everyone was murmuring, "That's Lanny Morris" to each other, which sounded an awful lot like *peas and carrots, peas and carrots.*

"I'm afraid my pen won't write on plastic," said Lanny.

She reached over to a seat pouch for the airline's magazine, *Sky Trails,* and held it out to him. "To Dolores," she requested.

Lanny knew (and I could see that he knew) that the instant he reached for his Scripto Admiral, he was a doomed man. As he scrawled his signature on the magazine, it seemed like half the passengers rose and came at us. We'd made the mistake of backing up into the center front row, directly by the movie screen. Before we could rethink this strategy, they were closing in on Lanny and me from both sides, crushing us against the now-buckling projected image of Charles Bronson and Michael Caine.

Lanny looked at me grimly. "Won't you join me in my worst nightmare?"

Stewardess Barbara, still in the aisle, was uselessly clapping her hands and asking everyone to return to their seats. I barked at her, "Tell the captain to turn on the FASTEN SEAT BELT sign." Barbara nodded and retreated to a wall phone by the large emergency-exit door. I tore the seat cushion off a vacant chair in front of me, grabbed the life jacket beneath it, and found the vest pocket that had a standard-issue emergency whistle in it. I blew it hard and its shrill sound quieted the crowd for a moment. Above me, the FASTEN SEAT BELT sign went on with a pleasant *ding.* Barbara spoke over the public-address system: "Ladies and gentlemen, Captain Anderson has again put on the FASTEN SEAT BELT sign. Please return to your seats now or be in violation of federal regulations and subject to arrest and prosecution." Barbara put this over well, and the passengers moved back to their seats.

As they began to sit, Barbara undid all the good she'd just done by announcing, "Now if you'll all remain seated, I'm sure Mr. Morris will be glad to sign any autographs by coming around the plane to you, starting with this left aisle and then back up the other!"

Lanny's shoulders instantly went limp, and he gaped incredulously at the stewardess. Some part of his brain turned up a back burner of loathing in his eyes. Barbara actually flinched when she saw it.

As you can imagine, Lanny spent most of the rest of the flight making the rounds of the heavily booked plane. Everyone over the age of twelve had something to tell Lanny about what their cousin thought of him or how they had seen him at his first professional performance. Lanny was polite and feigned interest in each related story, but he didn't seem to receive any inner gratification from the worship of the crowd. Walking this gauntlet was simply a professional obligation that he discharged honorably and without complaint. To him, things like this, regrettably, came with the deal.

If it was odd that I stayed with Lanny throughout his Grand Promenade of economy, he didn't seem to think so. As a journalist, of course, this was great stuff for me to observe, seeing how Lanny dealt with his public on a one-on-one basis. But Lanny didn't know I was a journalist. I guessed he was accustomed to having a woman at his side who was pleased to be photographed in the same frame with him, bearing the identifying tabloid caption of "current companion."

Irv and Reuben eventually came back to see what had happened to us, and each tried in their own way to get Lanny out of signing autographs for every person on the flight. But Lanny said the usual things about harm having already been done and putting toothpaste back in the tube. (My greatest wish is to see the day when toothpaste *is* successfully put back in the tube, but then again, I'm a hopeless dreamer.) Irv returned to first class to talk with Helen and the captain and also to make sure the airline's press office informed A.P. and U.P.I. of Lanny's generous intervention with hysterical Dolores and autograph session with the other passengers.

I was able to pretty much be myself around Lanny, with the exception of every factual detail of my life. Lanny himself was a genuine surprise to me. His private humor turned out to be quite low-key, but for the occasional horrendous pun, and he could talk for as much as five minutes without feeling the compulsion to make a joke. He had that self-taught intellectualism common to many celebrities; "smart" words like *egregious* and *ubiquitous* were used and pronounced with pride, as if they'd been learned recently and were making a special guest appearance in his conversation. All in all, he was not only unlike his public image and what I would have expected . . . he was also nothing like the voice I'd heard in the memoirs I'd read. Why would that be?

As Kim was telling us over the P.A. to restore our trays and return our seats to their upright position in preparation for our arrival at JFK, Helen knelt at the side of my chair. The bandage around her hand bore a rust-colored stain.

"Hon, the captain wants the company to send you something as a thank-you for helping out Lanny and American Airlines during the flight." She confided in a lower tone, "It probably will be something like a round-trip ticket somewhere, they usually do very nice things." Helen had a notepad and she clicked the end of the pen, poised to write. "We just need your name, address, phone number . . ."

Lanny had switched seats with Reuben so as better to converse with me, and was now looking right at me. I took a breath. "Oh, sure . . . Bonnie Trout, that's T-R-O-U-T, 235 East Thirty-third Street."

"That's a nice neighborhood," Lanny commented. "There's a CBS recording studio right in the middle of the apartment buildings. Can't record after ten P.M."

I nodded agreement.

Helen asked, "Is there an apartment number or . . ."

"Apartment 4D," I answered. "New York, New York, obviously. Zip is, uhhhh, one zero zero one six."

"Phone number?" asked Helen.

I gave her a number and saw that Reuben was leaning around from Lanny's seat and writing all this in a notebook. Lanny asked, "You don't mind if Reuben takes down your phone number as well, do you?" I said of course I didn't. He added, "Great. Anyone meeting you at JFK?" I said there wasn't and he said he'd give me a lift home. I couldn't think of a reason to say no. He told me to give Helen the luggage claim check that was stapled to my ticket and I explained I just had my carry-on garment bag.

At JFK, we were allowed to exit before everyone else. The word *security* was invoked a few times to pacify the Brit and the businessmen, who were annoyed at having to wait until Lanny had "cleared the gate area." There were cries of "Bye, Lanny" and "We love you!" from the economy passengers, and Lanny acknowledged them with a sideways wave of his hand.

I had apparently become part of Lanny's entourage. Reuben insisted on carrying my garment bag and looked as if it would offend him if I didn't allow this. Halfway up the gangway, an American Airlines employee opened a door in its side and the four of us descended a portable flight of stairs that had been rolled up to this side door leading down to the tarmac. A Lincoln Continental stretch limo was waiting not far from the very DC-10 we'd exited.

A big-chested driver stood with his hands clasped together. "Hi, Mr. Morris. Mr. Fleischmann. Hi, Reuben."

Fleischmann handed his carry-on bag to the driver. "You're uhm . . . ?"

"Michael Dougherty. From Dav-El. I've driven you a number of times. The airline says they'll bring your bags by hand over to the limo, you probably would like to wait inside the car. I kept the A.C. on. You remember me, Mr. Morris?"

Lanny looked at Michael. "Your mother is a typist for Senator Javits, right?"

Michael nodded proudly. "That's really nice you remember, Mr. Morris. I have no bigger fan than you."

Michael had opened the car door for us, and we scooted in. It was nearly midnight in the late summer, and even minus the sun the evening was still warm. It was nicer in the limo. Cool and dark. Through the tinted glass, I saw a uniformed American Airlines worker pull up in a mini-train. He had a load of luggage and quickly set about putting some of it into the trunk of the Lincoln Continental under the supervision of Reuben and Mike Dougherty.

Irv needled Lanny, "You should have let me set up a press conference here. It would have been good publicity."

Lanny rolled his eyes. "It's not like I landed the plane, Irving. Please. You'll get the word in a couple of columns that I'm a good scout, okay?

End of story. To hold a press conference would imply I'd done something heroic. That would be ostentatious." He produced this last word with some pleasure.

Mike sat himself down in the driver's seat and called back through the dividing window, "The Plaza, folks?"

Lanny looked at me. "First we're taking Miss Trout to . . ."

Two thirty-five was the number I had given Helen. "Two thirty-five East Thirty-third," I said.

"And thanks for dealing so nicely with the luggage, Michael," said Lanny.

"All I'd ever ask back is one question, Mr. Morris," said Michael.

"What's that?"

Michael steered the limo onto the Van Wyck Expressway. "When are you and Vince Collins gonna kiss and make up?"

"Make up what?" asked Lanny.

We all laughed, but a look of displeasure fluttered across Lanny's features.

No matter how excited I may be whenever I return to New York, the drive from either of its airports into Manhattan—past abandoned tenements, overcrowded cemeteries, and decrepit warehouses with rotted wooden facing only an arsonist could love—is enough to make me pine for the Santa Ana Freeway. At this hour, though, darkness served as a drop cloth over the worst of the view, leaving to be seen only the lovely cliché of the illuminated Manhattan skyline, promising absolutely everything.

"I hate New York in June, how about you?" Lanny asked, staring out the window. It was August, but I assumed he was paraphrasing the song.

"I like it," I said. "What's the matter with it?"

He shrugged. "My life here, as a kid in Brooklyn, wasn't very pleasant. I was brought up as a nice, middle-class Jewish boy, which was not the greatest idea since we were extremely poor and lived in a rough Puerto Rican slum. A handful of Italians, a few tough Irish. My aunt couldn't afford to live anywhere else. I owned two always clean white shirts, two pairs of corduroy pants, two black yarmulkes, and one green corduroy zippered jacket. Imagine if in Nazi Germany there had been only one Jew, and he was me. There you have my childhood."

He reached into a small ice bucket by the decanters, tossed a couple of cubes into a cut-glass tumbler, took out a decanter of vodka, and poured it over the ice. "This isn't vodka, it's bottled water," he advised. "You want some?"

I was dehydrated from the flight and joined him. As he fixed me a water on the rocks, he continued, "Look, *I've* met a few Jews I didn't like. My second wife, for example, was Exhibit A for the defense at the Nuremberg trials. What I minded was that not only did everybody in my neighborhood hate me, but they all tried to do something about it. Cheers."

I clinked water glasses with him.

"Every part of my career has been an effort to escape that neighborhood, those gangs— You ever have the dream that you're back in high school?"

"Once or twice a year," I confirmed. "Usually naked."

The limo slipped into the Queens Midtown Tunnel. The lighting was so brightly fluorescent that it penetrated our tinted windows, turning Reuben a sickly color and making Lanny pale. He mused, "Every week or so, I dream I'm a kid again, and I've made the mistake of coming back to New York. They've got me. All of them, in the alley behind the chop shop with the high wall and barbed wire on top, and this time they're going to use knives, not fists, and this time old man Quinn isn't going to see what's happening, so he won't run to get a cop."

We sipped our water until we came out of the tunnel and turned up a dark, narrow street of nondescript apartment buildings. There were no storefronts, restaurants, or (at the moment) pedestrians. There were only a few streetlamps, and one of those had burned out. Imagine if you had waited all your life to see Manhattan and someone told you this was it.

I could hardly see Lanny's face now. He was lost in another borough, another time. He downed the last of his water. Michael Dougherty lowered the divider window and asked over his right shoulder, "Number 235, miss, is that between Third and Second Avenue?"

"Mmmmm," I said in what I hoped was a noncommittal voice that might be taken for affirmation or negation, because I honestly wasn't sure of the answer.

Lanny continued softly, "One of the reasons I'm telling you this is because sometimes when you talk about something, you don't dream about it."

He didn't have my full attention. I was straining to see which side of the street 235 was on. I saw 217. It was a Laundromat. The next doorway led to apartments above the Laundromat.

"Along here?" asked Lanny.

A lit sign in an opaque storefront window read THE VELVET TOUCH—MASSAGE $12 AND UP and below it the words *Let our fingers do the walking.* (The presence of a massage parlor was, by the way, no indication that the neighborhood was bad; they had sprung up absolutely everywhere in the last few years.)

"I see 237, but not 235," Lanny murmured.

I looked back and barely perceived an unlit doorway, very old-fashioned, that looked like it was part of the massage parlor. "We overshot it," I said casually. "It's not very well lit, I'm afraid. But, well, it's home."

Michael Dougherty backed up the limo a few feet, popped the trunk, and hustled out and around to open my door. I got out and followed him back to the trunk, where Lanny was already standing, my garment bag in his right hand.

"Let me see you inside," he offered.

"It's not necessary."

"I'd feel bad if I didn't." He strode toward "my" apartment building, leaving me no chance for debate. I followed as he pushed open the outer door, which was not locked, and stood by the inner glass-and-steel doorway, which was. He nodded toward the lock. "Your turn, I think."

I started fumbling in my bag, making much of looking for a set of keys. Lanny smiled, in no particular hurry.

On the other side of the glass door, from a street-level apartment, came an old man in his eighties with a nicely manicured poodle on a short leash. He had on a plaid tam-o'-shanter (the man, not the poodle, although it would have looked quite a bit better on the dog). The old man wore a thin trench coat that he'd belted, not buttoned. The front of the trench coat flapped as he walked, and I could see he was wearing only blue boxer shorts and a sleeveless T-shirt beneath it. His feet were tucked into long, thin white socks and fluffy blue slippers. He opened the door, and I made a big deal out of keeping it open for him as he got the poodle out of the building.

"Hi there!" I chirped. "It's still pretty warm out tonight for you, thank goodness."

Any old man, straight or gay, will talk to any reasonably attractive girl who smiles at him. He sighed. "Thank goodness. Pepé doesn't keep banker's hours."

"Don't I know!" I said as if I did know, and as if I knew him and Pepé as well. I knelt down and scruffed up his head. The dog's, that is. "Pepé, have you been a good dog while I was away? Have you? Have you?" Pepé barked. Having established my longtime relationship with Pepé, I stood and warned the old man, "Don't be out there too long, now. Is the elevator working?" The question spoke of a familiarity with the place, and there could be no wrong answer unless (my heart jumped) the apartment was a walk-up. Luckily, I saw a lone elevator at the end of the drab hallway.

"Yes, thank goodness," he said as he left the building. "Took them long enough. Night," he added to Lanny, who kept his head down—to avoid an "Aren't you Lanny Morris?" scene, I assumed.

Lanny stood in the hallway with me. "Bet he's nuts about you."

"Oh, we're only acquainted by that kind of exchange; I don't even know his name," I replied with absolute accuracy. I looked up at Lanny. He was virtually the same height as Vince, which surprised me because in their movies it seemed as if Vince was always looking down at Lanny. "Well, this has been a remarkable day in my life."

"I'm seeing you inside your apartment door." He smiled, pressing the button for the elevator. Immediately I heard it start to descend. It was loud, like the conveyor belt in a silent melodrama's sawmill that is bearing the heroine to her certain doom.

"There's really no need," I said.

"Don't be silly—I won't try to come in, promise. But you've been away from your apartment for—how long now?"

"Ages," I admitted with that candor for which I'm known.

"Okay, well, you don't know if someone has broken in while you were gone. Let me just see you to your door. Believe me, I'm not trying to seduce you. I have to do the *Today* show at seven A.M. and they want me in makeup by six-fifteen." This was surely the first time anyone had ever used that particular line on me.

The elevator door opened and we stepped inside. It had the faint aroma of boiled cabbage, sautéed onions, and cigarette smoke. Lanny's hand poised over the buttons. "Which floor . . . ?"

For a second I couldn't remember. "Why, um . . . four." That was right, 4D, I'd said, and I saw that the elevator only went up to four. "The penthouse." I tried to make my hesitation seem like I'd been formulating a joke. He pushed the button and the elevator rose slowly as if being cranked up by hand. It had been designed for a maximum of only four people. My garment bag guaranteed we were fairly close to each other.

Lanny said, "I'm going to be in town for about a week. I'd like to see you again. How old are you?"

"Twenty-six."

"Well, look, okay, I'm old enough to be your father but only just barely. And for it to have been legal, I would have had to have been married in the state of Georgia with my parents' written consent at that. Is the age difference a big problem for you? We could double-date with the old fellow and his poodle downstairs. I'll seem like a spring chicken by comparison."

"How old are you?" I asked, knowing from his current press kit that his official admitted age was forty.

"Forty-two," he answered.

I liked that a lot. That he was honest with me, not that he was forty-two.

"No, I'm okay about that," I said.

The elevator stopped on the fourth floor. We stepped out into a short hall that went both left and right. "Which way?" asked Lanny. I looked for a helpful sign indicating which way 4D might be. There was none. But of course, if I really lived in Apartment 4D, I wouldn't need a sign to know which way it was, would I?

"Guess," I said coquettishly.

"Why?" he asked reasonably.

I leaned against the wall. "Oh, because if you have to search, we'll have another minute to talk."

He pulled my bag over his shoulder and trudged down the hall. I stayed by the elevator, looking all cutesy-poo. I must have been setting back the cause of women's rights by about twenty years.

"This it?" Lanny asked.

"You tell me," I moued.

He looked at the door. "4G. So it must be this way?"

He pointed in the other direction. I tried to look like I was playing the cutest little game, but actually I felt like a complete imbecile. He located a door at the far end of the hall. "4D," he said. "Last stop. Now let me just see you get in the door okay and I'll leave you alone till tomorrow." He looked at his watch and corrected himself. "Or actually, later today."

I saw that there were two locks on the door. I pulled out the keys I'd been fiddling with since we'd walked into the building. "This could take some time. I never get which key goes in which lock the first time." God, I was depicting myself as a total ditz here. One key was new and brass-colored and I fitted it into the upper lock of the door, which was new and brassy as well. The key turned and I felt the lock give. Hosanna. I tried a duller key in the much older lock below it, and the door opened. Well done, O'Connor.

"Well, thank you so much for everything." I smiled, stepping into the doorway. It was totally dark in the room. I reached for a light switch and didn't find one. I made the mistake of reaching for it on the other side of the door and found nothing there. I was afraid I had snatched defeat from the jaws of victory by looking like I didn't know where my own light switch was—I didn't—so I did the obvious thing, which was to kiss him.

I probably would have kissed him anyway. He took my kiss as if it were the most natural thing—maybe it was—and reciprocated very nicely, I want to tell you. It was a good kiss as these things go, something of which we could both be justifiably proud.

In this particular epoch of American culture, it would have been the expected thing for us to now have sex.

He set down my garment bag in the still-dark apartment and said, as if giving instructions to himself: "Okay, I'm going to leave now because I have Reuben and Irv sitting in the limo downstairs, and I also really have to get some sleep for the *Today* show or I'll look old enough to be your grandfather when they get me on camera. So I'm going to be well behaved now. But I want you to know that I have never hated Barbara Walters until this particular moment . . . and you should definitely not feel so safe with me again." Barbara Walters was cohosting the *Today* show at that time, and I took this statement to be a compliment.

"Do you need my number?" I asked.

"Reuben has it, remember? He's my human Rolodex, I'm terrible with numbers. If you want to call me at the Plaza—not tonight but any-time thereafter, I'm putting a 'Do not disturb' on my phone until five A.M.—you call and ask for 'Lenny Merwin' and they'll put you through to me. Or you might get Reuben, but you can leave a message with him. He likes you."

How Lanny knew Reuben liked me I wouldn't know, but it was nice to hear. I repeated the name he had told me. "Lenny Merwin."

"Right. If you forget, it's my character's name in my first movie with Vince."

"Smithereens," I said reflexively and foolishly.

"Yeah." He looked at me. "Hey, you're a bigger fan than you let on." His expression was almost one of disappointment.

"I'm afraid I've never seen it," I lied. "One of the people on the airplane mentioned seeing it when he was a kid. The name stuck in my head."

Lanny looked relieved. "Oh. I guess I didn't hear that. You get numb after a while. Well. I'll call you tomor—" He looked at his watch again. "I'll call you later. Lovely to meet you, Bonnie." He hurried down the hall, stepped into the elevator, and was gone.

I fumbled around, finding that the long-lost light switch was on the other side of a portal leading to what had once surely been a decent-sized storage closet and now was an indecently minuscule kitchen. That innovation only a New York landlord could have envisioned, the combination refrigerator-stove, took up most of the space. I moved past the kitchen-bath experience and into the living quarters, if you could call this living. Some prints of flowers, some photos of someone else's babies, and the scent of potpourri that managed to mask the dark odor of roach spray. Across half the room at a height of not quite six feet was a loft bed, a very full-sized one accessed by a ladder. It looked like an inviting expanse, but sitting up in bed would have to be negotiated very diplomatically with the ceiling. The underside of the bed also served as a ceiling for the area below it, where the occupant had an old writing desk, a gooseneck lamp, and what I sought more than anything else: a phone.

I picked up the Princess phone, which instantly lit (its best feature). Here in the darkness "under the arches" of the platform bed, its soft light helped me find the switch to the gooseneck lamp, and at last I could see a bit better around me.

I sat down in a beanbag chair against the wall opposite the desk and dialed the operator, who asked how she might direct my call. I told her I wanted to make a collect call to Los Angeles, and when asked, I gave the operator my own West Coast number. I heard a few rings on the line through the steady surf-noise of a transcontinental call. I knew those rings were sounding now on my own telephone. I imagined it purring in my somewhat overplush bedroom, filled with art nouveau prints and myriad decadent little touches, multicolored miniature perfume bottles, unusual drapery, perfect peacock feathers, leaded amber glass hanging in front of the window with an uninteresting view of the pool, a fountain gurgling just outside my kitchen window, and everywhere the lightest scent of Jungle Gardenia. Despite how pleasantly most of the day had gone, from this grim little Manhattan garret I envied the person who would be answering *that* phone in L.A. *My* phone.

On the fifth ring, Beejay, my roommate from college, picked up the receiver of my phone, told the operator she'd accept my call, and said hello.

"Hi," I said. "I'm in."

We'd remained friends after we left college and had always tried to see each other whenever I came back to New York. After I'd learned that Neuman and Newberry wanted to meet with me, I'd immediately called her to make plans. To our mutual chagrin, Beejay told me she'd just that afternoon taken advantage of a price war between American and TWA and bought herself a round-trip ticket to Los Angeles, good for the next twenty-one days, excluding Fridays and Sundays. That was when I suggested we swap apartments for a week, which would give her free use of my place in Studio City (which she had sort of planned to have anyway) while I would use her place in Fun City, which would give me Neuman and Newberry's sizable, Manhattan-calculated per diem to spend on something other than a matchbox-sized hotel room whose nightly cost was equal to the price of a Dunhill lighter.

She had flown into L.A. just the day before. I'd shown her how to open the valve to the gas fire under my ceramic logs and how to open the gas tank of my convertible. We'd exchanged keys and had dinner at Yamashiro, a restaurant some 250 feet above Hollywood Boulevard. It was a replica of a Kyoto castle of the same name and served not only as a restaurant but as a de facto Hollywood standing set, frequently used for TV and movies and as close to a Japanese fortress as you were likely to find within three miles of the Burbank Studios.

We had the most wonderful time at dinner, and I picked up the tab. I wasn't about to let Beejay pay any part of her first night out in Los Angeles. I knew what a big expenditure the discount plane ticket had been and how little her job paid, probably little more then sixteen to twenty thousand a year. I called her Beejay, because her initials were B.J. and she hated her full name, which was Bonnie Jean Trout. She was a public-school teacher at P.S. 29 on Orchard Street. Second grade.

TEN

Beejay was not all that entranced with me when I explained what had happened. She pointed out that when she'd offered to trade apartments with me for a week, she hadn't actually intended to throw in her birthright as a loss leader.

"I mean, what was on your mind, kiddo?" she asked in what had become a native New York accent—tragic, because she had grown up in Savannah, Georgia, among some of the world's most graciously spoken people. "Why the hell didn't you just make up a name?"

I tried my best to give her a rational reason. "I always try to work as much truth into a lie as I can. The thing a journalist learns early on is that the truth propagates a million details. Say a bank is robbed and the police ask me where I was at the time it happened. I say I was standing outside the A & P. Now, if I *really* was there, I saw lots of silly inconsequential things that you could never invent. The chicken on top of a Chicken Delight van parked outside was missing its head. Its driver wore a shirt with a mug of beer on it that read VIRGINIA IS FOR LIVERS. Four kids on a bus from Albertus Magnus High School mooned a cop. This is all stuff you could corroborate that you would never invent. But if you're lying, when you say you were outside the A & P, then that's all you've got. This afternoon, I was looking at a five-hour flight with Lanny Morris. If I had made up who I was, I'd have had to improvise a life story that wasn't attached to anything on earth—I couldn't have supported that. On the other hand, *you're* real, Beejay, your story comes equipped with all those little details, and I know a lot of them. So suddenly I could tell him where I work, where I live, where I was born, my father's name . . . instead of having to invent each fact question by question and, worse, keep track of it all."

I thought my explanation was reasoned and understandable.

Beejay replied casually, "I found a bag of Campfire marshmallows in your cupboard and I'm roasting them over the gas jets in your fireplace. They seem to be making quite a mess, you're going to have some cleanup job when you get back here. Tell me, how long do you plan to keep this scam going?"

I told her that this depended a lot on Lanny. Perhaps I'd never hear from him again. But if I did, I asked for her permission to—well, I was going to say "preserve the illusion" or "maintain the charade," but I suppose "continue to lie" was what I really meant. I said I'd promise to only be "Bonnie Trout" for a little while longer and only within his immediate circle.

"Well, for crying out loud, I hope so," she said. "So did you kiss him?"

I told her I did, and if a cringe is something you can hear over the phone, I heard her cringe. "Listen, kiddo: yuck. Lanny Morris is such a weasel-faced middle-aged wanker." I told her Lanny was very far from that. "Yeah yeah yeah, isn't it wonderful that out of all the world, Cupid singled out you and a considerably older, wealthy, internationally known grating entertainer. I guess true love conquers all. Oh, listen, you got a package. Not the post office. Messenger service. I signed your name."

"Aha! Thereby impersonating me, in my apartment."

"Yeah yeah yeah, the delivery guy had a clipboard with a space above your name so I signed it that way or else I got the feeling he wouldn't have left it."

I was curious about the package and asked what the return address on it was. She said there was none. I asked her to open it. She did. I heard a rustling, tearing sound. "It's a manuscript. About fifty pages long. Entitled 'Excerpt from the Memoirs of Lanny Morris.' Hey, he's writing you love letters already."

I reminded Beejay that when the manuscript had been sent, I hadn't even met Lanny. I didn't see any reason at this point to tell her about the previous manuscript I'd seen at Hillman's office. I asked if the package included a cover letter from anyone—Lanny, John Hillman, Warren Richter . . .

"Nothing. Just these pages, typed on an IBM, if I'm any judge and I am."

I wanted desperately to see those pages now. But there was no way to get printed matter across the country in an instant or even overnight. There were telex machines, but these were only good for telegram-length messages. There was first-class airmail but that would be two, maybe three days at best and I was dying to know what was in those pages before I next saw him, if that was to happen. "Beejay. You're going to hate me. I need you to read me that manuscript. Now. My dime, remember?"

It was only ten-thirty her time. I tried to think of the most persuasive words I could use. "Please? I'll give you half my sandwich."

There was silence on her end of the phone.

I added, "You don't actually have to read everything, just skim it and let me hear whatever looks significant."

I heard her sigh. Then: "I have to get some water."

"There's a water cooler with four gallons of Arrowhead spring water sitting in the kitchen."

"Okay. And I have to pee."

"Fine, fine, I'll wait."

I heard her scurry off. I went to get some New York tap water for myself from the kitchen. It was excellent if, like rice, water is healthier when it's brown.

"Okay, ready?" she asked, as I could hear her rustling into position within the down-filled comforter and the loving folds of the silky sheets on my lovely bed. "Just the highlights, okay?"

"More than okay," I said, trying to find some part of her beanbag chair that didn't contain beans.

The manuscript did not seem to pick up directly where the chapter I'd already read left off. A few days later, I would have the actual manuscript in hand, and that is what I will share with you here. It would almost certainly have been more helpful for me if I'd been able to read it in full the first time, rather than hear Lanny excerpted and paraphrased by Beejay. I will tell you in advance that in either format, Lanny's voice once again seemed nothing like the voice of the man I'd met that day, nor could I fathom why these words were being shared with me. But these were easily the least of the puzzles I faced.

ELEVEN

Let me explain to you here why two guys doing as good as we were doing at this point would find ourselves working in the state of New Jersey.

I'm old enough that I can remember trolleys. Tin cracker boxes on tin wheels heading down the middle of the street like they owned the place, which you found out they did if you ever stopped to tie your sneakers in front of one like poor Anthony Tedesco. In my grandmother's time, there were so many of them rolling around that they called the local baseball team the Brooklyn Trolley Dodgers, although by the time I was a kid the team had dropped the word *Trolley.* By the time I was a teenager the city had decided to drop the trolleys as well.

The thing I learned—from a guy who once told me exactly how he'd murdered a married couple, so why would he lie to me about public transportation?—is that back when the trolley companies ruled the boroughs and northern New Jersey, their owners had a big problem. Weekdays, business was great; the trolleys would be packed as tight as Lucky Strikes.

But on the weekends, the seats sat empty. So the trolley companies took it upon themselves to build all these fancy attractions as close to the end of the line as possible, so that people all along the route would have a reason on a Saturday or a Sunday to get aboard the same trolley or train they'd just said good-bye to on Friday. That's how places like Coney Island came to be. And nice picnic grounds with swimming and boating. But most of all amusement parks.

My favorite amusement park was set on the high Palisades cliffs in Bergen County, New Jersey. Once they'd finished the George Washington Bridge, you didn't need a ferry and a trolley to get there. You could take an IRT train to the old terminal at 168th, where you'd catch a public service bus across to Fort Lee and on to this place with beer gardens and bars and dancing and the most dangerous rides since Luna. It was called Palisades Park.

You had the saltwater pool with a machine that made artificial waves. You had a Bavarian Funhouse, where the most fun was standing outside of it, watching them shoot air up women's dresses on a little outdoor balcony that the customers had to step out onto to continue through the maze inside. The view of the girls from the ground below was spectacular.

And speaking of "ground below," to me the best thing about Palisades Park was that its big roller coaster was set right on the edge of the New Jersey cliffs. When you got to the top of the coaster, just before you took the first big plunge, if you looked down on your left, what you saw wasn't the drop to the ground that the Hurricane was built on but the drop to the Hudson River some sixty stories below that. The town at the foot of the cliffs was Edgewater, and they said that was where suicides landed when they jumped from their apartments in Fort Lee. It's not often in life you look straight down and see a different town than the one you're in. Every time you took that first big crash down the Hurricane at Palisades Park, it felt like you were trying to kill yourself.

Most of New Jersey was strictly from Yokelsville, having been farm country until very recently, but Palisades Park, that was something else again. There were as many big, nicely attired, heartless, neckless Italian murderers operating out of neighboring Leonia and Coyotesville as in the five boroughs, and let's face it: anywhere that killers hang out is automatically pretty hip. I mean, for starters you're going to have really good Italian food, at least of the red gravy kind. And since every Italian is an honorary half Jew, you're also going to have some pretty decent Cantonese joints as well. You automatically had good steakhouses, because a good steakhouse is determined mainly by a good steak, and a good steak is determined by what gets brought in from the Midwest on union trucks, and you know who controls the trucks and unions. And where trucks, unions, and gangsters go, liquor stores follow like Porta-Johns at a construction site, because there is money that needs to be dry-cleaned. The phrase "cash and carry" was invented for the mob, not the clientele.

There had been an unusual statute for a number of years that anyone could gamble in Bergen County except people who lived in Bergen County. To me, this seemed like the world's most open invitation to take the money and run. But by the fifties, gambling was definitely outlawed. The Boys had a nickname for the criminalization of gambling in New Jersey. They called it "the Renaissance."

At the center of all the prosperity was a big club adjoining the Park called the Casino del Mar. (The name was originally supposed to be "Casino del Mare" but they dropped the *e* to make it more American.) Almost a year before, we had played some of the last shows in the old nightclub attached to the casino itself, a four-hundred-seater (five hundred whenever *we* worked there, but that's because some people will call anything a table) named Tito's Cliffside Club, which had been plowed under to make way for a shiny new nightclub-restaurant-hotel complex. Not much was made of the shiny new illegal casino that was being built within the complex. Gambling was being moved from the front to the back room, which meant that the showroom had never been more accurately named, since it was all for show, and the front for everything.

It took the Boys a while to figure it out, but eventually they realized having a hot act in the showroom helped legitimize the entire operation. Why are all these cars coming across the bridge from the boroughs of New York City to go to this nightclub and hotel in New Jersey? If the showroom is featuring Penelope and her Trained Cockatoos, there *is* no reason, is there? Of course, everybody and his sister's cousin knew the reason was the gambling, but you can't be *that* obvious with it, or eventually the police or politicos will be shamed into doing something about it.

But if you get the hottest duo in show business to headline at the front room . . . well, *sure,* the crowds are flooding in to see Collins and Morris, and sometimes people get lost in crowds, and sometimes those people who get lost wander to the back of the lobby . . .

Near the doors marked GENTS and LADIES and MANAGER was another door marked CHILDREN'S SWIMMING POOL. If you went through this door, you found yourself in a long corridor, mirrored on both sides, with very bright lighting. What you didn't know was that the mirrors on the right-hand side were two-way, with several guards behind them looking you over and sniffing out whether or not you were kosher.

At the end of the corridor you'd go through another door, where you'd be greeted by a slim gentleman in a tuxedo, who welcomed you with a nice smile and ushered you through another doorway straight ahead of you. He'd even say a password, like you were being let into somewhere special, and he'd tell the guard behind the straight-ahead door to "take care of my personal friend, please," as if you were a privileged character. On the other side of this new door was a short hall leading to metal steps that led down to a loading dock for truck deliveries. It was all cinder block with a poured cement floor and the smell of exhaust in the air.

If it had been determined that you were harmless and had wandered into the corridor accidentally or out of dumb curiosity, you'd be directed to go back around to the front of the building to reenter the Casino del Mar.

But if you were some kind of fink, the loud motor of a

large truck would be started, its engine drowning all other noises. You'd be escorted by a couple of guys into the back of the truck, which had a long metal bench screwed into its side, upon which you would be told to sit between your escorts. The truck would drive to a private, fenced-in garbage dump called LATTANZI AND SONS—LANDFILL outside of East Rutherford. You wouldn't get to meet Lattanzi, but on the way to his dump, you'd be beaten up, either a little bit or an awful lot, depending on what they thought you'd had in mind when you walked down that mirrored corridor on the way to their nonexistent casino.

If you weren't going to be killed, the beating would serve as a warning, and you'd have to find your own way back home from East Rutherford, holding on to some part of your body that was now bent the wrong way.

If you were to die, they wouldn't beat you up much at all. They weren't trying to teach you a lesson you'd remember as long as you lived, because they didn't intend for you to live much longer. Once your fate had been made clear and you knew the true meaning of the words "despair" and "loneliness," they would put a bullet into you and bury you beneath a mountain of landfill. If the landfill didn't crush you, it would smother you soon enough. Hopefully, you were already gone before the backhoe started heaping generous servings of dirt over your body. No one checked first to see if you were dead or not. If you weren't dead yet, that was your dumb luck.

But if you had every right or reason to walk down that secret mirrored corridor, then when you got to the door at its end, the same tuxedoed gent would greet you with the same nice smile and direct you to an unmarked door on his far left, and you would enter one of the sweetest, plushest casinos ever located less than a half hour from Forty-second Street.

Most of the crowds that wandered into the casino were just fine by the Boys. These patrons followed the rules of etiquette that the Boys expected the clientele to observe: no cursing, no brawling, no cheating, and no winning.

As for Vince and myself, the situation was kind of like

that of the bookies who used a bakery as a front, but regrettably the bakery made the best brownies in all of Brooklyn and people kept buying the brownies and pretty soon the horse-racing operation started to cut into the profits of the bakery. We were such a hot draw that the Boys would get a little angry with us. By the time the high rollers hired the limo for themselves and their mistresses, ate a big fancy dinner in the Blue Grotto with lobster *fra diavolo* for ten and liquor for twenty, and greased every palm of every worker on up: the busboy, the water boy, the men's room attendant with the bottles of Pinaud and Vitalis and Aqua Velva, the ladies' powder-room attendant, the coat-check girl, the cigarette girl for a cigar or a fast blow job in the parking lot, the corsage girl, the camera girl who you'd pay for taking a picture (or pay even more for destroying the negative), the bartender who set you up with the cigarette girl, your waiter, your other waiter, your other waiter's brother who made the Caesar salad at your table, the sommelier, the captain, the maître d', the other maître d' who flambéed your cherries at your table, the coat-check girl again, the doorman, the parking-lot attendant, the tip for the limo driver, not to mention (which I'm mentioning) the cover charge, the music charge, the setup charge, and the drink minimum for forty minutes of the songs and comedy antics of Vince Collins and Lanny Morris . . . who the hell had any money left to gamble?

And that was if you went with your wife or girlfriend. God forbid you and your friends went stag. Then there'd be the hookers. And the hotel rooms for you and the hookers. And tipping the night clerk and the elevator operator to look the other way, and room service, and the whole thing would start up again.

There might also be the cost of drugs.

You gotta understand about drugs in the late fifties, early sixties. There were drug "addicts." These were blacks or jazz musicians (many of whom, you'll note, were already black to begin with). And then there were people who sometimes did drugs. But since they were white and had jobs and homes and none of them were full-time working musicians, they were not drug "addicts." They were just jet-setters. At least this was the thinking of the time. Pepsi used to have a jingle suggesting that their cola would keep you "young and fair and debonair." Affluent people who used drugs were just being *extremely* debonair.

To our limited way of thinking, anything you didn't take with a needle was okay. It wasn't *serious* serious. It was like running a red light. Everyone used bennies. Vince added them to his morning coffee like saccharine pills. We used to sing, to the tune of "Lollipop" by the Chordettes: "Benzedrine, methedrine, why not amphetamine . . ."

I realize this is a startling confession but we were . . . "up." All the time. We had figured out that if you slept eight hours a day (which I hear a lot of people like to do), this was one-third of your life gone, shot, lost forever. If you lived to be seventy-two and always slept eight hours a day, you were giving up your active time on earth from age twenty-one to forty-five. Well, come on. Would you have wanted to go from your college graduation ceremony directly to being forty-five, leaving out all you did in between?

When we did finally decide to flatten out (choosing to get unconscious was much less of a defeat than falling asleep), we'd take two or three Tuinals (or one or two *Three*-inals—joke, an old one, not mine). They were real good. Between the moment you took them and passing out, they felt really . . . sexy, you know?

The only drug problem Vince and I ever had was that sometimes we'd run a little low on drugs. Then we'd do our comedy bit with the audience: "Is there a doctor in the house?" We'd always find some smart young Jewish Dr. Stephen Something with his young wife in the audience. Backstage after the show, one of us would ask him, "Listen, as long as I'm giving you my autograph, you think you could give me yours for some medication I need? I'm out of town and they tell me I can't use my doctor's prescription out of state. It's just for some of those pills, the green-and-black ones, what are they called? Yeah, that's it. Just so I can sleep." Or, sometimes, "keep the weight off." The Dr. Steves were more than happy to oblige. They felt it made them our pal.

The Casino had built a brand-new showroom called the Blue Grotto, and it was a very nice place. Lots of good seafood with a Sicilian touch, meaning they shot the lobsters in the back of the head before broiling them (joke).

The showroom was actually belowground, leaving room for the hotel lobby and the hidden casino behind the long barricade of the front desk. The walls of the Blue Grotto were done to look like the walls of a cave, like a funhouse or a Tunnel of Love. They were made of Liquifoam, a mix of plaster and Styrofoam, flammable as all hell, but the Boys had learned that it was a lot cheaper to give a fire inspector two hundred bucks and a ringside table at our show than to spend thousands of dollars on fireproofing. Besides, it was always vital in a business enterprise of this sort to have available the option to torch the place at a moment's notice, should the need present itself.

So this tinderbox called the Blue Grotto sat twelve hundred patrons in total comfort and danger. There were four small waterfalls with catch basins in the four corners of the room—nothing too fancy, you understand, but the nice thing was that blue spotlights hit the basins and reflected the shimmer of running water on the walls of the cave, so the whole Blue Grotto seemed alive with rippling aquamarine light. You also could hear the sound of the fountains gurgling wherever you sat in the restaurant, which drove everyone to visit the rest rooms on a regular basis. The rest-room attendants, who worked strictly on tips, liked that feature a lot.

On a little Japanese-type bridge, you crossed a small pool filled with Maine lobsters. These Maine lobsters were flown in live from Miami each day. Don't ask.

All right, since you asked, I'll explain. See, the Versailles in Miami Beach (which was operated by the same people who operated the Casino del Mar) flew live lobsters from Maine down to Florida every day or two. The Blue Grotto planned to fly in lobsters from Maine as well. But when the Blue Grotto in New Jersey decided it would also fly in Florida stone crabs every day or two from the Versailles in Miami, they arranged for the Versailles to include some of the lobsters that had been flown in to them from Maine with the shipment of stone crabs being flown from the Versailles to the Blue Grotto. This saved the management a third flight from Maine to New Jersey each day, and that's why live Maine lobsters packed in ice (along with stone crabs) were flown in fresh from Miami each day. Sorry you asked?

The Casino del Mar operation was run by one of the biggest of the Big Boys, a man named Sally Santoro. Now, I know that every time you see the name Sally after this, your first reflex will be that I'm talking about a girl, so keep in mind that Sally was a man. He had more balls hanging than Sandy Koufax in spring training, and unlike Sandy, he was very good with a baseball bat in his hands. Sally's real name was Salvatore, but the only people who called him Salvatore were his mother and the politicians who accepted his donations but didn't want to appear to be his buddy.

I wish I could tell you that Sally was a slim, six-foot-six guy who looked like David Niven with glasses and spoke with an English accent. Then I wouldn't seem to be falling back on a stereotype. The trouble is, Sally was a respectable Italian gangster who looked and talked just like you'd expect from the movies. Maybe he'd seen those movies too and copied them. He was one of those cold sons o' bitches: five-ten, jet-black hair, strong arms, strong chest, dark black eyes, thin lips always a little in a frown even when he laughed at my jokes, which he did. He laughed a lot. He was scary.

Sally Santoro ran the Versailles and a few small clubs down in Miami, some strip joints and a really fine whorehouse in Baltimore, and the soon-to-open Casino del Mar in Palisades Park, New Jersey. We had flown out from Hollywood to be at the dedication ceremony for the entire Casino del Mar complex three months before the place would actually open. Sally had invited us up to bring some name value to the ceremony. As a rule you accepted these invitations, unless you had a really good reason, like your mother and father had been killed in a car crash. Loss of one parent alone probably wouldn't be enough.

After the dedication ceremony, which was also attended by Joni James, little Brenda Lee, Domenico Modugno, and actress Mara Corday, Vince and I were told to join Sally and his friends in his office, which was the first part of the new Casino del Mar to be completed. His friends were already sitting around this big, round table that went well with the Spanish Mediterranean decor. There was a lot of black velvet in the room. On the couches and chairs and in the draperies. A lot of the wall paintings were done on black velvet as well. A matador. A tastefully naked woman. A clown. There was a fantabulous view from a terrace of Manhattan, looking across the Hudson at the Cathedral of Saint John the Divine. I bet more than one person had seen that view upside down, while being hung by his ankles off the edge of that terrace.

We were shown seats and Sally said, "Vince, Lanny, I wanted you to meet my business partners here." He gestured to the other men and introduced them, first names only, then said collectively to them, "Guys, these are my very good friends Mr. Vince Collins and his spastic retard Jew partner, Lenny Something." I wondered what I'd done to make him angry. Then I saw him almost smiling and realized this was his brand of humor. Komedy for Killers. The Boys were making little laughing noises somewhere in their necks, so Vince and I laughed along. Hey, Sally, you're funny. *You* should be the comedian. No, says Sally, I leave that horseshit to cocksuckers like you. Laff riot!

A gimpy kid named Frankie brought in sandwiches on a tray. Everyone was happy to see the sandwiches and then absolutely nothing was eaten. Maybe coffee would be poured and reluctantly sipped, but questions like "You want the egg salad, did they send us any Russian dressing, is this ham or tongue?" were topics of as little interest to these gangsters as they were the very center of the universe to Jews like me. In all my life I don't think I've seen an Italian mobster eat a cold meal. Not a tuna-salad sandwich with lettuce, a BLT, or a hard-boiled egg. Okay, I lied: once I saw a mob boss eat a shrimp cocktail, but that took two minutes and then he was on to the fried calamari.

Then Sally and his associates had one of these amazing Mafia nonconversations. They sat there like the place was a steam room. They soaked up the silence, let it settle into their bones.

Finally, Sally started up. "So what's with our friend?" And after about four bars of nothing, one of the others tried back:

"You mean Joey."

Two-beat rest.

"Yeah."

Three-beat rest.

"Joey from Dallas?"

"Joey from *us*."

"Joey with the, yeah, Joey."

"He's okay with that? Because I wouldn't want it to be that he's sayin', you know—"

"No, he's okay."

Intermission.

"And his cousin. Tilio?"

"Yeah, I'm taking care of that. It's done, to be honest."

"So we're over, that's what you're saying."

"Yeah, Sally."

This is exactly how these nonconversations would go. Vince and I heard them many times. Maybe they did it for our benefit. Maybe when there was no else in the room, they talked like the Rotary Club.

There was another forty-five seconds of silence and then everybody but Sally stood, like some floor director had given some invisible cue. Tilio, in leaving, addressed us for the first time. "I saw you guys with Ed Sullivan last Sunday," he said. "That Ed Sullivan is some cold fish, huh?"

I answered, "Yeah, when we met I said, 'Gee, Ed, you look almost exactly like you did when you were alive.'"

Happy laughter.

Tilio nodded. "I love that thing you do walking on your ankles. Do that for me." I did it for him. He loved it. "That's great. Hey, one thing, though: every time I see you guys, Vince here tries to sing a song, he's just getting started, and you come out and interrupt him."

Well, of course, that was the whole departure point of our act, and I laughed at Tilio's joke. Then I saw he was serious. It was like complaining that in *Rhapsody in Blue,* the piano keeps coming in and drowning out the orchestra. "I'll watch it from now on," I nodded with a serious expression.

Tilio nodded back. "You should. Vince is a great singer and a good-looking guy too. Someday he may want to go out on his own, and then where would you be?"

I tried hard not to smile, for Vince's sake. For over a year now, columnists like Jack O'Brien, Moe Cohn, and Earl Wilson had raised the exact same point, only their argument was reversed: what would happen to poor Vince Collins if Lanny Morris ever left him high and dry? It was something we never talked about.

"Next time he cuts into your song, Vince," advised Tilio, "take my advice: just keep singing. The audience will tell him to get his loudmouth Jewish ass right off the stage."

I liked that Tilio was now in show business. Especially since I'd been told that the only time he'd ever killed an audience was when he'd shot a passerby who'd witnessed a rubout.

Vince, for his part, had been playing it very cool, simply smiling away in no general direction. His attitude, and I can't tell you he was wrong, was that you don't win an argument with these guys, so you smile and agree and hope that the next day it's all blown over.

But for me, I was getting a little annoyed. "What is this, the Italian Penny-Ante Defamation League? Keep in mind, Jesus was a Jew."

The Boys turned into a snapshot.

Big John asked very slowly, "What the *fuck* are you saying?"

It was as if one of their wives had said she'd given Sidney Poitier a blow job. They couldn't make sense of the statement, they couldn't envision it, maybe it was some sort of a joke that they just weren't getting. I tried to backpedal. "I'm not saying anything. It's just that Jesus and his family were all Jews who traveled to the, to the Holy Land." I saw their reaction and added, "From Naples, it's now believed."

Tilio didn't know if he should kill me or if he was just talking to the dumbest asshole on the face of the planet. He explained to me, like I was a baby: "Listen, if Jesus Christ wasn't a Christian, where do you think the word *Christian* comes from? The Holy Mother gave him that name."

"Sure, I was just saying that before there was a Christian religion, that Jesus was a Jew. Mary was a Jew too." Whoa. *Big* problem here. Lots of grunting noises from the Boys like I'd gone too far. I bailed: "Only in that there was no Christian Church until Jesus was born. There couldn't be. So Mary had to fall back on whatever religion that was around that was, you know, looking forward a lot to being Catholic."

I heard a chorus of grunts agreeing with this. Sally acted as Dag Hammarskjöld. "Tilio, hey, come on, Vince and Lanny here are comedians, you know? They say whatever they want and the crowd loves them for it. You'll see the show the boys are putting on tonight for the groundbreaking ceremony. You'll sit at my table."

There was going to be a little show that evening in the temporary lobby of the hotel. We were going to perform a song or two. We were the guests of honor, which meant we were working for free.

Sally moved the guys out the door, explaining that he had some business to discuss with us. We wondered what we had done wrong, but what we had done was done good. He sat us down and said he'd always liked us, liked the business we'd done at the old nightclub; he thought we were "a good fit" with his crowd, meaning we brought in an audience that was hip (or thought they were), meaning heavy drinkers, adulterers, and gamblers.

"Thanks for the compliment, Sally," I said.

He said we brought in people who liked to laugh, and people who like to laugh are more inclined to laugh off their losses.

"That's us," I said. "We got them laughing all the way to your bank."

Sally said I was fucking funny. "So what we want is for you guys to come back here three months from now and open our new showroom for us. A two-week, exclusive, limited engagement that we want you to give us for six weeks."

God help you when a killer takes a real shine to you. He'll move the earth over you. I looked at Vince and scratched my nose, which meant our strongest no.

Vince smiled warmly at Sally. "Sally, that's a very great honor."

"You damn fucking straight it is," he agreed.

"Only we've been really trying to cut down on the nightclub work. We just turned down the Sands so we could do a TV special. The only reason we still work the Versailles is out of friendship for you."

Sally just looked at him.

Vince asked, "What dates are we talking about?"

Sally named the date.

I smiled regretfully. "Sally, any other time and we'd be here in a flash. But that's the day we finish the next polio telethon, and we always take off two weeks after that, simply to recover."

Sally didn't even blink. He said he knew that, that he'd intentionally planned our first promotional appearance for the day after we finished our third annual polio telethon, which we'd be doing live from Miami. When it was over, and we were near dead, we were to fly up from Miami that same day, hold a press conference all haggard and hoarse so that people would know what great guys and heroes we were . . . and then we were just going to flatten out for three days of R&R. Which stood for Roche and Rorer, as far as Vince and I were concerned. "Look, boys, I know it's a big favor, but this one is for me, okay?"

I tried to figure out which of the big favors we'd done him in the past were *not* for him. The thing with a gangster is, give him an inch, he'll take a foot and cut it off you and stuff it in your mouth and then ask you if you understand better now that it's been explained to you. Sally's motto was "If you can't beat them, beat them."

He tried to soften the blow. "Look, when you're here, you'll have the run of the hotel. I'll keep a suite with the best hookers I got on your floor, your own personal cathouse— you like young girls? I mean like teenagers, of course. None of that degenerate stuff. Or how about a belly dancer? A real one, not a stripper."

I said, "My partner likes girls who majored in bobbing for apples in a barrel. Girls with really big ears. What do you call their ears, Vince?"

"Handles," smiled Vince.

Sally laughed that soundless laugh. "You fucking crack me up."

Vince said, "Thanks for the offer, but generally speaking we like to find our own talent. You know. The thrill of the chase."

Sally shrugged. "Tell you what, I'll give you your own masseuse, then. And I'll throw in five hundred dollars in chips for each of you every night, they'll be waiting inside the you know . . ."

Of course he couldn't say "casino." There *was* no casino at the Casino del Mar, right? This gift was an old trick they used with entertainers in Vegas and Reno, offering to pay them more if they'd take their salary nightly in chips. The entertainer would start to gamble, get into hock his first night out, and have to pay down his debt by working on a regular basis at the casino in return for just room and board. Sammy Davis was once booked for a long weekend that turned into three years that way.

". . . and I'll have them send you up here your own shipment of lobsters and stone crabs from the Versailles. You like lobster?"

We said we did, because we really did.

"And a case of these grapefruits I get special down there, you never tasted such a thing in your life, you need a towel when you're done eating them. You like Cuban cigars?"

We said we did. Sally frowned at Vince. "You, with your voice! I'll ship up some Cohibas and Saint Louis Reys, they're what Frank smokes, we'll ship those up here for you too. You'll thank me 'cause we don't know what the fuck is going to happen with this Castro guy taking over. Oh, and you like waffle irons, and cameras that take three-D pictures?"

Vince and I looked at each other. I was curious and asked, "Sally, what do those have to do with Florida?"

"Nothing, I'm just up to my balls in waffle irons and three-D cameras, you'll be doing me a favor if you take some. They make great presents. Oh, and I got chinchilla wraps for your mothers." He glared at us and grabbed my wrist hard as it lay on the table. "But only for them, you understand, you cocksucking bastards? I don't want some hooker walking around my lobby wearing the same chinchilla I gave *my* mother. Understood?"

We understood that we were going to return to the Casino del Mar three months from now, directly after finishing the 1959 Veterans Day Polio Telethon, which was the biggest as well as the last of our televised fund-raisers.

The truth is, polio was over. The vaccine had worked. Eventually we learned that the main reason we were still raising money was for all those scumbags at the American Polio Foundation who'd built themselves a very cushy operation with fancy headquarters in Stamford and extremely generous salaries. They used to say "Polio is Public Enemy Number One," but within the ranks, the enemy they really wanted to destroy was Jonas Salk and his goddamn vaccine, which was putting them all out of their sweet jobs.

Three months later we were back at the Versailles in Miami and had closed out our latest stint on Wednesday night. Louis Prima and Keely Smith along with Sam Butera and the Witnesses were taking over from us. They weren't us, obviously, but they did a good show, threw in a little comedy, and they could draw the same sort of crowd.

We spent most of the day out at the private pool the Versailles had. It wasn't much for swimming but it was railed off, which meant we could actually get some sun and a little seclusion. We got back up to the suite around seven and found that Sally had been more than good to his word. Laid out around the living room were various crates bearing the address of their destination, our suite at the Casino del Mar Hotel in Palisades Park, New Jersey. What I thought was a box of beach balls turned out to hold the thinnest-skinned, most dripping-wet grapefruits I ever tasted in my life. Likewise the promised six-foot metal locker filled with fruits of the sea, over a dozen lobsters shifting slowly across a bed of stone crabs and ice. A crate of cigars from Cuba. What cigars. And a box of eight waffle irons and four thirty-five-millimeter 3-D cameras, with viewer and slide projector.

We saw that the crates were closed up again, and having presented them to us for our approval like a fancy birthday cake, the Versailles was to ship these goodies up to New Jersey the next day, where they'd be waiting for us at the new Casino del Mar on Sunday. The insulated metal crate filled with ice and shellfish went to the hotel's meat locker for overnight storage. Sally had kept his word and now expected us to keep ours.

We purposely made it an early night Thursday because we knew we wouldn't have anything resembling a full night's sleep again until Monday afternoon. We called down for Maureen, the room-service girl with the gorgeous red hair that you stopped staring at once you got a look at her body, the same Maureen who'd brought me champagne while I was helping out Vince by boffing Denise. Maureen brought us up three steaks (one was for her) as her last official delivery of the day. Much as I love lobster, all that shellfish nested on ice in the living room had actually put us in the mood for hoofs, not claws. I didn't have much trouble convincing Maureen to also supply some attentive room service in my bedroom. Vince and I had both popped a couple of Tuinals to ensure that we'd sleep like babes, and Vince bought insurance on his bet by having a few babes on hand. Well, not exactly on his hand. The Tuinals, coupled with a nice amount of booze, guaranteed us the sleep of the dead. Late the next morning, Maureen was sent packing and Vince and I went about preparing ourselves for that night's broadcast.

The goal that year was $3.9 million "to stop polio from coming back," whatever the hell that meant. And how'd they arrive at $3.9 million, like four would have been too ostentatious? To remind the viewers of the goal, we had agreed that the telethon could run thirty-nine hours, nonstop. The show would begin at nine P.M. on Friday night and finish at noon on Sunday.

We paced it so that Vince and I were on from kickoff time Friday night to one A.M.; then Vince handled one to three alone, and our announcer, Ed Herlihy, handled three to six, which he really loved doing; then I did from six to nine A.M., catching the Saturday morning kids' cartoon audience. Vince and I worked from nine to three P.M. nice and light, lots of breathers, then we both took a four-hour nap, with people like Jack Narz, Art Linkletter, and Bill Cullen (very sweet guy) filling in. Then the two of us came back out for our big Saturday night, from seven P.M. to one A.M. Bert Parks handled one to six A.M., with Vince and myself dropping in if we felt like it—Vince never felt like it but by this point I was usually wired from lack of sleep, so I did—and then we caught the big wrap-up from six to noon, with Vince and me finishing it bleary and teary and weeping as America got ready to go to church. The effect was that it seemed as if Vince and I had been on the air from Friday to Sunday nonstop, and if we hadn't done exactly that, it was still a pretty heroic effort.

The TV studios in Miami were a miracle. They were one of the main reasons we wanted to do the telethon from there instead of New York. The heat from the overhead lighting for television at this time was a killer, I mean a *killer.* In Miami, they take heat seriously. It's a year-round issue. Until you've stood at the intersection of Fonseca and Ponce de Leon Boulevard for three minutes in any August, you don't know what it feels like to have your pants nicely steam-pressed while they're still on your body. In New York, if you didn't like the heat from the television lighting, they told you that was how it had to be. In Miami, they did something about it.

The Liftin Studios had cool blue walls everywhere, with glassy navy blue linoleum floors, as wet-looking as a rain slicker, covered with coats and coats of glassy Plastic Wax. As you first entered the doors to the studio, the air-conditioning hit you like you were dropping into your neighbor's vinyl pool, which had been filled from a garden hose. By the time you got to your dressing suite, you were rubbing your arms to keep warm, looking for a sweater, and asking about coffee. When you arrived on the stage, where the cameras and audience were, you were grateful to feel the caring warmth of those overhead TV lights. These Miami people knew how to handle heat.

I hadn't wanted to make a joint entrance with Vince, especially not now. Admission to the telethon was first come, first serve, so a good four hours before the broadcast (which was a transcontinental hookup over our own affiliation of local stations) there was already a long line of Collins and Morris fans wrapped twice around the block. This in ninety-six-degree heat.

We had already worked out that Vince and I would secretly enter the studios by crossing from the roof of the building next door, a big piano warehouse. This may sound ridiculous to you, but if you'd been there, you'd know what the mobs Vince and I dealt with were like. I entered the piano warehouse from its service entrance, where two members of the Miami police were waiting for me. The sun had been bright outside and it was pure gloom inside, so I didn't see them at first, until they stepped into a shaft of sunlight coming through the service door. They startled me and I jumped.

I reflexively cracked, "Hey, you got the wrong guy!" (Joke— not my best.) We all laughed.

We took a slow service elevator up, the open kind with a low corral fence in front of it. Then they led me up a short flight of stairs and out onto the roof. Pools of tar bubbled on the carpet of shingles around me. A light aluminum trestle bridge had been placed across the roofs of the two buildings. Although the two buildings were three feet apart at most, still, the four-story drop would kill you.

I told one of the cops, "The rule in Japan is that men walk ten paces ahead of the women except when strolling through a minefield. You first, please." He smiled and went ahead of me, then held the bridge steady on his end. I told the other cop to hold the side behind me and I scooted quickly from one building to another without looking down. Then the second cop crossed over and pulled the bridge over to the studio's roof, just in case anybody else got the idea of coming over that way.

"Just a second," I said. "What about Vince?"

"He's already here, Mr. Morris," said the cop. "We brought him over about fifteen minutes ago."

It was unusual for Vince to arrive anywhere ahead of me. He liked to wander in after I'd gotten the lay of the place, whether it was a TV studio, soundstage, nightclub, or state fair. But today, it made sense.

The cops walked me to what looked like an outhouse in the middle of the roof. One fumbled with a key, unlocked the door to this "privy," and there was a short staircase, which we headed down. A hall led to a bank of elevators, one of which was being held for me. I signed some autographs for the cops and the elevator operator as we went down to a hallway on the first floor, where they walked me to my dressing room, which had an intentionally anonymous sign on the door saying HOST 1. I looked across the hall and saw that Vince's dressing room was marked HOST 2. The police watched me walk into my dressing room and sat themselves down on either side of a small desk outside my door. They let me know they'd be there to make sure no unauthorized persons went into either of our dressing rooms while we were on the air, and particularly to make sure that no one disturbed us when we were napping. I thanked them and shut the door behind me.

There was a vanity with lightbulbs trimming three sets of mirrors. There was a wet bar, a large basket of fruit that would never be eaten, and the makings of a chef's salad laid out buffet-style on a tray. I heard the sound of a newspaper's pages being turned and I swiveled to see our agent, Billy Bishop, stretched out on the bed in a small room attached to my dressing room. I guess he'd told the cops he was authorized. He was dressed in a gray seersucker suit and patterned tie, looking as all Young Turk agents were supposed to look. I frowned at him.

"Shoes off my bed, Billy Boy," I said. "I'm really going to be sleeping there, not just fucking around."

He got up at the right speed, not so fast as to seem like he'd done something wrong, not so slow as to seem arrogant. "Sorry, Maestro," he said, smiling nicely with lots of small teeth. He had been calling me "Maestro" since the day we met, and I'd done nothing to stop him. "See what happened to Cornel Wilde?" he asked, indicating the trade paper on the bed.

Unlike Billy, I had never been that interested in Cornel Wilde. "I want Vince and myself and you to have a quick meeting. Go let him know, will you?"

Billy nodded. "Mind telling me what it's about?"

"No, I don't mind telling you, that's why you're invited to the meeting. Go get Vince." I nodded toward the door. He started to speak, but I guess he saw something in my face that made him cancel the idea and he left the room.

A Kelvinator refrigerator was stocked as per our rider. I found a bottle opener, popped the cap off a C&C Cola (that was the cola I liked) and sat in a chair with my back to the makeup mirror so the bulbs framed me from behind and made it a little harder to look at me in the windowless room.

Vince came in, looking attentive. His eyes went around the small room. "Reuben's not here?" he asked quietly.

As I took out a cigarette, Billy joined us and closed the door behind him. I answered Vince. "He's packing up the stuff at the hotel that we don't need here. I thought this meeting should be private anyway." Vince eyed Billy, and I added, "Except for Billy. He should be part of this."

Vince sat down in the chair next to mine, in front of its own bulb-framed mirror, and looked at me as if I were a waiter setting a plate of warm, green, funny-smelling raw clams in front of him. "Your call," he said.

Billy asked, "Okay if I get one of those sodas for myself, Lanny?"

"Yeah, in a second. Sit down," I advised Billy, and he did so. I took a nice last drag on my cigarette and dropped it into the C&C Cola bottle. "At some point over the next three days, everyone who owns a TV set will watch us. I've thought a lot about it, and I think from the start of the telethon right to the end, we should be talking about our next movie."

Billy disagreed. "You have a movie out right now, Lanny. Plug that."

"Plug you, Billy, it's already out and already it's out, if you know what I mean."

"It did fine."

"It did okay, but we need to change some things." Billy looked at Vince, who seemed as passive about this as I thought he might be. "So what I want us to do is to announce tonight, and repeat through all the hours ahead of us, that our next picture is going to be *A Night at the Opera* for MGM. We're going to accept Shelly Deutsch's offer. Billy, you'll call and tell him we're going to announce."

Vince lit a cigarette and exhaled. He looked vaguely amused.

Billy said, "We've been up and down this, Lanny. It's not a good idea. As a matter of fact, it's one of the really bad ideas. There's no way you're going to get away with remaking the Marx Brothers."

I shook my head. "It's not a remake. It's a whole different take on the story."

Billy said, "So you really want to play Groucho and Chico and Harpo. What, with trick photography?"

"Yeah. Not just split-screen. They have these things called traveling mattes. If Alec Guinness could do it in *Kind Hearts and Coronets,* I sure as hell can. I'm thinking I'll play Harpo as a circus clown, Chico as an American zoot-suit Jazzbo-type, and Groucho as an egghead, my German-professor character."

Billy got up from where he was sitting, opened the refrigerator, and took out an Orange Crush. He uncapped it and took a long drink. "You ever consider the fact that you're one half of a duo, Lanny?"

I looked at Vince. "Vince would do the Allan Jones role," I said.

Vince looked down as if his cue card had fallen onto the carpet and murmured, "Lanny, the Allan Jones role isn't a real part. The Marx Brothers wouldn't have given it to Zeppo. What, I'd sing three songs and marry— Who would I marry at the end?"

"The Kitty Carlisle part."

"So it'll be *'Yes, it's Lanny Morris as you've never seen him before—three times as dizzy—three times as daffy—three times as wonderful, with Vince Collins and Giselle MacKenzie in a duet you won't forget!'* I don't mind playing second fiddle to you, Lanny. But this. I'd be fourth violin."

I aimed my explanation, not that any was owed anyone, at Billy. "MGM doesn't know who the hell they are anymore—they're running around like Chicken Little over in Culver City, I got Shelly Deutsch there throwing money at us to do this project. It's a classic title, they don't owe Kaufman or Ryskind a thing, it was a total buyout." I turned to Vince. "And listen: not that it matters, but when people think 'opera,' what do you think they think? They think singing, they think Italians. Who's the singing Italian in this room? It's perfect. It could get you into a whole Mario Lanza kind of thing."

Vince looked up at me. "Why would I want to get into a Mario Lanza kind of thing?"

Billy brought the bottle of Orange Crush down hard on the buffet table. For the first time since I'd known him, he looked at me without masking his contempt. He had always been chummier with Vince. "Listen, for fuck's sake, Lanny, you'd be telegraphing to everyone, not just the trade but your fans as well, that you think the team is all you. That goes against the whole appeal of the act. People want to think that you think of Vince as your big brother."

"Abel had a big brother," I commented, but I don't think he got the point.

"Even if you think only of yourself, Lanny, this is a terrible move. If this picture is anything less than a smash, people are going to start talking about how you're in love with yourself and how you shat on Vince. The audience will have stopped believing in the love you guys have between you."

"Shut up, Billy," Vince snapped in a quiet tone.

Billy looked at him in surprise. "Come on, Vince, back me up on this."

"What . . . Vince back people up?" I asked. "Joke."

Vince stubbed out his cigarette with his foot on the linoleum floor, even though there was an ashtray on the counter behind him. "Whatever Lanny wants."

I nodded in agreement. "I'd at least like to know that my partner will never try to stab me in the back. You know I have absolutely no interest in ever ramming the knife into you, don't you, Vince? Not ever. Not fucking ever."

Vince held out his hand. "Okay."

I shook my head. "We don't have to shake on anything. We can just say we agree."

Billy retied his tie as if getting ready to leave. "May I be blunt with you, Lanny? Sometimes you are the biggest fucking prick around."

I smiled at Vince. "What do you think, Vince?" I asked. "You think I qualify for biggest fucking prick?"

Vince mumbled something about us having a show to do and left the room. Billy left the room too, not mumbling.

"Live—until they drop dead—from beautiful Miami Beach, Florida! For the next thirty-nine hours, it's the Veterans Day Pooooo-lio Telethon! This is little ol' me, Ed Herlihy, introducing that guy with a voice that's simply from heaven—and his pal with a face that's strictly from hunger. That's right, here they are, folks: your hosts, Vince Collins and Lanny Morris!"

Ed Herlihy's announcing was always right on the money. The perfect blend of formal and informal. As always, Vince came out first, smooth, debonair, smiling at the audience. He sidled up to the standing microphone in front of our orchestra under the direction of Russ Cummings and started working the mike and the crowd and, most of all, the camera. Vince always played to the fullest part of the studio, which he'd smartly realized early on was the camera. All TV cameras had a red light on top that lit up whenever the public was looking at you through its particular lens. Vince really knew his way around that red-light district. Jesus, was he ever a natural.

His first song, "Pennies from Heaven," got a big hand. Let me tell you something: Vince Collins could have carried any show we ever did all on his own. The years since then have only gone to prove that. Great singer, sure, but just as great a straight man. And a great straight man usually has better comedy timing than his partner.

Now out I came to a huge roar from the audience. I was dressed up like I was a Good Humor salesman with my own pushcart, and I started selling, "Ice cream, hey ice cream!"—first to our orchestra, then climbing up into and onto the audience, shaking hands, throwing Popsicles, planting big fat kisses on hysterical fat ladies, and all the while Vince is following me, trying to coax me back to the stage, the band vamping the whole time. How long could this go on? On a show like this, that was left up to me. And since we had thirty-nine hours to fill, I felt generous.

Eventually, the studio audience and most of America being in stitches, we calmed down and got on mike to sing our usual "Two Lost Souls"/"Side by Side" medley. No one on earth would ever have known from looking at that performance that there was anything wrong with our partnership.

The dynamic of our style was brilliant, if I do say so immodestly, since I pretty much invented it myself. What I'd hit on was that Vince and I were really doing a boy-girl act. A few years after this, George Burns pointed out the same thing to me over soup and martinis at the Hillcrest Country Club. Except we were two heterosexual men, one (me) idolizing the other (Vince). So Vince was the guy and I was the equivalent of the goofy dame. The underbelly of Collins and Morris was: Lanny needs to know that Vince likes (loves) him. "I did good, I did good, huuuuh?" was the trademark question I always asked Vince. When he slapped me around, it was the slap that every guy wants to give every broad who angers him; obviously, unless he's a wife beater, he can't hit her. But Vince could slap me all over the moon and the audience would just laugh so much. When a guest star like Rosie Clooney or Marilyn Maxwell flirted with Vince, I'd act insulted that the lady didn't like me as much as she liked him. But the hidden message was: Vince wouldn't leave me for a (another) woman, would he?

I'm not saying anyone ever thought it through that far. They just laughed at us. But there's all kinds of laughter. When people laughed at us, they felt good about it, because underneath all the slapping and the insults was a loving relationship. One that I, monkey-Lanny, hoped and prayed for; one that he, dreamboat-Vince, was saddled with and resigned to.

This all sounds very intellectual, but of course it was also about me falling on my *tuchus* and Vince breaking a prop violin over my head.

I'm not going to get into every minute of the telethon here. I donated the kinescope to the Newhouse School of

Journalism at Syracuse University, and you can check it out there if you want to.

The fact is, Vince and I were never off camera for more than six hours at any given time. That's important to remember. And just for the record, there's no way anybody on earth in 1959 could get to New Jersey and back in under six hours unless he flew in a supersonic jet, landed, had the jet turn around, and took off the next minute. And that probably would have been noticed by, say, the Civil Aeronautics Board, or an airport, or somebody. So that's that.

The Friday night broadcast from nine P.M. to one A.M. was nothing for us, absolutely nothing, just a slightly longer version of our nightclub act. The one to three A.M. slot that Vince did alone was easy enough. He just introduced people from these little file cards he had. Abbe Lane did her whole nightclub act minus Xavier Cugat and that was forty minutes right there. Vince sang "Two Sleepy People" with her and then he introduced Richard Hearne as Mr. Pastry doing his impression of an old man dancing "The Rounders." Pinky Lee followed with his xylophone bit, then ventriloquist Jimmy Nelson with dummies Danny O'Day and Farfel, and by then all Vince had to do was briefly leave Abbe Lane when he and she were having drinks in his dressing room, go back on camera, and tell everyone he really had to get to bed right away.

Ed Herlihy filled in from three to six with the acts that had circled the date of the telethon on their calendars six months ago and had been counting down to the big day.

I was back on the air at six A.M., urging kids to go out and get nickels and dimes from their neighbors. This was for me the most tiring part, because I was without Vince and I had to talk slow and non-showbiz to all the kiddies. You try being Miss Frances from Ding-Dong School for three hours and see what it's like. Thank God for Shari Lewis or I would have passed out then and there.

It was a big relief to see Vince at nine. For about the fifth time that morning, we just happened to accidentally let slip news about our next project.

LANNY: Wow, you sang that song just swell, pal!

VINCE: Thanks very much, Lan.

LANNY: You should be singing somewhere like at the Metropolitan Opera, where they have all the nice costumes and the fat ladies with the German "oh-hoh!" and all like that, huuuuh? Wouldn't you say?

VINCE: Well now, funny you say that . . .

LANNY: Funny I say that *why,* huuuuh?

VINCE: Now, now, Lanny, you know we're not supposed to let slip the big news.

LANNY: What big news would that be, Prince Vince?

VINCE: The news about our next motion picture, *A Night at the Opera,* with you *and* you *and* you and me taking on the world of classical music in our rowdiest romp yet, for MGM.

LANNY: MGM?

VINCE: Yeah, the people who make those movies that always start out with the (*Vince's impression of a lion's roar; my standard scared leap onto Vince's back in fear*).

Professionally speaking, I could only admire what a pro Vince was at every hour, especially considering what had happened. Whenever we hit the talk about *A Night at the Opera,* I wondered if Vince might crack or lash out at me. We were live, you remember. There was no rewind.

By late Saturday night, when we felt like someone had injected scrap metal into our veins, I was very much at the breaking point. That's when Jack Lescoulie, who was helping us out, came on at midnight with a big black telephone that had cables attached to it and told us we had a very important phone call from a very important person. Usually this would be someone like Dwight Eisenhower or Richard Nixon or Bishop Fulton J. Sheen or Eleanor Roosevelt.

"Hello, Lanny, this is Sheldon Deutsch, president of Metro-Goldwyn-Mayer motion pictures."

I looked at Vince in mock shock. He reacted in kind. What total ecstasy we pretended to be feeling, to be receiving a phone call from an old, short Jew who normally would have barely deserved a wave from us at Musso and Frank's on any Tuesday afternoon.

"Sheldon *Deutsch*?" I questioned Vince with a throb in my voice. "He's, he's, he, he, he, he, he, ha, ha, ha—" Vince slapped me across the face, maybe a little harder than was necessary. "He's the head of MGM motion pictures, hello Mr. Shel-*dun.*"

"Hello Lanny and hello Vince," Sheldon read aloud over the phone. His voice was piped onto the floor monitors. We stared at the phone as if God had just come up with an eleventh commandment and had called to let us know about it. *"As the president of Metro-Goldwyn-Mayer motion pictures, now celebrating its fortieth anniversary, it's my pleasure to talk to you via transcontinental hookup from station KDRA here in Hollywood."*

"Transcontinental hiccup?" I joked.

Vince slapped me. "That's *hook*up. He's got a hookup from Hollywood!"

"I thought they arrested all the hookups in Hollywood—or at least got them off the streets," I ad-libbed. It was pretty risqué for the time, especially for TV. But since it was live they couldn't bleep it, and since it was in the name of charity, no one could condemn it. The crowd went nuts for like a minute while Vince mock-beat me over the head for my vulgarity. When we let the audience finally calm down, Vince took the phone from me and said respectfully:

"Mr. Deutsch, this is Vince Collins. We're very pleased to hear from you."

"Thank you, Vince, and thank you, Lanny. We here at MGM have a long history of supporting those who cannot always physically support themselves. That is why it is our pleasure to announce an endowment from MGM to your wonderful cause, to celebrate the release of our latest movies, which we hope will get all your able-bodied viewers off their feet and into their local movie theater: Ask Any Girl, *starring Shirley MacLaine and David Niven, and* The Gazebo, *starring Glenn Ford and Debbie Reynolds."*

I mugged, "An endowment, Vince? With Debbie Reynolds and Shirley MacLaine, I bet they're very well-endowed, huuuh?" Walk on ankles, Vince slaps me, tells me to listen to Mr. Deutsch.

"Therefore, it is my pleasure to donate the grand sum of ten thousand dollars to your cause on behalf of MGM and all its upcoming motion pictures."

We and the crowd went crazy. Ten thousand dollars? So much! So unexpected!

"Ah, ah, ah. But there is one little catch to this," says Shelly Deutsch over the phone, interrupting my mad Irish jig. It was really great to hear him try to do comedy delivery. Sort of like watching your CPA perform open-heart surgery. *"If you want this money for your polio pals and gals . . . we at MGM want you boys to say yes to starring in our biggest musical comedy ever:* A Night at the Opera, *with you, Lanny, playing all the roles that the Marx Brothers played in our classic comedy years ago . . . and with you, Vince, singing your heart out to Miss . . . Jayne Mansfield!"*

The crowd went crazy yet again. What a great thing to hear about. Me and Vince looked sheepishly at each other . . . me trailing my toe in a line in front of me like some reluctant coed, Vince looking at the audience as if to say, "Should we . . . should we?"

Vince and I locked eyes, slowly nodded in sync, slammed handshakes together. "Mr. Deutsch," I shouted into the phone, "we'll *do* it!"

The band struck up *Pagliacci,* I started dancing with Jack Lescoulie, Vince smiled at the merriment. What a wonderful spontaneous moment. Jack yelled, "You heard it here first, folks!" I could see our agent, Billy, who had set up the call as per my instructions, standing out of camera range. He was not applauding. He was just looking at Vince.

By the last two hours of Sunday morning, I was croaking, literally. The schedule had been arranged so that Vince and I could drop in or out of the proceedings as we saw fit between naps in our respective dressing rooms. Usually that meant I would fiddle while the Roman slept, but not this year. Vince seemed to have forgotten the meaning of the word "sleep," or discovered a pharmaceutical better than what he'd previously been using. Maybe Vince didn't want to leave me alone on camera too long. I had the opposite point of view: I was more worried about what might happen when both of us were on camera. That old feeling that we were there to defend each other was gone.

It had worked so perfectly for us over the years. It was an almost foolproof way of intimidating an audience into loving us. If Vince tried a joke and it failed, I would leave the stage and go right out into the audience and yell at them, explaining the logic of the joke and why they *had* to laugh. Now, this worked gorgeous, because no one took my abuse seriously. I was the monkey, right? So here was the little kid yelling at the grown-ups for not appreciating his big brother. How are you going to be offended by that?

And then Vince would yell at *me,* he'd slap me on the head and say, "Now stop that, Lanny, these nice people have every right not to laugh if they want to, they've paid a lot of money to be here, and we should be privileged to perform for them." And I'd act sorry for what I'd done. Vince would tell me to apologize and I'd wet my eyebrows with my fingertips and put on a posh accent and say how sorry, et cetera, and then flip it by snarling, "You rat finks!" (on TV) or "You rat bastards!" (in a nightclub). Vince would slap me again, the audience would howl, and look what we'd done: through my harmless kid's mouth, we'd criticized them for their response, abused them, vented all our loathing for them, bullied them, demanded they respond better . . . then, through Vince's charming mouth, we'd brown-nosed them, paid tribute to them, told them how appreciative we were, so all the men in the audience could feel like hotshots and big spenders, and I'd still gotten in one final shot. We were mugging the audience, working them over, calling it comedy, and they were loving it.

And we could invert the formula. If I was dying with that night's crowd, Vince could act like I was this pathetic schlemiel (yeah, sure, a schlemiel in a six-hundred-dollar tux with custom silk shirt and diamond-studded cuff links). He'd put his arm around me and say, "My little partner here"—I'd be slumped over—"is working his heart out to make you folks laugh and you, you sophisticated people, you're too cosmopolitan to give a chuckle at somebody who is willing to take this"—he'd throw me around the room—"and this"—another flip, concluding with my patented death pratfall—"but no, you're too jaded, too urbane, for that kind of humor." By now the audience would be screaming, not only because what I was doing was spectacular slapstick, but also because Vince had let them know they had been letting us down. Since they really *did* want us to like them, to belong to our gang, to be in our club, they would always laugh, if for no other reason than to gain our approval.

And if at some strange second show on a Tuesday the audience was stiff or talkative and we couldn't get them in line, then we'd just play to each other, or to the band, and we'd cut the ad-libs out of the show and be offstage in thirty-two minutes, fuck the rat bastards, and back to the dressing room to boff the broads we'd noticed sitting at tables eight and seventeen.

It had all worked so perfectly for us. Good-bye to that.

I was worried about Vince. Publicly, he'd taken the *Night at the Opera* thing fine, but all worms turn and Vince had never been much of a worm in the first place. If he was going to have some kind of blowout with me, it would not be good to do it on live TV.

In past years, it had turned out that our very best ratings came in the last hours of the polio telethon. It was the same thing that brings people to sports car races. In this case, Vince and I were the sports cars, and the audience tuned in hoping one of us would crash. By the last hour or two of the telethon, it was as if *we* were the charity. I would hobble around, reading the latest figures on the tote board, squinting to see through puffy eyes. Ed Herlihy, who had gotten a good night's sleep, would point at me as if *I* were handicapped. "Look at this man here," he'd implore, "God only knows what's holding him up, he's killing himself for you, pick up that phone and pledge your dollars. The number to call is being flashed on your screen as I speak." We made it like I was staggering my way to Calvary and anyone who didn't contribute was Pontius Pilate.

This was where we got to the ever-popular "Lanny is going to have a heart attack on camera" segment. I'd wait until Vince was resting. I'd do a tap routine with the Nicholas Brothers, which would leave me panting and unable to regain my breath. I would then sit on a stool and sing "Smile." I would barely be able to get out the notes. My voice would break. I would gasp and wheeze and mop my head with a handkerchief. A glass of water would be handed to me and my hand would tremble. Sometimes I'd just stop singing but the band would keep playing. *"Smile—"* I'd attempt to rejoin them, but my breath would fail me. "Go to the band," I'd say to the cameraman—while I was still on camera, you understand?—and the cameraman would pan to the Russ Cummings Orchestra, and the musicians would take over, playing the song as an instrumental. I'd let Ed Herlihy walk me off the set to applause. Ed would come back and reassure everyone that Lanny was okay, just overcome with fatigue and I'd be back in a little while, but he didn't want me to come back until we were within striking distance of our goal. This would usually tie up the switchboards.

This year, just as I was about to tell the camera to pan to the band, Vince strolled out from behind our show curtain, looking equally haggard, and he'd been smart enough not to shave. He took over the melody from me in that voice of his, which *is* fucking gorgeous after all, and the audience went nuts. I had no choice but to pretend I'd found some new last reserve of strength, and so I managed to catch my breath and sing in thirds with him. We went for the last notes and he sang the D, so I went for the F sharp above that. He smiled, put his arm around me, and joined me on my note, then slid up to an A that was like a major ninth or something, which I didn't have in my range even on a good day. He *was* the fucking singer, after all.

So I did the only thing I could do, which was to collapse. There were screams, but Vince caught me. Somebody snapped a picture and I thought, "Front page tomorrow's *Miami Herald*." I told them I'd just hyperventilated from the singing and the heat and I'd be back at the top of the next hour. Vince said he'd carry the ball from there, and I walked off on my own steam, feeling like a quarterback who takes himself out of a tie game in the fourth quarter because he's feeling a little woozy, while his coach stares at him in disgust.

I went back to my dressing room to lie down for a minute. I actually needed to, because the fake collapse had taken the wind out of me. I was assisted, as I had been since the telethon began, by a cute kid who attended either the University of Miami or a store where they sold their T-shirts. You can't expect me to remember her name, but the way her rack distorted the M's in MIAMI will live in my memory forever.

One of the two Miami cops who had gotten me into the building (who now alternated as security guards outside our dressing rooms) looked up from his paper and asked, "You okay, Mr. Morris? I saw you had a little accident." He nodded to a TV monitor next to Vince's dressing-room door. I told him I was okay.

The cute girl with the defiant torpedoes expressed her concern for me. "You sure you don't want someone to watch out for you, Lanny?" she said, all worried-looking. "Maybe you shouldn't be left alone."

I smiled at her and kissed her forehead. "Listen, sweetheart, two days ago when you wouldn't leave me alone, I loved it. Right now, I'm beat. But thanks, you were great." She looked disappointed that this was the end of it and she knew that it was.

Now I was alone in my dressing room and I turned up the volume on the wall speaker that monitored the broadcast. I heard Vince's voice, so I turned the knob of the speaker to "off." I got up and looked closely at myself in the mirror, as I always do in dressing rooms. I didn't look too bad, unless you compared me to a heartthrob like Vince Collins. If I wasn't twisting my face around trying to look like a monkey all the time, I probably looked just fine. Maybe even handsome. Hey, I got laid with the ladies more than Vince did, for all his looks. I could play the romantic lead in my own movies. Why not? Monkey meets girl, monkey loses girl, monkey gets girl. Darwin would love it.

I heard the door open. I had to admire the Miami T-shirt girl, who was so determined to achieve some kind of record with me.

"Sweetheart . . ." I protested.

"Sweetheart," said a mellow baritone back. Vince.

"You've got the wrong room," I said. It was awkward now with us. It was hard to talk to each other. I nodded to the speaker on the wall that monitored the broadcast. "If you're in here, who's driving the bus?"

Through the doorway I saw him reach into the fridge for a beer. "The local stations have it for three more minutes. You think I can risk drinking a beer?"

"You?"

"I don't mean because of getting drunk. I mean will it put me to sleep? I never wanted a beer or a night's sleep so bad in my life, and I don't even like beer. Or sleeping." He opened the beer and came into the bedroom, sat down next to me, offered me a cigarette, which I turned down. He lit his. "You were faking that collapse, right?"

"Right."

"Uh-huh. Tired all the same?"

His eyes looked like twin entrances to a cave. We were both exhausted. I could hear words, but I was having a hard time remembering what they meant. I knew that everybody hated me. And that the room we were in was suddenly lit very strangely, as if the parts that were supposed to be dark were light, and vice versa.

"I'm fine," I told him.

Vince was saying something to me now, but it was very hard for me to take it all in. I kept wondering whether his head was as big as it seemed, like a weather balloon.

"I thought about it, pally," Vince said from this immense

head of his. "You think you have me over a barrel but listen: you don't. You want to shoot me with a shotgun in a telephone booth? Fine. Anything you do to me is going to splatter all over you. The ricochet might even kill you. No matter what, you'd come out of it looking like one helluva mess." *In somnia veritas,* I thought. Vince took a long swill of the Pabst beer. "So let's play nice."

"Go play with yourself, you goddamn Mediterranean," I said in a steady voice and stared him down. For a second I thought he would hit me, and if he hit me, it was going to hurt, I knew that. But he didn't.

He got up. "I'm finishing out the last hour. Would be swell as hell if you dropped in."

He walked out of the room, a little uncertain in his steps but not because he was drunk. He was just really tired. Me, I wanted to stay on the bed past forever, but I knew if I did, Vince would be glad to end the show without me, and then there'd be talk about my health at the press conference, the one we had agreed to hold in New Jersey late this afternoon. Why had we ever agreed to it? I knew why. We were afraid of Sally Santoro.

We could sleep on the plane, though. That's right, we could sleep on the plane. I forced myself onto my feet and walked out of the dressing room. The nameless cutie was still waiting for me.

"Sweetheart, walk me to the stage, okay?" I asked her. She answered, but again, it was very difficult to understand her, because she was speaking in English and I was hearing in Braille. I asked her to try talking faster, but that didn't help. She was saying something to me about when we might see each other again and I told her not to be ridiculous, that of course we weren't ever going to see each other again and she started to cry. I asked her if she'd like to lie down on the floor and do her impression of a couch with two big fluffed-up pillows for me. She just stood there as I found my mark near Vince on camera and the audience cheered my return after my dramatic collapse.

We told the audience that we *had* to reach our goal of $3.9 million in pledges. Actually, we had reached it about two hours earlier, but they purposely held back the real totals, because the big boost always came in the last hour, when people at home called in droves to get us over the magic number.

Now the numbers moved rapidly on the tote board, and when we hit $3.9 million the whole place went hysterical, like Ben Grauer reporting from Times Square on New Year's Eve.

With gravelly throats, we told the audience to watch for *A Night at the Opera* from MGM, and Vince and I sang "Side by Side" to finish the show. We had no voices, and as we sang to each other, we each looked at the other's earlobe, shoulder, Adam's apple, anywhere but each other's eyes.

I walked quickly to my dressing room, but Billy Bishop was there with a couple of Sally Santoro's friends. Billy told us that they were taking us right to the airport, where the twelve-thirty American flight to New York was going to be held for us.

A motorcade led by both the police and Sally's friends took Vince, myself, and Billy Bishop to the airport at about ninety miles an hour. We boarded the American Airlines flight bound for Atlanta, Washington, D.C., Philadelphia, and New York's Idlewild. Vince and I fell into a stupor without the assistance of booze or Tuinals, and we weren't awakened until we'd landed in the fourth and final city. I was told that during the flight I'd wake for a minute, ask for water like a four-year-old, have a sip, and then pass out again. Billy Bishop and the stewardesses made sure no one bothered us.

When we landed in New York and they shook the two of us awake, I felt completely groggy, like a dentist had put an entire box of cotton pads into my mouth and rammed a few up my sinuses as well. As we came down the roll-up stairway onto the tarmac, we were hit by a twenty-one flash-gun salute going off in our faces. The press was told we wouldn't be making a statement until we got to the new Casino del Mar, so off we all went like a funeral cortege that had entered the

Indy 500. Apparently, we were a pretty big deal. We had a police car in front and in back of the limo that Sally Santoro had provided for the two of us, along with several bodyguards, who were there to protect us from any thoughts we might have of going AWOL prior to our press conference.

Our limo pulled up to the front of the hotel itself, which was a wall of windows, each with that gray plastic curtain lining taking up different amounts of the window's frame. We stepped out, and a stiff, cold breeze that you'd never have found outside the Versailles in Miami flapped around our tuxedo jackets, which we were still wearing.

We were greeted by what turned out to be the lead publicist for the Santoro operation, a thin, sharp-edged, dark-haired woman in her early thirties. "Hello! Jackie Biderman, I'm running public relations for El Toro Enterprises, welcome to the *new* Casino del Mar."

Vince looked at me. In earlier days, when we met these P.R. women (this Jackie could have been the older sister of Denise, the skinny brunette we'd dumped from the Versailles, but then they all could have been), Vince would mutter softly to me, "Yours." Unless I beat him to it. In this case, he didn't say anything.

I turned to Billy Bishop, who'd been with us all the way from Miami and said, "We have to clean up a little. See where Reuben is." Vince's five o'clock shadow had him looking like a saddle bum, and I was beginning to resemble the caricature of me that occupied the right half of the bass drum in the Russ Cummings Orchestra.

Billy conveyed our needs to Jackie, who smiled no, explaining that Mr. Santoro wanted us to look like the heroes we were. He was being very smart from a publicity angle. Vince and I had just finished a nationally televised broadcast. We were the Good Guys. We had broken all box-office records for a disease. Now, before the telethon had a chance to fade out of the public's mind, here we were talking about the next huge event in our lives: the opening of a hotel in Bergen County, New Jersey. And it would make it to the local seven o'clock news in the tristate area if we moved our butts (as Jackie was instructing us) into the main reception hall, where we were about to hold a press conference.

A pair of New Jersey state policemen walked on either side of us as we entered the lobby of the hotel. They stayed with us throughout. It was an indication of how legitimate Sally had gone that he could bring in the local police to guard the facade of his racket.

You could see that the hotel wasn't completely finished because a wall between the public rest rooms and the lobby hadn't been built yet. A gorgeous view of Manhattan's Riverside Drive from the hotel's cocktail lounge was completely unobstructed by glass, and the wind whipped through us in the lobby more than it did in the driveway outside.

Jackie showed us into a room marked GRAND BALLROOM (*which is also how I describe a lady wearing an athletic supporter—joke, not mine*). Already seated at a long dais were Sally Santoro and some people who looked like attorneys. Jackie indicated that the two vacant center chairs were for us. Sally hugged us both. That was a first.

It seemed as if Jackie Biderman was going to serve as emcee because that was what she was now telling the newspaper people she was going to do. "*B-i-d-e-r-m-a-n,* with one *n,*" she explained to the press, who weren't writing anything down. "Well now. I want to welcome all our friends to this very special press conference with three very special people." I was hoping she was not counting herself. "Mr. Salvatore Santoro, that's *S—*" and she spelled his name for them. When the members of the press saw that Sally's boys were taking down the names of those who didn't take down Sally's name, the fourth estate instantly whipped out their pencils and scribbled away. "And of course two gentlemen on my right who need no introduction and who, as you can see, have come here directly from their record-breaking polio telethon in Miami, Florida."

The first thing she did was announce that Mr. Santoro, on behalf of the El Toro corporation, was pledging $20,000 to the American Polio Foundation. She had a quick whispered word with one of Sally's boys, asking if they had the oversized check to hand to us for the benefit of the newspaper cameras. They looked around at one another like altar boys. No, gee, uh-no, we don't. She inquired in another whisper if they had a normal-sized check that Mr. Salvatore could hand to us for the benefit of the newspaper cameras. The Boys gazed idly around the room, like maybe the check had been taped to the chandelier.

Sally stared straight ahead throughout all this.

Jackie announced into the microphone that regretfully, through a mix-up, the check itself wasn't here at the press conference, but she was pleased to be able to announce Mr. Santoro's magnificent pledge. "And in addition, it is my very great pleasure to announce that Mr. Santoro is also donating to the American Polio Foundation over . . ." She consulted a file card in her hand. ". . . over two thousand Kenmore waffle irons, so that those afflicted with this terrible disease can enjoy waffles any time of the day . . . and I'm sure we all applaud him in this humane effort."

Santoro had a word in the ear of his associate, who whispered a word in Jackie's ear. She nodded and added, "And also over five hundred three-D photographic cameras, because the crippled are entitled to a beautiful world just like the rest of us."

She sat and Sally waited while lots of flash cameras went off. He had a whispered word with the attorney at his side and leaned in to the microphone to speak. How he managed not to reflexively say, "I refuse to answer upon the grounds that it might tend to incriminate me," I have no idea. Instead, he read a little speech about how proud he was that the United States had launched the Vanguard rocket into space and he was proud that New Jersey was launching its own rocket, the new Casino del Mar. Then he jumped off the prepared text and talked about how he would never forget all the people who helped and all the people who didn't, because that was who he was.

Jackie looked at her watch and said that since we were a little ahead of schedule, she would let the press ask us a few questions before our live TV interview with the local ABC affiliate. That's when these sophisticated New York journalists started trading wits with us, and man, was it hard to keep up with them.

"Ralph Latiff, *Bergen Record,* question for Mr. Morris: are you tired?"

"You bet I am. Yes?"

"Rose Wanamaker, *Daily Mirror,* how did it feel—this question for Mr. Collins—how did it feel raising all that money for polio?"

Vince answered, "It felt great. Really, really great."

A guy from a Trenton newspaper asked from the back of the room about the movie we had announced, *A Night at the Opera.* "Will the movie be in color?" And they wonder where the *new* Edward R. Murrows will come from.

Vince answered: "We don't know. I hope it will be. Everyone ought to see how pink my eyes get some mornings." The press laughed and I saw a lot of pencils moving. So Vince had drawn first comedy blood, huh?

The Trenton newspaper had a follow-up question. "Will it be a wide-screen movie?"

I leaned in to my mike. "If Jayne Mansfield is in it, it'll have to be."

Now here was Cindy Goldner, a local gossip columnist. She wasn't a guaranteed pushover. "Vince, with Lanny playing three roles, aren't you actually taking fourth billing?"

Vince started to speak into his mike but I overrode that. "This is a Collins and Morris movie. Vince has always had top billing."

Vince looked at me with a slightly crooked smile. "I think Lanny means sixth billing, don't you, pally?"

Cindy pressed him. "How do you figure sixth, Vince?"

Vince drawled, "Well, as I understand it, Lanny is going to play a trio of wonderful roles, and Jayne Mansfield has quite a pair." Laughter from the press. "I figure that puts me sixth."

The guy from the *Daily Mirror* tried his professional best to goad Vince. "You sound like you'd be okay about Miss Mansfield getting billing above you, Vince."

"I always prefer my women on top," smiled Vince.

Rich laughter from the press. We all knew they could never print a comment like that in a newspaper, and they knew that too, so you could say it strictly for the amusement of the press without having to go off the record. The only ones who didn't always live by this gentlemen's agreement weren't there today: Kilgallen, O'Brien, and Winchell hadn't felt like hiking all the way to New Jersey for a puff piece like this, Hedda Hopper and Louella Parsons were in L.A., and Moe Cohn only wrote his column for Miami, so thank God we'd escaped his raking.

Jackie Biderman had gone a little pale at this last exchange and advised us that when we went on the air with George Gromire from the local ABC affiliate, Mr. Santoro hoped we'd mention the Casino del Mar and the Blue Grotto and the dates of our engagement there.

At six minutes after seven, local ABC correspondent George Gromire got his cue and thrust a mike in our faces. "Vince Collins, Lanny Morris, welcome to New Jersey. We all saw you on the telethon that ended this morning. Are you tired?"

I said in that voice, "Oh no, Mr. Gromire, we're both fresh as dai—" and pretended to pass out, my head hitting the table hard enough to cause a loud comic impact and even to hurt me a little. I instantly started snoring real loud. Let Vince do the interview.

Gromire pushed the mike toward Vince with a weak laugh. "Well, as long as your partner seems to have departed for dreamland, Vince, tell us why you're here, won't you?"

Vince said the right things about how we were honored that our good friend Mr. Santoro had asked us to be the first act in this magnificent entertainment center so close to Manhattan yet so high above the Hudson River, that this area had always been very special to us, et cetera. I snored a loud snore.

"We also hear you're about to film a remake of that wonderful Marx Brothers movie *A Night at the Opera,*" lobbed Gromire.

"Yes." Vince nodded. "And on top of that, I'm very excited to announce my motion-picture debut as a straight dramatic actor in *The Maginot Line,* about an American soldier during World War Two trying to escape from a prisoner-of-war camp in Nazi-occupied France."

Gromire and I were both very interested to hear this, but only he showed it. "This would be a solo effort, without your partner?" he asked. Now I felt like a real dickhead stuck in the middle of this fucking stupid snoring bit I'd gotten into.

Vince said, "Well, I know I'll welcome all the advice and guidance my pally here can give me, if he ever wakes up."

I pretended to wake up and shot upright. "Starting this Friday at the Blue Grotto here at the Casino del Mar in Boigen County for the next two weeks!" I said, plugging like I was supposed to. The jack-in-the-box bit would have been funny in another context. Suddenly it felt lame.

Gromire turned to the camera. "Well, a very full calendar for two guys full of talent and goodwill, Vince Collins and the dizzy, dozy Lanny Morris." He froze his smile for about fifteen seconds, until someone relayed that he was clear. "Thank you very much," he said to both of us.

I looked to my left and saw Billy Bishop smiling at Vince. He gave Vince a little wink. This solo project had clearly been in the making for some time.

Jackie Biderman was not happy at all. Through a smile of icicle teeth, she hissed, "It would be better if in any future interviews we set up, you mention show times and how to get to the Casino from both New York and Connecticut."

Vince leaned toward her, and said in a voice that only she and I could hear, "It would be better if you never told us what to do again, because if you do, I'll set fire to your lacquered hair and put out the flames by pissing on you. Thanks a million."

She looked like she had been hit direct center in her starved stomach. "Oh my Guh—God," she moaned.

I got up, stepped over to Sally, and, for the benefit of his hired photographer, did the pose I'd done a million times without ever really understanding it. I, famous person, have my left arm around a not-famous person and with my free right hand, I point at the not-famous person. What am I indicating when I point at him? What does that mean? Throughout this world are millions of photos of me pointing at strangers. What is the message of my pointing? *"Look, he momentarily exists alongside me!"*

It was hard not to imagine a congressional committee someday questioning me about every photo I've had taken with my arm around gangsters, mass murderers, extortionists, arsonists, and child molesters. And in every case, I have a stupid grin on my face and am pointing at them.

At last we were led by Sally and company away from the Grand Ballroom and toward the elevators to our suite, which had been completed weeks ago, they assured us. Sleep, priceless sleep, awaited.

An assistant to the ABC TV reporter hurried over to Vince in the lobby and handed him a folded slip of paper. She was very pretty, maybe twenty-three, with the sweetest pair of partridges for breasts. She looked like a breathless, blond Natalie Wood. I could hear her say in a low voice to Vince, "Hi, I work with George Gromire, just an assistant, my name is Joan, I'm married and I absolutely love my husband, but when we got married, I told him, 'Listen, no joke, I'll always be faithful to you but if I ever meet Vince Collins, I get to cheat, at least for one night.' He agreed, so if you would like to spend the night with me while you're here, that's my phone number. Or even right now." She sort of presented herself with good posture and a hopefulness that was so lovely. "It's all right with my husband. It really is."

Vince pocketed the slip of paper and said, "That's just the nicest compliment, Joan. Sounds to me like you have a wonderful relationship with your husband. That's not easy to come by in this world, and I'd hate to intrude on that, tempting as the offer might be."

We stepped toward the elevator bank, where the door was being held open for us.

"It would be all right," she said. She cupped her small hand around his ear and said in a voice that I could still hear: "I'm really good in bed. You'd really like it."

Vince smiled at her. "You don't have to tell me that. I know you would be." He stared at her, pretending to take a mental picture of her as he got on the elevator. "I promise I'll never forget you. Joan."

We joined him on the elevator, myself, Jackie, Sally, the two state policemen who had been with us since the outset, and a bellman who had the carry-on luggage from our flight.

The good suites were as far away from the elevators as they could be, toward the southern end of the corridor, so that their view favored Manhattan.

At the end of the hall was a door into a vestibule, from which branched three doors numbered 501, 500, and 502. There was a maid's service wagon outside 501 and the door was ajar. The bellman nodded at the cart. "The maid is turning down your beds."

"Nobody ever turns down Vince's bed," I said as a knee-jerk reaction, forgetting that the press conference was over.

Sally nodded. "We guessed you might want some sleep. We gave you our best bridal suite."

The bellman opened the living room door and we walked in. Not bad. The view was fantabulous. You could see the Empire State Building, the RCA building, and the sparkling brown of the polluted midtown harbor. Standing on four angled legs, Danish modern in an antique white finish, was a giant RCA console TV, and I would not be a bit surprised if it was a compatible color model. On top of the TV was a turntable stacked with LPs, probably all Vince's recordings. The immediate left wall of the living room was mirrored, a tan marbleized watermark rippling through it. There was a stocked wet bar on my right and art on all the walls, most of it on black velvet: a matador, a tastefully naked woman, a clown. If you couldn't get laid in this suite, you couldn't get laid.

"Fucking nice, huh?" asked Sally. Vince and I agreed it was very fucking nice. "People talk about having fancy hotel rooms and apartments on the West Side of Manhattan and what do they get to see? Fucking New Jersey. Here, you see the skyline of New York City."

There was a scream. Not a funny scream. A real scream on our left.

A mother hears her daughter scream a million times and it's almost always because another kid took her daughter's toy, or because she fell off her tricycle, or because she's scared of the witch in *Snow White.* And the mother will slowly stop a conversation she's having with a friend and walk into the kid's room to see what the problem is. But sometimes a mother hears her kid scream because her kid's hand is caught in the garbage disposal, and the mother knows instantly that this scream is different from all the others and she runs to her child faster than she's ever run in her life. Vince and I had heard a million screams in the last few years and we usually smiled and said, "Thank you." This scream made us run to the source.

It took us a second to realize that it was coming from behind the living room door that led into one of the two bedrooms, the one on the west side of the suite. I ran to the door and tried to open it, but it was locked from the inside, as was usually the case with a hotel suite when you first check in. The two state police who had been admiring the living room with us had moved fast to the hall, where the door to 501 was open, with the maid's cart still outside it. I ran after them, Vince following me.

"Oh, man," I heard one of the cops say as I entered the bedroom. It was obviously a nice bedroom, but I didn't take time to look at the decor. A woman in a maid's outfit, about fifty or so with a squat Dutch face and braided hair, was kneeling on the floor near the end of the bed, vomiting onto the nice green carpet. I turned away, feeling reflex-sick myself, and saw the cops standing in the bathroom, looking at the bathtub.

Lying in the narrow tub was a young woman. The tub had just enough water in it to cover her face and drown her. An inch less and her nostrils would have been above the surface.

I remembered a cleaning woman in Crown Heights who'd banged her head on an overhead pipe and fallen unconscious into her bucket of water. She'd drowned in that little bucket, in a big basement room that was otherwise bone-dry.

The young woman in the tub would have been extremely attractive if she hadn't been dead. Her red hair was still rich in color against her blue-gray face.

The medical examiner, who was summoned immediately by the state patrolmen, estimated she'd been dead somewhere between two and four hours. The good news was that both Vince and I had been watched by everyone from security police to airline stewardesses to a live TV audience of millions from Friday to Sunday, nonstop. Even when we'd been alone, we'd been guarded. And of course, we'd only been in the New York area for a few hours, during which time we were constantly with cops, reporters, and other witnesses.

This was more than a little important, because both Vince and I were acquainted with the young dead woman in the bathroom of what had been meant to be my hotel bedroom in New Jersey.

Her last name, we were to learn, was O'Flaherty.

Her first name was Maureen. She was the girl from room service at the Versailles Hotel in Miami, Florida. The girl Vince and I had both come to know.

TWELVE

I was dead, or at least dead tired even as I awoke. I felt like a battery that had spent the night in a recharging device that no one had remembered to plug in. The oxygen-rich air on my plane ride with Lanny had inspired me to drink well past my usual limit, and each burst of giddiness I'd felt yesterday was now memorialized by a burst capillary in my brain.

A Princess phone was ringing somewhere below me. To evade its miserable chirp, I tried to incorporate the sound into my dream, in which I was the pilot of the world's first commercial hang glider (seating eighty in the folding chairs my family used to bring out each Thanksgiving). I was, of course, naked in the cockpit and there was a Princess phone on the instrument panel of the plane just above the eight-track player. The phone kept ringing so I asked my father, who was copiloting, to take over the controls while I awoke in order to determine who was calling.

I sat up in bed and cracked my forehead hard against the ceiling above me as if I were in the opening scene of a bad sitcom. My hand reached up to feel a smooth solid surface over my head, like the lid of a coffin. Panic genuinely overtook me, and I rolled to my left to determine if I was boxed in on all sides; I realized in the same instant that I was *not* buried alive but merely in that damn loft bed in Beejay's apartment, perched just below her low ceiling—and with that comforting thought came the accompanying realization that my rolling to the left meant I was no longer on that damn loft bed but falling off its edge and now dropping to the floor, which I then hit. Why is there never a laugh track around when you really need it? Worse, a heavy metal bar landed on my shoulder; another sitcom moment. It was supposed to help barricade the front door, but Beejay said she preferred having the metal bar in bed with her, where she could use it on the intruder after he'd broken in. Such was Beejay's logic.

Luckily, I hadn't broken anything, though I'd banged my left shin quite painfully against the metal ladder that led from the floor up to the bed. The phone had stopped ringing on the fifth ring, after which all calls were automatically relayed to Beejay's answering service, so my injuries were for naught.

What time was it? I had no idea. The chirping noise started again, and I scuttled under the roof of Beejay's bed and found the Princess phone.

"Hello?"

Lanny's voice said, "Bonnie?"

I started to pronounce "Yes," but the word put up a struggle. God, how I loathed beginning the day by verifying this immense lie of mine, particularly before I'd had coffee. I'd hitherto thought I possessed some halfway decent ethics as a journalist, certainly more than rock writers of the period, who had no qualms about sampling a rock band's cocaine while interviewing them in the men's room at the launch party for their new album.

"Bonnie, you there?" Until such time as I could admit my deception to Lanny (and how I was already looking forward to that little chat!), perhaps I could at least reply to him without overtly perpetuating or progressing the already-scummy falsehood I'd conjured so glibly on the plane. From this moment on, I vowed to do my best not to actually confirm or embroider the lie. So instead of replying "Yes" to his "Bonnie?" I simply responded, "Lanny? Is that you?"

"No, it's the Four Seasons featuring the sound of Frankie Valli. How'd you like the show?"

The show. "What show?"

"The *Today* show. You did watch, didn't you?" He sounded almost shaken. "You didn't watch. Wow, that's scary."

I stumbled, "I'm sorry, I had more than I usually drink—I didn't know I was supposed to watch. I've offended you."

"No, you don't understand, I'm not offended, just scared. When you're a star, you live in terror, wondering if it's all over yet. You find yourself looking for signs. You're shooting a scene for a movie on a New York street and a crowd doesn't form. You show up at Lutèce without a reservation and the maître d' seats the couple ahead of you first. You meet a girl on a plane and tell her you'll be on the *Today* show the next morning and she doesn't wake up early to watch. Very scary. You know, I mentioned you on TV. On the *Today* show."

"You did?"

"Yeah, I proposed to you on the air and everything. My guess is your apartment building is surrounded by photographers at this very moment."

"You're kidding."

"Yeah, sure I'm kidding. But look, help me out here. After I left you last night, you *did* call someone and tell them you'd met me and I went up with you in your elevator, saw you to your door, we kissed, we're supposed to see each other today?"

"Yes, I told a girl I know, my best friend."

"Okay, that's okay then." He sounded very relieved. "By the way, when you told her I kissed you, she said, 'Lanny Morris, oh, he's such a geek,' didn't she?"

I hesitated. "No."

"Sure she did. So when do you want to have lunch?"

I told him truthfully that I had a business appointment in midtown at eleven-thirty and that I wasn't sure when it might end. He was surprised that a teacher would have a business appointment during summer vacation, but I explained I was exploring the possibility of a different kind of job, something in publishing, a copywriter or editor or proofreader, anything along those lines. I was trying to work my way toward the day when I would tell him I was in fact already in publishing and that I'd recently had occasion to review a portion of his own writing.

He sighed. "Okay, I'll see if I can take a morning nap—I only got a few hours' sleep last night. Why don't you just come here to the Plaza when your meeting is done? Suite 2302. Mr. Merwin, remember? If I'm napping, Reuben will let you in. You remember Reuben." I told him I remembered. He ventured, "You have anything else to do after your business meeting, or can I have you for the whole day?"

I said in so many words that he could, without knowing exactly what "have you for the whole day" might entail. I told myself it was what Neuman and Newberry would have wanted me to say. We hung up cordially, if not cooingly, and I reached for the cigarettes I'd been eyeing the entire time I'd been on the phone with him.

I always smoke when I'm uneasy and now, awake and sober, I needed very much to smoke. Of course I had every reason to feel anxious, with the curtain of lies hanging like a scrim between me and Lanny, a scrim that could be rendered transparent with the merest change in backlighting. I was also a smidge uneasy about my approaching business appointment at eleven-thirty. But I knew that the disquieting wariness I was feeling emanated primarily from something in the chapter that Beejay had alternately read and paraphrased the night before. And I didn't know what that something was.

It wasn't the identification of the Girl in New Jersey as sad Maureen O'Flaherty, the vividly redheaded room-service girl from Miami inexplicably found dead in the tub of Vince and Lanny's virginal bridal suite in New Jersey. I had learned a lot about her already, having researched what there was to learn, until I likely knew more about the Girl in New Jersey than anyone, outside of the boys or the police who had originally handled the case.

Maureen was so absurdly Irish that simply stating her family background made it sound like you were starting up a joke. Her father was an Irish bartender, the son of an Irish cop whose brother was an Irish-Catholic priest, and her mother was either a niece or cousin to the great George M. Cohan himself. And like that Yankee Doodle Dandy, Maureen had lived in New Rochelle (a town in Westchester that is only "forty-five minutes from Broadway," as goes the title of one of Cohan's songs), and yes, of course, her mother's name was Mary. Maureen had reportedly been a "good" girl throughout her adolescence and had talked about being an English teacher, possibly at a parochial school. During her senior year at Hunter College, she took a spring vacation in Miami for a week, which turned into a month, which turned into a few years, which turned into forever in a bathtub in Palisades Park, New Jersey.

All this I already knew, so hearing Beejay report the discovery of Maureen's corpse wasn't likely to be the cause of my uneasiness. No, it was something else lurking in or about the text I'd heard that was giving me low-lying jitters, and unlike a caffeine or nicotine fix, I didn't know exactly where to find its remedy.

In times of inner panic, I find it comforting to make lists. The very useless act of setting down information in a numbered column with check boxes to the left of each item can infuse a sense of peace and purpose to my day.

So I spent the next hour making up a list. In the drawer of Beejay's little desk I found a ream of paper obviously filched from P.S. 29 on Orchard Street. It had been a long time since I'd seen unholed, blue-lined notepaper with a red-lined left margin, the kind of paper history teachers handed out when a test included essay questions. I could hear the groans of old classmates in my head as I wrote:

1. The deep-abiding puzzlement I first felt during my time with Lanny's manuscript at Hillman's office has only increased. Why is Lanny Morris sending me these chapters? His lawyer's explanation, at the time, had placated me: Lanny wanted to discourage me from continuing further work on my book by showing me that he was writing one of his own, one that would easily trump my own efforts by virtue of its authenticity. Fine. But with that established, why now send me another chapter?
2. Why is the Lanny I've met on the plane and on the drive to this apartment so different from the Lanny in the pages I've read and heard? Admittedly, nearly fifteen years have elapsed since the described events, but am I really thinking these pages were written when these events occurred? No, there are several comparisons to the present that indicate Lanny has written this fairly recently. Which Lanny is the real one?
3. Most unsettling: within the course of this new chapter, it's obvious that something has changed in the working relationship of Lanny and Vince. There's a sense of resentment and distrust, but I can't immediately tell who is the more offended party.
4. Had the late Maureen O'Flaherty been invited to await Vince and Lanny in New Jersey while they were on TV in Florida, or did she go there planning to surprise—

I looked up at Beejay's Felix the Cat clock and realized I'd have no time for the very good coffee at the Pantheon Diner across the street from my publisher if I didn't get ready for my meeting now. It wasn't, after all, as if I felt on the verge of answering any of the questions I'd just posed to myself.

I opted for the same outfit I'd worn when I took my walk around the Burbank Studios with Vince. It was more summery than I'd normally wear to a business meeting, but after that I was going to join Lanny.

At that time, Neuman and Newberry had its offices on the top three floors of the Flatiron Building. I took a taxi there without even considering the Twenty-third Street crosstown bus; what I was saving by staying at Beejay's instead of at a hotel allowed me to indulge myself in such lesser luxuries without a second thought.

My meeting was with the three people most immediately overseeing my project: Connie Wechsler, Greg Gavin, and Neuman and Newberry's editor in chief, Lil Walker. Some N&N attorneys might be on hand as well.

Connie was my editor. She was about fifteen years older than I, half a foot shorter, with hair that was dark and frizzy with hard, natural waves. She was the essence of frumpy, and comfortable with that. She knew my work and understood me, even gave the impression that she liked me.

Lil Walker was the person to whom Connie reported. When Lil talked about the writers she'd edited in her twenties, one had the distinct feeling that much of the male contingent of the Lost Generation could have been found in her bedroom on any given weekend. She referred to Hemingway as "Ernie" without pretension and once made a comment about Steinbeck being at Gertrude Stein's beck and call that had the ring of firsthand information to it. She clearly didn't know my work very well, but she knew Connie and tended to reflexively back her up whenever she needed support, so that worked out just fine for me.

Greg Gavin was that anomaly that is (paradoxically) common within most large companies: the mystery man whom everyone believes was hired by someone else. His arrival at Neuman and Newberry was apparently never formally announced or explained. I had first noticed him when I'd inked my deal with N&N at an impromptu signing party (meaning Yago sangria in paper cups in the reception area). He was sitting alone on the receptionist's desktop, sniffing at the bowl of his empty pipe. He smiled vaguely across the room at Connie and gave the pipe a few hard spanks on the flat of his left hand. I asked Connie as a matter of course who he was, because he looked like he owned the place, or was at least leasing with an option to buy.

Connie murmured, "His name's Greg Gavin. Everybody's a little scared of him and no one knows why. One day he just suddenly appeared at a meeting of the editorial board, very nicely outfitted, sucking at an unlit briar pipe. I thought he was working with Harv Prescott because he kept smiling these smiles at Harv, so I asked Harv and Harv said he'd assumed Greg and I were working together because he'd kept smirking at *me.*"

A consensus had gradually formed within N&N that Gavin was in charge of special marketing. No one was very sure what that was, either. He had asked the senior secretary of each department to carbon all inter-office memos to him, and after that, he seemed to simply pick and choose which meetings he attended according to an agenda he kept entirely to himself.

The Flatiron's elevator rose to my floor in approximately the same amount of time as it took Richard, Duke of Gloucester, to ascend to the throne. The doors opened. There was no receptionist, and security was nonexistent. After all, this was a publishing house, not a bank or a radio station. What was someone going to do—break in and demand that their manifesto be published in hardcover by the late fall of next year or hostages would die?

I stepped down the old-fashioned hall, each of the corridor's tightly spaced doors highlighted by a yellowing translucent glass panel that bore the office's number and the name of its current resident. I half-expected to see one labeled SAM SPADE AND MILES ARCHER—PRIVATE INVESTIGATIONS.

I let myself into Connie's office. She always seemed out of place there, since Connie was neither a published book nor a manuscript, which happened to be the only other things visible in the room. Her desk, the top of which had long ago been rendered inaccessible by a glacier of accumulated reading matter, now served solely as a beam bridge creating a tunnel where her lap could go amid all the books that filled the little room. She smiled. "Hey, you got here. How's tricks?"

I told her tricks were fine. She tossed a thick manuscript she was reading onto a heap. "Peeee-yew! Another Kennedy conspiracy book. Should have been written in crayon. According to this one, the mysterious third bullet came from *within* the limousine. The author claims Jackie did it. Derringer hidden in the pillbox hat, which served as a—as a pillbox."

I nodded at the pile onto which she had tossed the manuscript. "For the scrap heap?"

"What scrap heap? It's going straight to the original-paperback department downstairs. Something has to pay for this book you're writing." She got up, adjusting her sweater so the various bulges were where they were meant to be. "C'mon, we have to explain to business affairs why we should give Vince Collins, who has lots of money, a lot of money."

Their best conference room had been renovated out of several small offices and a storage closet in the narrow prow of the landmark building, creating a pizza slice of a room, with a curved glass window at the building's prow. The overall effect was of being in a *bateau-mouche* that was anchored gracefully high above the river of Broadway, looking north toward Herald Square—and I promise not to mention George M. yet again.

Lil was late because she could be anything she wanted, but Greg Gavin was already there, as was the head of business affairs, the likable Bernard Besser (who pronounced his first name *Burr*-nurd), and a much younger attorney with severe acne named Jay Drelitch. After niceties about my trip (from which I excluded any mention of Lanny), we sat down at a long triangular conference table that would have been laughable anywhere except in this three-sided room. As if he were in charge of the meeting, Greg dealt six slim binders, one to each of us around the table. I stifled the urge to say *"Suivi,"* as if he were a baccarat dealer, and took a quick look at the first page.

Its heading read: "Suggested Questions for Vince Collins." The questions appeared to easily outnumber those in the memo I'd written to myself back in Beejay's apartment.

I closed the binder, feeling rage rising within me.

Bernard, a nice enough fellow in his late fifties whose light-gray suit and cream-colored tie were his version of going casual, asked me to review for everyone at the table what I had verbally agreed to with Vince. Understandably, he wanted to know what I had stuck him with (and what he might have to renege upon) in terms of translating my proffers into a legally binding document.

I repeated for Bernard and Jay what I had already told them on the phone. I omitted the highly personal compact I had made with Mr. Collins in L.A., as I viewed our sexual covenant to be more of a personal side bet than a formal wager against the house. With some assistance from

Connie, I helped elucidate what I had and hadn't guaranteed, and it was my perception that Bernard was both surprised and relieved that I hadn't painted him into more of a corner. I had certainly built into my offer various safeguards for Neuman and Newberry should Vince be less than forthcoming with information or less than cooperative in terms of his schedule.

Bernard said he was grateful that I had been watching out for N&N's interests, but of course I had also been watching out for myself. He concluded, "Well, I think Jay and I can hammer out something resembling a contract we can all live or litigate with. The only thing I don't quite understand is why Mr. Collins is willing to allow what could end up being an exposé of himself."

"I've thought a lot about this," I offered. "Vince is a realist. The days of his box-office drawing power are drawing to a close, and his record label just dropped every artist on their roster over the age of thirty except him and Mahalia Jackson, and the only reason they haven't let her go is they're afraid God will make locusts fly into the vinyl at their pressing plant. For Vince, this is an easy way of getting some fast 'fuck you' money that he can afford to lose." I offered, by way of apology, "The phrase isn't mine. I think it's credited to Humphrey Bogart."

A low, bronze female voice sounded: "Sorry I'm late, all." It was Lil, who walked with a cane that she clearly enjoyed smacking down onto the conference table as she took a seat across from me. "Miss O'Connor. Bernard." She looked at Greg Gavin and gave him a nod that clearly indicated she didn't remember his name.

Greg erroneously took this nod to be his cue. "Well. Since the investment in Mr. Collins is quite sizable, and since Miss O'Connor has indicated that her book will be largely in the form of a transcript, I've compiled a list of questions I'm sure we as the publisher would want to see addressed. Turning to the first page . . ."

My hands trembled from anger mixed with the shame of asserting myself as I said in a voice I borrowed from somewhere else, "Um, I'd rather not turn to the first page, if you don't mind. Frankly, I'd prefer not to read any of these questions at all. Once I see them, my tendency will be to avoid asking any of them like the plague. God forbid that among them would be some questions I would have asked anyway, in my own words and manner, when I thought the moment was right. That's part of what you're paying me to do." I pushed the binder aside to make my point. "I already landlocked myself creatively when I volunteered that the interviews would be published in transcript form. I hope and assume I'll be able to cheat around this somewhere, maybe in a preface to each chapter, making my points as a biographer and journalist like the narrator of a documentary. *Playboy* does transcript interviews, but the interviewer leads with almost a full page of editorial comment."

Greg Gavin made sucking noises on his empty pipe. "We're not paying a million for what you have to say about Vince Collins, we're paying for what *he* has to say."

"To *me*. What he has to say to *me*. If you start telling me what you want me to say and when, you'll throw me off my game. Pretty soon, I'll have as much to do with the creative process of this book as a French interpreter at the U.N. has of solving the problem of world famine." I took a breath. "Who *are* you, anyway?"

"Okay now," murmured Connie to me.

"No reason to cop an attitude," said Greg, showing he'd known people who smoked dope in the sixties.

Lil rapped the head of her cane against the table. "Now, let's quit this." She indicated the binder in front of her. "Connie, are these your questions?"

Connie shook her head. "All news to me."

Lil gave Greg a smile combining immense reasonability and loathing. "Well, as I've always understood this company's policy, while the book is being written or rewritten, the relationship between author and editor is sacrosanct. Miss O'Connor is a wonderful writer—" Lil looked at Connie and inquired, "She's okay, isn't she?" Connie nodded with a smile and Lil continued, "So until we actually have a book, I think we'll let Miss Wechsler, in whom I have the utmost confidence . . . I do, don't I, Connie?" Connie nodded again. "Good. Then let's let these two women do what we've hired them to do, assuming business affairs is okay with the structure of the deal with Vince Collins. . . . Are you all right with the deal, Bernard and Mr. . . . ?" She wafted a look at Bernard Besser that included the pimply Jay Drelitch.

Bernard nodded. "I think we'll be fine, Lil."

"With all due respect," piped up Greg with no respect intended, "this isn't your typical book deal. We're really just leasing an oil well named

Vince Collins and granting Miss O'Connor here the right to tap it, and I think we should have some say in monitoring the drilling." He opened the list of questions, which everyone else had closed and which everyone else left closed.

Connie clearly decided she'd better speak before I did. "It's not as easy as it looks, Greg. If you go to Vince Collins and ask him your questions, you'll come back here with a three-hundred-page press handout and puff piece. There's an art to building trust over the long term with your subject, a way to judge what to press them on and when. You have to know more about the person than they do, be historian, shrink, lover, father confessor, mother superior. When the police need to get a confession from someone, they don't just send any cop into the room. The job takes more than just a solid writer, it takes—"

I stood up. "Here's what I'll do. You can put it in writing." I looked over at Bernard. "As a matter of fact, I prefer it in writing, and if you draft a rider to my existing agreement to the following effect, I'll sign it before I leave town." Bernard gave Jay Drelitch a look and suddenly Jay's Bic pen was scribbling on a legal pad everything I was saying.

"Greg, you'll pay for a typing service on the West Coast to transcribe the tapes of my interviews with Vince. As each transcript gets typed up, I'll send it to you, edited and pruned as I see fit. This way you can review my work as I go along. But I will not talk to you about the transcripts, read any memos, or take any phone calls from you about them. If after reading the transcripts you think I'm really screwing up in a big way, fire me. No explanation will be necessary. But other than to give me my pink slip, you will have no further communication with me. That's the deal. But do keep in mind that if you let me go, this company will then have to find someone Vince Collins is equally willing to open up to, and good luck with that."

What on earth was I doing playing brinksmanship with Greg Gavin? Never would I have dreamed of doing this had I not been feeling my oats from my burgeoning relationship (and agreement) with Vince and my budding relationship with his ex-buddy. I felt connected to the guys in a way that these civilians didn't know about and couldn't understand. Perhaps Lil might. Yes, Lil and I could have a good old talk over boilermakers at the Old Town Bar some night, she with her Ernie and Gertie, me with my Vinny and Lanny. For the moment, I had the swagger of success (see *fleeting* and *illusory*), buoyed solely by the merest moment outside Vince's trailer and a date I'd made with Lanny Morris to . . . do what? I had no idea.

I felt like my high school boyfriend's erection after I'd innocently asked him, "Is that as big as it's going to get?" Like "it," I now began to shrink perceptibly with each pulse of my heart; but luckily my bluff had deflated Greg first.

"There's no need to put it in writing," he mumbled, closing his binder sulkily. "I'm sure your word is good enough for all of us."

The three men left us, as if they were heading for brandy and cigars in the billiard room and we three women were now free to discuss childbirth and the crocheting of antimacassars.

After an appropriate silence, giving the men time to get down the hall, Lil asked Connie in a modulated tone, "Who the hell is he?"

Connie shrugged and looked at me. "I was secretly *kvelling* when you asked him straight out. No one else ever has." She looked wistful. "But we still don't know."

She offered Lil an assisting arm to help her to her feet. As Lil fumbled a bit with her cane, she advised me, "Look, forgetting—what's his name, Gavin?—forgetting that he's clearly an idiot, there is something I feel I should pass along to you. There are unique concerns with a book where a large sum of money is being paid in the hope that a large number of copies will be sold. You must try to come up with something that the newspapers will consider a story all on its own. Not for the gossip columns or book-review section or arts supplement. Something they could run on the front page, as news. Quoting the book. Quoting you. No price can be put on that kind of publicity."

She leaned on the cane for support and put her right hand on my arm. "Where you put yourself in all this requires careful judgement. I'm assuming Connie here will help you with that. You can't underestimate your readers' interest in Mr. Collins, nor overestimate their interest in you. On the other hand, you're standing in for the reader, who is in the company of this famous person courtesy of you. So although it goes against all my principles of what reportage should be, I tell you that, in this instance, it will be acceptable, even desirable, to let your presence be felt in a very small way—to let yourself be tasted, if only so much as a dash of nutmeg floating on a punch bowl of well-spiked eggnog." She looked at

Connie. "I think in this case, it would be all right." Connie nodded and Lil looked back at me, issuing final dispensation. "It's all right to make yourself a part of the story."

I smiled thankfully, and I really did respect her, but the truth is, I wasn't paying much attention. For the last five minutes, I had been far more concerned with whether I should have the taxi go uptown on Sixth or on Madison to get me to the Plaza hotel, where I had a date with Vince Collins's ex-partner, Lanny Morris, who was apparently going to have me for the whole day.

THIRTEEN

I walked up the Plaza's main steps, at 750 Fifth Avenue. (Yes, it has a street number like any other building.) Above me the flags of whatever foreign dignitaries were staying in the hotel that day hung motionless in the heat between banners for Old Glory (Betsy Ross, 1775) and Old Money (the Plaza hotel, 1909).

I never thought of the area just inside its Fifth Avenue entrance as a lobby. It wasn't as if you could sit there and read a newspaper. It was simply the largest and most elegantly carpeted vestibule in midtown. Directly up one flight to my right were hair salons and a barbershop. I'd once been treated to a pedicure there as a gift from a rock singer whom I'd interviewed. Later he asked to see the results, and it wasn't until I felt his tongue eeling its way between my toes that I realized he expected a gift in return.

On my left was the former entrance to El Morocco, recently closed while the management debated whether to make the nightclub into a discotheque or lease it out as a clothing store. Below me, I knew from past experience, were the mysterious yet graceful cloisters of an underground ballroom, floored in rosy marble and framed by creamy arches, as if it were a petite cathedral for society's divine.

I crossed the threshold into the Palm Court, which I considered to be the Plaza's true lobby, then passed the cloakroom for the Edwardian Room, now rechristened the Green Tulip. The management was hoping to somehow blur the line between nouveau design and nouvelle cuisine with a kind of hippie herbal attitude thrown in for good measure, as if when Oscar Wilde had walked about London with a lily in his hand, he had intended to smoke it. The overall effect was that of Bob Hope growing long sideburns to become relevant to the youth movement.

I reached the Plaza's small reception area and a bank of manned elevators, one of whose exquisite cages opened to take on passengers. I stepped in.

"Twenty-three, please," I murmured.

"Who do you want?" asked a mutty-looking attendant none too politely.

"Merwin."

"Hold on." Mutt the attendant took a step out of the elevator and signaled to a man in a blue suit standing near the check-in desk. "Bob? She wants to see Merwin."

Bob stepped over. He could have been the long-term president of any junior chamber of commerce in the Midwest. He gave me the twice-over through steel-rimmed glasses and nodded to Mutt. "She's okay." The question in my mind was whether my being "okay" meant that Lanny had described me to the front desk and I fit the description, or whether it simply meant that Bob knew Lanny's taste in women and I met those standards. Or maybe he just wanted to make certain I wasn't too overt a hooker, meaning that I was white, properly attired, and could pass for a schoolteacher as I circulated about the hotel. On the schoolteacher part of the disguise, I had apparently been doing quite well since yesterday.

The twenty-third floor was swiftly reached. Mutt terminated the car's ascent with a lackadaisical double-clutching of his hand throttle, and I felt that sick-making feeling as my stomach slightly overshot the elevator for a full second, then slid back down within me. It was a nauseating sensation achievable only by the ineptitude of human hands, one I'd not felt since automation had replaced elevator operators. Mutt pointed to the end of the corridor.

"End of the hall, the three doors after the uh—"

"Alcove?"

"Yeah. Center door is the living room. Tell him Mickey says, 'Hi.'"

I walked down the hallway, waiting to hear the elevator cage close behind me, but it stayed open. I didn't mean to flatter myself, but Mickey was no doubt checking out his rear view of me. I walked in as close to a military gait as I could muster in order to display minimal buttock-toggling for his viewing pleasure.

The hallway was not decorated all that beautifully, considering the hotel's reputation. A major hotel chain had acquired the dowager Plaza and was more than pleased to call it their flagship, but beyond changing their corporate stationery to denote this, they didn't want to do too much else about it. They'd splashed a coat of white paint everywhere, but it was that sloppy, thick slapping-on of paint that leaves the window jambs sealed and closets difficult to open.

The main door to Lanny's suite had a doorbell to the right. I reached out to it, then hesitated, realizing I should collect my thoughts.

My name is Bonnie Trout. I am an elementary-school teacher, although we're going to try not to talk about that anymore. A new school year will begin shortly. I've just come from a job interview at . . . well, if I had to name somewhere, Neuman and Newberry would do. Even if Lanny checked, he'd be asking about a girl named Bonnie Trout, wouldn't he? My meeting could have been with any one of a hundred people there.

I also had to remember that I had not read what I'd read in Hillman's offices. That I had no special insights into Lanny's personality, that all I knew of him was what I'd encountered on the plane and at Beejay's—*my*—apartment. That Vince Collins was a total stranger to me. That I wasn't even a particularly big fan of the duo. And I knew nothing about the Girl in New Jersey, not who she was, nor what her connection was to the two men, nor anything at all that was mentioned in the second chapter that Lanny had sent to me.

But *why* had he sent it to me?

Then again, he hadn't sent it to me. He'd sent it to a journalist named O'Connor who lives in Los Angeles. He'd had no idea that I was—

Did he know who I was?

I had made a convincing case for why it was not all that odd for a celebrity and a civilian, both flying first-class to New York, to end up sitting next to each other.

But would it be that hard for someone like Lanny Morris to hire some bright young fellow with a master's degree in criminology and personal security to find out which flight I'd booked and to purchase the three seats next to mine? Was a flirtatious Lanny really interested in the seemingly susceptible Bonnie Trout, or was he more—

The door opened. I hadn't rung the bell.

Reuben was standing there with a wastebasket in his hand. His golden skin seemed even more saturated in hue against the white houseboy jacket he was wearing, apparently oblivious to its "Hey boy, chop-chop" connotations. I couldn't imagine Lanny forcing him to wear it. It must have been what Reuben felt most comfortable or appropriate in. It did have a stylish look to it, the line between a busboy's outfit and a Nehru jacket at that time being thinner than Gandhi.

Reuben seemed as flustered as his Sea of Tranquillity face would allow. "I'm sorry, I didn't hear you ring," he said, instantly setting down the offending wastebasket. "Won't you come in, please?" He really had the warmest voice. He gestured for me to enter, looking guilty that he'd been derelict in his duties.

"I didn't ring," I reassured him. "I was just composing my thoughts, as Mozart was wont to say." My cajolery registered nil on him, as my cajoleries often register on people from Earth. "After all, it isn't every afternoon you meet *the* Lanny Morris." The regret I felt at this schoolgirl simpering was in the next moment replaced with a much greater regret as I realized that this comment could be overheard by *the* Lanny Morris, who was seated on a couch to my extreme right and engaged in an energetic phone conversation with someone.

"Okay, but if I do it, you got to have a Lanny's Club Day next season," he negotiated, giving me a lovely wave. "For all my club members." Lanny's Club was the dread tag phrase for preteen burn victims, who had become Lanny's new charity since polio had been regrettably stopped in its tracks. The phrase "Lanny's Club" still brings horror to my heart. Believe me, the last thing in life you ever wanted was to be a new inductee into Lanny's Club, unless debriding dead skin from your own body is your idea of a hobby. "And I don't mean you put my club members in the grandstand, either . . . field box. Yeah, you heard me. In the shade, under the press-level overhang. Okay, deal. I'll be at the players' entrance at three." He hung up the phone and appraised me. "Hope you like baseball. The Mets need somebody famous to sing the National Anthem this afternoon. Vikki Carr was going to do it, but she didn't make her connection in Denver."

"So you're singing it?"

"Yeah, it's no big deal. I do this for them, they come up with eighty seats the next time they play an expansion team. You like Chinese?"

"There's a Chinese expansion team?"

"Food. Or did you have lunch already?"

I said I hadn't. He turned to Reuben. "Look, we'll never get down to Chinatown on four wheels fast enough—we'll take the subway. Call Dav-El limos, we'll meet that Mike Whatever-His-Name-Is down there." Lanny turned quickly to me and asked, "You were okay with him, right?" as if such issues were subject to my approval.

As he was saying all this, he did something that was new to my range of experience. He put on a disguise, as if this were no different from putting on a blazer and a tie. He reached into a hatbox near the couch and adjusted a blond wig that gave him a coif not unlike that of the late Brian Jones from the Rolling Stones. To this he added a pair of granny glasses with smoked lenses. He took off his shirt in front of me (he had a much nicer physique and quite a bit less chest hair than I had imagined) and donned a silk one that bore a hand-painted western landscape, over which he wore a light-navy sports jacket with gold piping. A beaded choker around his neck completed what was, in that era, quite a smart outfit and which, in any other era, would have caused him to be laughed out of town.

We took the service elevator down to the Plaza's kitchens, then up a flight of stairs that Lanny knew about and out a service entrance onto Fifty-eighth Street. Soon I was doing the best I could to keep up with Lanny, who kept his head bowed but chivalrously took my arm as we plunged down the steps of the Lexington Avenue line. Amazingly, Lanny had a platinum subway-token dispenser in his pocket (probably worth three or four hundred times the price of the five tokens it contained). He put a token into a turnstile and, ever the gentleman, gestured for me to pass through first. As I did, a Number 4 train rasped into and against the platform; its doors opened with the snorting sound of a Brahman bull.

There were no two seats alongside each other free, so we stood holding on to a pole by the doors, my hand and Lanny's hand and the hand of a man who didn't know us stacked as if we were all swearing to some solemn pact. Lanny obviously didn't want to speak for fear of betraying his identity, so I occupied myself by reading the banner ads along the top of the car. Channel 11 was now showing reruns of *Perry Mason* every weeknight at eleven. Women were being warned in Spanish not to do some particular thing if they were pregnant. It was apparently assumed that women who spoke English already knew not to do this. Anbesol was recommended to relieve the pain of those jagged red lightning bolts that so often float in the air outside your jaw whenever you look pained. Alongside that, it was fervently suggested that we not move between the cars while the train was in motion and that we not spit on the train or platform. I had, of course, just been about to spit in front of the mop-topped Lanny Morris, but somehow managed to squelch the impulse.

By now the Canal Street station had rolled into place outside our subway car. We got off the train and headed up the stairs.

These were the days before Chinatown became overrun with Asians. To be sure, there were lots of quaint Chinese men and women neatly tucked away behind glass-topped counters by the cash registers of Chinese restaurants, fronted by a bowl of after-dinner mints and a juice glass full of loose toothpicks, or in little Chinese shops selling funny things like Chinese daily newspapers or Chinese girlie magazines with pretty, flat-bottomed girls in pastel-colored bikinis on the cover.

But it was still largely a place for Occidentals to eat dirt-cheap Chinese food served by hurried, irritated waiters. Oh, on the streets you'd see the occasional old Chinese man in a gray suit and brown hat going to get a haircut, but mainly the neighborhood, like the country of Jamaica, existed primarily for the amusement of white people. "Oh look, a Chinese hamburger stand!" you'd hear. The pagoda roof on an outdoor payphone was adorable.

Lanny said his first sentence to me since we had boarded the subway. "You ever had Sesh-wan cuisine?"

I thought he had sneezed. "What?" I asked.

"Sesh-wan. Most amazing food you'll ever have." I had no idea what he was talking about, but he was clearly pleased that he did. "It's a place in China."

"Oh. As in the Brecht play. *The Good Woman of Sze-chu-an.*" I said the word in three syllables, the way I'd been taught by the same English professor who'd personally introduced me to the word *frenulum.*

Lanny frowned. "I thought Brecht was German or something."

"A good German," I advised. We turned a corner into Doyers Street, which curved beyond our sight line.

"My favorite street in Manhattan," he commented. "You know why? It looks like a movie set." It did, but I remarked that, other than the Chinese neon signs and the shop windows featuring gnarled medicinal roots and gnarled roasted pork carcasses, I couldn't tell just why.

He explained for my edification: "Every backlot wide shot in every Hollywood movie that's set in New York shows either a T-shaped intersection or a curved street. That's because if you showed a real intersection, you'd have to show block after city block going back to infinity. So when I grew up, to me the real Manhattan—meaning the one in the movies—was full of T-shaped streets where gangsters' cars come screeching around the corner . . . or curved streets where some guy standing by a lamppost casts a long, arcing shadow across the wet pavement."

He trotted up three steps into an unpromising canteen named Szechuan Garden. Its decor was a cross between that of my high school cafeteria and a travel agency for slow boats to Mandalay.

Lanny pulled off his wig and greeted the obvious owner, who had been standing by a counter in a wash-and-wear short-sleeved shirt and slacks, picking his teeth. "Oh, Missah Morris!" the restaurateur cried with an accent and jargon and elated demeanor I fully suspected he employed because Caucasians expected it. "Me so happy see you. Got picture you up on wall, see? That make it 'Great Wall'!" It was surely not the first time he had said this. He indicated an eight-by-ten glossy of Lanny over the register, autographed, "Thanks, Lee, for a HOT time in Chinatown!" Lanny nodded, introduced me, and murmured a food order to Lee, who showed us to a large table toward the back of the room and scurried off to the kitchen.

Lanny explained that he needed to save his voice a little for "The Star-Spangled Banner" (which he described as the worst waltz ever written) and apologized in advance for making me do most of the talking. Of course, I was eager to talk about anything under the sun as long as it wasn't about myself, since I was already completely compromised on that topic. This led us into a strangely abstract and esoteric monologue on my part, punctuated now and then by Lanny's "Oh really?" New lovers talk only about themselves. (This is one of the great appeals of a new love.) But no one listening to our conversation would have mistaken us for lovers, nor should they have.

I'd heard that the reason for the cooking style of Chinese food, the ingredients diced small in advance to cook in a flash over high heat spread across the width of a wok, was due to the lack of firewood in China. You had to make the most of the heat while you had it. The verity of this (as well as Lanny's priority as a customer) was demonstrated by the fact that within minutes, our dishes were being brought to our table, presented not in the usual silver tureens with silver tops but simply on open oval plates. And the dishes contained something I had never before seen in a Chinese entrée: the color red. Not the usual pale gray-green-white-brown palette of every Cantonese-American restaurant's dishes (the principle ingredients of which were always cornstarch and bamboo shoots with a little julienned meat sprinkled on top) but livid, troubling colors. Red bell peppers, strange sienna husks I could not identify, blood-orange peel alongside the shrapnel of corrugated cabbage—and peanuts, for God's sake!

In the midst of all this, I found myself saying three words hitherto unspoken by me in a Chinese restaurant: "I smell lamb."

Lanny nodded. "That's lamb in tea sauce, this is twice-cooked pork with shredded pickled cabbage, and this, my friend, is kung-pao chicken." He looked at me blissfully. "I really envy you. You're about to meet a whole bunch of flavors you've never tasted before."

The next half hour was a truly hallucinogenic experience. Flavors cascaded and tumbled around my mouth like a troupe of Chinese acrobats and fire jugglers performing a noisy circus there. Salt and tang and sharp and deep—I found myself forking white rice into my mouth directly from the individual bowl provided, using it like a sorbet between courses in a swank restaurant, restoring my tongue to a semblance of neutrality between bites, rather than making the rice into a bland flatbed for one's entrées, as was the American custom.

"Well?" asked Lanny with a grin. We'd not talked much once the food was served, other than my fevered oohs and aahs. I felt as if he'd brought me to an orgy dedicated solely to my pleasure. He intently studied the rapturous expressions on my face. It was sexual, a bit perverse, and thoroughly enjoyable.

These men, I thought. And by "these men," I meant Lanny and Vince. I wondered what it would be like to spend time with either in a normal place. Or would a normal place instantly be made abnormal simply by their presence?

Lee approached the table with a long plate upon which lay a nearly two-pound lobster, its most abundant locations of meat skillfully plumed up and blooming from within its cracked and unfolded shell, drowned in a livid red sauce that made the carapace of the lobster modestly rosy by comparison. The sauce was flecked throughout with tons of diced scallion.

Lee announced, "I make my special lobster in chile sauce with tangerine peel for you and your lovely lady friend, Missah Morris."

To my surprise, I heard Lanny snap: "You shouldn't have done that, Lee. I don't eat lobster. I'm a Jew."

Lee looked bewildered. "But . . . you eat pork." He gestured to the shredded-cabbage dish Lanny had already ladled onto his own plate.

"I'm a New York Jew, we get dispensation from Milton Berle. I'm allowed spareribs and meatball-parm wedges, but I don't eat shrimp or lobster. They're roaches on plutonium, Lee, they're disgusting. I'll pay for the dish, but take it away."

Lee shrugged. "If you don't want it, I'm not going to put it on the bill," he said in absolutely unbroken English. He carried away the dish, slighted.

Lanny looked back at me with a wisp of contrition in his face. "Sorry. Forgot to ask—maybe you love lobster."

"Well, not after the analogy to roaches I don't," I said with what I hoped was a wry smile.

"Sorry," he said again.

Today I'd been waiting for the slightest sign of vulnerability in Lanny, and this was perhaps as close as I might get. "I feel sorry for you, actually. If you complain to the manager of a restaurant, you're not some bastard at table five. You're Lanny Morris. You have no cloak of anonymity. If you buy rubbers at a drugstore, the man behind the counter will spend the rest of his life talking about how he once sold Lanny Morris rubbers. I've read lots of books about the lives of famous people, but what would be truly interesting would be a book on what it's like to forever relinquish all anonymity. The way you've done." I placed some food in my mouth and intentionally spoke with my mouth full to make myself sound even more casual. "You ever think about writing a book?"

Lanny drank some tea. "When I'm dead."

I ventured that this sounded moderately challenging, and he explained, "No, I mean, if I ever wrote the book I'd like to write, it would have to be published after I died. When I wouldn't care what anybody thought about me. Man, that would be something. To write a book where I just . . . told the truth. Not put a nice face on everything." He signaled to Lee for a fresh pot of tea. "Can you imagine? Like, I've met four presidents and the truth is, each one seemed to me totally out of it. As if they hardly knew what was going on. Like meeting the principal of a high school where the kids are smoking hash and getting knocked up, and he's in a blue suit talking about young minds. Even JFK left me unimpressed. Felt like I was with the boss's son."

"But you don't think you could say that."

"Not if I was planning to live in this country. I don't think Edith Piaf was such a great singer. I'd get killed for saying that. Or that Marilyn Monroe didn't act any better after she got with Lee Strasberg than before. Oh God, just saying what I really felt. That would be something. Having to be a nice guy is the toughest job in the world when you're not."

"You don't think you're a nice guy?"

"You think you're a nice girl?" he parried with the inflection of a Jewish mother. I bit down upon what I thought was a piece of lamb crackling and was immediately assaulted by hot spears of pain in my mouth, not unlike the radiating red lightning bolts from the Anbesol ad in the subway. I gasped and reached for a tumbler of water.

"Oh, no, you don't eat those, honey," he admonished. "Those are dried chile peppers." My eyes streamed and my nose began to run as if I'd been servicing a proportionately endowed basketball star. "Here, just eat more of the rice, and—" He summoned Lee with a wave of his hand. "Club soda, quick." (It had been discovered in recent times that all things were solved by club soda. Stains, damage to silk, tumors . . . "Could you bring me some club soda, please?") Lee returned with a glass of sparkling water, which I downed. The cold and carbonation bit into the burn in a helpful way.

"I should have warned you," Lanny apologized, pouring tea for us very much in the manner of a nice guy. "You know why Chinese teacups have no handles? Because the Chinese are smarter than we are. If the cup is too hot to hold with your fingers, then the tea is too hot to drink. But what do we do? We put a handle on the teacup, so we can't tell how hot the tea is. That way we get to pour boiling hot tea right into our mouths, cauterizing our tongues."

As my mouth still burned from the chile peppers to which he had so very nicely introduced me, I entertained the thought that perhaps men like Lanny and Vince were cups with handles, who would nicely stroll you down unreal streets and feed you full of dreamy food until you allowed yourself to be nicely manhandled by them and suddenly felt the surge of their boiling brew scalding your mouth. But I had a rule about going three deep on any metaphor and promptly exited the thought as we were brought orange segments for dessert, instead of the standard lump of melting ice cream in a small silver bowl. Two fortune cookies were nestled among the orange slices and Lanny invited me to pick one, which I did. Lanny took the other and cracked it open. I asked him what his fortune said. "Well, it's supposed to be a joke, but . . ."

He pushed it across the tablecloth to me. Its red ink was no doubt intended to read "Eat, drink and be merry, for tomorrow you diet." But it had been printed off center to the right and the *t* in *diet* was missing.

Lanny smiled. "What about yours?"

I cracked mine open and tried to locate the slip of paper that revealed my fate, but disconcertingly, I discovered that the cookie was empty.

FOURTEEN

We found ourselves scurrying like laboratory mice through a maze of corridors that had been decorated by someone with a flair for submarines. We hung a left turn and raced up a concrete incline that held the promise of a clear blue sky at its end, until suddenly, as if in an agoraphobic's worst nightmare, we burst out of the square tunnel onto a huge, flat lawn flanked by two walls of humanity, each wall composed of some twenty-five thousand faces. An usher in an orange sports jacket, cloud-white shirt, and sky-blue pants pointed us to our immediate right, where various New York Mets were lounging in their dugout. We sought momentary shelter there.

"Hey, Lanny!" cried a mustachioed fellow whom I recognized from hot-shaving-lather commercials. The rest of the Mets cascaded their greetings. One would have thought from their familiarity that Lanny did this on a regular basis, but I later learned he had never met any of the team before.

A stentorian voice rang out from all four corners of the globe, reading copy that had no doubt been supplied by Lanny's P.R. agent.

"Ladies and gentlemen . . . if you will kindly direct your attention to the playing field . . . to sing our national anthem . . . please welcome one of the world's most

beloved comedians, film actors, and vocal artists . . . performing on behalf of his own charity, 'Lanny's Club.' . . . Would you give a magnificent New York Mets welcome to New York's favorite native son . . . Mr. Lanny Morris!"

Lanny winked at me and strolled jauntily toward a microphone that had been placed halfway between home plate and the pitching mound. He gave a manly wave to the crowd, more like a ballplayer's self-assured salute than a politician's frantic acknowledgment. He stood at the mike and waited confidently for their silence. The crowd quieted down as much as a crowd can. I was close enough to him that I could hear his unamplified voice sing: *"Oh, say can you see . . ."*

I was alarmed to hear, or rather not hear, that the P.A. system wasn't working. It may have been something as simple as the mike not being switched on. I was curious how a veteran like Lanny would handle such an awkward moment. Would he stop and wait for the mike to be fixed? Continue without amplification out of patriotic deference to the anthem itself? But after the half second it took me to ponder the above, Lanny's amplified voice bombarded me from speakers all around the stadium: *"Oh, say can you see . . ."* I'd never realized how long the inherent delay in public-address systems was and suddenly found myself far more sympathetic to sporting-event vocalists who got themselves radically out of sync with marching bands, so that the band was playing *"And the rockets' red glare"* somewhere around the time the vocalist reached *"And the home of the brave!"*

It was strange to stand there and watch Lanny's lips mouthing words in advance of his own voice, which was blaring live over the stadium's P.A., as if he were the leading man of a Godzilla movie. As he reached the last stanza, a roar began to build within the crowd, not so much in response to Lanny's rendition (which was a surprisingly smooth-voiced interpretation, neither operatic nor croony) but because our national anthem was almost over and our national pastime was about to begin.

But in this instance there was an added catalytic force. A man in his early thirties with oily brown hair and an oily brown raincoat had vaulted over the right-field wall and onto the playing field. He quickly discarded his coat, beneath which he was stark naked. Lately, this had become a thing. Lanny was the last person in the stadium who could see what was happening, and as the noise of the spectators increased, he started to extend his arms to receive the seeming adulation of the crowd. The streaker dashed in front of the microphone and yelled into it, "Nixon is a warmonger! Kissinger is being used as a—" Lanny grabbed the microphone away from the streaker and the stadium was assaulted by the massively amplified sound of that grab, a veritable cannonade favoring the frequencies below 150 cycles. Someone in the press box had enough wit about them to close down the mike as Lanny began to wrestle for control of it. Lanny suddenly realized that he was struggling with a naked man, whose puny physique and not very awesome genitalia were evoking little of the Greco-Roman spirit. Wisely, he trotted away from the man, laughing and shaking his head to the crowd as if to position himself above this sorry spectacle, as the Mets players raced out of the dugout and began to punch and kick their naked victim. The Shea Stadium security force eventually got the players to calm down; the man's raincoat was fetched from right field, and he was ushered to the locker room to a frightening wave of catcalls, most of which linked the streaker to Communists, peace advocates, civil rights activists, and people who copulated with their matriarch.

"You believe that bastard?" Lanny said to me after the game, when he could talk without being overheard. We were walking back to the limousine, which was parked in the fenced-in lot reserved for the players. "All I need is for one person in that crowd to have taken a decent snapshot of me wrestling with that guy and they'll sell it to the tabloids. *'That ugly rumor about Lanny Morris being caught in a clinch with a naked man is in the right ballpark—and we have the pictures to prove it!'*"

"No one on earth is going to believe anything like that," I assured him, as I spotted Michael Dougherty standing by his limousine. He was getting an autograph from Tug McGraw, who didn't look too pleased about it.

"Oh, I'm not worried about people believing that. It's just that there's a zoning regulation in show business that you can publicly look stupid three times, and after that, guess what, people figure you're stupid."

I had expected us to get onto the same ugly highway that had led us from JFK to Manhattan the previous evening. But only a minute or two after we stole our way out of Shea Stadium, the limousine began ambling through some pleasant residential streets, small houses each with a tree on the front lawn. Then Michael Dougherty cut a sharp turn and we were back on another access road with large cracks in its pale, dirty concrete. We veered onto what looked like some sort of abandoned boulevard and now we were passing by the Unisphere, a steel-ribbed globe that had been the symbol of the 1964–65 World's Fair. Shea Stadium was at our back and before us was a structure that looked like a one-story building that had been lifted from a corporate park and pointlessly placed upon four tall turrets no less than ten stories in height. The building bore the words TOP OF THE FAIR. (Even though, obviously, there was no longer a fair for it to top.)

Michael Dougherty stopped the limo and dashed around to my door. I looked at Lanny, puzzled.

"We're dining?"

"Leaving."

He strolled me onto the cement esplanade, which was totally deserted, and through doors marked PORT OF AUTHORITY NEW YORK. Beyond them was a small lectern manned by a middle-aged fellow in a business suit. He referred to a clipboard. "Hello, Mr. Morris. All set for you. If you'll sign here."

Lanny scribbled a signature. "Who's driving?"

"Cubby."

Lanny nodded approval and stepped to the already open doors of a narrow elevator, gesturing for me to enter. Once we were in, he pushed the only button other than G for Ground. It was discreetly labeled H.

"What's 'H'?" I asked as we ascended very quickly.

"Hroof garden." The elevator stopped, the doors opened, and a stiff breeze hit us. Correction. Many stiff, measured breezes hit us. "And heliport," he added in what I'm sure was intended to sound like an offhand comment.

We were standing on the roof of the building, and slapping its five rotary forearms against the air with its trademark chopping sound was a commercial helicopter. Lanny nodded toward it. "Our ride home."

I happened to know that the helicopter was a Sikorsky S-61L. I knew that its cruising speed was 115 nautical miles an hour. I also knew that I was supposed to be impressed. I was, but enough already, I thought. Lanny was putting on an admirable floor show, no doubt designed to sweep me off my feet and him against my labia, but it was calculated for what he believed was a starry-eyed schoolmarm named Bonnie Trout. Meet the celeb at his Plaza suite, have an incredibly low-profile lunch at a delicious dive on Doyers Street where the yellow press won't discover or publicize "Lanny's New Lady." Then on to watch Lanny be the darling of fifty-five thousand at Shea Stadium. After all, let's give the devil his due: how many people can, on two hours' notice, arrange to sing for a gathered multitude and be cheered despite performing only one musical selection, and an *a cappella* one at that? Then into a private whirlybird, where Lanny is taking his new bird for a little whirl—how to respond to all this?

Fuck. I'm Bonnie Trout.

"Wow," I said.

"Oh, you like?" replied Lanny as if he'd hardly noticed the Sikorsky that was slashing at the air around us and requiring him to raise his voice about twenty decibels. "Yeah, it's all ours. Hey, Cubby!"

He walked us toward the helicopter, thoughtfully putting his hand on the back of my head and gently pressuring it downward to ensure that it was well below the overhead blades. It was the first time a man had pushed my head down that way where I didn't snap, *"Don't ever do that again!"* in a voice that invariably reduced his erection by a good two inches.

"You ever been on a helicopter?" he asked me as Cubby, a nice-looking guy in his twenties, helped me up some steps. The interior looked as if it could easily seat a dozen or more (I'd been on commuter airplanes that had smaller cabins than this), but we were the only passengers.

"No, never," I replied truthfully. Not that I hadn't had the opportunity once or twice, but I'd always managed to find a reason to decline the invitation. And now here I was on an S-61L. Oh good.

I'm by no means knowledgeable about aviation, but my journalism thesis had been a piece I'd written (which actually ran in *The Christian Science Monitor*) about the estimable Sikorsky S-61L and its two accidents in California, causing the deaths of all on board. Passengers and crew. Both times. No survivors. In 1968, the S-61L had been a commercial shuttle from LAX to Anaheim. I called it the Disneyland Death Train. Within six months, the S-61L had twice decided to drop out of the sky en route. Metal fatigue was cited as a possible cause. Gee, don't you just hate it when metal gets tired?

"So where are we taking this?"

"Just back to Manhattan. You should sit on the left side." He indicated a window seat. Cubby stepped into a kind of pilot's cabin separated from the passengers' seats. "No copilot?" I asked.

Lanny laughed. "The whole flight takes less than ten minutes." I was about to comment that, in the event of metal fatigue or pilot stroke, it would probably not take us all of ten minutes to plummet to where the ground would provide all the stopping power we'd ever need. But as if to illustrate the brevity of our trip, the copter immediately buoyed itself into the air. We scooted off the rooftop as carelessly as Peter Pan and were already passing by Shea Stadium, at an altitude not much higher than its cheapest seats. Ah, that incredibly attenuated island toward the west, the one with all those ridiculously tall buildings—would that be the fabled Manhattan now? The hot orange sun was currently playing peekaboo with us, popping out from behind the cover of the Chrysler and Empire State buildings.

I assumed we'd be landing at the Heliport on the East River, which we were already closing in on. I pointed in its general direction, below a phalanx of polka-dot-painted cement trucks that were huddled a little north of Ninety-sixth. "We landing down there?" I asked.

Lanny shook his head. "Not down. Up."

As if on cue, the trustworthy S-61L seemed to take off again and trampolined us into the thick of New York's tallest spires. We were above them, but only just slightly, and it felt as if we were dodging the buildings rather than scraping by above them. Then it seemed as if we had stopped (we had, more or less), and I saw to my horror that we were poised above midtown Manhattan at an elevation equivalent to, say, the ninety-ninth floor of a building, except that said building had ceased to exist and we were now in its lone remaining office, supported by nothing.

When I look down from a terrace mounted to a high apartment building, where I can see the laws of perspective in action, the side of the building dropping away beneath me and my feet . . . this is the kind of vertigo from which I suffer. To suddenly be a hundred feet above the top of the Pan Am Building, which was now yawing up at me, its facade like a ninety-degree ski slope of glass terminating in the grid between Lexington and Vanderbilt avenues . . .

"You okay?" asked Lanny. I closed my eyes for a second, swallowed. There was a very strong bump as we dropped onto our tiny perch, and I correctly assumed we'd landed. Instantly there was a change in the volume of the motors. All confidence now, I chattily commented, "I thought the Pan Am heliport had been closed down."

"They closed it in sixty-eight because there just wasn't enough business. But there's a new group wants to reopen it. In a year or two. I'm a stockholder. Meantime, you can get clearance to land four hours in advance if you know who to ask and you don't mind paying for the privilege."

Cubby had already opened the door and slid some steps up to it, and Lanny walked me out. Again he placed his hand above my hand and pressed gently down until we cleared the rotors. It was something like the hands-on blessing the priest would give you as a child in lieu of Christ's blood and body. I had always found it very comforting.

I was currently feeling quite weak, grateful to be alive, and tough as runny Camembert. A private elevator dove us down to the street, the same fall I'd been afraid the helicopter might make. Context is everything. The ugly lobby of the Pan Am Building was easy to leave, and Lanny quickly nabbed us a cab on Vanderbilt.

"Fifty-ninth and Fifth," he told the driver, keeping his head down so as not to be recognized. That was the Plaza. Would we eat there? Would we eat at all?

We got out of the cab, however, by the General Motors Building, on the other side of the Grand Army Plaza from Lanny's hotel. Lanny handed the driver a more than handsome tip, the driver said, "Hey . . ." in the first dawning of recognition, but Lanny smiled and scooted us away.

Lanny took my hand, which was all right I suppose, and trotted us down a long flight of white steps that verged onto an open-air café one floor below street level. It was already quieter on this level beneath the traffic, and it got better as Lanny walked us over to a revolving door directly underneath the General Motors showroom and we entered the Autopub.

In Manhattan, theme restaurants were blooming like plastic flowers in winter. I confess to enjoying such places: Trader Vic's, which made me feel like I was in the Enchanted Tiki Room in Disneyland; Chateau Henri IV, where you crossed a bridge over an indoor stream to reach your table by a stained-glass window; the Monk's Inn on Sixty-fourth, where the waiters were dressed in cowled robes and your Emmenthaler fondue and dusty bottle of red wine were accompanied by a Gregorian chant, or A Quiet Little Table in the Corner, where every booth was as the name implied, each hidden behind a beaded curtain, to which you summoned your waitress by pulling a cord that illuminated a red lightbulb. The Cattleman had set the stage, or rather the stagecoach, for such funhouse eateries, supposedly patterned after a Kansas City steer palace, as was also (surprise) the Steer Palace. The ubiquitous Steak and Brew chain's mock–British publican atmosphere offered you all the beer you could drink and all the lettuce you could assemble. Enrico E Paglieri offered the same deal but with all the sangria you could drink ("red wine and 7UP," translated the waitress) and all the antipasto you could eat (Oscar Mayer cold cuts and health salad). Some lunatic soul opened a similar restaurant named Chicago with the astounding offer of All the Booze You Could Drink, but apparently in its third month one frat party from Princeton buried the place for good.

The Autopub's theme was cars. Get it? General Motors Building? When you walked in, you were directed (by a gossamer young thing—my, how they get around) to one of several dining areas within the long, low-ceilinged, windowless facility. There was the Pit Stop, a brightly lit white Formica area with orange banquettes, delineated by trendy globular white lights. Very Euro. Behind the wide bar, with its decorative racing helmets, were the more-coveted booths, where four people could dine inside replications of a Model T or vintage Oldsmobile. Some of the cars were hardtops, meaning that you dined under their roofs and within their rolled-up windows, making it the coziest, most claustrophobic sit-down dinner in Manhattan.

"Merwin," murmured Lanny to the hostess, who was clearly expecting him.

"Oh yes, Mr. *Mer*-win," she delivered like a stripper enlisted into a burlesque routine. "Your table is waiting."

She took two menus and strutted her way down the restaurant's interminable corridor. We followed. A very Kiwanis-looking man stepped away from the bar and pumped Lanny's hand. "Mr. Morris, Jim Mackendorf, general manager, just want to say how delighted we are to have you here. If you need anything . . ." He forced his business card on Lanny, who pocketed it graciously. "Perhaps later we could take a photograph for our Wall of Fame . . . ?" Lanny said yes, on our way out, but please not while we were eating.

We continued to follow Gossamer Gertie for some time. When she'd reached what I assumed were the restrooms, she stopped in front of an inauspicious door labeled DRIVE-IN. A sign on a little easel outside the door said, "Our apologies. The Drive-In is closed for a private party." She opened the door for us, gesturing within. "Please sit anywhere you like, obviously. Tracy will be your waitress. I'll send her in now." The private party was apparently a party of two.

I'd heard about the Drive-In. It was a tunnel of a room, dark and cool as eleven P.M. in September. Black light caused Lanny's white shirt to glow. Instead of tables, the room had three single files of truncated mock automobiles mounted on three long platforms, the front seats of the cars with flat dashboards that served as one's table. The truncated cars (all "tables for two" with side-by-side seating, as if you'd been placed in the front seat of a Chevy Nova) were pointed toward a movie screen at the end of the room. The back of each "car" had lit red taillights, so as you were led to your assigned convertible, you were immediately seduced by the illusion that the drive-in was full and that you were merely making your way back from the popcorn concession. All it lacked was a kiddie railroad ride. We slid into a vehicle five cars back from the screen.

"Hi, I'm Tracy," said our waitress perkily. Everyone was named Tracy these days. Even people named Dawn were secretly named Tracy. She was dressed like a carhop attendant. "You pretty much have the run of the place, so do you want to see our menu . . . ?"

"Well, what do most people have when they come here?" Lanny asked.

"The Drive-In special. That's a big cheeseburger, and it's really big and really good, with shoestring fries and a martini. The martini is really big too." She smiled.

Lanny looked at me. I noticed that he had really nice eyes and accompanying lashes. "That okay with you?"

I said it was. I had the feeling that a big hamburger was one of the items the Autopub's culinary staff might handle best. And at this point I could use a big martini. Really big. Of course, I could have ordered a martini no matter what I ate, but the fact that it came with the hamburger made it seem almost unavoidable. "Vodka martini," I said. "On the rocks."

"Olive or onion?"

I thought of my breath and opted for the olive. (I was about to have a burger and I was worried about the scent of a cocktail onion!) Lanny ordered his martini with Beefeater gin, straight up, a little extra vermouth, four olives. Like me, he asked for his burger medium rare, without cheese. Maybe we were both thinking about our breath.

Tracy went hopping off to fetch our drinks, and the movie screen came to life. So there we were, parked in the fifth car from the screen, surrounded by other cars whose dashboard lights glowed warmly in the crisp blue night, but we were very much alone. If Lanny and I had decided to have it off right there in the front seat (and it was doubtful the management would have been likely to stop us), only Tracy and perhaps the projectionist would have known.

Lanny seemed the most relaxed he'd been today. Work (meaning the *Today* show and "The Star-Spangled Banner") was over, he explained. "And I love drive-ins. When we first started making movies, Vince and I would go rent a Thunderbird convertible or a Caddy, and we'd take out some local girls to see our pictures. Sometimes they didn't even know who we were until they started watching the movie. The girls would keep looking up at the screen and then back at us— God, if you could have seen their expressions!"

"I imagine you and Vince did quite well with those wide-eyed girls in those wide convertibles with their tops down," I observed as Woody Woodpecker pecked out the opening title to one of his cartoons. "Referring to the convertibles, of course."

He shrugged apologetically. "What should I say? We were young men with normal hormones who discovered there were only eleven women on Earth who wouldn't sleep with us on a first date."

I smiled. "Who were the eleven women?"

"Eleanor Roosevelt was one. Princess Margaret was fine about petting but nothing below the waist. You really want me to go on?"

Tracy returned with my martini, which came in something akin to a crystal horse trough. My lone stuffed olive looked like a green-and-red beach ball hopelessly adrift on an ice-filled silvery ocean, miles from civilization.

"My God," I muttered in awe.

"Told you they were big," chirped Tracy. "We've had people order second rounds, but I don't know if anyone's ever finished three of them." She set down Lanny's Beefeater straight-up martini, which trembled in a beaker about the size of an upright flügelhorn in both height and size of bell. "I'll be back in a moment with your food."

As if responding to some Shakespearean "Exuent, flourish" cue, she departed with an accompanying brass fanfare that actually emanated from the movie screen, as appeared the monochrome proclamation "Our Feature Presentation."

Now there was the logo of Republic Pictures, followed by the breathless news that Harold Stolman and George Piselli present: *A Republic Picture under the supervision of E. Bennett Lodge.* Then (single title card, festive theme): SMITHEREENS! New card: *Starring John Derek, Vera-Ellen . . . and introducing Vince Collins and Lanny Morris as "Vince and Lanny."*

I looked mock-accusingly at Lanny, who rushed to assure me, "They were showing this anyway, I swear to you. I thought you might enjoy it with a running commentary. Hey, I'm trying to impress you, all right?" He gave me a sheepish grin that was either sweetly studious or studiously sweet. "Now let me tell you how we did this opening dolly shot."

And he did. As we sat side by side in our Naugahyde love seat, reflecting pools of vodka and gin gleaming before us, Lanny relived for me the making of *Smithereens.*

It was a little eerie, as you can imagine. Lanny was on the screen, selling ice cream to kids in a Hollywood rendition of Central Park. Then his warm breath, with a pleasant scent of cool juniper laced with olive, would make some comment into my right ear. I'd turn and see the right profile of Lanny, almost as monochromatic in the blue light of the Drive-In as the slightly green-tinged image onscreen, whispering who in the cast had been evil, who'd had a drinking problem, and who'd been doing whom during principal photography.

My hamburger arrived, the size of a forty-five RPM record—or, rather, a stack of about fifteen such records—and it was a really good one, tasting of Memorial Day picnics. I took demure bites and, combined with *Smithereen*'s unassuming charms, Lanny's inside stories, the extremely long french fries, and most of my second martini, the evening floated along like a dreamy rowboat ride up the Thames. When Lanny wasn't narrating, he'd watch my reactions to the movie the way a novice writer watches his girlfriend's face when she reads his latest story. Every now and then, he'd give me a gentle nudge, or murmur "This" to alert me to a particular sight gag or one-liner. It might have been annoying, but his boyish enthusiasm for his early work was so sincere and affectionate as to be almost enviable.

By the unspooling of the last reel, we were sipping liqueurs, as of course people so often do at a drive-in. I'd ordered a crème de menthe for the sole purpose of freshening my breath, a Scope mouthwash you can swallow. The film ended with an astounding twist: over the image of Vince crooning the last chorus of "Just My Pal and My Gal," the words *The End* appeared, upon which Lanny slapped a big question mark as suffix while winking broadly at the camera. Fadeout, cast credits, *A Republic Picture.*

With the movie's end, the overhead lights came up, which startled and momentarily disoriented me. After all, at an outdoor drive-in movie, if the overhead lights came up, it would indicate the aurora borealis, Armageddon, or the conclusion of a horror marathon that ran until dawn. I had, in fact, forgotten for the moment exactly where we were. The two bountiful martinis had nestled me into the most comfortable cocoon. Now I looked with vodka-infused affection at this man with whom I'd been spending a near-hallucinogenic twenty-four hours within my already surreal life. Vince Collins had strolled me around the cloud-capped towers and gorgeous palaces of the Burbank Studios and elicited from me the guarantee of a sweet and easy lay at the end of our intended work together. Then, with hardly time to return to whatever passes for reality in Los Angeles, I'd been catapulted into this strange, long arc of a first date with his ex-partner, Lanny.

He'd really been funny in the film. The script itself was disgracefully clunky, even for its time, but Vince and Lanny had their own unscripted movie percolating within the film, one that consisted of looks and takes, the love-hate of their brotherly love, and, particularly, Lanny's outrageous mugging, which seemed to have been filmed at a different frame rate than the rest of the cast. He made a five-syllable word out of "Hello," a punch line out of "Why's that?," and he was unable to take three steps without knocking something down, which he then caught, then dropped as he reached to catch something else he'd knocked down. Onscreen, he was also an awful lot more like the man who'd written the two chapters that I'd read than the sometimes pensive fellow in the seat next to me.

I looked at him. In repose, his face really was quite lovely. Somebody kisses clowns after they take off their makeup, I thought. Emmett Kelly must have gotten laid in his lifetime or there wouldn't have been an Emmett Kelly Jr. Maybe Lanny was very good in bed. Why wouldn't he be? To be a clown is to take on a calling, isn't it? Like being a surgeon or a counselor. Such people can be sensitive, expressive . . . some of the qualities you might hope for in a bed partner.

What was I doing? I knew what I was doing. I was making the case for becoming one of the women in his memoirs, and having very little problem doing so.

Outside the Autopub, as we mounted the stairs up to Fifth Avenue, the night and I were warm and susceptible to anything that might happen. What is the halfway mark between giddiness and drunkenness? I was there. Lanny didn't say where we were going next, but gee gosh, his hotel *was* just across the street. He wrapped his arm around my waist and we walked slowly across Fifth Avenue toward the southern boundary of Central Park. At this relatively early hour of the evening, the hansom cabs were still lined up across from the Fifty-ninth Street entrance to the Plaza. The farmlike smell of horses and their hay created in me a sensory conflict as my retina processed images of the cosmopolitan facades of Central Park South while my olfactory lobes told me I was back in the barnyard.

Lanny turned to a driver of a hansom cab, a bearded young man in an Ascot cutaway suit whose long hippie hair was crowned by a dove-gray top hat.

"Cleopatra's Needle and back?" he asked the cabby.

"Fifty," he was quoted.

"Thirty," Lanny countered.

"Forty," offered the driver.

"Sixty," Lanny smiled, completely confusing him. He handed the driver some money and helped me into the cab, which was a true hansom (whereas most of the others were carriages). The swing door closed in front of us and we were obliged to snuggle together more tightly than in our convertible at the Drive-In. I leaned against his chest and he wrapped his arm around my shoulders.

I hardly knew which Central Park this was: the one seen in *Smithereens,* where Lanny was a Good Humor salesman, or the one that Vince had strolled me by at the Burbank Studios. There was even the laughable possibility that this was the real Central Park.

"You know, we've hardly talked about *you,* Bonnie," murmured Lanny. It was probably a sentence he had considerately learned to say to women over the years, since he obviously was going to be Topic A in any conversation with most civilians.

As you can imagine, the last thing I wanted to be talking about with Lanny was Bonnie Trout.

"Oh, do we have to talk?" I asked and kissed him. I've heard tell that

I'm a pretty good kisser, but whatever I was, he was easily my match. We found enough to keep us occupied until the hansom cab pulled up to the Plaza's main entrance.

"I can take you home now," Lanny said. "Unless you'd like to come back to my suite."

I nodded slowly. "Oh . . . of course, yes, have me," I heard myself say, without even a tinge of sarcasm. "By all means," I added.

We didn't say a word on the way up to his suite. He let himself in. Reuben was nowhere to be seen. (My impression was that he had a room of his own, apart from Lanny's suite.) I let Lanny lead me to his bedroom, where Reuben had laid out a neatly folded silk robe for him. I took the liberty of filching it, and excused myself to the attached bathroom with the assurance that I'd be but a minute.

After little more than that, I stepped back into the bedroom, making sure the bathroom light was already off, so that I wouldn't be seen backlit in shadow, which would have ruined the effect. Lanny had thoughtfully turned off all the lights except a lamp near the bed. He'd kicked off his shoes and was lying atop the blanket and sheets; the bedspread was now heaped in the room's far corner. His incredibly expensive watch was on the night table.

He could see that I was wearing his robe. I stood by his side, looked down at him, and let the robe drop to the carpet. I'd left my bra and panties back in the bathroom, so in that instant, Lanny became very much better acquainted with me.

The air-conditioning in the room had been left on high, and that, combined with the voluptuous internal shiver induced by the boldness of what I was doing, gave my skin what I hoped was a desirably goose-bumped texture. My nipples were hard, but that would have been the case without the air-conditioning. I was aroused by my own forwardness, and I could see from the ridge outlined in the fabric of his pants that I more than had his interest as well. He tugged me down to him on the bed with just the correct amount of forcefulness . . . and soon my breasts, my arms, my stomach, my sex (as I'd come to call it), my neck, my ass, my back, my lips were brushing against his shirt, his pants, his skin, his cock (as I'd come to call it) as he so hurriedly undressed himself beneath me. Our curious, adroit, gliding tongues were everywhere, delighting with one lovely discovery after another. Either we were both very good together or he was so incredible that he was good enough for the both of us. As he finally entered me and God, God I felt so filled, his steady, confident thrusts that showed no sign of ever ending causing a scarily ecstatic pressure that I could feel all the way back to my cervix and yes I began to give myself over to this unceasing engine we'd together constructed on this bed in this hotel room, a turbine with him and me as mindless pistons, and it was using me, as I so wanted it to, and I thought, I thought as I gave myself up to it, "*Now* am I part of the story? Was *this* what you wanted?" and as I began to scream wordlessly in a hosanna of glorious despair, I had no idea to whom this thought was addressed.

FIFTEEN

Lanny (who had risen early the previous morning to appear on the *Today* show) was again up early, I deduced as I awoke and found myself alone in bed. He'd clearly been thoughtful enough not to wake me, and I was grateful for the extra sleep. We'd followed our first rage of lovemaking with talking—almost shyly and not about much, especially where I was concerned. I tried to keep my limited comments philosophical and nonbiographical. We both happily and idly explored each other's bodies as we conversed. Eventually, he decided to devote his focused attention upon one fixed orb in the constellation of my already so totally exploited body. It began almost casually, but it continued, in a reassuringly mindless, steady way. I had been hypersensitive there only thirty minutes earlier, but now I was not and could allow him to do what he insisted he needed to do. It became difficult to tell which was his clever tongue and which were his fingers. The sensations were as if several very different types of men were simultaneously having their complete way with me, trading off tasks, comparing notes, pooling information about my responses, all totally dedicated to creating this dangerous, deep-seated rising within me.

I will tell you, because this is part of my job, that my second orgasm with Lanny was almost certainly the longest I'd ever known, even at my own hand. It would not peak, not for the most harrowing time. I actually thought I might lose consciousness, from lack of air and heartbeat. Surely it was over now. No? No. Still more to take. Slow breaths now. Take more of it now. "Stop," I beseeched.

"No" was Lanny's witty riposte.

"I'll die," I confessed.

"Not yet," he managed to reply. It was so cruel of him. I had only given him whatever he wanted and here he was, causing me to die, and still I was not yet dead.

"Now you can die," Lanny murmured.

My cries became so loud, truly as if I were being murdered, that Lanny had no choice but to clamp his hand over my mouth. I understood, even as he half-suffocated me. I, too, was afraid security guards might at any second break into the room.

Later I returned the favor. I can't review my own work, but I had him so demonstrably hard and on the edge for such a time that I have to assume it was good. I was first a veritable hummingbird, then warm quicksand, and finally a belly dancer creating ornate spirals upon him with my hips. To my surprise, I found myself peaking yet again, even as he hoarsely cried out his own wordless epitaph beneath me.

After several long minutes of silence, we walked together to the bathroom and ran the cold-water tap in the sink at the Plaza Hotel, leaning down to drink at it like it was the high school water fountain, until we'd slaked our near-rabid thirst. Then we walked back to the bed together, intertwined ourselves comfortably, and instantly fell into sleep.

When I woke, I looked at the G.E. clock radio provided by the Plaza, but it had apparently become unplugged at 2:26 A.M., most likely due to our thrashing about. I had a watch, but I'd left it in the bathroom along with all my clothes, and I just wasn't ready to get up. In two consecutive Manhattan mornings, I'd awakened in two strange beds, and jet lag always hits me hardest on the second day. Considering the state I'd been in when I went to bed (there was a soreness within me whose cause I savored for a moment), I decided I still needed to sleep a good hour or two longer. I reached around for my new darling, but he wasn't there. I considered getting up to find him, but thought I might shift the pillow a bit first. Perhaps he was in the bathroom or more likely making incredible breakfast plans—renting a Circle Line boat and having it catered by the Regency or

Ratner's . . . or maybe we'd have eggs Benedict here in bed. I pictured black olives dotting pastel-yellow hollandaise and livid-yellow yolks sacrificed on an altar of crimson bacon and charred muffin. I burrowed into the pillows.

I was slowly awakened again by the annoying drone of a vacuum cleaner outside our bedroom door, in the suite's living room. That Reuben was one fastidious fellow, I'll tell you.

I didn't love the idea of greeting Reuben, who would justifiably regard me simply as the girl Lanny had picked up on the plane. Which, of course, I was. But it bothered me that I'd be perceived as a starstruck groupie. I was a published and trendy writer, I'd interviewed people just as famous as Lanny Morris, and I'd already chummed up to Vince Collins. I possessed documents from major publishing companies confirming my professional status.

Reuben's vacuum cleaner banged against the bedroom door. I assumed he was doing that intentionally to get me out of bed. I looked for the robe I'd shed, but it wasn't there. My purse and clothing had been moved from the bathroom and laid out for me neatly in a row on the dresser. I could not imagine Lanny doing this; it bore all the signs of the fussy Reuben. I didn't like that he had done this while I was asleep. Was it really necessary for the room to be straight before I awoke?

I scooped up my clothes from the dresser and stumbled into the bathroom, where I dressed and did my best to make my hair and face look acceptable. Then I walked out through the bedroom door to the living room.

But it wasn't Reuben who was vacuuming.

It was a maid in a blue-and-white Plaza Hotel uniform. She looked at me as if I were one of the toilets along her route. "Checkout today?" she said with a South American accent. I asked her, first in English, then in dreadful Spanish, if she could come back in half an hour. She looked annoyed, indicated her own wristwatch, and departed.

The room was bare of everything except that which the Plaza had provided. Already knowing the answer, I searched the suite for Lanny, for Reuben, for some note Lanny might have left me. Nothing. The second bedroom in the suite had clearly never been slept in. My guess was that Lanny had used it merely as a clothes closet.

I went to the bedroom's phone, hit nine, got a dial tone, and dialed the number of the Plaza Hotel displayed on the phone itself, as if from the outside world. I asked the operator for Mr. Merwin. I was told (after a moment) that he had checked out.

What do you know? The dork had ditched me.

Technically speaking, I was now staying at the Plaza illegally. And I certainly felt very much like a squatter. Or diddly-squat. What was that Italian movie? *Seduced and Abandoned.* When any of my past couplings had ended with one of us leaving in the morning before the other awoke, it had invariably been me, and I'd at least left a note on my pillow, the bathroom mirror, or the refrigerator.

Bastard.

My initial impulse was to order a couple of bottles of Dom Pérignon from room service to run up Lanny's tab, but I was already feeling far too much like a cheap slut who'd spread my legs in return for a ride in a limo, a burger, and a couple of drinks.

I had the sudden need to shower. The Plaza bathroom's plumbing was ancient, with separate faucets for hot and cold welded into the tub, perhaps by rust. I turned on the higher-placed knob for the shower, waited a minute, and discovered that hot water was apparently hard for the management to come by. Perhaps some other hotel guest was taking a shower at this particular moment. Just as well, I thought, remembering the fate of previous women who'd occupied the tubs of hotel rooms reserved for Lanny Morris. Besides, once cleansed, I wouldn't much feel like changing back into the bra and panties that I'd dirtied in my mind by the very act of removing them for his amusement.

I left the suite almost as hastily as had Lanny. The elevator was manned by Mutty Mickey, who'd given me a leering lift just yesterday. I saw the slightest tug of a smile on the far side of his mouth as he noted that my outfit was the same as the day before.

"Shut up," I said.

In the lobby I went to the front desk and asked if either Mr. Merwin or Mr. Lanny Morris had left any message for a Ms. Bonnie Trout. The desk clerk instantly replied without consulting anything or anyone, "No, may we get you a taxicab?" His way of telling me to beat it.

I hit the Fifty-ninth Street exit. The wind was blowing south, wafting the smell of horseshit in my face all the way over from the hansoms and carriages on the opposite side of the street. I turned my back on the Plaza and the Autopub and started trudging west.

Why *had* I slept with Lanny? I couldn't blame it solely on the two oversized martinis I'd downed, which was nowhere near my limit. And certainly I'd already interviewed enough celebrities to make it unlikely I'd been starstruck.

I entertained the possibility that subconsciously I'd slept with him as a delayed response to Vince's overtures, that with Lanny I was simply completing the pass that Vince had thrown me. I couldn't copulate with Vince, because we had lots of work to do first, but I could sleep with Lanny, because he wasn't going to be part of the deal.

I liked this explanation a lot and decided to embrace it until further notice.

Meanwhile: that bastard.

He'd made me look worse than a slut. He'd made me look foolish. If only he'd acted like the repugnant Lanny Morris from the memoirs I'd read, I'd never have gotten into this situation. At the very least, I would have expected absolutely nothing more from him than the distinction of being Boff No. 331 and a leading contender for this year's title of Miss Receptacle. I surely would have been more measured and calculated in the bestowing of my apertures and embouchures.

Ah well. In life, what's important is to learn from your mistakes, to identify why others might have led you into making them, and to kill them. I am a person who, if someone steps on my foot, reflexively says, "I'm sorry!" Beware such people, my friends. We are, as Dickens once said, "secret and revengeful."

I'd suddenly found an additional driving purpose for my book with Vince. It could be not only a fascinating study of *the* comedy team of the fifties, but also a fine opportunity to tarnish Lanny's reputation, especially if it could be done with impeccable accuracy, detail, and documentation. (*See also* "hatchet job.")

For the first time since I'd begun this project, I knew how to handle the dilemma of balancing Vince's story (which I would be hearing directly from him with my own two ears) against Lanny's story (which I hadn't expected to hear at all).

The way I would handle balancing their sides of the story would be that I wouldn't.

I reached Columbus Circle invigorated. This would be the finest payback I could manage. Whatever dirt I might find would have to be the truth, of course. But I would seek out "the truth" and, like the tabloids, accept only the data that confirmed my working hypothesis. Like a graph chart at an annual stockholders' meeting, the truth can be most anything you need it to be.

I was at the stairs to the subway, where you could take the IRT or IND trains in any number of directions. I advised myself, "You should take the A train to get to Sugar Hill at 145th in Harlem, and after that to 175th." There were two grand destinations at that last stop. One was the Tabernacle of Reverend Ike, which prior to being a tabernacle had been one of the great Loew's movie dream palaces. The other was the Port Authority George Washington Bridge Bus Station.

I walked the dank concrete corridor from the subway steeply up to the station itself, which was definitely the poor sister to the huge bus terminal near Times Square. I knew that almost any bus leaving Manhattan via the George Washington Bridge stopped at the Bridge Plaza in Fort Lee, New Jersey, the way every northbound train out of Grand Central stops at 125th Street. I had a quick cup of coffee at the coffee shop (and was reminded that the coffee at most coffee shops isn't very good) and took an escalator up to the outdoor shed, where all buses were launched directly onto the bridge.

A few minutes later, I climbed thirty concrete steps from the Bridge Plaza up to Lemoine Avenue in Fort Lee, where there was a line of about forty custard-yellow Checker cabs standing idle in the early-afternoon sun, each with a big white baseball painted on its side bearing the name Babe's Taxi. The first man on the stand, a burly muttonchopped fellow, waved me into the roomy backseat.

"Where to?"

"Palisades Park."

He looked back at me. "The town or the amusement park? Some people get off the bus and want to go to the amusement park, but they closed it down a couple of years ago."

"Shame."

"Damn shame." He scowled, turning the ignition. The Checker's engine sounded like a tractor. "No reason on earth it had to close. Just people got greedy."

"Can you take me to the police station there?" I asked.

"Sure, but complaining to them about it won't do much good now," he counseled, pulling away from the taxi stand.

I always think of police stations as having two big globe lights outside and a cigar-smoking sergeant at an elevated admitting desk. This one could have been the local library, except that if your book was overdue, they'd put you in a cell.

I asked the uniformed officer behind the desk if there was anyone still working there who might have been involved in the investigation of Maureen O'Flaherty's death. I showed him the letter that permanently resided in my pocketbook, written by Connie Wechsler on Neuman and Newberry's letterhead, confirming that I was researching a book commissioned by them about Lanny Morris and Vince Collins. If I'd been a male newspaper reporter, he'd probably have shrugged me off, but as I was a personable young woman writing a *book,* of all things—"Good for you, sweetheart," he said and I half-expected a pat on the head—he was willing to help this little girl as best he could. After some consultation with his peers, he said that the only person anyone could think of who was still around the area was Jack Scaglia (he pronounced the *g*), who'd been one of the two patrolmen who'd first seen Maureen's body. He'd taken an early retirement and now headed corporate security for Lipton in Englewood Cliffs, just a few miles up Lemoine Avenue. The officer gave me the general number for Lipton's corporate offices and I was able to get Jack Scaglia on the line. I didn't pronounce the *g* in his name, and that, coupled with my celebrated ability to impersonate the vocal timbre of Ann-Margret over the phone, was enough to gain me an immediate audience.

Scaglia had been in his mid-thirties when he'd escorted Lanny and Vince to their press conference for the Casino del Mar and then on to their hotel suite. He had a pleasant office now, with a plastic cube on his desk containing photos of his wife and two daughters, and a small plastic Oscar award inscribed BEST DAD IN THE WORLD.

I explained that I had no official standing, saying simply that if he were to provide me with information I would give him credit for his contribution within my book. He asked if I could make clear that his name was pronounced without the *g,* and I said that if I were to quote him in my book, I would do that. Thus assured, he offered, "Sally Santoro and his people—" He stopped and asked me, "Can this part be off the record?"

I nodded solemnly and assured him that I always retained total discretion in the event of such a request, which he foolishly took to mean yes.

Reassured, he explained, "Sally had a pretty tight relationship with the state police—he still does—so when somebody said Sally needed some cops to work security for him, we were always glad to help. As long as he wasn't committing an actual felony, we tried to keep a respectful, cooperative relationship with Sally's people. They were very supportive of the police, except of course where crime was concerned. But they brought a tremendous amount of income into the area, as you can imagine."

I could. It turned out it was Jack who'd found the cleaning lady (who was the first to discover the body) and then Maureen O'Flaherty herself.

"I'd never seen such a beautiful dead woman before," he confided as I passed on his offer of a drink and watched him pour a Four Roses for himself in his office at three in the afternoon. "The water came just a little above her nose." He held out his thumb and index finger to indicate. "That much. Imagine that much water being the difference between life and death."

I asked him if the coroner had actually determined the cause of death. I knew most of this already from newspaper files, but I hoped maybe he'd have something new to say on the subject, especially if it might make Lanny look bad. He smiled patiently as he added some water to the Four Roses from a small pitcher on his desk. "You try lying underwater in a bathtub for a couple of hours without a snorkel. What do you think you'd die from?"

"So she drowned?"

"Of course she drowned."

"Why?" I asked.

He looked at his watch. "Look, I thought— What do you mean, 'Why?'"

I indicated a pack of Benson & Hedges cigarettes on his desk. "May I?" I asked. He looked annoyed but nodded his assent. I took my time extracting one from the pack. "I mean, you and I take baths all the time. We don't drown in them."

He reached into his desk drawer and retrieved a book of matches from somewhere called the Bicycle Club and lit me. "There was some talk that she'd mixed sleeping pills and booze—not that she was a suicide, you understand. Just passed out."

"No signs of violence?"

Funny. I felt like I knew more about this than he did, and he'd been there. He sat down in the chair next to mine and pulled at his lower lip. "Are we still off the record?"

People hear what they want to hear. I said, "Jack, no one is going to hear anything unless it's with my say-so, and I guess you can imagine how I would feel about that. Do you even see me writing anything down? I'm looking for context here." I said it fast and smooth and none of it was technically a lie.

Jack lit one of his hundred-millimeter-length cigarettes. "Okay. Well, look. The Casino del Mar was a huge deal for Sally Santoro, for everyone. It was a chance to turn the town into what Atlantic City thinks it's going to be. Only we were close to Manhattan, so it could have been even bigger. It got launched with this tremendous publicity push from Vince and Lanny . . . and this dumb girl shows up dead. Nothing was going to resurrect her. It was in everyone's interest"—he lowered his voice a little—"especially Sally's interest, for this not to get blown way out of proportion. So the whole investigation was sped along, and she was cremated here, and that was that."

I nodded. "I think I asked you if there were any signs of violence on her body."

"The coroner said—"

"Jack, I'm asking you. You saw her body long before the coroner did. I'm just asking you what you saw, for gosh sakes."

So he told me. Her body was blue. There were scratches on her torso, but they were a little unusual looking, because they weren't really cuts but more like welts. The medical examiner hadn't thought much of the marks, but Scaglia also conveyed in as many words that there weren't a lot of great medical examiners outside of the big cities back then. In those days, a forensic specialist was generally assumed to be an alcoholic doctor with a strong conscience who'd opted to perform surgery only on people he couldn't possibly kill.

The medical examiner had ventured that the marks might have come from some activity prior to Maureen's death, perhaps something sexual. Scaglia told me that any time something couldn't be explained, the coroner's office tended to imply that there was a range of perverse sexual activity indulged in by the kinds of shameless people who allowed themselves to be discovered dead.

Looking for any wiggle room in Lanny's alibi, I asked Scaglia what the consensus had been regarding the time of death. He said the coroner had based his finding on the onset of rigor mortis, the stiffening contraction of muscles after death. Where present, rigor mortis tends to start setting in about six to nine hours after the fact, or at least that was the rule of thumb back in the late fifties. However, in the case of Maureen O'Flaherty, the estimated time of death was placed as being considerably more recent than six hours, owing to the fact that the victim had died while taking a bath. The warmer the temperature, the sooner the stiffening kicks in. In a hot or even warm bath, her body would have responded as if she were living (or rather, dying) in a tropical climate, where rigor mortis often occurs almost instantly. When her body was found by Scaglia and examined by the coroner, the stiffening effect had just started. The coroner placed the time of death as being two to three hours, at the very most, before she was discovered.

The numbers provided by the coroner completely exonerated both of the boys. Even at the most outside time of twelve hours for the onset of rigor mortis, Vince and Lanny still had the best alibi available in the twentieth century: they'd been on camera, live, in front of millions of witnesses. Their "nap" breaks had been in their dressing rooms, which in the Miami studios had no windows; there was a guard posted outside their doors to ensure that no one accidentally or intentionally interrupted their sleep. Most important, the naps never went longer than a few hours, and the fastest private airplane could not get from Florida to New Jersey and back in that amount of time, even discounting traveling to and from the airports and, of course, the few additional minutes required to commit a murder.

The coroner had tested for the presence of semen—Scaglia had a little trouble telling me this part and even blushed a bit—and the response was a clinical positive, but he could find no actual presence of ejaculate (as Scaglia chose to put it). So the indication was that, yes, the victim had had sex sometime in the week before she died but with the limited science of the late fifties, that was all that could be deduced.

"Then from when you and your partner first arrived at the Casino, there was no time when Lanny or Vince wasn't in full view of more than one other person?" I asked, knowing the answer. Scaglia said it was impossible for them to have slipped away, that not only had he and his partner, a man named Ted Dolinger, been at their side right up until Maureen's body was found, but that the press had been watching them too, in large numbers. They'd even done a live television interview.

So my trip to Palisades Park had only affirmed what the gossip columnists had reluctantly been forced to concede at the time: that Vince and Lanny couldn't be pinned to the girl's death, despite the fact that she was found in their hotel suite and (as later came out) was acquainted with them. What she was doing in their hotel (and in their bathtub, for that matter), how she had gotten there from Miami, and whether her death was by accident or foul play were unsolved mysteries and likely to remain so as the years went by. Through a supposed clerical error, Maureen's body had been converted into ashes shortly after a lackadaisical autopsy had left a ton of unturned stones lying about in a heap. Her cremation's inferno ensured that the scent would grow cold for any future investigations.

Once it was clear that our boys could not be directly connected to Maureen's death, the powerful columnists of the time handled the story a variety of ways. Kilgallen's was the cleverest: she immediately became their champion, countering all the wicked rumors and falsehoods that were circulating, thereby doing a splendid job of circulating all the wicked rumors and falsehoods. Winchell (who was slipping in popularity) saw the Mafia's black hand in the girl's death, and certainly Lanny and Vince had some gaudy mob ties that they weren't shy of wearing in public. In a similar vein, Jack O'Brien speculated that the late Miss O'Flaherty had caught the eye of Sally Santoro in Florida and when the mob boss had learned that she had the hots for one of the duo, he'd had her laid out dead as a big wet surprise for our two lads. From his viper's den in Miami, Moe Cohn was a spoilsport about the boys' alibi; apparently, if he couldn't say anything bad about Vince or Lanny, he opted to say nothing at all. He never mentioned them in his column again but instead heaped lavish, bland praise on their competition. It didn't make for interesting reading, and by the end of the year, his column had been dropped, the *Miami Sentinel* opting for shorter, racier items with lurid pictures to go with them.

But although Maureen's death couldn't be pinned on Vince and Lanny, the yellow press had not hesitated to wonder aloud what she'd been doing in their intended suite. Perhaps she'd been taking a bath with the plan of slipping herself between the cool sheets to lie in wait (and wait in heat) for one of our two boys to tuck himself into her. If so, was this meant to be a surprise for one or both of the boys (perhaps coordinated by a grateful Sally Santoro) . . . or was Maureen there at Lanny's or Vince's request? There had been nothing in Lanny's memoir to indicate that either man was genuinely smitten with Ms. O'Flaherty. Why would she be recruited all the way from Miami when there were undoubtedly a score of superbly skilled courtesans in the New York area?

Scaglia relayed most of what little new information he had to offer at the Bicycle Club, an upscale singles bar near the entrance to the Palisades Parkway. He'd said he could talk more freely there. Certainly he had to talk more loudly. Although he was a family man, I noticed that our waitress knew Scaglia by his first name and relayed an urgent message to him from someone named Cheryl, who was wondering why she hadn't heard from him.

I asked him, with a look of passionate interest that I assumed he would overinterpret: "But is there anything else you can remember, Jack, something you alone might have noticed or heard at the time that might have been overlooked by others?"

He peered around furtively at the happy-hour crowd, then returned his eyes to me. "Listen, as it happens there *is* something else. But this wouldn't be the place to talk about it. We'd have to . . . go somewhere private."

Where would that be? I asked. He suggested a motel about four minutes away. *Quelle surprise!* So we got in his orange Datsun station wagon and drove down to the Cresskill Inn, nice as flophouses go but a bit tawdry for a Norman Rockwell type of village. He made the check-in arrangements with the manager, who, from my vantage point parked outside his office, seemed to know Jack almost as well as did the waitress at the Bicycle Club.

The motel room had all the amenities: a bed. There was also a chair by the combination desk and dresser. I sat on the amenable bed as Jack looked around the room, elated over its ice bucket. He suggested that he get some ice from the machine outside. He had a bottle of Four Roses in the glove compartment of his car—

"Jack," I smiled. "We're here so we can speak more privately. So let's get business out of the way first and then . . . well, the night is young." Actually it was a little after five P.M. and the sun was still shining brightly, so the night was barely embryonic.

Scaglia exhaled with a sigh. "You can't say where you heard this," he cautioned.

I laughed. "Would I be likely to put in my book that I checked into the Cresskill Inn with you?"

He frowned. "I mean that you heard it from me."

"Oh, I would just say the information came from a reliable source."

Jack Scaglia looked relieved. A Reliable Source took another drag of his Benson & Hedges cigarette and began: "The police like to withhold some information about a crime scene from the media and the public. It helps them sort out who might know something and who's lying. So there *was* something strange about the girl's body that was never mentioned in the press."

"You mean the marks on her torso and legs?"

He shook his head. "No. This was something a little more unusual. I'm not sure if anyone noticed right away. Two of her toes were cut off."

Okay.

"Two toes on one foot or one on each?" I asked.

"Two on one foot. Pinkie toe and the one next to it. Like they were cut at the same time, maybe with the same blade."

"Was there blood in the tub water?"

"The water wasn't bloody or anything, no. There was a little 'stuff' in the water . . . bodies can, um, leak a bit after death."

"Was the cut clean?"

"Well, I heard it was. The coroner pointed it out to some of the detectives involved in the investigation. I didn't notice her toes when I found the body. I mean, what I was looking at was not her toes."

I'd heard of the Mafia cutting off someone's fingers, professional cardsharps or dealers who were caught manipulating cards. Never toes.

People with diabetes might have to have a toe cut off if they developed oozing gangrene, but Maureen hadn't been diabetic. If she had been, there would have been speculation that she'd suffered from insulin shock or gone into a diabetic coma.

One of Cinderella's stepsisters cut off her toes to try to fit into the glass slipper (not in the Disney version, of course). Men used to shoot off their toes to stay out of the army. There were jokes I might have made, but we were talking about a dead young woman who, as far as I might tell from Mr. Morris's memoirs, had done nothing worse than sleep with Lanny very shortly after meeting him. Anyone might have done that.

"Did they think she lost her toes before she died?"

"Actually, they thought it might have happened after. There being so little clotted blood where they were cut off."

And that was the full extent of his secret. It made absolutely no sense to me, nor to him. I couldn't see how it would help me taint Lanny's reputation.

"Now how about that drink?" he asked.

I nodded agreeably. "You get the Four Roses from your car and I'll get the ice," I said, snagging the square ice bucket from the desktop. "And maybe I'll ask the manager if there's a pizza place that delivers. We might get hungry, sooner or later."

Oh, he liked me talking this way. One edge that women have over men in the game-playing department is that men are unfailingly prepared to believe they're desirable to any woman who hints that they are. Out of kindness, Christie Brinkley might say to a seventy-year-old deliveryman named Murray with hair growing out of his ears and a mole on his right cheek, "You're so cute!" Murray would have no problem with that concept. "I guess I *am* pretty damn cute at that," he admits. "Maybe Christie and I will go out sometime." Here's married Jack Scaglia and he really thinks I'm opting for a water glass full of rye, some slices of pizza, and a quick suck-and-fuck at the Cresskill Inn. And off he goes to his car, totally confident that this will happen.

By the ice machine, I picked up a yellow Babe's Taxi courtesy phone mounted on the wall and asked for their flat rate to the East Thirties of Manhattan. Twenty-six dollars had me covered nicely. The cab pulled up two minutes later at the Rite-Way Dry Cleaners across the street from the motel, as I'd requested. The cab ride only took about forty minutes. Happily, I was going opposite the rush-hour traffic departing Manhattan for New Jersey.

Back in Beejay's apartment, I finally took off the outfit that I had previously removed in Lanny's bathroom at the Plaza while donning his silk robe. At the time, I had hoped he'd check out my body and find it desirable. Yes, he'd found it desirable to check out.

I looked at my naked self in the mirror as I called Beejay's answering service, on the off chance that Lanny had left some explanation for his departure that might make everything lovely again. After all, he had called me here yesterday morning, so I knew he did have the number.

There were no messages for Ms. Trout.

I turned on the water in the shower. It was very hot, much hotter and stronger than the inexcusably tepid dribble at the Plaza. I let the water assail me. I stood closer and closer to the showerhead, and adjusted it so that instead of a steady downpour, it beat against me like the blades of a helicopter or a well-deserved caning from the headmistress. Eventually, I switched the showerhead back from massage to fine spray. This allowed me to make the water hotter still, and huge billows of steam filled the bathroom. I was having trouble with the lathering-and-cleaning-myself part, though. It's not that Beejay didn't have many, many bars of soap in her apartment. It's just that there simply weren't enough in the world.

SIXTEEN

It was a lovely house. Really just such a lovely, gracious house. Someone went to great trouble with it, each day. Troubled over the flower beds along the walk. Troubled with trimming back the privet hedges. It was the kind of house where someone came out each morning with a broom and swept away the dust on the porch, then repeated the same task at midday. It was certainly not an upper-class home, but it had more intrinsic class than many a millionaire's mullion-windowed mausoleum.

I rang the doorbell by turning a little metal wheel in the door.

The door opened and the lovely smell of sweet flowers and flowering vines from the front yard was met by the aroma of well-oiled wood and cherry potpourri from within. It was like stepping from a wild garden into a warm plum pudding.

The woman who opened the door looked kindly but fearful, as if she wondered what bad news I might be bringing and if there was any way to stop me from delivering it.

"Yes?" She'd realized she'd forgotten to smile and did so. "Hello."

"Mrs. O'Flaherty?"

"Yes."

"My name's O'Connor, I'm the one writing a book . . ."

She nodded and told me to come in. It had been a relatively easy trip, taking the commuter train to New Rochelle (the local service took exactly forty-five minutes, as guaranteed in the song written by Mrs. O'Flaherty's uncle) and then a Bluebird Taxi to her door.

She offered me tea or coffee. It was quite warm out, and I opted for tea, thinking it would be iced. She brought me a hot cup of Constant Comment. Still, the house was tolerably cool, despite the absence of air-conditioning. I commented on this.

"High ceilings, stone floor, plenty of cross-ventilation," explained the mother of Maureen O'Flaherty. "Of course in the winter I have the devil to pay. But I just wear more layers. Cardigans. You can always put more on, my father used to say, but there's a limit to how much you can take off before the police step in." She started to laugh, but the mention of the police put a sad little appoggiatura on her melodic line, and she looked away. "So you're doing a book about those men?" she asked. She put no undue emphasis on "those men," but it was clear from her face that she regretted having to say such unclean words.

"About Vince Collins, first and foremost," I said, giving her my most updated answer. "I'll be asking him a lot of questions, and I wanted to know if there were some you'd like to have answered yourself."

It was as good (and as honest) a way as I'd been able to find to talk with her about her daughter. I thought I'd taken a decent tack on the matter.

She peered into me. "Not to seem rude, Miss O'Connor, but why is it that you are the one who will get to ask these questions?"

I'd explained to her on the phone, but I guess it hadn't properly registered. "This won't be a legal proceeding, Mrs. O'Flaherty. It's not what they call a 'deposition.'"

She looked a bit peeved. "I know what a deposition is. I mean, why does your publisher think you're the one who should do this?"

"Actually, the book was my idea. I pushed for it."

"And do you have some personal involvement? Did you know either of these men before you proposed writing this book?"

I hoped answering the second question would seem to be answering both. "I never knew either of them before my publisher gave me the green light. And as to why *me* . . . my publisher knows I don't ask soft questions of celebrities. The deal that I've negotiated with Vince Collins . . . Well, I've made it clear to him that I will be asking some very direct questions, and if I do my job right, I might even get some direct answers. I thought, on behalf of you and your daughter, I might be able to slip in a few questions that you might have for him." I leaned forward. "I'm trying to be a friend here, Mrs. O'Flaherty."

She stood and asked if I'd come outside with her for a moment. I followed her through a kitchen in which everything knew its place and out into an equally well-organized yard. There were four or five trees, perhaps a few too many for the small square lawn, but they all seemed to coexist just fine. A warm afternoon breeze stirred their overlapping layers of leaves, rustling them like crinoline.

She walked me over to a good-sized tree dotted with little, yellowish peaches. Apparently not a one had fallen to the ground. She patted its trunk lovingly. "Maureen and I planted this on her fifth birthday. Her father did most of the digging. She'd be thirty-eight. I'm sixty-three myself. If she were alive now, we'd be able to talk about things back and forth like two women, like you and I are doing, except that she'd be older than you, of course. After Maureen, they told me I couldn't have any other children, but one can be more than enough, believe me. Especially if you get to keep her."

She led me back into the house and up a narrow staircase that cowered against a dark wall papered in a brown flowered pattern. At the top of the stairs, off a landing, was a bathroom, flanked on either side by two bedrooms of equal size that ran the width of the house. "That was my daughter's room," she said, nodding to my left. I moved toward the doorway but she shook her head. "Her things have all been packed away. It's the guest room now, but it must be, oh gosh, six years since I had a guest and then it was just for Frank's funeral."

I asked how her husband had died. She gave a diminutive smile. "Very thoughtfully, I must say. He told me to go visit my cousin in Chicago. She's single, in her late nineties now, and besides perpetuating our celebrated family name, I have no idea what keeps her going. While I was gone, Frank drove around and around the county until the gas tank on our old DeSoto was at three-quarters empty. Then he drove it into the garage, shut the door, and left the motor running. He had the radio tuned to the classical station, QXR, playing so loudly that it covered the sound of the car motor. Then he unfolded one of the canvas lawn chairs we used to take on picnics and made himself comfortable right near the tailpipe. By the time the car ran out of gas, he was dead. This was on a Sunday. He'd arranged for Con Edison to come on Monday to check our gas meter—which he'd told them was broken—and when they opened the garage door, they discovered his body, with a bottle of John Jameson in his lap. He didn't want any of our neighbors to be the ones to find him. He was very thoughtful in how he did it. Much like he'd been before Maureen passed away."

I conveyed my sympathy, but she shook her head. "Oh, it's all right. After she died, he went a bit 'off' in his head. It got so that I really didn't know him any longer. He slept in her room a great deal, on top of the covers. In the middle of my own grief, I discovered there was this strange man living here, roaming about the house, falling, accidentally breaking things. I felt like I'd taken in a boarder. A boarder who was allowed to let himself into my bedroom."

Her bedroom smelled clean, perhaps of wood soap. Austere, without making a show of its bareness; it could have been the room of a nun.

She walked me over to a windowed door that opened out onto a little perch that was too small to call a terrace and not romantic enough to be a balcony. It was intimately shaded by the limbs of the peach tree she'd shown me moments before. "Higher than the house now, and yet I planted it with her," she smiled. She reached out and easily stole one of the yellow peaches from an encroaching bough; it made a lovely popping sound as she wrested it away from its mother branch.

"Frank, at the worst of his depression, if we're going to call it that, did a rather awful thing one night while I was asleep. He dug up the earth around the peach tree, without harming the tree of course. Then he took the urn that had Maureen's ashes in it, which we kept downstairs, and spread the ashes around its roots. Then he put the earth back where he'd overturned it, and watered the ground lightly with our rotary sprinkler, moving it about the tree over the course of the next two days."

She walked over to a bureau where there was a score of framed photographs of Maureen: baby picture, kindergarten, ballet recital, junior high cheerleader, serious and waxen-faced high school graduate. Laid flat on the table were report cards, prize ribbons for best essay, student leader, a letter of acceptance from Hunter College, a postcard Maureen had sent her parents from Florida with an amusing return address that I noted, a photograph of her in room-service uniform in front of the Versailles

Hotel . . . this was Mary O'Flaherty's miniature shrine for her daughter. She shrugged and looked back out at the tree. "Frank got the idea that Maureen's ashes were now a part of that tree, and the tree bore fruit . . . when he was really drunk, he'd eat one peach after another, hoping that somehow, if he ate enough of them, Maureen would be inside him, inside his mind, and that she would then be alive through him. That's when I knew it would be all right if he wanted to take his own life."

She set the peach down on the bureau by Maureen's photos. "So . . . that's my daughter," she said, indicating the yellow fruit. It was as if she were introducing me. "That's what I have of her, Miss O'Connor."

I nodded.

"Are you Catholic?" she asked.

"I was christened and confirmed in the Catholic faith," I put forward.

"Then perhaps you will understand my dilemma. I would like to see my daughter again. You can imagine a mother wanting to see her daughter again?"

I said I could.

"Well, then I am going to have to hope for an afterlife, aren't I? Luckily, my faith offers one. But suicide would condemn me to Hell, as you know. Therefore, I can't kill myself, much as I might have wanted to these fifteen and a half years. A daughter needs her mother. And so I have to live out this life our Father has provided me, as free from sin as I can manage, although of course we all of us sin in one way or another. I'm hoping that when I die, I'll be with my daughter again, although by the tenets of my faith this will mean I will never see my husband again, who has consigned himself to Hell, may God have bountiful mercy on him."

She had led me back down the narrow stairs, carrying the peach with her. Her demeanor was in no way bizarre. She was just explaining things, laying out for me what she had to do within the constraints of certain logical and ethical assumptions. She went again through the kitchen and out into the yard.

Just outside the back door, a garden spade rested in an empty flower pot, alongside a pair of gardening gloves. She put on the gloves and moved to the foot of the peach tree, all the while continuing, conversationally:

"My added dilemma is that some people think my daughter may have committed suicide. I don't for a moment believe this, but what if they're right? Then she is in Hell, with my husband, and the life I'm trying to lead may lead me to Heaven's grace, where I'll hear their screams of torment but be unable to help them. Surely that would make a Hell of any Heaven. You understand."

She was kneeling now at the foot of the peach tree and digging a small hole with the spade. She dropped the peach into the hole and smiled up at me. "Once Frank had planted the idea in my head that Maureen was now part of the tree, I couldn't let the fruit rot on the ground, to be pecked at or carried away by the birds, like vultures would do to carrion. So I have to bury every peach that falls. Which helps replenish the tree."

I watched her as she covered over the peach with dirt.

"That must be a tremendous amount of work," I said sympathetically.

"Next month it will take every minute of my day," she said, patting the earth flat. "It keeps me occupied. I'm grateful to God for that."

She got up, put the spade back in the empty flower pot, wiped her hands on a thin towel in the kitchen, and led me to the front door. I thanked her for her valuable time. She nodded slowly.

"My daughter was studying to be an English teacher. She went to Miami Beach for a spring vacation. After that, all we got from her for a few years were postcards and phone calls. When she died, I received a check with a typed letter calling it an 'anonymous gift of bereavement.'"

"May I ask the amount of the check?"

"Fifty thousand dollars." She laughed bitterly. "If it were a hundred times that, what good would it do? I put it in a savings account, and when I die, it will all go to the church."

"Do you remember the account the check was drawn on?"

"It was what they call a bank check. The note itself was typewritten on plain paper. Frank kept it. Later he said he'd thrown it away." She opened the front door, and indicated the path. "So, Miss O'Connor, I can tell you the question I would most like you to ask Mr. Vince Collins, or anyone else who might have the answer to it, for that matter. I hope you'll commit it to memory. It's a question that I hope *you* never have to ask yourself. Why did my daughter die?"

I said I would ask the question and told her where she could contact me if she wanted to. I thanked her for her time and apologized if I'd stirred up any painful feelings. She said I hadn't stirred up a thing.

I walked down the path and for a long time after that. I could have called the Bluebird Taxi company from the O'Flaherty house, but I opted not to. I simply walked downhill on the assumption that towns are rarely uphill of the residential area.

My slow descent eventually brought me onto Huguenot Street, where I saw a sign directing me to the train station. As I walked through New Rochelle's rendition of an urban ghetto, I realized that there is no such thing as the right side of the tracks. Respectable people live nowhere near the tracks.

I didn't ask when the next train was, but merely stood on the Manhattan-bound platform until one pulled in. I may have waited for twenty or thirty minutes. There was an additional charge for purchasing my ticket on the train.

I looked out the window. When Maureen O'Flaherty was born, a great deal of New Rochelle had still been farmland. That had all gone away, but someone here was still working the soil with her own two hands.

SEVENTEEN

We had intentionally timed it so that I wouldn't leave for Los Angeles until after Beejay had returned to New York. Her morning flight was scheduled to arrive in the late afternoon; mine was to leave at nine that night. If there were no delays on her end, we would have dinner together before I took a cab to JFK.

I opened her apartment door and she screamed a loud, shrill howl of delight that would have put a car alarm to shame. "Oh God, it is *so* weird for you to be on that side of the door and me to be on this side!" she laughed. She walked in, her suitcase banging into a small table she ought to have remembered was there, sending a deluxe box of Crayolas flying.

"Beejay, I've needed you." I poured myself into her arms for sympathy, but she was having none of that. She'd already talked through the dearly departed Mr. Morris with me over the phone several times during the course of the past week. She gave me a quick hug and shook me off.

"Yeah yeah, there you were, saving yourself all these years for that special someone and then the Big Movie Star passes through town and he deflowers you." She hoisted her suitcase onto the elevated bed. "I refuse to let you act victimized here. What were you thinking, that you'd be the third Mrs. Morris?"

I sat down in her uncomfortable beanbag chair. "If I'd known I was going to be tossed out with the empty bottles of complimentary shampoo, I would have at least questioned him more about his career, about Vince, and especially about the Girl in New Jersey. But no, I had to get all dewy-breathed and exchange sweet nothings. So totally unprofessional of me."

"Yeah yeah. He was good, huh?"

"Yes."

"How big?"

"I had no complaints."

"Come on, this is me, length and girth, please: two, four, six, eight, who do we appreciate . . . ?"

I gave her the details she craved and a blow-by-blow description of what we did and she was placated for the moment. The fact that the sex had been really good made her slightly more sympathetic to me. Oddly, I'd found myself no less wounded or angry or rejected over the last several days. I hoped that putting New York three thousand miles away from me would put Lanny well behind me. I started packing the last of my clothes.

Beejay tossed a manuscript alongside the pantsuit I was folding. It was the chapter from Lanny's autobiography that had been sent to my apartment under such odd circumstances. I'd decided that some paralegal or trainee from the offices of Weisner, Hillman and Dumont had relayed it to me without a cover letter explaining its why and wherefore. I put the pages into my flight bag. I'd only heard Beejay's synopsized version of the manuscript; my flight home would be a fine chance to read through it carefully.

Beejay lit a cigarette. "When are you going to start interviewing Vince Collins?"

"I'm planning to call him tomorrow and set up something for as early as the next day."

"You going to tell him about you and Lanny?"

I'd been thinking about this all day. "I don't see that I need to, or that I really owe him that information. Our agreement allows me to research his life, interview the people he's worked with—"

Beejay smiled. "'Interview.' Is that what we're going to call what you did with Lanny Morris?"

"No, if it'd been that, I'd have gotten something more useful out of him. But honestly, do I have any moral obligation to tell Vince who I've slept with in the past?"

"Well, it's pretty bogus of you not to let him know, but then again, I suppose it could really screw up your working relationship with Vincenzo." She was using the nickname that absolutely none of Vince's friends ever used.

I'd been so busy calculating my side and Lanny's side of the equation that I'd not thought much about how Vince might react to the revelation. He and Lanny had had a marriage of sorts, or at least their split-up had been like a divorce. *"Excuse me, Elizabeth Taylor, I'd like to write a book in which you reveal to me all your innermost thoughts, fears, and desires—and oh, by the way, may I mention what a fantastic lay your ex-husband Richard Burton is! Yes, we just had sex yesterday. But back to you, Liz, and remember, you can open up to me as much as you want."*

God, I really *had* been stupid, hadn't I? Beejay stubbed out her cigarette hastily. "Can we eat right away? I'm starving."

"You didn't eat on the plane?"

She looked annoyed with me. "I don't get to fly like you do, I'm stuck back in coach. The choice of entrées was 'meat' or 'not meat.' I told the stewardess I was hungry enough to eat a horse and she said I should definitely have the meat entrée. I haven't had a good meal in over a week." I asked why that was and a pained look came over her face. "Honeycake, may I be blunt with you about that painted desert with a sprinkler system you call Los Angeles? Your apartment is lovely, the men are prettier than I am, but what in God's name do you people do for *food* out there? There's nowhere ethnic, it's all Robert Redford Restaurants, the blond leading the bland! Italian cuisine means a pizza burger, Japanese is a teriyaki burger, French means fries. Mexico is less than a hundred and fifty miles away, but despite that, they've come up with this thing called 'Taco Bell,' and when I ate one of their burritos, I found myself saying, 'Gee, Toto, I think we're still in Kansas!'"

I'd only been half-listening while picking up her scattered deluxe Crayolas. "So—where do you want to eat, Beejay?" I asked.

She grabbed my arm. "Spice. Flavor. Nothing with cheese. No ground beef. I want to go to a restaurant where no waiter named Brad asks us if we've ever dined here before and then explains to us how it all 'works.' As a matter of fact, I'd prefer it if our waiter hardly spoke English at all. I want jagged, ballsy New York foreign food."

The obvious answer struck me. "Look, Beejay, I know you're the New Yorker here, but have you ever had Szechuan cuisine?"

Fuck Lanny Morris, I thought (while noting that I'd recently acquired much personal insight into that particular profanity). I considered how nice it would be to reclaim the Szechuan Garden on Doyers Street with Beejay, wrest it from Lanny, and make it our own. And it would be fun to watch Beejay's expression as she tasted these shocking new flavors, like taking a friend to a clever whodunit you've already seen, and watching their reaction as they encounter the surprise twist you now already know.

We headed up a few steps into the restaurant. I wondered if Lee, the manager, would recognize me.

"Oh, I know you!" called out Lee, pointing at me with the index fingers of both hands. "You come here with Mr. Lanny Morris!" he proclaimed so that others in the restaurant would hear him, employing what I now firmly believed was a completely fraudulent accent. He showed me the autographed photo on the wall he had shown me before. "You bring your friend"—he pumped Beejay's hand—"to the hottest restaurant in New York! Ah, you bring champagne, good, we open for you. Where you want to sit, here?"

He made it seem as if it were our choice, but in fact he steered us quite emphatically to a small table against the wall; there really wasn't much else available. In an instant a metal ice bucket was set down on the table and a bottle of cold Mumm's we'd bought near Beejay's apartment was plonked into the sloshing ice and water. Two old-fashioned champagne goblets were set down in front of us. A waiter efficiently opened our bottle and filled them.

Lee was at our side. "You want me to order dishes that Mr. Lanny Morris likes? *He come here often,*" he added loudly for the benefit of any nearby tables.

I very much wanted Beejay to taste the cascading flavors I'd recently experienced, which had gloriously flambéed themselves on my palate. She'd love every mouthful, I knew. But I was also smarting that Lanny had been fanfared by Lee more than I liked. We had walked in on our own, we had brought our own booze, and we would be paying our own check. But Lee was making me feel as if we were Lanny's guests.

Then I realized the one thing I could order that would make me feel as if I'd momentarily trumped the Loathsome Lanny.

"Lee," I said, "we'd love to have the, uh, king-pow chicken and the lamb in tea sauce, but you know what we'd also like to try? That, um, dish that Lanny sent back, lobster in chile sauce with, with . . . ?"

"Lobster! I knew you weren't a Jew!" he said more loudly than he probably intended. The restaurant went silent for just a moment. Apparently the predominantly Asian clientele understood English perfectly. As conversation resumed, Lee asked, "You ladies want to pick your lobster?"

Beejay, feeling her second glass of champagne, nodded. "Yeah yeah, I always like it when I go to a steakhouse and pick which cow will be slaughtered. Even better when I'm having veal piccata." She got up boisterously, I fell in line with her, and we followed Lee.

The lobsters shared their bubbling water tank with a bed of understandably sullen crabs. To Lee's credit, the water in the tank was as clear as a mountain brook. Black rubber bands held the claws of the crustaceans in check, to stop them from attacking one another.

"You see any particular lobster that looks delicious?" asked Lee. I wanted to inform Lee that "delicious" was a hard term to apply to any greenish-blue skeletal creature with antennae.

Beejay apparently didn't have any qualms about selecting which arthropod would go to its doom. "Look at that guy," she smiled. "He's got a lot of fight." Beejay's lobster had broken the rubber band that had been intended to emasculate him. "That's the one I want," she declared and, ever game, started to reach into the tank to pluck him out. "Where do I grab him?"

Lee caught her wrist with surprising abruptness and pulled it away from the tank. "Don't do that! His cutter claw is totally capable of shearing off your finger!" he snapped, simultaneously betraying the sham of his Charlie Chan accent.

Lee had a net that was used to scoop up the doomed one, and we went back to our table, where a waiter was topping off our champagne glasses for us, but from that moment on . . .

. . . the rest of the meal, Beejay's reaction to Szechuan cuisine, the taxi ride back to Beejay's place, dropping her off and getting my bags, the limo I'd booked to JFK, boarding the 747, taking my favorite seat, more champagne, the takeoff, Captain Anderson's reassuring prediction of smooth weather on the way to Los Angeles, the food that I waved away . . .

. . . not one bit of it went into the cerebral cortex where memory is stored. The events around me just sailed into and out of my cute little hippocampus as if it were the revolving door at Macy's on December 23.

Something huge was troubling me, something so immense I couldn't step back far enough to see what it was.

The lights were low in the airplane's cabin. A number of people were watching the in-flight movie (I believe it starred Michael Caine); others were napping. I took Lanny's manuscript from my flight bag and went up the spiral stairs to the first-class lounge.

It was empty. I sat down on the orange-cushioned couch that ran around three sides of the lounge and lit a cigarette. Out the window, a stark white moon held total dominion over a flat sea of cloud caps. Myself and the moon. Everything else was below us.

I began reading Lanny's manuscript.

> Let me explain to you here why two guys doing as good as we were doing at this point would find ourselves working in the state of New Jersey.

I was amused again by their gangster friend Sally Santoro. There really were such people. I'd met more than one, and it was always easy, or perhaps I should say convenient, to forget that one of the things such people did in the course of their workday was to arrange for other people to be killed.

And like so many of these gangsters, they tended—

Oh God.

The plane stopped. Or at least that's what it felt like. The plane stopped, my heart stopped, the moon stopped.

In truth, nothing had stopped, outside of my brain. But a door barricading a terrible darkness was creaking open in my mind, and the acrid black fog behind that door was rolling toward me and into my thoughts as if it carried a plague.

Because of what I'd read. The huge troubling thing was still too big for my limited field of vision to see, but now I was getting glimpses from other angles, and it was beginning to take form. I reread the part where Sally was trying to bribe the boys with gifts.

> ". . . and I'll have them send you up here your own shipment of lobsters and stone crabs from the Versailles. You like lobster?"
>
> We said we did, because we really did.
>
> "And a case of these grapefruits I get special down there, you never tasted—"

Lanny was saying that they liked lobster.

Maybe he was just saying it to humor Sally. I flipped the pages, searching for— There it was. When the boys were at the Versailles in Miami, the night before the telethon.

> We got back up to the suite around seven and found that Sally had been more than good to his word. Laid out around the living room were various crates bearing the address of their destination, our suite at the Casino del Mar Hotel in Palisades Park, New Jersey. What I thought was a box of beach balls turned out to hold the thinnest-skinned, most dripping-wet grapefruits I ever tasted in my life. Likewise the promised six-foot metal locker filled with fruits of the sea, over a dozen lobsters shifting slowly across a bed of stone crabs and ice.

I read on.

> . . . having presented them to us for our approval like a fancy birthday cake, the Versailles was to ship these goodies up to New Jersey the next day, where they'd be waiting for us at the new Casino del Mar on Sunday. . . .

And just a little farther down the page:

> We called down for Maureen, the room-service girl with the gorgeous red hair that you stopped staring at once you got a look at her body, the same Maureen who'd brought me champagne while I was helping out Vince by boffing Denise. Maureen brought us up three steaks (one was for her) as her last

official delivery of the day. Much as I love lobster, all that shellfish nested on ice in the living room had actually put us in the mood for hoofs, not claws . . .

"Much as I love lobster."

It was all there. He had told the truth without meaning to.

He loved lobster, according to his memoirs, or at least he did up to the night before the telethon. The same night (and the last time) he and Vince saw Maureen O'Flaherty alive.

In a hotel-room suite where there had been a coffin-sized metal case filled with lobsters and crabs packed in ice.

But by the time we dined together at Lee's Szechuan Garden, Lanny detested lobster. Roaches, he'd called them. Creatures that (manager Lee had just warned Beejay) could nip a finger right off you. They had done the same to people wading in the water at the beach who'd made the mistake of treading near them. Those people had ended up missing toes.

Maureen O'Flaherty was missing some toes.

But she hadn't been swimming or walking along the beach. The water she'd been in was bathtub water.

Because rigor mortis was in the process of setting in when her body was discovered, the medical examiner knew she couldn't have died much more than six hours earlier. In fact, because her body was lying in hot water, rigor mortis might have started even sooner; she might have died as recently as two hours before she was found.

And then I could see the truth, and the truth was a terrible thing to see.

The only factor that could have changed the time of death would have been if Maureen had taken a bath in ice water. That would have delayed the onset of rigor mortis and some of the other earmarks by which a time of death is established.

But who on this earth would ever take a bath in ice?

A corpse might.

A corpse in a hotel suite in Miami who must be disposed of.

And so the corpse is placed in a six-foot insulated metal trunk filled with ice and lobsters and crabs and delivered to another hotel suite in New Jersey. And en route, one of the lobsters breaks the rubber band that stops its strong right claw from opening and closing and as it falls asleep from the cold, it snaps at whatever it can grab hold of and takes away two of the corpse's toes. And it or another crustacean is also responsible for the weltlike marks on Maureen's torso that brought no blood to the surface because her blood was no longer circulating.

And when the trunk arrives in New Jersey, perhaps one of Sally Santoro's soldiers—for reasons unknown—puts her body in the bathtub and covers her in the ice, which puts a hold on the contraction of Maureen's muscles. The lobsters (those creatures that Lanny Morris will never eat again) are taken away from the room. And slowly the solid ice becomes ice water becomes cold water becomes cool water becomes room-temperature water, and finally rigor mortis begins.

The truth was all there in a dreadful throwaway sentence, referring to the day after the night they'd last seen the girl. "Late the next morning, Maureen was sent packing." Had he known what he was saying? Was it his cold-blooded little joke or simply a monumentally revealing slip in what he'd intended to be a lie?

Vince and Lanny's alibis meant nothing. Every part of me knew that Maureen O'Flaherty had died before the telethon had even started.

She could have been murdered by Lanny. Or Vince. It could have been either one of the boys . . . or, for that matter, the both of them.

EIGHTEEN

I had myself a secret, oh yes I had. And I intended to keep it all to myself, idiot that I am.

Certainly I could have walked my brilliant deduction into a police station, although I had no idea how the generous bequest of an amateur sleuth's inferences would be received. For that matter, to *which* police would I report my precious insight: Miami, Palisades Park, Bel Air? Who had jurisdiction?

What did it matter and whom was I kidding? I wasn't about to tell anyone anything. Without intending to, I'd fathomed my way to exactly the scandalous revelation that Lil Walker had stressed would be so helpful in selling the book. Whatever anyone was going to hear about the secrets I'd unearthed, they were going to hear from the media quoting from (and thereby plugging) my book . . . not from the police. I wasn't about to tell anyone anything.

Of course, it would be infinitely better to know more. Such as, say, who murdered Maureen O'Flaherty. But I'd already managed to unravel something, leaving me with the same reassuring feeling one has after extracting the first knot from a child's tangled shoelace and knowing that the rest of the task is now doable.

To be sure, it had always been assumed that Vince and Lanny knew more about (or were more directly involved with) the death of the Girl in New Jersey than had ever been revealed to the Public, and said Public seemed just fine about this. Collins and Morris were a national treat, like Fritos or Skippy peanut butter, and no one was prepared to abstain from the pleasure of watching them simply because some tramp had turned up dead in their hotel room.

But as ready to forgive them as the Public had been, the boys were not prepared to resume business as usual post-Maureen. Something had happened in the vicinity of that last telethon, something that had truly soured the team. They no longer behaved like brothers on stage. They behaved like brothers-in-law. The put-downs, always a mainstay of their act, seemed to hang in the air a half second longer than before. When Vince said his trademark "I'd kill you if you weren't already brain-dead!" the audience laughed a half decibel less, and perhaps some of their minds flickered for the duration of an eye blink to the imagined image of that girl's body in the bathtub.

The start date for shooting *A Night at the Opera* was pushed back six months because of "casting problems." As production of *The Maginot Line* began (its roster including Vince Collins but not Lanny Morris), no one was very surprised when Lanny announced that he'd be playing his first dramatic film role in the Warner–Seven Arts motion picture *Royal Flush,* a heist picture with a juicy role for Lanny as a safecracker gone straight who is forced to return to crime to protect his ex-wife. Both movies were supposed to win the boys Oscar nominations, if not the prize itself. Neither film did, nor should have. The boys showed their good sportsmanship by appearing together at the Oscar ceremony to present the Best Supporting Actor award (Vince quipped that he'd been supporting Lanny for years), and that marked the last time the two appeared in public together and, as best I could tell, the last time either saw the other in person.

There are things that everybody knows. It doesn't mean they're true. It's just that everybody knows about them and so they "are." Documented U.S. Air Force encounters with alien spacecraft, the marriage of Rock Hudson to Jim Nabors, Dr Pepper containing prune juice, champagne goblets being made in the shape of Empress Josephine's breasts (not referring to the stems, of course—there's an image), Fidel Castro's involvement in the assassination of JFK. We have no outright proof of any of this, and yet we all know it to be true because we've talked about it so much. We assumed Peter Lawford and Robert Kennedy were involved in the death of Marilyn Monroe, but that just made them more interesting, more worldly. They knew things we didn't know, and we subconsciously admired them for this.

And we felt that way about Vince Collins and Lanny Morris, whom we *knew* had something to do with the death of Maureen O'Flaherty. Since it was reported that she'd been involved with one or both of the comics and had turned up dead a few days later in their hotel suite, we knew they were both knee-deep in it without hip boots . . . because we'd read it, said it, thought it, even if their impeccable alibi proved they couldn't have been directly involved in killing her.

And now I alone—hurrah!—knew that their alibi meant nothing.

So here I was again about to have lunch with Vince, a man who might have done A Terrible Thing. Only now I knew he'd had the opportunity, if not yet an acknowledged motive. And astutely as ever, I was having lunch with him alone. In his home.

What was I supposed to do? When he suggested that our first interview take place at his house, would it have been diplomatic to say, "Do you mind if I bring a friend? Because I'm concerned that you might, in the course of my questioning, murder me."

To be sure, I didn't think I was *really* in any major danger. It wasn't as if the further careers of Vince and Lanny had been littered with the corpses of other women. I wasn't some room-service valet. I had an editor, a publisher; there were contracts signed with this man with whom I was about to lunch; people knew where I was going, they would know if I didn't get back, and if anything happened to me, the police would rain down hard on Vince Collins. You can get away with murder, but usually not twice.

Still, I decided to regularly mail myself an updated copy of all I've been relating here. Today I again sent to myself all but these last two pages, and on the back of the manila envelope I'd printed in discreet block letters, so as not to alarm the postman, the melodramatic phrase TO BE OPENED ONLY IN THE EVENT OF MY DEATH, and I will repeat this procedure every day or two. (I do hope you're not reading this now because that event has taken place.)

I was so happy to be back in my home. My glorious day with Lanny, culminating in my utter ravishment, had been a total lie that still sat sour in my stomach. But I had remedies. The best medicine is not laughter but rather, of course, revenge. It would be wonderful if in writing about Vince, I could find evidence that Lanny had been directly involved in Maureen's death. This would indeed regally reciprocate Lanny's royal screwing of me.

And in the far more unlikely instance that I found Vince to be the guilty party, well, I'd just have to console myself with a monstrous best-seller. Although every part of me reverberated with the belief that while Vince might know more than he had ever spoken about the death of Maureen O'Flaherty, he was not a murderer.

God, I was so glad I hadn't slept with Vince. Imagine if I'd compromised myself so disgracefully with *both* men! At least I still could begin my work with him feeling halfway clean. There was, to be sure, the agreement I had made to sleep with him when we completed the project. At the time I'd thought I was being quite the alluring libertine. Now I thought differently.

Vince had a villa in Bel Air, built in the late forties by John Lautner. Vince had dictated detailed directions to his home over the telephone. I was now wheeling my really-just-awful canary-colored convertible (which lacked power steering) up the privileged pathways of Bel Air, careening and nearly caroming along the twisted turns of its upper tiers like a tarnished pinball, yellowed with age. America might in theory be a democracy, but I was truly extending the Jeffersonian ideal by daring to drive the wretched refuse of my jalopy through what was a de facto private sector.

I'd been alternately referring to Vince's directions and cursing them for the last forty-five minutes. I'd passed Anzio, looped onto Roberto, turned down the redundantly named Via Verone Street, swiveled up Portofina Place, turned back onto Stradella, now firmly convinced that Vince lived in Tuscany.

He'd said, "You'll need to hang a right on Tortuoso, and after you pass a kind of Cape Cod house with blue shutters, you'll see an unmarked driveway on your left. It has some painted white stones on either side. Head up that until you get to a tall white iron gate. There's an intercom on the left—the name on it is Otto Bloodwort."

"Who's that?" I'd asked.

"Nobody. I just assume that no one on earth wants to talk with anyone named Otto Bloodwort. Push the button, say today's password, which is 'Hi, it's me, I'm here,' and I'll buzz you in."

The route conveyed to me by Vince was like one of those maze puzzles in a kid's comic book that resemble the upper intestine. Now my "car" was finally coiling its way up the torturous Tortuoso and my instincts were telling me that Vince had by no means given me the most direct route from my apartment to his estate. In fact, I learned much later (and not from Vince) that years before he'd had mapped out for his use the most circuitous route to his home from all points of the compass, which he relayed to first-time visitors in the hope they'd be unable to retrace their path without written instructions or a road map, lowering the odds on uninvited return guests who might contemplate dropping by without warning.

"Yes?" asked the voice that emanated from the speaker grille below the name Otto Bloodwort on the gate's intercom.

"Hi, it's me, I'm here," I said. I was standing by the intercom, as I'd been unable to reach the intercom button from where I'd stopped my hideous car.

There was no reply but simply a low buzz akin to what I'd imagined the hum of the electric chair might sound like, and after a dramatic pause, the metal gate swung slowly open. I ran back to my vile vehicle, fearful that there was a time limit on how long the gate stayed open. "Lady Journalist Crushed in Dreadful Convertible."

There was still quite a bit more driveway ahead of me after the gate. I eventually pulled my unforgivable transport into a motor court the size of a playground. Vince was framed in his doorway at the far end of a walled courtyard. He wore a fisherman's sweater, charcoal gabardines, socks that looked like cashmere, and Bass Weejuns.

"Any trouble with the directions I gave you?" he asked.

"Only with the parts where I had to turn. It doesn't usually take me an hour and a half to travel fourteen miles as the crow flies." My, what an ornery cuss I was for the moment.

Vince shrugged. "I'm sorry. The price of seclusion."

"Have you considered Yucca Flats?" I responded, pushing my luck. "Actually, it's my fault, not yours. My car turns on a dime store."

We walked into his home, stepping through a foyer that might have been an art gallery and down five softly carpeted steps into the living room. It was as handsome as I knew it would be and as comfortable with its manliness as Vince was with himself. Hues in every shade in which coffee can be taken: black, and with varying amounts of heavy cream, and simply cream itself. I was surprised to see so many books, not a one of them about show business.

There was a De Chirico hanging on the left wall, not one I knew but the usual setting: a sunny, eerily deserted Italian town square, a self-important statue, the long shadows of two people talking in an archway of the piazza. As always, the painter's work looked to me like a holiday photograph taken a few seconds before something dreadful happened. Its muted oranges and yellows went well with the room, which had as its main ornamentation a marvelously slung-out view of Los Angeles, as if from the verandah of a manor house that oversees the valley that is its domain. "Good for you, Vince," I couldn't help but murmur to myself.

Vince asked if I'd like the grand tour, but we had work to do and some of it would not benefit from my being Vince's pal. I was, at the very best, morally positioned somewhere between a matador and a surgeon. "You know," I said, slinging the bag that contained my cassette tape recorder and my writing tools onto a leather couch studded in dull brass, "we're going to be doing this every day, and I'm sure I'll have occasion to look around. We have so much terrain to cover—"

He nodded and went into the kitchen to get some coffee. I lavished praise on his taste in Italian modern art. He laughed. "What were you expecting, wide-eyed moppets? Or matadors, nude women, and clowns on black velvet?" Again, I had reflexively been patronizing him. As I set up the tape recorder, I asked him if he always fended for himself.

The thought of having live-in help was poisonous to him. "I'd have to talk with them, ask all about how their family was doing, hear what they thought about this and that, introduce them to guests and then tell the guests all about how their family was doing, so I'd seem to be a nice guy. . . . That's a lot of work, considering that what I most cherish in life these days is to not have to be 'Vince Collins.' " That was why Reuben had been (and remained) Lanny's valet exclusively, whom Lanny always paid directly. "I like to read, to think, and have the freedom to get up and leave any time of day without having to tell anyone about it, or even having to say good-bye."

That first day we started with his parents and his childhood. I knew he half-expected me to open with the topic of Maureen. But I wanted to make it easy at the beginning for Vince.

It wasn't so much that I wanted him to trust me. I wanted him to trust himself, to feel like a trial witness given the kid-glove treatment from opposing counsel for the first hour of a cross-examination. After a while, he begins to feel, Hey, there's not much to this. He starts to get more expansive. He follows up his own answers. He knows you'll understand since he's already explained to you how things were. Eventually, he'll tell you everything. The truth is: everybody wants to confess.

Of course, I couldn't wait too long to get to Topic A. I knew I had Greg Gavin all antsy in New York for hot copy and N&N's *Master* magazine ready to run stunning excerpts from our book in its premier issue. But it could wait three, even four days. I rationed myself that long to enjoy chatting with Vince Collins.

It was easy. He was self-effacing, funny, a nice mix of warm and tangy, like a perfect circle of lemon slice floating in a straight-up Manhattan. And when he talked about his childhood, I pictured how hard he'd worked to better his lot in life. Somewhere in his early teens, he must have looked in the mirror, messing with his hair and some Wildroot Cream Oil, appraised his looks, and thought, "I can work this. I can get myself somewhere with this face."

His father's American name was Domenico Collins. Vince had been told that Collins was really some customs official's version of Colline Metallifere, which is the mountain range in southern Tuscany where his father's family came from. His father's Italian name was Domenico Vincenzo d'Ambrosio. He'd always wondered why the customs official didn't dub his father Domenico Ambrose.

I asked him, "Making you Vince Ambrose?"

"Does sound a bit lavender, doesn't it?" he acknowledged.

His father came to the New World in his late teens, either because he'd heard there were lots of good prospects for northern Italian chefs in this country or because he had murdered an ex-boyfriend of his wife's. "Oh, Madon', what a goddess my mother was!" Vince reflected. He said he would look through his mother's face and see from the Renaissance all the way back to ancient Rome. She was the one who'd encouraged Vince to sing, although he'd inherited his voice from his father, who was known for singing (not just robustly but memorably) while he cooked.

By a quarter to six, I heard the slightest rasp in Vince's voice and I suggested we pack it in.

"Would you like to get some dinner?" he asked. I hesitated and he added, "We wouldn't have to talk about me."

Recent experience should certainly have caused me to say no to Vince's suggestion, but I knew that if I searched my mind, I could find a justification for saying yes.

My real reason for wanting to acquiesce should have been obvious enough for anyone to understand. If George Harrison of the Beatles meets you at a bar, takes you on a mini–Magical Mystery Tour, makes you feel that something special and unique is happening to you, has his way with you (which is exactly the way you'd have it), and then unceremoniously dumps you, what would be the one thing that could make you instantly feel better about losing George Harrison?

Correct, very good: John Lennon, of course. If I was Dorothy Lamour, then Lanny was definitely Bob Hope and Vince was Bing Crosby.

Not that Lanny was unattractive. But though his face could look fascinating and sensitive in the glow of a Plaza bedside table lamp, and though he had one of the three most adorable *tuchus*es it had ever been my privilege to grab, and though he was certainly (God fucking damn it) the best one-night stand I'd ever had, anyone but anyone would tell you that it was Vince who was the looker of the two, the man of the two, the more soulful of the two.

Aha. I'd thought of the rationale. Great. It hadn't really taken very long. Being social and chummy with Vince would be a great way to, again, make him further drop his guard. Not to sleep with him yet, of course (of course), for, as a rule, when a man sleeps with a woman, this causes him to afterward *raise* his guard.

He took us to a favorite restaurant of his, across the street from the Riot House (which is what we in the trade had taken to calling the Continental Hyatt House, because this, along with the Sunset Marquis, had become the lodging place for second-tier rock bands or the roadies for first-tier rock bands).

The restaurant's address may have been 8426 Sunset Boulevard, but you certainly couldn't find it if you were standing at that address on the sidewalk. At this point, the streets off the Sunset Strip nosedived downhill to Santa Monica Boulevard, as if you were in San Francisco. At number 8426 there was simply a metal gate and a flight of stone steps descending into what seemed like an empty lot alongside a tattoo parlor. Vince opened the gate and gestured that I should follow him.

Once again I was being led down a long flight of steps by Vince Collins to an unknown terminus. This time there were Japanese lanterns hanging above the wrought-iron balustrades and thick foliage on either side of me. The air was wonderfully sweet. After descending some forty steps, we emerged onto a patio enclosed by shrubbery and trees far below the boulevard, where very smart people were dining as if in the garden of someone's house, which in fact it was. Gas sconces challenged nature, negating the hint of a chill in the night. Well behind and above me, I could hear the soft whisking of traffic along Sunset Boulevard like distant comets sweeping across the night sky.

A fair-haired young captain instantly spotted Vince and ushered us to a table tucked into a corner of the sunken patio. It was a lovely place to be.

I learned that the restaurant, called Butterfield's (and who Butterfield was I have yet to glean), had at one time been the guest house of John Barrymore and was preserved as such. Its most illustrious guest was Barrymore's drinking buddy Errol Flynn.

Without Vince uttering a word, a fair-haired young waiter had placed before us fried parsley on a silver salver. We picked at it strand by strand as we talked. It was hot, greaseless, and sophisticated, as if Cole Porter had reinvented the potato chip.

I had a cream of watercress soup that was pleasingly thin with a mysterious flavor something like smoky asparagus. Vince started with sand dabs, which were new to me, a flat fish like a thumb-length halibut. They'd been dredged in flour, then pan-fried in olive oil and served with a green tartar sauce that I suspected contained Japanese horseradish. Vince had me try one of the sand dabs, neatly ushering it onto my bread plate. It was wonderful. He was wonderful. We were having such a nice time, talking not one bit about show business or his career but simply what each of us thought about all sorts of matters.

Maybe it hadn't been such a bad thing after all, I thought, that I'd agreed to make love with him when the book was finished. It was as if, having come to that agreement, the issue of sex was now off the table. Flirtation was unnecessary. Lecherous innuendo need not lurk at the end of every sentence. Some men I'd known would have made endless references to the promise, trying to make sure it hadn't all been a joke on my part, reminding me of their intention to cash in the promissory note I'd issued, seeing if the redemption date could be advanced a little. Not Vince. Apparently when we were done with this project, he would get to de-flower me of whatever was left of my petals, and that was that. So there was no need for either of us to toy around with each other. We could actually talk, as if we were people.

And that, undramatically, was how our evening went. No kiss, not even a "kiss-kiss," no plaintive voicing of "God, if only we weren't working together!" Just this sane, rational, very atypical for the time "See you tomorrow."

For several days, it went just this way. We would progress through Vince's life (by Day Three we were only up to his entry into the army, and there were still some points in his teens I needed to go back over) and then have a relaxed dinner, where we would make a graceful transition from narrator and inquisitor to two adults having a genuine conversation. We went to relatively low-profile places where Vince could dine as anonymously as was possible. By "anonymously," I mean simply that people he didn't know didn't come over to our table and introduce themselves, asking for photographs to be taken or menus to be signed. Vince treasured certain restaurants where the majority of the patrons understood this code of behavior. Don't think I'm saying that Vince could go anywhere without being recognized.

He did have a "don't recognize me" face, which he sported on those rare occasions when he was momentarily out in public and vulnerable. He'd apologize, saying, "Sorry, I'll be right back" and tilt his head downward, keeping his eyes up and wearing what I could best describe as a stupid, openmouthed grin. He'd also raise the key of his voice a fifth and adopt a flat, genial midwestern twang, pushing the words a little. "Well, thanks very much, sir," he'd say to the parking attendant, "we'd just like to have it back in one piece," and one would see this shy but good-natured rube standing where Vince had been a second earlier. As we got to know each other better, he stopped apologizing and simply whipped out the face when necessary, as one might whip out a hankie if about to sneeze.

Thursday night he'd suggested a place out in Malibu, the Sandpiper, whose management guaranteed that the sun would set into the Pacific Ocean each evening. Vince being Vince, we had the best table, providing us with a clear view of the slick, hollow stone that jutted far out into the water, ocean spray spuming up through its ventilated surface like a rock garden of geysers.

As a kind of a test, I had casually asked Vince that night if he liked lobster. His response had no special tinge to it. He said he loved cold lobster, served in a salad, loved the look and feel of the red shell and red radishes set upon a bed of green leaves. Loved lobster bisque, especially at Wheeler's in London, where they would flambé cognac and literally ladle the mysterious blue flames into the soup as it sat before you. He wasn't nuts about boiled lobster, the meat sometimes getting too mushy or stringy, but split and char-grilled, that was heaven. Didn't like dipping it in butter, though. "Then it just tastes like good popcorn at the movies, so why not have good popcorn and see a movie?" Enjoyed the act of cracking the lobster for the first few bites, but then it became simply too much work, considering that he was paying for the lobster in the first place.

He answered me in such a genuine, balanced way that I gratefully took this as further reassurance that if lobsters had been a part of any dark episode in his life, Vince probably didn't know about it.

We had started our work on a Tuesday. At the end of Friday, as we unwound from reliving his first year in the army (he was almost court-martialed for addressing a colonel as "Kern"), he asked me if I wanted to continue through the weekend. I opted not to, for my own sake. I thought it was important I have the weekend to myself, to stay in touch with that world where people do laundry, buy groceries, and park their own cars. It would be too easy to lose all context, and that might take me off my game.

He seemed to understand but stressed that he was blocking all other activities out of his schedule to accommodate the book, and said that anytime I wanted to work straight through the week would be not only fine with him but preferable. I suggested Sunday as a possibility, but asked if he could give me until Saturday afternoon to confirm because it would require moving some things around. In point of fact, I had nothing planned for Sunday but simply wanted to keep my options open.

That evening I dropped off my four cassettes at the offices of Cynthia R. Lehman Stenographic Services, which were located in the dining room and sometimes also the kitchen of Cynthia R.'s little stucco house on a street called Formosa in West Hollywood. When I got home, I poured myself a white Graves and sat powwow style on my bed with Cynthia's transcribed pages from the day before. Flanked by my Klimt prints and antique perfume bottles, I read them with some satisfaction. I had drawn out Vince quite nicely, I thought, bobbing and weaving during his narrative like a sheepdog moving his flock through the paddock gate with a minimal amount of backtracking. None of what I'd acquired so far would cause Greg Gavin to click his heels and deem it a best-seller. But things would perk up next week when I asked Vince about Maureen O'Flaherty. I'd let him have smooth sailing as we began another week. But then I would ask him, perhaps on Wednesday. After that, I expected I would know much more. Oh yes I would.

NINETEEN

Saturday started lazily, much to my liking. It was great not to think for a while. I dropped off my edited pages at Cynthia Lehman's place, so they could be retyped and mailed to the East Coast. I took some laundry to a place on Ventura Boulevard called the Soapermarket. I didn't even leave while the washer was on. I watched Dick Clark's *American Bandstand* on a black-and-white set mounted on a shelf above the Coke machine. That's how mindless I intended my afternoon to be. I'd interviewed Dick once in conjunction with a piece I was doing about the Philadelphia recording scene and had asked him the secret of his youthfulness. He said that he took an aspirin every day. He told me this in the course of the ninety minutes he spent in a barber chair while an ABC makeup artist plied her craft with his face.

After that, I went to do some food shopping. I never make a list. I just wait until I'm absolutely famished, go to the Safeway, and walk up and down absolutely every aisle. This way my ravenous sense of hunger can inform me if something I see is something I might want to eat, if not today then certainly someday.

I wheeled up aisle two, very interested in their selection of herbed cheese spreads with French-sounding names. As I leaned into the open, refrigerated shelf to better examine garlic-chive and honey-jalapeño, my breath formed a condensed cloud in the chill, through which I discerned the dignified figure of Reuben, valet for Lanny Morris.

He didn't see me. He was in the produce section, examining tomatoes with a calm, efficient intensity. He rejected three and then found another that met his criteria. He moved along to pass judgment on both red and green peppers in a similarly expert and assured way. He *did* have a list, and he consulted it now and then with the methodical manner of a respected attorney citing legal precedents.

I reflexively pushed my cart away from him and made a sharp turn around the end of the aisle, swerving neatly into paper products and pet supplies.

I collected my thoughts. It wasn't particularly odd that I'd crossed his path. I knew better than anyone that Reuben and his boss had left the East Coast. The particular Safeway I liked was almost as convenient to Lanny's home address in Beverly Glen as it was to mine in Studio City. And certainly Lanny couldn't venture into any supermarket in America without unintentionally inciting the public to riot, so Reuben clearly was entrusted with the household food shopping.

What would be the consequences of Reuben spotting me? Would he even recognize me—had I made that much of an impression? Or did Lanny have a revolving door/whore policy that made me a case of "if you've seen one, you've seen them all"? Maybe Reuben would look at me and draw a complete blank. It was this last part that made me want to confront him. How he reacted to me might tell me something about how I'd been appraised (and was now viewed) by both servant and master. Business, logic, diplomacy all flew right out the window—there they go, bye-bye! I was seeing red; literally, a red corona had framed my vision as I again thought of how I'd been fucked and shucked.

I tailed him all over the store. "Follow that cart" was my modus operandi. I was ridiculous, shadowing him past preserves and canned soups, ducking up an alleyway of salad dressings and behind a display of Kellogg's Sugar Smacks. One time he started back in my direction and I cleverly leaned into the frozen foods and extracted a Hampton's Hog Wild Pork Chop Dinner with a side of macaroni and cheese, carrots, and a small square of applesauce. Tossing it into my rapidly filling cart, I then nosed my way slowly around a corner and saw him enter checkout lane number five. I smoothly glided into place behind him, cutting off a little old lady.

She started to protest, but I glared at her with such intensity that she switched to an adjacent checkout.

Reuben finished placing his Safeway selections on the conveyor belt and moved the wooden divider bar to the end of his purchases. I started to casually place the contents of my cart behind his, positioning the Hog Wild Pork Chop Dinner on Reuben's side of the divider. Then I set back on my haunches and allowed the profound implications of my gambit to play itself out. Reuben did an almost cartoonish double-take as he saw the package in the checkout lady's hands. My safe guess was that Lanny Morris did not eat many frozen TV dinners, and if he did, they were probably not pork chops with a side of cheddar macaroni.

"Excuse me," demurred Reuben to the checkout lady. "I don't think that's mine."

I dedicated myself to making a neat row of flatbread boxes on the black conveyor belt.

"Miss?" the checkout lady called to me. I pretended there were lots of other misses she might be talking to and continued to deposit herbed cheese spreads onto my portion of the belt.

"Miss?" she repeated. I finally looked up. "Is this yours?" she asked, holding up the Hampton's dinner. She wore a name tag that told me she was Lois.

"Oh yes, thanks," I said, giving Reuben one snapshot of my face and then going back to the process of unloading my cart. There would be time for me to "recognize" him if I had to. First I would see if he recognized me.

Reuben was busy locating a BankAmericard in his wallet and handed it to Lois, who sighed at this rare mode of payment. "Really?" she asked. "You don't have it in cash?"

"I'm sorry. I'm purchasing the food for someone else," said Reuben. "Here is my identification, if you need it." He offered his driver's license.

Lois left the register. "I don't have the thing. Hold on." She went off to a counter marked CUSTOMER SERVICE to fetch the swiping device and a triplicate carbon-copy form, giving Reuben a dirty look in the process.

Reuben turned away from Lois's glare and found himself looking at me again. He smiled as if to apologize, and then recognition dawned over his golden face. He ventured, "Excuse me . . . aren't you Miss Trout? We met on the plane to New York."

I allowed slow realization to dawn upon me, but I couldn't overplay my surprise too much. "Reuben!" I said. "Hello. Yes, my gosh, what a surprise. Who would have thought I'd see you so soon after the Plaza . . ."

I paused, keeping my face in neutral while keeping my eyes on his. I wanted to see what he knew of how I'd been dealt with. God love him. He blushed, his skin turning an autumnal orange. "Oh, I'm *so* deeply sorry, Miss Trout. The way you were treated . . ." He couldn't finish the sentence, but his shame was eloquent. It seemed as if he felt that, like a dedicated servant from a different time and place, he must bear or share responsibility for his master's behavior.

I murmured in a low, hurt tone that was in no way a distortion of how I truly felt, "Well, yes, I do think something should have been said to me. At least—and I mean at the *very* least—a note, a call."

Reuben nodded painfully. "Of course."

"I realize he's a big star and that big stars can rewrite the rules of nature—"

"No, you don't understand," he interrupted. "There's a saying: *'No man is a hero to his valet.'* I'm valet to Lanny Morris."

Lois arrived with the credit-card device and angrily jammed Reuben's card and the carbon-copy form into it. After signing with his own pen rather than the one proffered, Reuben waited a respectful few feet from the checkout while I paid for my groceries. He then offered to help load my bags into my trunk. We walked our carts out into the cheerlessly sunny afternoon and stopped at my inexcusable car. Orange and yellow pennants were tied to the light posts in celebration of nothing; they stood dead still in the big heat. As I opened the loathsome trunk of my leprous convertible, he asked what I was doing in Los Angeles. I said I'd been looking into the possibility of a new job, perhaps editorial work, and that I'd had a few signs of interest from a company in the Los Angeles area. I was staying with a friend for a few days. I was curious to see if he would ask me where I could be reached. It would indicate that I might have at least achieved the status of "serviceable lay" in Lanny Morris's Book of Books. (Look at me, look at what I'm saying!)

He did ask, and I am horrified to admit that I was relieved, although I had no intention of giving him my address. I told him that in light of what had happened, I didn't think I wanted Lanny contacting me again.

He pushed his shopping cart forward and back a few inches on the hot asphalt as if rocking a baby in a pram. He was clearly uneasy to be speaking so openly about Lanny, but to his credit, personal honor won out over professional duty. "Miss Trout, telling you this—it's quite a breach of my position, which is one of trust, but I would like you to understand. I'm getting older; pretty soon I will retire, if he'll ever let me. I look forward to that. I have on the one hand great loyalty to Mr. Morris. He has shown generosity to myself and to my family whenever we have needed his help. I am very grateful. He has done wonderful things for many people, including such a simple but important thing as to make them laugh. I like him very much. I have been privileged to be in his employ."

I said I understood. This was clearly difficult for him. He continued, "But I have certain principles. Some of us in the Philippines descend from Spanish nobility, and though the fortunes of our families may have declined, we still have strong feelings about how women are to be treated and respected. It has been the most difficult part of my job over the years, to let his behavior go by."

A security guard of the Fresno redneck variety pulled up alongside us in an unmarked car. "How you doin' here, miss?" he asked.

It was so gratingly obvious that his inquiry was simply because he saw a youngish white girl being talked to at close quarters by a man with darker-colored skin. "Just fine, thanks," I replied.

He nodded dubiously and asked of Reuben, "How about you, sir?" He leaned on the word "sir" with condescension. Reuben said that he, too, was fine and thanked the guard for his thoughtfulness. The guard gave me one last look, checking to see if I was trying to signal for help by blinking my eyes to the beat of the International Distress Signal, then reluctantly continued on his never-ending quest to protect the loins of California girls from the onslaught of mongrel races.

Reuben shrugged at me as if to say, "This is what I deal with every day." He turned his shopping cart around to indicate to the redneck that he was indeed hitting the trail. He said, "I'd like to believe that our paths crossed at this store not without some greater intervention."

I didn't bother to explain that our paths had crossed largely because I'd been stalking him past boxed cereals and bottled beverages for the last fifteen minutes.

"I want you to know that the way Mr. Morris behaved had nothing to do with you personally. Not with anything you are, anything you did, anything you said. The truth is, he does this with all the women he meets.

This is his way with women. He can be very attentive and genteel, but once he has a woman. . . . I think it's almost a sickness." He touched my arm. "When he left you that morning, you may have felt bad for a moment. Perhaps even for days after that. But I am telling you, Miss Trout, to have him out of your life . . . it is the best thing that could ever have happened to you. At that point, you may have felt your life was wounded. It wasn't. It was saved."

He wheeled the cart away. I watched him get into a ten-year-old beige Ford Falcon that was as clean today as when it was purchased. He drove off. I turned to put my groceries into my car and saw the pork-chop dinner sitting at the top of the bag. I tossed the package back into the shopping cart, which I then shoved away from my hopeless dud of a car.

TWENTY

Certainly what Reuben had shared with me had extinguished any little pilot light of hope I might have had for Lanny's affection. No, I had been made an honorary member of Lanny's Club, placed at the end of a long line of women who'd been burned by the club's founder and who now stood out in the cold, cooling their heels. Enough. Shaping a successful book about Vince Collins that revealed some injurious facts about Lanny Morris would have to be my consolation prize.

I'd had a chance to think through how events in New York would affect my immediate schedule. I'd pick up the revised typed pages from Cynthia this evening, airmail them to N&N first thing Monday morning, and with any luck they'd be there by Thursday. I would certainly then receive a self-important call from Gavin, saying that the stuff I'd sent was far too innocuous and that the entire project was in trouble. (Gavin's type had a constant need for projects to be in trouble so that he could come in, all furrowed brow with much pipe sucking, telling everyone to remain calm, with the air of the Man Who Will Sort Things Out; never mind, of course, that the whole frenzy had been created by him.) It would be good if, during that phone call, I could tell him something juicy that would silence him for the remainder of my tenure.

Toward this end, I called Vince and told him that I wanted to take him up on his offer to work Sunday. Sounding regretful that he'd volunteered this, he asked if we could do it while he got in some golf, which he tried to make time for at least every other day. I advised him that I didn't know the first thing about golf. He said that wouldn't matter, I could just walk the course with him while he played. I considered that it might be the only chance I'd ever have to make the rounds of the Bel Air Country Club, short of becoming a caddy, and agreed to meet him there.

I had always found golf courses beautiful and frightening, looking a little too much like cemeteries minus the gravestones. They gave me the same uneasiness I felt looking at Vince's De Chirico painting, where the marketplace and town square are inexplicably deserted at midday of all but two denizens, who cast long shadows even though the sun is high overhead, and who share whispered words about things that no one must know. It was in that sort of eerie, sun-filled midday that I found myself telling Vince we would wrap up his big-band years by tomorrow and, on Tuesday, jump ahead in chronology to discuss the Girl Found Dead in New Jersey.

He started to walk briskly away from me to where his last drive had landed. "Why do you need to jump ahead in the time line?" he asked. I told him a variant on the truth: Neuman and Newberry's *Master* magazine, which would be publishing an advance excerpt from our book in its first issue, needed the material much sooner than did N&N. I watched him carefully as I elaborated: "They have to work out what the placement on the cover and the wording might be—you know, '*Vince Collins Comes Clean About a Dirty Secret*' or '*We Ask Vince Collins the Hard One.*' They're going to want a grabber—"

He kept walking but glared at me. "Boy, you're really blunt, aren't you?"

I had to take a little extra run-step, as he had half a foot on me. "Vince, I was very direct about this from the outset. I'm not going to play games with you. This is in large part why you're being paid such a huge sum of money." He looked at me questioningly and I snapped, "A million dollars is a huge sum of money, Vince. That's more than the budget of your first Colt Carrera film, and not a whole lot less than the gross of your fourth one." That was nasty of me and not altogether accurate. "Sorry, that was stupid."

He kept moving. I had to take two run-steps this time. He said, "The Carrera series is played out, I know it."

"You've spent days telling me what it was like to grow up poor in Pittsburgh, so it irks me if you don't take seriously the amount I fought for you to get. You'd have to make two films to get this kind of money." In this I was being generous, to compensate for my previous insult. I knew what Vince's current going rate was, and while certainly that of a Hollywood star, it was not on a level commensurate with anyone over at First Artists, meaning McQueen, Newman, Streisand, or Poitier. Vince would have to make more than a pair of films to pull in a million dollars.

Vince putted cool, long, and straight into the cup. The dimpled sphere made the satisfying sound of a roulette ball settling down into the very number on which you've bet. Vince didn't even watch.

"It's your show," he said flatly. "I thought all of my life was of some general interest, but if my brief encounter with a girl named Maureen O'Flaherty, who worked a room-service job in Miami and was found dead in a New Jersey hotel that I'd never set foot in before, is all you really want to hear about, then Tuesday it is. Now, do you want me to tell you about the boring stuff . . . like when the Elgart band played for Harry Truman's inaugural ball and what I did at the request of his daughter Margaret while two Secret Service men stood guard outside the ladies' lounge and why from that day on I always called her Peg? Or do you think that's not going to be of much interest to the reading public?"

He moved on to the fourth hole, not brusquely, just more than anything a bit hurt. Or was he nervous? I felt guilty if it was the first, and a bit excited if it was the second. But either way, I knew that I still liked him, liked his reasonability even when he was angered. I felt certain (and I'm pretty good with these things) that whatever I might ultimately learn about the events in question, I would not think any less of him after that.

Vince played through the rest of the course quickly, as if there were points given for the shortest time. He took no pleasure in his game now, but worked the green more like a champion billiards player, efficiently lining up his shots and making them before he had a chance to second-guess the angles. I was out of breath the entire time, even though he was doing the talking, but some part of me didn't want to ask him to slow down, perhaps because I felt I'd ruined the day for him. Under my breath I asked his caddie if this was Vince's usual style of play, and he said he hadn't seen him behave this way before. When Vince finished the course, he didn't even tally his score, as if when each hole was finished, it no longer counted.

We didn't have dinner together that night. We got a lot accomplished in the afternoon at his home, and when his stories were funny, which most of them were, we both laughed. But there was definitely a different feeling in the air. It was the atmosphere that emerges in a doctor's examining room, when the doctor (myself) comes in and makes a few lighthearted jokes to the patient (Vince) prior to using sharp instruments to perform a surgical procedure that he knows will hurt a great deal.

For dinner that night I stopped at Barney's Beanery. The waitress, who was dressed like a drugged-out groupie who'd made it with Sly and the entire Family Stone, took my order by sitting down across from me in my booth. I asked for a draft Coors and a bowl of chili, which the menu proclaimed to be the second best in the world. "Who makes the first-best chili?" I asked. She scowled and pointed at a flyer on one side of the table as she walked away. I picked it up. It read: "Don't ask your waitress who makes the first-best chili. She doesn't know."

The next morning I was assembling my notes in the kitchen, in preparation for our day's work, when there came a knock on my door. It was Vince, looking all chipper in a silk shirt the color of lemon sorbet and smart black jeans with a wide black leather belt. I didn't like bell-bottoms (although men were wearing them as if America had turned into one gigantic naval academy), but these were flared so slightly that you didn't notice them at all. He looked great, and to my relief he didn't seem upset with me.

"Hi," I said. "I didn't know you knew where I live." Which was perhaps not the warmest greeting but was certainly the first thought that popped into my head. He reminded me that my earliest letters proposing the book had all borne my home address.

I offered him some coffee, but he waved me off. "Look, here's the thing: tomorrow we get to the grim stuff, so you're going to have to let me off easy today. You can ask me any questions you want on the drive down to Anaheim and back, but in between, you have to let me have my four hours of recreational therapy. I try to do it once a month to stay sane."

I asked him what this therapy was. He looked embarrassed and sat down on a flower-patterned love seat by my window, which overlooked the fountain in the courtyard.

"Okay, let me explain. Every month or so, I have to clean out my brain, totally, of all the poisonous pressure of this god-awful town. It's stupid but it's therapeutic for me, so why should I apologize? Some people listen to Bach. Some people chant mantras. Carol Lynley does needlepoint while she's being interviewed on talk shows. Lots of people go fishing. Others go to hypnotists. I go to Disneyland. Please don't laugh."

I looked at him, not sure if he was ribbing me. I knew from my research that Vince enjoyed playing the occasional, well-constructed practical joke. But he seemed serious, if admittedly chagrined. "I'm not trying to be cutesy or adorable or anything. Honest, I just really like the place. I like its corniness and its technology. To me, hearing five hundred choruses of 'It's a Small World' sung by nine-fucking-thousand figurines all smiling at each other while I glide along in my canal boat with a family from Topeka, Kansas, is better than a million transcendental 'oooms.' It's Disneyland. Walt says, 'I Am That I Am.'" He smiled. "It's just that I like the place."

I took my bag off the kitchen table. "Me too," I said and started to walk out my door. "But if we squander some of the day's work for the Magic Kingdom, I've a couple of stipulations: we either have to have lunch at the Blue Bayou or eat StarKist tuna sandwiches alongside Captain Hook's ship under the Skull Rock waterfall. We go to the Enchanted Tiki Room, and when the audio-animatronic parrots cry out, 'Oh applause, applause!' at the end of each song and the audience doesn't applaud because they know the parrots can't hear them applauding, *we* have to applaud. And we have to laugh at all the jokes on the Jungle Boat ride, right up to the end when the Skipper says, 'And now we reach the most dangerous part of our journey. That's right, the return to civilization and those California freeways!'"

He looked at me as if he'd suddenly learned that his loyal secretary, whom he'd come to love and who had helped him through his years of amnesia, was in actuality his loyal wife. I checked my makeup in the antique Mucha-style mirror by the door. "And in the Haunted Mansion, coming out of the stretching-room elevator, we have to lag behind the crowd in the gallery until we're alone."

He nodded slowly. "You mean the room with the three-dimensional busts that turn whichever way you move?"

I adjusted the air-conditioning before leaving. "It's the only place on one of the indoor dark rides where you can stay inside the environment for as long as you like. If we let everyone else in our group go ahead of us, we'll have the gallery to ourselves for at least a minute, maybe two, before the next elevator unloads."

Vince's expression was of exquisite joy and profound gratitude, as if I'd just given him his first hand job. "Oh, this is wonderful."

The car parked outside was a 1957 Ford Skyliner, looking like the mating of a Thunderbird and a 1955 Chevrolet Bel Air. Its prow was all optimism, and its tail fins scalloped out gracefully like inverted single quotation marks. It was a pert-busted girl with a tail that was just begging for it, a two-tone in "Starmist Blue" and "Colonial White," Vince later informed me. He'd retracted its patented "Hideaway Hardtop," and it was now in convertible mode. I had the sweet suspicion that this was the car Vince had longed for as a teenager. "I don't take it out very often," he said, and I was glad he didn't call the car "her."

We didn't do much interviewing on the way down, which was fine because we had covered as much of "the Elgart Years" as any reader would find interesting. The bothered mood he'd been in yesterday had made us work efficiently and was now dissipated.

The L.A. sun was shining big, and the wind felt good. My name was as close to Peggy Sue as it was ever going to get.

Vince didn't take the usual exit to the Disneyland parking lot.

(You may have gathered that I'd been there more than a few times. When I first came out to the West Coast, I'd been hired to trash the place for the *L.A. Free Press* before that paper became a sex rag. There'd been rumors—untrue—that the Disney company was thinking of reinstating the dress code of the sixties, which had barred men with long hair from attending the park. Not just from working there, but from actually going on the rides or walking around the place. This was supposedly to prevent another yippie invasion, which had closed down the park for a day in 1970. My assignment was to savage Disney's simplistic, sanitized spin on America past and future, with the additional directive to search the fairy tales for latent pederasty and anal fixation. I spent a week at a cut-rate motel only a few blocks from the main gate and patrolled the park armed with pencils sharpened to a dartlike point . . . and came away by the end of the week completely smitten with the place.)

Instead of the regular exit, Vince turned off earlier onto a local street, made a left, and approached a gate marked WED ENTERPRISES—PLEASE SHOW PASS. There was a guard there, not an old fellow but more of an ex-marine. Vince greeted the guard by his first name and said in modest fashion that he believed there might be a pass waiting there from Mr. Byram's office. The guard looked through a file box, found the desired memo, and opened a drawer, from which he pulled out two rectangles of blue plastic, each the size of a MasterCharge card. It said WED GUEST and bore today's date. On the back was a three-digit number and letter, which Vince later explained was a code that got changed every day so that the card could not be counterfeited.

We drove past many low buildings with small lawns around them, mostly warehouse-type structures but some two-story offices as well. Vince pulled up to a brick building with a broader front lawn and a sign marked ADMINISTRATION AND GUEST SERVICES. Past it, I could easily see the turrets of Sleeping Beauty's castle and the Matterhorn's peak. I could also see the backs of the Victorian buildings that commenced the park; Walt Disney, with his admirable attention to detail, had insisted that the rear of the mock buildings be as complete as the front, even though no paying guests would ever see them.

We parked and were greeted by a charming Disney brunette, a stewardess-type whose bright smile evoked "coffee, tea" but no "me." Her name, on the oval I.D. pin that all Disney staff wore, was Pam. She apologized to Vince, saying that unfortunately she'd been unable to obtain any seating on Royal Street (whatever that meant) because it was closed for the installation of a new ventilation system. However, if we wished, we could have a table held for us at the Blue Bayou on the semiprivate part of the patio. Vince smiled and said, "But the strongest thing in the mint juleps will be the mint, right?" Pam said yes, the only spirits permitted there were those that wandered over from the Haunted Mansion. I tried to picture the manual Pam had studied containing all these answers to oft-asked questions.

She walked us down a long, blue-carpeted corridor where lots of people were typing and filing as if they were in any office in the world. At the end of the short hall was a narrow door, and by it stood a guard who was dressed as a policeman in an O. Henry story. He had a short handlebar mustache that was clearly his own. "Hello, Ken," said Pam. "Will you show our guests in, please?" I'd thought we *were* in.

Ken rapped two short knocks on the door. After a pause, two knocks sounded from the other side. Ken said, "This way, please." He opened the door just a crack and nodded at a man dressed in a straw hat, a shirt with blue vertical stripes, a white apron, and gray pin-striped pants. Getting a nod from this fellow, who looked like he had been plucked from a barbershop quartet, Ken opened the door wider and indicated that we should step through. We did and found ourselves outdoors. The door shut quickly behind us. The barbershop fellow beamed at us. He was standing behind a tall pushcart of plastic flowers that obscured our view of anything else. "Have a great day in the Magic Kingdom, Mr. Collins, ma'am," he said. Vince led me around the flower stand, and I immediately saw that we were at the end of a narrow courtyard. I heard horse's hooves clopping by, the bell of a trolley, and the oscillation of a thousand people. We stepped through the brick-paved area, past an artist in similar period costume seated at a small table. She was busy with black paper and scissors creating a silhouette cameo of a girl dressed in a Partridge Family T-shirt and Ditto jeans for kids. A double-decker bus puttered by and I realized that we were in Main Street USA, halfway along its length, equidistant from the train station by the entrance gates and the circular park out from which all the Disney "lands" radiated. Not since Blanche Sewell, who'd edited *The Wizard of Oz,* had spliced from the last frame of Dorothy's monochromatic house to the Technicolor door into Munchkinland had anyone experienced a more abrupt change of locales. Vince smiled at me and we headed up Main Street, past the Sunkist Citrus House on our left, whose tangy scent of a thousand freshly squeezed oranges seemed appropriate with the California sun high overhead. Vince had donned aviator sunglasses and a beat-up, broad-brimmed cowboy hat he'd brought with him. If you didn't expect to see him (and who would expect this big swinger at Disneyland?), you'd never have known him.

We stopped in front of the Crystal Palace–styled Carnation Plaza Gardens. There you go. Lanny had taken me to the Szechuan Garden, where the flavors were strange and erotic and hot, so hot that they had at one point literally caused me pain. Vince had brought me somewhere safe, sunny, and soothing, as soothing as Carnation evaporated milk drawn from contented cows and poured over cornflakes. At that moment, I much preferred where I was to where I had been.

We stepped over to the Plaza Park, hub for all the Disney "lands." Vince smiled at me. "So? Where first?"

"Ummm, Tomorrowland?"

Vince winced enough that I could see it even behind his sunglasses and hat brim. "No, we don't like tomorrow," he muttered. I had unintentionally reminded him of the topic we'd be covering the next day.

We decided to go straight to Adventureland, which was as appropriate a destination for me, I would grimly come to realize, as Tomorrowland was for him.

TWENTY-ONE

Our plastic passes got us onto the rides without requiring the pastel-colored A through E coupons, an A coupon at ten cents being good for nothing more than a one-way horse-drawn trolley, double-decker bus, fire wagon, or horseless-carriage ride up or down Main Street, an E coupon at eighty-five cents being required for the most expensive attractions: Haunted Mansion, Pirates of the Caribbean. More important, we could even bypass the lines when we wanted to. In some cases this could be done subtly: for Pirates, we were walked by a cast member in a buccaneer outfit to where passengers disembarked, and were seated in a just vacated boat before it was floated around to the boarding area. We pulled up to the dock already perched in the prow, and the mere civilians who'd been queued up for an hour enviously wondered who we were to have achieved first-class status while they'd stood on line for economy.

Whatever mindless pleasure Vince was taking in his surroundings, I was taking every bit an equal share. As the day evolved, I realized we were having our own personal prom night. He was the high school quarterback who was also the school rebel. I was, well, I let myself imagine I'd been pinned by Vince. I hadn't given myself to him yet, and he, being a sensitive rebel, had never pushed the issue. But I knew that someday, when the time was right, it would happen. And I knew it would be wonderful for the both of us.

Vince fired a rifle at the Frontierland shooting gallery and, thanks to the training he'd had for films like *Return to the Alamo,* won me a Davy Crockett coonskin cap. On the Matterhorn, my date put his arm around me just before we skidded hard into the hidden pool, shielding me from the plumes of water that shot into the air upon impact. On the Mad Tea Party ride, my beau spun the center wheel of our baby-blue teacup so that we rotated far more dizzily than I thought possible on such an innocuous-looking attraction. Our motion rivaled the twisted turns of Bel Air. I found myself laughing uncontrollably until after the ride had come to a full and complete stop.

In the Blue Bayou, the restaurant built within the "prologue" of the Pirates of the Caribbean, it is always a perfect, deep blue evening, even at high noon. One sits "outside" on the terrace of a handsome antebellum mansion designed in neo–Ashley Wilkes. Spanish moss clings both to the creamy-white trellises and an immense tree whose boughs reach to the water like drinking straws. The evening sky is full of uncountable stars and the odd comet. The moon fades away behind a cloud and then reappears, this with reassuring regularity. A bullfrog recites his low, sad poem. The placid surface of the Louisiana bayou sloshes as a gator slides sideways off the riverbank. "O Susanna" is picked out slowly on a banjo played by an old man in a shack across the water from our table, where we consume absolutely forgettable food in a memorable setting. We had been placed by the water's edge, at the best and most private table in the house. Vince sat with his back to the rest of the patrons, and so was able to remove his sunglasses and hat. We watched the boatloads of passengers gliding by in silence, some of them deceived by the languid faux evening around them and the easy glide of their craft. If they had never been this way before, they might be blithely unaware that in a matter of seconds they would enter a dark tunnel and go toppling over the edge of a precipice, borne down by cascading waters. Vince placed his hand over mine at one point, and I turned my hand around so as to cup his hand back. Peggy Sue and Bobby Joe.

I was having a dreamy time with Vince, and I took comfort from its being so different from my day with Lanny. Lanny's itinerary had been for me to witness him. Eat his food. Hear him sing. Fly his helicopter. Watch his film. Ride his thing. Vince, on the other hand, seemed so eager for things to *not* be about him. Whenever we had gone out, we had hardly ever mentioned his career.

And sex was not an issue, because we were definitely not going to have sex until our work was done, and we definitely *were* going to have sex upon its completion. What a brainstorm that had been. It gave me (and presumably Vince) an inviolable comfort zone.

As a child, I had savored Christmas Eve more than Christmas itself. I loved to stave off the opening of my presents for as long as possible, ecstatically sitting in their midst, wriggling within the thrill of expectation. I was wonderfully comfortable now with Vince, and every time I looked at him, I saw a continent of Christmas presents, gleaming and unopened in the first light of dawn on December 25.

And today Vince seemed the happiest he'd been since we'd met. The dark rides were particularly enjoyable for him because as we entered them, he could remove his sunglasses and become everybody else. For anywhere from three to seven minutes, he didn't have to be Vince Collins.

The one time he publicly owned up to his identity that day was, significantly, a moment of openhearted generosity, as you'll see.

We both liked the Alice in Wonderland ride. But it was very much an orphan in the park. Disney himself had never been totally comfortable with Alice's story (though not so uncomfortable that he didn't replace Lewis Carroll's name with his own in the movie's opening credits: Walt Disney's *Alice in Wonderland*). The feverish, surrealistic story, with its neurotic cast, centered on a young girl who took unknown medicines without a prescription, passed through mirrors unscathed, ate mushrooms that caused her to change shape, this—how can I put it?—this was not your quintessential Disney girl. A Disney girl did not unquestioningly eat food simply because it was labeled EAT ME or imbibe unidentified liquids just because their bottle advised DRINK ME.

Perhaps because of this, the ride looked and felt very different from the Fantasyland dark rides that had preceded it: Snow White, Mr. Toad, Peter Pan. Its use of myriad muted pastels glowing under gobs of black light seemed to have anticipated the psychedelic sixties, even though it had been built in the late fifties. You moved more slowly and languorously than on the other rides. Appropriately, your vehicle on this journey was the Caterpillar, whom, we all smugly noted, smoked a water pipe. Not for nothing did we drift pleasantly through Alice's world of wonderment as if sweetly stoned, gliding upside down across the ceiling and floating through fields of Day-Glo flowers, who hummed fitfully about the golden afternoon.

The ultimate sign that the ride was the troubled child of Disneyland was the value given her by the company. She was a B coupon. Twenty-five cents, two bits, just one notch better than a one-way bus ticket. No other dark ride was a B coupon.

After we got off the ride, we heard an amplified female voice singing. "Who's that?" I asked Vince. The voice was one moment similar to Astrud Gilberto, then Ella Fitzgerald, then Marianne Faithfull.

"I don't know," said Vince. "She's good, whoever she is."

We walked a few steps over to an area of tables and chairs that had been cordoned off just outside the Salada Tea concession. Signs standing on the pavement identified this as being the Salada "High Tea" Party. At four o'clock each afternoon you could sit at a table (if you could find one vacant), drink iced tea, and hear live entertainment.

The singing voice we heard was that of Alice herself. Understand that in the world of the Disney theme parks, there are "atmosphere characters" (those who dress up as Mickey, Goofy, Captain Hook) and "face characters" (costumed but unmasked, such as Snow White, Peter Pan, and Alice). The search for a Snow White or Alice was always particularly challenging because the faces of the animated characters had such a very distinctive look. Replicating this in real life couldn't be done simply by makeup because the face actors had to interact with the crowd from a foot or two away, in bright sunlight. In essence, they had to really *be* Snow White or Alice.

This exquisite, fairer-than-fair Alice was flanked by Tweedledee and Tweedledum, who were there both to work the crowd and to dance behind her as she sang songs from the musical score that bore her character's name.

She was singing my favorite song from that underappreciated score, "I Give Myself Very Good Advice," in which Alice laments that, while she certainly knows the difference between right and wrong and is able to give herself wise counsel, she tends to ignore her own advice and instead await the moment when something "strange" will begin. And no, it was *not* my favorite in the score because I in any way identified with it. Perish the thought.

A backup band dressed like four playing-card Jacks accompanied this otherworldly Alice who sang in such haunting fashion. She sounded a bit like a folksinger, a Joni Mitchell or a Judy Collins, although her voice transcended any category with its clarity and lilt. I looked at Vince and the crowd that had gathered. They were all listening intently.

And looking. Alice was so breathtakingly lovely that I could not even be jealous; it would have been like being jealous of Bardot when she was discovered by Roger Vadim at seventeen, or of a cave painting on the isle of Minos representing the ideal of youth. Her hair was fine but luxuriant, golden yellow with a rich bounce that had been waved into it. Her face was truly Alice's face (from the Disney version), unspeakably pretty with a small bow mouth and a dainty nose. As she sang, her lower lip would unknowingly pout a bit and her jaw tremble, not from fear but from her ethereal vibrato. Her eyes were full of white, and where they were watery blue, they were big and accepting. If you were close to her, you'd want to take that face in your hands and search it, trying to find what in its composition made it so exquisite.

She wore Alice's mandatory blue-and-white pinafore, the well-starched front of its "apron" stiff across her breasts. Her legs were in white stockings that ran for cover up the hem of her dress with a graceful curve, hiding amid a slew of petticoats. In this she differed a bit from Disney's Alice, who, I always thought, had been given cow legs. This Alice's legs were beautifully slim and tapered. Despite the absolute respectability of her hose, I am sure there were men in the crowd who looked at those white stockings and at where they went, and envisioned what they met there.

Her singing had momentarily transformed this small corner of the sun-drenched park into an intimate cabaret. She'd made her Alice song into a torch song, or perhaps it would be more accurate to call it a yearning song, like "Over the Rainbow." When she finished, the crowd that had gathered applauded her so loudly that passersby wondered what had elicited such a response and came over to see what they were missing.

Clapping enthusiastically, Vince asked me, "What do you think of her?"

I shouted over the applause to him, "How can she be that beautiful and sing so wonderfully?"

He nodded his head. "You know, they're probably paying her not a cent more than Tweedledee and Tweedledum there. I bet she's nonunion, too. So you definitely do think she's good?"

"I love her," I shouted back.

Alice was now making the rounds of the audience, which had formed a circle around the bandstand: curtseying to those who had something to say to her, shaking hands gently with children, introducing them to her friends Tweedle A and B, who were proficient at bumping into each other in a funny way and waving busy-fingered waves to the crowd. When someone in the crowd reached to touch Alice's hair, one Tweedle interposed his big belly between them and shook a scolding finger at the offender. It was clear that the two Tweedles were also doubling as "handlers," those who ventured out with Disney characters to serve as their bodyguards.

A determined look came over Vince's face, even behind his sunglasses and broad-brimmed hat. "Look, I want to help her out. She's too talented to be doing this for the next ten years. Trouble is, if I have my manager contact Disney, they'll give him a total runaround, we won't find out who she is, and meanwhile they'll realize what they've got and they'll sign her to a five-year contract. She'll never be heard of again. I've got to let her know who I am. Is that okay with you?" It was so different with Vince. Here he was, asking for my approval, my permission for him to be Vince Collins. He warned me, "I mean, you know if I get spotted by this crowd, it could get messy. You okay with that?"

"Speak to her. I'll try to block you as best as I can."

Alice was working her way around the circle. She shook hands with a little girl next to us.

"I hope you are having a nice time here today," she said in a skillful imitation of Kathryn Beaumont's voice from the Disney movie. She gestured at her costumed cohorts, who were playing a game of patty-cake behind her. One took a roundhouse swing at the other, who ducked it. Alice laughed to a nine-year-old, "I'm afraid my friends Tweedledee and Tweedledum are making quite a spectacle of themselves. What silly boys they are!" One of the "boys" hugged the other, and both were back to being friends. Alice smiled. "And the more they fight, the closer they become!"

She passed by us, and Vince called out, "Miss Alice!" and asked her for an autograph. When she saw the WED Guest card he offered for her to sign, she looked up at him, aware that this was someone whom the management viewed as a VIP.

Vince whipped off his sunglasses as I blocked the side view of his face. "Kiddo, listen, my name is Vince Collins, I do some singing myself. Do you recognize me?"

She put her hand to her chest in a very un-Alice gesture. She said, minus her British accent, "Oh, Mr. Collins. I grew up listening to your albums."

Vince smiled at me, amused by how her response aged him. He said to Alice, "Great, look, you sing incredibly well. Like Peggy Lee when she started, with some Blossom Dearie, too. I want you to promise me you'll keep at it. It's very hard in our industry. No one makes it. But you can make it." Vince pulled a business card from his wallet. He put a big grin on his face, so that anyone looking would think he was saying what a nice time he and the little woman were having here in Disneyland. He beamed at her, "Listen, I know you can't talk. This is the card of my manager, his name is Billy Bishop. Call him tomorrow. When the secretary tells you he's not in, say that 'Sir Ron Lyman' told you to call."

"Sir Ron Lyman," Alice repeated.

"Sir Ron Lyman. Billy will take your call when he hears that. We'll see if we can set up some auditions for you, for TV, records. You may not see me again, but the world is going to see you again. I want you to know that."

Alice took the card and quickly hid it in a pocket in her pinafore. She reverted to her British accent and cried out to the crowd, "Oh, I think I see the White Rabbit, I must follow him." She waved to Tweedledee and Tweedledum. "We must leave or the Queen of Hearts will be wanting my head! Good-bye everyone! Have a golden afternoon here in the Magic Kingdom!"

The two Tweedles flanked her protectively as she turned and rounded a corner. They were as effective at manipulating the crowd as entertaining it. As people started to follow the lovely blonde, the two intervened, pretending to be fighting again, allowing Alice to step over to an unmarked door in the side of the Mad Hatter's Hats concession. A Fantasyland security officer (dressed in a purple frock coat and green top hat) was keeping the door just slightly open. Alice ducked in and began her descent into the underground of the park—which Disney cast members referred to as "backstage"—where there were changing rooms for the employees and a break room where one could have a soda, a sandwich, or a smoke.

"Do you think she'll call?" I asked Vince as Dee and Dum followed Alice through the doorway and the crowd dissipated. We were now walking back toward Main Street, to depart via the same secret passage by which we'd arrived. Vince took off his cowboy hat for a moment and ran his fingers through his hair.

"Hard to say. She'd be risking her job if she did. But she can't play Alice in Wonderland forever." He looked at me as if he'd been foolish. "I wasn't trying to show off, you know."

"I know that." I did know that.

"You don't hear many fresh-sounding voices. I was a shameless Como impersonator when I started out; there was nothing original about me. It's exciting when somebody comes up with a new instrument."

Here Vince had taken the time to help this girl, running the risk that someone in the crowd would spot him and a mob scene would ensue, and he was afraid I'd think he was showing off. He and Lanny might at one time have been a duo, but they certainly were not a matching pair.

The drive back to L.A. was a bit depressing. We both knew that tomorrow we had things to discuss that were not going to be pleasant. We didn't talk about it, not one bit. Vince had put up the Skyliner's patented Hideaway roof, which lifted automatically out of the trunk, as the evening had gone quite cool. On the push-button radio, he tuned in a "Beautiful Music" station (a format that usually called for large doses of Mantovani and Tony Bennett) and we talked about the passing scenery until Vince's voice came over the radio singing *"Non Dimenticar."* He snapped off the radio and we drove for a long time without talking.

For dinner, he took me to the restaurant at the Hotel Bel-Air. It was quiet and comfortable there, he said, and very private. We parked near the reception office, which was in its own building, separate from the hotel. Getting to the restaurant required crossing over a lovely footbridge that spanned an idyllic pond. We stopped midbridge to look at the swan that floated sedately near a willow whose tendrils grazed the surface of the water. It looked to all intents and purposes exactly like the Disney rendition of the riverbank where Alice's older sister had been reading to her when her adventures began.

The swan was the logo of the Hotel Bel-Air. I'd seen its likeness at the main gate.

I indicated the swan to Vince, who looked more vulnerable without his cowboy hat and sunglasses, squinting into the setting sun. "Look at her," I said. "She's a trademark and doesn't even know it."

Vince grimaced. "There's a lot more she doesn't know. See, there are coyotes in these hills." He gestured to the scrubby slopes behind and above the low, elegant bungalows of the hotel. "Some nights they come down here and manage to kill the swan. There's no effective way to stop the coyotes, so it's easier for the hotel to simply have a ready supply of swans available to replace the dead ones on a regular basis."

I looked at him to see if he was joking, but clearly he wasn't. "That's horrible!" I responded. "But do coyotes swim?"

He shook his head. "They come down in pairs. The first coyote races toward the east bank of the pond, snarling like crazy, and this frightens the swan, who swims away and gets out of the water on the west bank. Where the other coyote is silently waiting. He kills her, and then the other coyote comes around the pond or over this bridge and the two of them share the feast."

I could picture the entire scenario. And as I pictured it, for some silly reason, I gave the coyotes the names Tweedledee and Tweedledum.

TWENTY-TWO

The next afternoon found me pulling up to Vince's home around three P.M. He had asked if we could start late, and I was all for obliging him. I wanted to be as reasonable as possible prior to giving him the third degree.

I parked my car in the motor court outside his home.

Basically, I had one edge going into this. I knew something about Vince (and Lanny) that he didn't know I knew. I had to play this one little ace up my sleeve as if I were holding a flush. First I had to question Vince all around the topic of the last night the two of them saw Maureen, knowing—as no one else knew—that she had died there in Florida at the Versailles, almost certainly in their hotel suite. If I watched Vince carefully, led him disingenuously around the terrain of that time period, perhaps he'd slip.

After I'd covered that time frame as much as I felt was credible, I then planned to lead him into related areas so that he'd feel as if he were out of the woods. I'd ask him how he felt about her death, how it had affected his working relationship with Lanny, did he believe the public's response to their partnership was altered by the sordid event, et cetera. I would let this become an airy and philosophical discussion.

That's when I'd have to steel my nerves and play my ace for its full worth. There would be one moment, and one moment only, when I could calmly say to him something like "*Yes, but when you packed her in the case with the lobsters and crabs, did you alert Sally Santoro's boys in New Jersey about this or were you planning to unpack her yourselves after you checked into the hotel?*" Perhaps this would not be the exact question (the moment and context would decide that), but it would certainly be the one and only time I could knock the wind out of him with one blow to the solar plexus. Then I'd have to bluff impeccably, putting across that this was merely one of many bits of inside information I had gleaned about Maureen's death.

The beauty of my position was that I was not with the police. I did not have to read Vince his rights. In point of fact, he did *not* have the right to remain silent. Just the opposite. He was contractually obligated to N&N to cough up what he knew. To any other interviewer, he could simply say, "No comment." Saying that to me would cost him a million dollars.

I walked through the walled-in courtyard to Vince's door. I liked him. I had a crush on him. I was going to sleep with him no matter what. Oh, I suppose if I found out that he was a murderer and turned him over to the Miami authorities, he should probably not expect a conjugal visit from me in prison. That reminded me that an electric chair nicknamed Old Sparky was still percolating away in Florida, doing an inhumanely inefficient and protracted job of burning its victims from the inside out.

Here comes Vince to the door. I hear his footsteps. Yes, there he is in a lightweight olive sweater with a turtleneck collar, black-and-gray trousers, black socks, black loafers. Someday I would help him off with his clothes. Let me see if I (eager and self-promoting young thing that I am) can bait and spring a saw-toothed trap for him.

"Hi." He smiled with a set about his lips that indicated this was not going to be his favorite afternoon. "Thanks for accommodating me on the time. We can go as late as you like."

Anything he casually offered I was going to nail to the table while it was out there. "That's good," I murmured. "I do think this may take us late into the evening."

He shut the door behind me and followed me into the house. He indicated the dining room. "I thought that might be the case," he said. "So I've arranged for a hot and cold smorgasbord to be brought in from Scandia's. I had them lay out the dining room for us. We can work through dinner if you like."

I looked in the dining room and saw place settings and matching linen, water and wineglasses, a full set of cutlery, including fish and salad forks, dessert plates, and coffee cups.

The table was set for three.

"We'll be having company?" I asked, a bit annoyed. If he thought that he was going to checkmate me by bringing in a third party, he was well mistaken. I watched from the dining room as he walked over to the living room couch, sat down, and lit a cigarette.

"Yes, I have a fairly big surprise for you." He took a drag and exhaled. "Actually it's a big thing for me as well. I've asked Lanny to join us today."

I felt as if an intravenous drip of ice water had just hit my bloodstream, and yet at the same time my mouth went dry.

"Lanny?"

Vince nodded, biting at his lower lip. "Yeah. You know, this will be the first time we've seen each other alone, at close quarters, in over thirteen years. Look at me." He stretched out his hand and there was a small shake to it, although Vince the actor could have been faking that quite easily. "I'm nervous as hell."

I sat down across from him. "Well, this is something," I tried to purr. "Neuman and Newberry are certainly getting their money's worth."

Vince shook his head. "I thought that if I was going to discuss for the record something that made such an impact on both of our lives, professionally and personally—we've declined to comment about the incident since it happened—I thought it would be only fair for Lanny to hear what I have to say and be given the chance to respond. There may be something he wants to add from his own recollection, or even contradict. My memory isn't always the best." He nodded toward his bar. "A lot of my gray cells have been put out of their misery over the years."

I started to unpack my tape recorder, still trying to figure what the hell I would do, but not wanting Vince to think I was anything but pleased about this development. "Well, it's going to be fabulous to meet Lanny," I chirped, reaching for my microphone. "I mean, in researching you, I've certainly read a ton about him as well." Oh, God help me, I couldn't get my brain to operate. I kept picturing Lanny walking in the door and seeing me for the first time. The first time since Bonnie Trout had fallen asleep in his arms at the Plaza hotel. "I'm sure I'll have a ton of questions for him. When is he due to arrive?"

"He couldn't be here until three-thirty, but he's always right on time.

I didn't even have his number—I had to have my manager call Irv Fleischmann to track it down." He took a last drag and stubbed out his cigarette. "I can't tell you what it was like to call him."

I smiled to cover my inner hysteria. "Oh, I think you *should* tell me. This is a huge event in both of your lives, and I'm just thrilled that I'll be here for it." Thrilled, yeah. The structure of my universe was being picked apart like a game of jackstraws.

What would I say when Lanny saw me? A fabulous wash of absolutely opposite and extreme emotions was churning inside me, like the first, formal introduction of nitro to glycerine. Yes, I was angry at Lanny. Yes, I was hurt. But this was simply that stupid "love" stuff. Lanny would say, "Bonnie?" And Vince would say, "What do you mean 'Bonnie'?" And then Lanny would no doubt explain to Vince that I had apparently wangled my way next to him on a flight to New York, lied about who and what I was, flirted with him until he had me right where I wanted him. Vince would look at me, think of our little agreement, and recall that I had certainly done my share of the propositioning with him—oh God, I was sunk. At best, Vince might continue to work on the book with me, but he'd hereafter perceive me as an unscrupulous whore who was not to be trusted in any way. Far more likely, he'd get on the phone with Neuman and Newberry and state that my behavior with his ex-partner was unethical and duplicitous, that he wanted me off the book, and that all my work thus far should be barred from publication. Oh, would Greg Gavin have a pipe-sucking festival with *that* crisis. If word ever got out in the trade (and it would, rest assured) that I'd blown their million-dollar advance by becoming sexually involved with one of the two men about whom I was writing, and done so while lying about my name, my address, my profession, my life story—in fact, being fraudulent about virtually everything except my orgasms . . .

My first reflex was to tell the truth. (I know. "Fancy that.") But what I'd done was so damning, even given my best presentation of the facts, that the truth offered me little more than the option of shooting myself in the head rather than facing a firing squad.

I had one dim candle of hope but very little time before Lanny's breezing in would snuff that right out. "Well, this is very exciting." I beamed. "If you don't mind, I'd just like to run to the powder room before Lanny gets here."

Vince looked wounded. "Oh, your makeup was fine for me, but for Lanny you need to touch yourself up?"

"No, actually, it's a 'woman thing,'" I said and excused myself. No man has ever challenged that answer and, to my knowledge, none has ever requested more specific information.

Vince's guest bathroom was, thankfully, not by the front door but down a dark paneled hallway to the right of the foyer. I opened the door and checked to see if Vince could see me, but luckily, I was angled out of his sight line, assuming he stayed put. I entered the bathroom, leaving the door open. It was all done in black lacquer, and I recognized the engravings on the wall by Piranesi, from his *Imaginary Prisons of Rome:* incredible vaulting arches supported narrow galleries bridging the way to staircases that descended hundreds of feet into the hopeless gloom of secret dungeons. I turned on the cold-water tap and then left the bathroom, shutting its door loudly as if I'd closed it behind me and I were still inside. I moved down the hall toward what Vince had once indicated to me was his bedroom. I'd not seen it yet, but I was about to.

I opened the door as quietly as I could manage. I had no time to note details, but it was done in various shades of rust and navy blue and very smart indeed. The bed was low and as big as a dance floor in a small nightclub; I still hoped to dance there with Vince someday.

I was praying he had a bedside phone, and my prayers were answered. It was a custom Italian designer model in maroon, and it was so sleek and stylish that I couldn't figure out where you talked into it or how you dialed. Fuck! I had to decrypt a MoMA award-winning designer's rethinking of a touch-tone. I found a button flush with the receiver and pushed it, heard the purr of an open line. I then hit zero and dialed a New York City number. The operator kicked in. "Collect call, Operator," I advised her in a whisper. She asked for (and I gave her) my name. I listened to dead air for about ten seconds. If Vince caught me making a surreptitious call here in his bedroom, I had no idea what explanation I could give, but it didn't matter. I was at least unhampered by doubts about the wisdom of what I was doing, just as a basketball player in the last second of a losing effort has no second thoughts about shooting an eighty-three-foot basket in an attempt to tie the game. Neither of us had any choice.

There was a discernible *click,* and the other end of the connection rang on the line. It was six-twenty P.M. in New York. Everything depended on

Beejay having gotten home on time and not having gone anywhere since. On the fourth ring I actually felt the sting of self-pity welling in the corners of my eyes; then I was pulled back to life by a sharp *click* on the line. I wiped away my twin tears with my left index finger as I heard Beejay's voice, heard her say yes to accepting the phone call, and I had her.

"Beejay, I have to talk fast."

"I'm glad, kiddo, 'cause if you're in L.A., I can't afford you calling collect."

"Beejay, I need you to do exactly what I tell you, and I have no time to tell you why, okay?"

"Yeah yeah yeah, shoot."

One minute later I walked out of Vince's bedroom. I heard him doing something in the kitchen and was able to duck into the bathroom, quietly opening and closing the door behind me. I turned off the faucet and flushed the toilet for further effect.

It was three twenty-four, and if Lanny was even a minute early, this wasn't going to work. I strolled back from the bathroom and found Vince staring at the view that filled his wide windows, a veritable relief map of downtown Los Angeles. He gazed thoughtfully at nothing in particular. I adopted the most casual, glib manner I could muster, considering that I wanted to make like Peter Lorre in *Casablanca* and beg, "Rick, hide me!"

"Sorry if I was long," I said breezily.

Vince half-smiled. "You never hear *men* apologizing on that account." He stepped away from the window. As he did so, I noticed that behind him on an end table alongside one of his low couches was a multiline telephone with five clear, square buttons and a red hold button to the left of them. I realized that if, as was likely, the bedroom phone was one of those lines, then when I had picked up the phone in Vince's bedroom, it would have illuminated one of the buttons on the master phone in the living room. Of course, as long as Vince was staring out the window at that time, or occupied in the kitchen, or doing anything but looking at the phone, I was okay. If not, I was surely suspect, as there was no one else in the house. But again, in a strangely blissful way, I had no choice but to brazen it out until either I escaped or the whole mess exploded in my face. Like an expert defusing an atomic bomb while a timer ticked down from sixty seconds, I could only try to clip the right wire. At this point, running for cover would be of no use.

I flopped down on the couch as if I'd be staying there forever. "Well, this is pretty damn exciting, Vince," I gushed, plugging my microphone into the recorder. "The only question for me is, will Lanny let me record what he has to say? I guess we'll have to ask him that when he gets h—"

The phone rang. I saw the third translucent button flash slowly.

It rang a second time. I waited for Vince to answer it, but he was looking only at me, interested in the end of my sentence. The phone rang for the third time. I smiled casually. "It's okay, you can get that."

Vince waved dismissively. "No, that's the number I give to the press, people I'm working with short-term, you know, landscapers." Of course, this was the number that Vince had given *me,* which I had given Beejay. "I don't answer it unless I'm expecting one of them to call. Otherwise it rolls over to my office."

The ringing stopped.

At this point my fate was in the hands of Beejay. I could only act as if everything was sunny and fine. "Well, tell me, did you speak to Lanny directly on the phone?" I asked in as reportorial a fashion as I could manage. Vince nodded a grim yes and I pressed ahead: "What was that like? I know you haven't seen each other in over a decade, but have you ever spoken on the—"

There was a louder ringing sound from his phone than before, and my eyes could see the right-most button flashing.

Vince muttered, "Excuse me, that might actually be Lanny," and instantly picked up the phone. He listened and looked at me with concern. "It's my office, there's a woman, a friend or relative of yours, it wasn't clear. She says she called on the number you gave her, my number. Says there's a problem, your family . . ."

I stepped quickly to the phone, and Vince handed it over watchfully. "Yes?" I asked. I was speaking to Vince's secretary, the woman I'd met at the Burbank Studios. She told me much the same as Vince had just said, and that my friend or relative would call back again on the same line as before, only Vince would pick up this time.

Almost in the same instant, the third line rang. Vince took the phone back from me, answered, and handed me the receiver.

"Hello?" I asked, concerned.

"Hi, kiddo," said Beejay. "Now listen, your brother Clifford has just been rushed to the hospital. He was doing some construction work when a thing—"

"A steel girder?" I asked in a concerned voice.

"That's it. So you better get back to the city and make your peace with him, 'cause the doctors don't think he'll last the night. I've booked you on the next flight via American Airlines, I'm waiting here for you in front of the terminal. I'll drive your car home for you."

"Thank you, Sharon," I said to Beejay and hung up. Vince watched what I hoped was my controlled hysteria as I first started packing up my recorder, then abandoned the task. It was three twenty-seven. "Can I leave this stuff here, Vince? I have to go to the airport. It's my brother. They say he may have very little time."

"How can I help?" he asked, concerned.

I shook my head. "They've reserved me a seat on the next American flight to New York. I have to get to the airport this instant." I grabbed my pocketbook and was already moving to the door. I hoped he would view my rudeness simply as touching, sisterly concern.

Vince walked with me. "I'll get you a ride there."

Behind me, I heard the loud "hot" line of his phone ringing again, but Vince ignored it. I waved him off. "No, Sharon is waiting at the airport for me. I'll turn my car over to her at the white zone for the loading and unloading, you know. It will be quicker than if I wait for someone to pick me up here." I was through the courtyard now.

"I'll drive you in my car," he said.

"What, and have you stand up Lanny Morris? Then the two of you won't talk for another dozen years. It's easier and faster this way." I had reached my Caprice. A few more steps and Lanny would never see my face. "My deepest apologies to Mr. Morris and, of course, to you, Vince."

I was behind the wheel, turning the ignition. Even if Lanny arrived now, if I could just be pulling out of the driveway, I could probably angle my face so he wouldn't recognize me through the windshield as I drove by. In a movie, the car wouldn't start and I'd struggle with the ignition, but the car did start (suddenly my car wasn't so pathetic) and the wheels spat gravel as I pulled away from Vince.

All down Tortuoso, I kept waiting for Lanny's car or limousine to pass me as he ascended the hill. I'd quickly put on my sunglasses and wrapped a scarf around my head. I thought that under the circumstances it would be difficult for him to recognize "Bonnie Trout" behind the wheel, and I kept my head as low as I could without losing sight of the road. I also twisted my mouth like a character out of *Dick Tracy* to further distort my appearance. I wished I could take the descent faster than thirty miles per hour, but with the road's extreme turns and unrailed edge, there was simply no way. However, by the time I got to Sunset Boulevard, I'd encountered no limos nor had I passed any driver who looked anything like Lanny.

Now my body allowed the adrenaline level in my system to drop to normal. All the icy thoughts of dread and panic that I had fended off were melting into a flood of slush, which I felt rushing down into the pit of me. It was terrifying how close I'd come to being exposed in the most awful way. I could hardly breathe, and I found myself jumping a red light to try to outrun the feeling, but it was no use. Once paranoia is in full bloom, it's difficult to uproot, and in my case, my anxiety had been as justified as that of a whore strolling the alleys of Whitechapel circa 1888.

Home was the one place I didn't want to go for the moment. Vince might have noticed his bedroom phone line being lit only two minutes before my emergency phone call. As a matter of fact, there'd been a click on the line that I'd assumed was the phone system, but that might have been Vince on the living room extension. Vince knew where I lived, and in case he had his doubts about my poor brother's accident, or if he good-naturedly decided to leave a note for me, I didn't want him to find me walking in or out my door when I was supposedly on a plane to New York.

I turned right on Sunset, away from both our homes. Fairly soon, I saw a sign for the San Diego Freeway south. It came into my head that if I wanted to work as much truth as I could into my lie, as was my policy, it would be a good idea to take the Freeway to LAX, as if I *had* in fact been going to catch the next American Airlines flight to New York. I could see how long that would have taken, see what flight would have been the logical one for "Sharon" to have booked me on, and when it was supposed to arrive at either JFK or La Guardia. For all I knew, Vince, who was a very thoughtful guy, might call American Airlines himself to see when that was, when I might arrive, if the flight was delayed. It would help my recounting to base it on as much reality as possible. I certainly had nothing better to do with my afternoon.

I parked my car in the lot near the American Airlines terminal and headed over to the ticket counter to look at the Arrivals and Departures display. There was a nonstop to JFK at 4:30 P.M. Flight 49. It was the last of their flights out of LAX to New York until the red-eye left at ten P.M. for a dawn arrival. The 4:30 P.M. was the flight I would have taken, and I would have just barely made it had I really been trying to catch it, but the Departures board said it was now scheduled to leave thirty minutes later. That was good to know. I'd have to wait and see when the plane actually left, in case the flight got canceled. Fearful of being caught in a lie, I was collecting data as if creating a detailed alibi for a murder I planned to commit.

I thought of another piece of information that would be useful to know. I walked over to the ticket counter and asked a pleasant-faced women, "Could you tell me how much a ticket is to New York if I bought it right now, one-way, economy?"

She nodded enthusiastically. "I know," she said, apparently agreeing with me about something. "People come up to me and they've heard about it and they still don't believe it. Up through next Thursday, ninety-nine dollars each way. The flight can't be rescheduled, though, without having to pay the regular full fare, and you have to return within fourteen days." She looked very pleased. "People ask me what the catch is, and I tell them the catch is that TWA lowered their rates, so our boss is undercutting them. American can absorb the loss because we're bigger. And, we like to think, better. When did you want to leave?"

I instantly decided it would be worth eating ninety-nine dollars to have a receipt for my emergency flight. The tickets always came in layers of three. I could "accidentally" leave the receipt for the ticket on Vince's coffee table one day, and later call and ask if he'd found it, since I needed it for tax purposes. To have concrete validation of my flight seemed cheap at any price. I wondered if there would be any problem when I didn't take the plane. The airlines were getting warier of letting a plane take off when a no-show passenger's luggage had already been checked on board. But I wasn't *going* to be checking any luggage. People missed their flights all the time. I'd missed more than one, and no one had ever held the plane for me. It would be fine. I'd stay at the cheapest hotel at LAX and "return" to Los Angeles and my home late tomorrow night. Instead of killing off my nonexistent brother Clifford (which would necessitate my having to stay in New York for his funeral, et cetera), I'd plunge him into a deep coma and let him remain a vegetable until well after my book with Vince was published.

I gave the American Airlines clerk my MasterCharge card and told her pointedly that I had no luggage to check. She took a look at the Departures board; the flight was now scheduled to depart from Gate 4A at five-fifteen.

I went up to the Flight Deck Bar and readied myself to have a leisurely, much needed Scotch and soda while I waited to see when the flight I would miss actually managed to leave. I sat back against a black leatherette banquette and eagerly caught the eye of a waitress. She was still in the miniskirt and black mesh stockings she'd been issued in the mid-sixties, and even then she'd been a little too old for the outfit. Her name was Teena, or she had stolen Teena's name tag out of sheer envy. I looked and saw that the bar had neither Ballantine's nor Chivas. "Dewar's and soda, please."

I sat there, eyeing the Departures board to see if Flight 49 to JFK was being delayed further (and what did I care?), listening to Tom Jones sing "Delilah" over the American Airlines P.A. system, when Tom suddenly spoke my name. He said my name twice and asked me to pick up the nearest courtesy phone and ask for Guest Relations. It took me a moment to realize that the music had stopped and that this was an American Airlines employee speaking over the P.A. I asked Teena if the bar had a courtesy phone. It did.

The woman at the Guest Relations extension said there was an emergency phone call for me and that she was connecting me now. It was Vince. "I'm amazed I caught you," he said. "When does your flight leave?"

What an absolute godsend that I was here when he called. Now my story was rock solid. "It was supposed to leave twenty minutes ago. At the moment they're saying five-fifteen, but who knows." I looked at my ticket and reeled off the detailed information impressively. "American Airlines Flight 49 departs LAX four-thirty P.M., arrives JFK twelve forty-five A.M."

"Flight 49, that's what I figured. You said American, and I know that's the last one of the day. I've taken it myself a couple of times. You get the tailwinds, which knocks fifteen, twenty minutes off the flight. Listen, I ordered a limousine to pick you up at JFK. He'll be holding a sign that says 'O'Connor.' This way, no matter how long the flight is delayed, you'll have someone who can take you directly to your brother."

Oh God. "Oh no, Vince, no. My family's going to meet me."

He wouldn't have any of this. "I'm sure they don't want to leave your brother's side. And they'd have to get out to JFK after midnight and they'd have to park the car. It's already booked with Fugazy. The driver's name is

Adolfo, I know him—the airport police always let him park right by the baggage claim area, so you'll walk out and you'll be on your way. He knows all the quickest routes. You want me to call your family for you? I'll let them know they don't have to pick you up. What's their number?"

"No, no, I'll call them," I said. "It's very nice of you, Vince. Very thoughtful. But really, you know, I'd much prefer—"

"Have you heard anything about how your brother is doing, and what hospital he's at?"

What hospital. If I said anything, he'd have flowers or surgeons on their way. Even if I didn't, he would just have his secretary start calling every hospital in Manhattan searching for a patient named O'Connor who'd been admitted in the last six hours. I had to at least block that from happening. "Vince, he's not in Manhattan, he's in—hold on, I think they may be calling—and his name isn't O'Connor, he's my half brother, it's—Vince, sorry, they're boarding my plane, thanks so much, I'll call you when I know where I'm staying and let you know what's going on." Go ahead, let his goddamn secretary accrue a list of every patient in every borough except Manhattan whose name is anything other than O'Connor.

"Hey, wait, you haven't—" Vince began.

"I have to call my family and tell them they don't have to meet me. Thanks so much for the limo, Vince." I hung up the phone. Fuck. "Fuck-fuck-fuck-fuck-fuck!" I cursed, causing Teena to race my drink over to me and fearfully set it down at the bar.

I was going to have to take the next frigging plane to New Fucking York. For no good reason other than to let Adolfo report that he had picked me up successfully.

I could think of no way around it. If I didn't show up, Adolfo would call his dispatcher at Fugazy, and Vince, worried, would start searching even harder for me and my brother Clifford. The only hope I had was that goddamned Flight 49 would be scrubbed completely. If so, I'd kill off Clifford tonight and say that in his will, he'd requested there be no funeral.

I took a big pull on the ample Dewar's and soda that Teena had brought over. My mouth reacted, my lips reflexively drew back across my teeth. It tasted really weird, but I didn't think Scotch could go bad. I tried the drink again and detected the strange sweet-tartness of quinine.

"You made me a Scotch and *tonic*!" I yelled at the bartender. His stupid thumb had hit the Q button on one of those hateful multifunction spritzers instead of the S button.

He was going over receipts with Teena. "Oops. Call me Mr. Dumb-Thumb!" he laughed, forgiving himself with ease. "Make you a fresh one in a minute," he said affably. "No extra charge."

"All passengers for Flight 49 destined for New York JFK International Airport must now be boarding at Gate 4A. This will be the only boarding call for all passengers in economy and first class. Final call for Flight 49—"

The bartender was nowhere close to finishing his totals. I took the Scotch and tonic, gritted my teeth, and downed it in two long pulls. I slammed a five-dollar bill onto the bar and started rushing and cursing my way to Gate 4A, which I knew would be nowhere as near as "4A" might sound, and I was right. God help me, I was taking a cross-country flight for no purpose, I'd have a limo waiting to take me to a hospital where I had no business—and then I also remembered I was flying economy on the last flight home for the day, seating configuration three-five-three with an undoubtedly packed house. I'd have to beg and cajole the stewardess for a miniature of Dewar's at two bucks a pop, and when I wanted a third, she'd tell me they'd locked up the liquor cabinet because they were arriving so late, whatever that would mean. The meal would be meat à la thing with a tiny roll and a three-greens salad, meaning that's how many lettuce leaves there'd be to soak up my plastic thimble of Kraft French dressing. I had no book to read, no yellow legal tablet, no bevy of Bic pens with which to write. And the in-flight movie would turn out to be *The Black Windmill.* Arguably the worst film ever made that starred Michael Caine.

TWENTY-THREE

It got worse, of course. I found myself in the highly uncoveted center seat of three, between a keypunch operator named Rory who wore a necklace of hand-carved African fertility symbols (although he himself was Caucasian) whose various symbolisms he felt compelled to explain to me in detail and a heavyset fellow who never introduced himself because he was busy snoring.

I determined that there had to be something good or useful I could harvest out of this astoundingly pointless trip other than seeing Beejay, who at two A.M. was not going to be that thrilled about seeing me.

I knew I had already played around far too much with both of these boys. Some aphorism my mother had imparted to me about mud and lying with pigs came vaguely to mind, although only Lanny could sustain the analogy. Vince had been far from hoggish and nothing but a gentleman. I, on the other hand, had been every bit the unsavory sow. Once, after a particularly unpleasant sexual encounter when I was nineteen, I had had the momentary wish that I could move to another town and be a virgin all over again. I wished there was a way to do that now, to get clean again.

Another town.

As before, the most clean I ever felt in this matter was when I dedicated my concern to Maureen O'Flaherty. I had no idea how much danger either of the boys represented to me nor how dark that unholy night in Miami had been, and I would never know any of that until I had answered the question Maureen's mother had wanted me to ask the boys. I would now make it *my* overriding question as well.

Why did Maureen have to die?

Not whether it was Vince or Lanny or both of them. Not which minion of Sally Santoro's might have put her dead body in the tub or what hold the mob boss would then have had over either of the boys. Simply the "why" of her death. Once I had that, I suspected that the answers to all my other questions would come rushing at me like sharks to a swimmer with a nosebleed.

Nothing in my research in either Los Angeles or New York had brought me closer to the truth. I'd gleaned little from Palisades Park or the O'Flahertys' home in New Rochelle. But wedged in my economy seat, I remembered the little shrine Mrs. O'Flaherty had assembled on the dresser in her austere bedroom. And I remembered being amused by the return address on a postcard Maureen had mailed her parents from Florida. It would be easy enough to call Mrs. O'Flaherty in the morning and ask her to give me the full address over the phone.

I was flying to the East Coast for no good reason. There was nothing I could do about that now. But if tomorrow I then flew from JFK to Miami, the flight would be two and a half hours shorter than if I'd flown to Miami from Los Angeles. It was not a powerful rationale for the flight I was currently taking, but it would make me feel a shade less stupid about having taken it.

We landed at something close to our originally scheduled ETA, there being at that hour no delay in getting landing clearance. The charming Adolfo was indeed there at the exit from the baggage-claim area, holding a sign marked O. CONNER, which I took to be me. I asked Adolfo to wait while I made a call from a pay phone. I called Information and, in what I hoped for Adolfo's benefit was an agitated voice, told the operator I needed the phone number of a hospital where my injured brother had been taken. All I knew was that it was not too far from JFK airport.

"Do you have a name for the hospital?" the operator asked. I said that I thought it began with the word *Saint*. She said she had a number of those in the area. She named a Saint Mary's in Far Rockaway, which seemed a credible distance, not too far, but enough of a drive to give Adolfo something to do. She gave me the address as well as the number and wished my brother a speedy recovery.

I told Adolfo the address and he said he knew where that was. I sat back in the limo and noticed three cut-glass decanters, a small bucket of ice, and some sparkling-clean tumblers set into a mahogany bar planted midway between my seat and two rear-facing jump seats. I helped myself to ice and reached for the decanter filled with brown liquid. It was probably Johnnie Walker Red, not my favorite, but who was I to complain? I would have asked Adolfo to play some music, but I thought that might seem odd. A woman flying in to visit her dying brother might need a stiff drink to bolster her nerves, but she probably wouldn't need to hear Steely Dan.

We pulled up to the emergency-room dock at Saint Mary's, the only entrance open at this hour. Adolfo intended to go in with me, but I told him there was no need for him to be waiting in an emergency room full of sick people and the victims of knife and gun wounds. This depiction mollified his eagerness, and he told me he'd stay right there until I knew more.

A small desk served as the sentry post for the emergency room, manned by a Russian woman who'd seen everything and was reading a romance novel. I asked her if anyone had been admitted there in the last twelve hours with a head injury. She said she'd need a name. I said the name was "Cledrow Gommelfarver." I spelled it for her and made her check for the name twice. I figured that if anyone (such as this mythical and unlikely private detective whom I'd fantasized Vince hiring) were to ask her the name that *I'd* asked for, even if she remembered it accurately it would sound like she hadn't heard it properly. "Something like Cledrow Gommelfarver," she'd say in her heavy accent, and the detective would roll his eyes. That's if she remembered. My guess was she'd simply say it was a funny name she'd never heard before.

I didn't actually think Vince was going to hire a private detective. I didn't even think he doubted my story. I just wanted to play it safe.

I returned to the car, looking grim and heartbroken. Adolfo looked concerned.

"I was too late," I said bitterly.

Bye, Cliffy. We hardly knew ye.

Adolfo crossed himself and apologized for not having gotten here faster. I reassured him: "No, no, he passed away before my plane landed. His last words were 'No tears.'" I said this primarily because I wasn't a good enough actress to credibly cry on demand. Better I play the stoic. "His body isn't even here; it's at a funeral home in Rego Park."

Adolfo offered to drive me there, even if it was now well after midnight. I shook my head. "No, they're flying his ashes down to South Florida tomorrow, where he was born. There will be a ceremony there, and his remains will be scattered throughout the Everglades he loved so well." Adolfo nodded compassionately.

I asked Adolfo if he'd be kind enough to drive me back to JFK. I'd check in at the Hilton hotel there ("Not that I'll get any sleep," I sighed) and take the first available flight to Miami in the morning.

Adolfo got me to the Hilton, gave me his personalized Fugazy card, and said if I needed anything at all, I should not hesitate to call him. I pointed out that the regular airport shuttle would get me to the Air Florida ticket window in under ten minutes. I tried to tip him but he refused it, saying it was included in the billing.

The Hilton was used to individuals staggering in at three A.M. minus their luggage, their connecting flight canceled, who preferred to rent a room for a few hours than to spend the night in a plastic chair at the terminal. The night clerk asked if I needed a wake-up call in the morning. I asked for a seven A.M. call.

I got to my room, took off all my clothes, and hung them in the bathroom, where I'd let my morning shower steam some of the wrinkles out of them for me. I flipped on the TV, turned to Channel 2 for what was left of the Late, Late Show, and yanked the bedspread and the thin blanket off the bed. As I lay down on the cool sheets, a public service commercial ended and we went back to the movie. It would have been fitting if the movie had featured Vince and Lanny, or at least Michael Caine, but it was *The Quiet Man,* with John Wayne and the hauntingly lovely Maureen O'Hara. The two were being driven by Barry Fitzgerald on their first date; John looked handsome, but I only had eyes at this moment for Maureen, lovely Maureen, her opulently red hair giving the TV set quite a challenge in the tint-and-hue department. As I fell asleep, Maureen was smiling sadly on the screen, with a questioning look in her eyes that was surely intended only for me.

TWENTY-FOUR

Before she'd died, Maureen O'Flaherty had lived in Hollywood, Florida, if one believed the return address on a postcard she'd sent her mother. When I called Mrs. O'Flaherty early that next morning from my hotel room, I'd needed the first line of the address—"7GW c/o Ludlow"—and the street number I'd seen on the postcard, but I'd remembered the street's name, because at the time, it had amused me: "North Dixie." Surely an oxymoron to rival "Glen Campbell Special." Living fifteen miles north of Miami Beach, Maureen would have had an easy commute to the several hotels and nightclubs at which she'd worked as a waitress.

So having been to Manhattan on the West Coast by way of the New York street set Vince had shown me, I was now surveying a Hollywood on the East Coast for whatever remnants I could find of Maureen O'Flaherty.

I located 1350 North Dixie at the corner of McKinley Street (the cross streets to Hollywood's Dixie Highway being named after our chief executives from Washington through Coolidge, rising from the south to north in order of succession). It was one of many porcelain-white, gray-mortar mid-rise apartment buildings that had been slapped up twenty-five years ago. Its facing was now cracked and spackled by time, heat, and the occasional fusillade of a tropical rainstorm. Just outside its entrance, a man in his early sixties was seated in an aluminum lawn chair with a webbing of interwoven white and teal plastic. He sported a uniform that only partially conceded he was the building's doorman: dark brown pants with a gold stripe running up each trouser leg, teamed with a yellow T-shirt that said I CAN'T BELIEVE I ATE THE WHOLE THING! His comb-over began virtually at one ear and ended just short of the other to form a shiny helmet over his skull. To make it worse, he'd streaked his hair with blond highlights. I could smell his Hai Karate aftershave from the end of the walk.

Upon my arrival in Miami, I'd rented a cool blue Camaro and driven it to Burn, Baby, Burn, a very trendy boutique that dished up dreamy, elegant outfits that seemed always on the verge of slipping off one's body. I'd opted for a conservative number that still looked like I'd jumped into something comfortable and nearly missed. I could see the doorman perking up as I sashayed toward him.

"Hot out." I smiled.

"I got cold Budweiser in the fridge in my apartment," he offered. Jesus. It was eleven-thirty in the morning, he was at least thirty years older than me, I hadn't said more than two words, and *still* he was giving it a shot. "My name's Tony," he added.

"I could go for one and that's for sure, but," I sighed, "can you give me a rain check till later this afternoon? Right now I'm working." I tilted my hips to one side as if to explain. "I'm Jill. You run this place, right?"

He nodded. "Pretty much."

I lowered my voice. "You remember a party in Apartment 7GW named Ludlow? Back in the late fifties?"

"I ought to. I talked with him about an hour ago."

As they say in the sacred liturgy of the Catholic Church: bingo. Forty bucks cash got Tony Gebbia to open up like a blown-glass piñata.

Ludlow in 7G West was Kef Ludlow, and judging by both his appearance and some idle conversation over the last fifteen years, Tony estimated the man's age to be about the same as his own. Kef's occupation had always been a murky issue. The one thing Tony knew for sure was that Ludlow was enslaved to the dog races, attending them five days a week. He'd have gone seven days, but they were closed on Sundays and Mondays, not so the dogs might rest but so that the personnel could.

Sometimes Tony got the impression that Ludlow had something to do with the gambling that was associated with greyhound racing. Tony ventured that he might be a bookie. This, in the family tree of organized crime, seemed very low to the ground, being to gambling what podiatry was to medicine. The local betting at the dog tracks in Florida was done on a pari-mutuel basis, with the track and the state deducting their cut, and it was hard to envision any big-time gamblers getting worked up because Bowser in the fifth was showing long odds and Spot had just been spayed.

In the late fifties, it seemed as if Ludlow had hit a run of luck, either because he was picking a string of winners or (if he *was* in fact a bookie) because his customers were not. He'd stopped taking public transportation and had purchased a used Buick LeSabre the size of a small yacht. Ludlow started bringing home fewer groceries and eating out more. The doggie bags he came home with were from places like the Embers and the Lobster Trap, first-class steak-and-seafood joints. One year at Christmas he tipped Tony a twenty-dollar bill.

Sunday through Thursday in this time frame he'd leave the building at eight in the morning. He'd be wearing a straw panama and a lightweight white jacket with blue vertical stripes (Tony said it was made from thin crinkly material, which I took to mean seersucker) over a blue wash-and-wear short-sleeved shirt with white pants and a white belt. Some days Ludlow wore a tie. On these mornings he always sported a pair of prescription sunglasses (at the dog races, he wore only his regular glasses, as he felt that shades limited his powers of observation). He'd usually be whistling; "Lemon Tree" was a recurring favorite. In his hand would be a manila envelope. About a half hour later, still whistling, he'd return to his apartment. On Tuesdays, Wednesdays, and Thursdays he'd reappear ten minutes later, having changed into a more casual outfit of polo shirt and navy blue polyester pants, and he'd be off to the dog races. On Sundays and Mondays, when the track wasn't open, he'd come back from his errand and stay in his apartment. You could hear his TV through the door; he tended to like wrestling, jai alai, and baseball.

On Fridays and Saturdays he would not go out in the early morning but simply head straight to the greyhound track around eleven, dressed in his more casual outfit.

The lucky streak lasted only so long. By 1960, he'd sold his LeSabre, complaining that it used too much gas for city driving, and instead waited for the Number 24 bus two blocks north on Taft to take him to the races each day. He'd leave only at eleven, no longer at eight, with a brown-bag lunch he'd made the night before. He didn't whistle much anymore, nor did he eat out. Hamburger Helper started to appear at the top of his grocery bags. He said you didn't even need the hamburger most of the time, or certainly nowhere near as much as the box suggested; a little Mazola oil and oleomargarine added to the mix would serve you just fine.

Of Ludlow's family, Tony knew nothing. His mail, when Tony saw it, was very ordinary and usually addressed to "Occupant." In the glory years, he got *TV Guide* every week, but later he said that the schedule in the newspaper was just as good. Packages that wouldn't fit in the mailbox would be under Tony's supervision, but Tony couldn't remember anything unusual arriving for Ludlow in all the time he'd been there. Every five years, maybe a box of new checks from Florida First National Bank. Once, a package from Marboro Books had been delivered half-opened and Tony had seen its contents. One volume was called *How to Beat the Pari-Mutuel Racket!* The other was a photo essay book called *The Art of the Nude,* with lots of color photos.

After I'd drained Tony Gebbia (a process that made me feel like Dracula sucking on a hemophiliac) on the topic of Kef Ludlow—who took no vacations, had no visitors, and was a relative stranger to those who lived alongside him on the seventh floor west—I then produced two more twenties and explained to Tony that the focus of my interest was much more in a roommate Ludlow might have had during the late fifties.

Tony's eyes narrowed a bit. "You mean the redhead?" I nodded and he warmed to the subject. "What a piece of ass *she* was. She could've sat on my face all day like I was a lawn chair and you'd never have heard me complain about it. When I read she was dead, up in New Jersey, I said, 'Hey, if nobody else wants the body, I'll take it.'" He smirked at the pithiness of his observation.

I wanted to spit in his face, but I needed to know what he knew. I asked how long she'd lived with Ludlow.

"Not so long and not very often. I don't think it was a full-time thing. I never knew what their story was. He was, I don't know, maybe twenty years older than her. He was no ladies' man, I'll tell you, even back then. Has a nose like Durante. I think he may have just been putting her up but not getting anything, although he liked us thinking he was. She must have been coming in like at two or three in the morning, 'cause although I saw her leave the building once or twice a week, usually in the late afternoon, I hardly ever saw her getting in. The only times I did were when she came in so late she'd be walking in as I went to meet the garbage pickup. She used to joke about us both wearing uniforms." He indicated his pants. "Back then I wore the whole thing, shirt, clip-on bow tie, even the jacket, if it wasn't too hot. She always wore her hotel uniform home 'cause she worked part-time in different hotels and it was easier to keep all her outfits in one place. She'd had the pants altered so they really tucked tight around her ass, then she had the jackets shortened so you could see it, and then she moved the buttons on her jacket and shirt so you could see some of her tits."

My guess was that Maureen prided herself on her looks and that her work uniforms were standard issue, designed for men. I'm sure she found, pragmatically, that men tipped attractive women better than dumpy women. It was likely worth the investment on her part in order to garner sizable gratuities from the Miami Beach fat cats and celebrities she served.

Tony Vermin was still prattling on. "She liked me a lot. We could have had a thing, but our schedules were too different." Yeah, that was it. Just the scheduling. Otherwise, Tony would have been a shoo-in for getting into Maureen's tailored pants. Same problem for Tony with Kim Novak. Opposite coasts. Ah, what might have been.

She'd gotten a couple of letters at Ludlow's address; he knew this because the postman had been confused and had asked Tony if there was an O'Flaherty in 7GW. He admitted to snapping back, "Yeah, but it doesn't mean Ludlow's dicking her," which was probably more of an answer than the U.S. postal worker had required. Not a lot of mail had come to her, though. What letters he'd seen were from New Rochelle, New York.

Sometimes a week or two would go by without him seeing her at all. He'd ask Ludlow about her, and Ludlow always had a similar response. He'd say something along the lines of "I'm a lucky guy, Tony" or "She's beautiful, isn't she?" Answers that told Tony next to nothing but allowed Ludlow to lord it over him for a moment.

When she'd died, *The Miami Herald* had printed a photo of her in her Versailles uniform, identifying her as Maureen O'Flaherty. Tony said that when he saw it, he thought, "Now I'm *never* gonna screw her," and in a dark way, it was the funniest thing I'd ever heard said in conjunction with the poor girl's death.

Ludlow had apparently taken it very hard. He barely emerged from his apartment for almost a month. Finally, the call of the hounds must have drawn him out of his seclusion. His life evolved into what it was now, a shuttle between Hallandale Beach, where the Hollywood Greyhound Track was located, and McKinley Street. For the months in the summer when the dogs didn't run, you could still play poker or dominoes there, but Ludlow wasn't crazy about this, and he was more inclined to restlessly hang around Gulfstream Park, the nearby horse-racing track, where they ran the Breeders' Cup each year. He'd bet only on the daily double and almost never won.

Exactly what he did by way of vocation to meet the cost of his meager lifestyle was as much a mystery fifteen years after Maureen's death as it had been in the fifties. Maybe he did just well enough with the dogs to keep him in Hamburger Helper for the rest of his life.

I asked Tony if there was somewhere at the greyhound track I could find Ludlow. He said he knew from talking with Ludlow that, just as in horse racing, there was a paddock area where the greyhounds were paraded around before the races started, at two. Ludlow tried never to miss this. He considered himself good at determining from this look-see which dogs were likely to win. "Like I said, you can't miss him. Nose like Durante. Big black head of hair for a man his age, probably a toup'. All you have to do is ask anyone who works there. They all know him."

I thanked him for his trouble and slipped him another twenty. He smiled seductively. "How about that Budweiser?" he asked.

I nodded enthusiastically. "I know, that Budweiser is really something, isn't it?"

To me it was a pretend racetrack, like one of those children's play kitchens with miniature boxes of Pillsbury cake mix with which you could make a cupcake in an oven heated by a lightbulb. It had one pair of washrooms, one cocktail lounge, and three ticket windows, like a train station in Utica. There was an undernourished feel about it, but nowhere near as undernourished as the wretched canines who worked there.

The greyhounds were raised to be fast, desperate, thin, and, in particular, famished. This fourth commodity somewhat guaranteed the first three. The only part about starving that was counterproductive was that when they had no food, they had less energy. But that's where desperate (for the reward of food) kicked in.

I found Ludlow in the paddock, looking over today's and tomorrow's contenders. He fit the description Tony had given me, and his identity was verified by a sleepy security guard.

Ludlow was taking lots of notes on a racing form, flipping back a page now and then to cross-reference some bitch's progeny. Imagine Walter Matthau without the charm and you have Kef Ludlow: a sour-faced man with a shock of black hair of which he was not the original owner, a prominent nose that instantly evoked the Great Schnozzola without the greatness, and beady eyes so rheumy he seemed permanently on the verge of weeping. Or perhaps his eyes weren't rheumy at all.

He was tall, perhaps over six feet, but his stooped shoulders and receding chest brought him right back down to earth. He didn't have a potbelly, but his stomach and thighs were those of a slightly stockier person.

He got right in there with the greyhounds as if he were the judge of a dog show at Madison Square Garden. More than once it looked as if he was smelling their breath, in the manner of a mother checking her teenage son for the scent of liquor. He petted them, but there was nothing goodhearted about it. He was appraising them, with all the warmth of a slave trader pinching the breasts of a nubile Nubian girl. Some of those displaying the dogs looked offended by his handling of their charges, but apparently a fixture like Ludlow was given wide latitude in this department.

I trailed him into the enclosed grandstand, which, blessedly, was air-conditioned. The back wall was a hideous pale pink with blue and green vertical stripes that had lost their color over the years in the direct sunlight. Everyone knew Kef, and perhaps for this reason, everyone left him alone. I, luckily, didn't know him at all, so I plonked myself down next to him. I still was looking pretty smart in my newly purchased outfit, but he appeared to resent the intrusion.

"Mr. Ludlow?" I asked.

He looked down into his racing form. "I have no tips for you, miss. If you want tips, pay for a copy of the *Miami Racing Gazette,* it's an eight-page daily, you can get it at the cigarette counter to the right of where you first walk in. It's a dollar." He looked at me and his snarl softened a bit, probably because he liked the sight of my nipples through the thin fabric of my outfit as they reacted to the icy air in the grandstand. "I'm sorry," he added.

"Mr. Ludlow, I'm a journalist." I took from my purse a small plastic sleeve one-fourth the size of a page in *Cosmopolitan.* For official inquiries about Vince and Lanny, I had my folded-up letter from Connie Wechsler on Neuman and Newberry stationery, which I kept with me at all times, confirming that a book about the duo had been commissioned by a reputable publisher. But for all other interviews, I used the contents of the plastic sleeve as my "letters of transit," as this was my temporary visa when venturing unprepared into unknown territories. From the sleeve I withdrew five folded slick magazine pages, each the first page of an interview with or an article I'd written about a famous person, and I'd picked the five for their diversity: Edgar Winter, Viveca Lindfors, Cesar Chavez, Buckminster Fuller, Judy Carne. Somewhere in there, at least one name meant something to most everyone.

Kef looked through the package and said suspiciously, "Miss O'Connor, you know all these famous people, why are you talking to me? I don't know anybody."

I put the articles away. "I'm writing a series of pieces for a new magazine coming out here soon called *Hooray for Hollywood.* Each piece of mine is going to be about some interesting facet of life in this area, past and present. Greyhound racing, politicians who started out here, celebrities who retired here, you get the idea. You're quite the legend, Mr. Ludlow. I'm told you know more about this track than the people who run it."

It was a very safe bet on my part to say this. Find me a sports fan who thinks the owners of his team know or care as much about the sport or the team as he does.

Ludlow sniffed. "The people who own this place are running it into the ground. Look around you." The grandstand was dotted with perhaps thirty people, all but a few well over sixty. "The first race starts in fifteen minutes. Sure, the crowd'll get bigger but not by much." He set down his racing form. "So what's your angle? The cruelty of dog racing? Been done a million times. You're not going to get anything from me on that topic."

"No, very much the opposite, Mr. Ludlow. Actually, I think that dog racing is a beautiful thing."

He raised his eyebrows. "Yeah? How so?"

The thing I'd always loved about the debating team in college was that you had to be prepared on a moment's notice to argue either the pro or the con of the question, with equal passion and conviction. Your true feelings were completely irrelevant. All that mattered was the argument.

I said to him fervidly, "Mr. Ludlow, the starting point for my article is that a dog race has it over a horse race any day. Horses are beautiful animals, no doubt about that. But sorry, they're not really smart. We don't think a cow is smart, right? A horse is just a cow that runs fast and looks pretty." The idea of containers of homogenized horse milk came to mind and momentarily nauseated me. "But a dog? A dog is a smart animal. A dog *knows* he's in a race. A dog has pride, wants to be liked, wants to win. You ever see a horse at the end of a race? If he came in fifth, does he look disgraced? No. But a dog, a dog would know, Mr. Ludlow. A dog would bow his head in shame." I sat back, pleased with my improv.

Ludlow looked at me in disbelief. "Dogs . . . dogs are dumb, pathetic animals, Miss O'Connor. Hitler had one, you know. That's how much these dogs know about character. Give a stray dog a steak, he'll be your friend for life until you don't have a steak and somebody else does. These animals are meat whores. And stupid? Greyhounds will chase a metal rabbit that has no scent around the same oval loop five, six times a day for the most useful portion of their lives. The reason they do it is not because they're hungry for fame, praise, or affection. It's because they're hungry for food." He smiled a dry smile. "But if you think writing the kind of romantic claptrap you're spouting will help keep this crummy place on its feet a few more years, you go right ahead. You feel free to put your words in my mouth and then quote me. Just get my name right."

I told him I had it right already and spelled it for him. He seemed pleased. I tried to make him feel as if he were some sort of local legend, like Toots Shor or Jack Dempsey. I laughed at things he said that weren't intended to be jokes, and when I complimented him on his sense of humor, he said, "Well, you can't take life too seriously now, can you?" It was said that Charles Dickens would allow no man to be a bore, and I refused to let Kef Ludlow be a crab. Perhaps it had been a while since a girl in her twenties had treated him warmly.

The dogs were funneled into their respective stalls at the starting line by a trainer who had the wisdom to wear leather gloves. The sides of the stalls were high enough that the dogs couldn't see one another, but they yelped within their abhorrent muzzles, as if challenging one another, or perhaps calling out, "This time can't we just ignore the rabbit? Can't we, guys?"

They wore muzzles only to protect their noses and to help officials determine the winner in a photo finish, said the management. Right.

There was a shot, the gates opened, and they were off. A greyhound can see clearly up to a half mile away, but these animals had never been allowed to look that far. They weren't even allowed to chase cars, many of which they could have caught.

As the dog wearing a red vest bearing the number 5 took the early lead, Ludlow leaned over to me and said, "He's the favorite but he's going to fade; watch number three." Number 3 wore a royal blue vest and was currently running fourth. His name was Proud Fella. As the hounds rounded into the home stretch, the crowd of thirty came to life, or as much as a crowd can come to life when the vast majority had received a senior discount. The greyhound's pace was approaching thirty-five, maybe forty miles an hour. One of the dogs growled as if to alert the others that this was the finish. Proud Fella surged forward, as predicted, but several of the others surged forward even more. Ludlow had been trying for a quinella, picking Bobby's Baby and Proud Fella to finish first and second, but since Proud Fella came in fifth, it didn't matter that Bobby's Baby won.

Ludlow didn't seem to mind talking to me while the races transpired. It was as if the real action was before the race, in the calculating of the odds, and at the finish line, where the results of his wager were totaled. Everything in between was merely passing scenery.

After the third race, I treated us to franks and fries as I asked him what had attracted him to the sport in the first place. He didn't take his eyes off the tote board as he answered, "I'm not attracted to *the* sport or *a* sport or any sport. I don't like sports. I like gambling. That's what I'm attracted to, the gambling. But dice, roulette, cards, slots, they have no consciousness, they don't know what they're doing, they're just 'the odds.' So you can't blame them. You can only blame yourself. With football, you blame the quarterback or the coach, real people, and when I lose there, it makes me churned up and upset inside. Same thing with baseball, hockey, basketball: some other guy screwed me over, and I hate that, because that's the way real life works, every single cruddy day. Even betting on the horses, there's a jockey. A midget from the Dominican Republic screws up and I get screwed over. Who wouldn't hate that? But when you lose your money here, with the greyhounds . . . it's all the fault of one scrawny mutt." I laughed at his drollery and he laughed, too. "That's what I love about the greyhounds. No jockeys, no coaches—if you lose, it's only because of one dumb dog."

I smiled back warmly and wrote this down as if it were the eleventh commandment. "What a wonderful way to put it," I cooed, and he glowed as much as a broken lightbulb can.

Ludlow did fairly well that day. He boxed a trifecta and also picked up an exacta in the twelfth, which was the last race of the matinee, as they call it. He also picked the winner in the fourth. On some rather small bets, he was walking away with several hundred dollars. I got the feeling that this was not often the case.

Flush with victory, we retired to the Dog Pound, the track's murky cocktail lounge. It's amazing how you can illuminate a maroon bar with only the light from a jukebox, the beer signs, and a gooseneck lamp by the register. Why, if it were any brighter in the place, they'd have had to clean the tables and vacuum the carpet.

We talked at length about the Florida dog-racing scene, the track over at Flagler particularly arousing his ire. It was about as scintillating a topic as you might imagine, but in the light of the shaded candle that I'd lit at our table, I dutifully wrote down some minimal notes in one of the spiral-bound pads I always keep in my bag. I like the kind with the spiral on top so my hand doesn't rub up against the metal coil by the left margin. I'd gone through about thirty such notebooks thus far on the project.

My note-taking took us through a third drink for him and a switch to 7UP for me after an initial Scotch. I picked up the tab, which he liked a great deal and which I said was the very least I could do in return for all the valuable insights he'd been generous enough to give me. Finally, the moment had come. I asked him for his address so I could mail him a tear sheet of the article. He told me it was 1350 North Dixie Highway, Apartment 7GW.

I let myself enact what I hoped was a sufficiently flabbergasted expression and said in a low, stunned voice, "Why, that's astounding."

He looked confused. "Why's that?"

I shook my head slowly. "Unless I'm mistaken . . ." I rummaged in my bag for another of my spiral-bound notebooks, which I'd rigged for this moment. It had a hot-pink cover. I flipped to a single page where I'd written down the address I'd gotten over the phone from Maureen's mother and showed it to him. "Look. It's the exact same address as yours." I put the notebook back in my bag. "One of the other pieces I'm doing in my series is about this girl, Maureen O'Flaherty. The one who was found dead in the hotel room of that comedy team . . . ?"

"Collins and Morris," he said.

"Yes, that's them. I came across the fact that she lived here in the year or two before she was murdered, and the address her mother gave me is the same as yours. I mean, this must be the most remarkable coincidence I've ever— Talk about killing two birds with one stone! I guess— Would you mind, as long as I have you here? I mean, you've already told me you've lived at the same address for almost twenty years, so you *must* have known her."

He had three gimlets in him, and I offered to buy him a fourth. He said yes to this, but once the order was in, he said, "I don't talk about her."

I told him I wouldn't quote him directly in the *Hooray for Hollywood* article (which was easy to promise, since the magazine didn't exist) and that he didn't have to tell me anything he didn't want to (which I hoped he'd forgotten was already his right as an American citizen). I said I just needed some background on *her,* as if this would keep him out of it, that it was probably information I could get from someone at the apartment building. . . . At that point, his look changed; he may have decided that it was preferable to tell me his version of the story rather than have Tony the doorman recount what he knew.

(I did know that if Kef Ludlow and Tony ever talked to each other about me, they'd both realize that I'd been completely deceptive with them, but that didn't concern me, as I had no plan to speak with either ever again.)

The fourth gimlet arrived, and with a sip of it, he told me a small ration of what he knew about Maureen.

He'd met her here, literally, in the Dog Pound Lounge. She'd been working as a cocktail waitress a couple of matinees a week to fill out her afternoons. They would talk. She was new in town, just out of college, had no money, and was holding down several part-time jobs in a number of Miami Beach hotels. It was hard breaking into the hotel scene, especially for a woman, but she'd told the management she was okay with working the graveyard shifts, from eleven P.M. until morning. Sometimes, on a Monday or Tuesday, she'd wait for hours without a single order, and with room service you made decent money only if you got tips; but she considered the wasted time an investment. The management appreciated those who didn't complain at the start; someone had to work the unprofitable shifts, and since the veterans had families to support, it fell to newcomers to bear the burden. In time, a newcomer would acquire veteran status. It was just a matter of patience.

Maureen was sweet but quite smart; she got her orders right the first time and delivered them efficiently. She looked nice as well, with a warm, natural quality that was different from so many of the bleached-blond waitress-types that applied for such jobs. Her speaking voice was lilting, not Miami-courtesy-of-Brooklyn. She had a college degree. She didn't chew gum on the job. She was, in fact, a touch of class, and the management knew that such a staff member was an asset to the operation. Big-spending guests will return to a specific hotel for so simple a reason as liking a certain waiter or desk clerk.

Soon the different hotels were assigning her to the guests who needed kid-glove treatment: celebrities, big-time brokers (Florida's Hollywood was called "the Wall Street of the South"), real estate developers . . . It would have been an ideal situation for Maureen to land herself a fat-cat husband.

"But she wasn't in it for that," asserted Ludlow. "She was real independent, just wanted to make good while she could. When she had a little bundle saved away, she was going to write, and that's all she was going to do. No day job for her. The biggest problem she had was finding the right living arrangements. See, the hotels were more than happy to put her up for the night when she was working the graveyard shift there. There are always two or three rooms that any first-class Miami hotel prefers not to sell: rooms with a view of a dumpster or ventilator, rooms across from the elevator or directly above the ballroom. They know most paying customers would complain, and it's not worth the grief to them. So when a room-service valet like Maureen or other staff members were working lousy hours, the management would make one of these unwanted rooms available to them. If between midnight and five A.M. it got to be slow going, Maureen could go to a room and nap, rest her legs, watch TV. If someone ordered something in the middle of the night, the front desk would call her room and she'd be down in the kitchen setting up the cart with linen and silver before the steak and fried eggs even hit the grill. All the hotel asked was that she make her own bed and leave the room the way she found it, so the maids wouldn't have to make it up all over again the next morning."

Ludlow ran his finger around the rim of the glass. "So she really only needed somewhere to stay three, maybe four days a week, when either the hotel was all filled up or she wasn't working the hotels but working afternoons somewhere like here, or when, God forbid, she wanted a day off. Of course, like all women, she needed a place to keep her, you know . . ."

"Clothes," I prompted.

"Exactly. So that's when I suggested that she could rent space from me. See, my apartment is only a one-bedroom, but the couple who lived there before me had a baby. They put up one of those plastic room dividers to section the dining area off from the living room. Made it into a nursery. I told her, 'Look, put a mattress down on the floor in there and you have your own room, privacy, an address.' I'm not fancy with the clothes, so she had most of my closet space, too."

I took the check from a bleached-blond, gum-chewing waitress and looked it over. "And you got?"

"I got thirty dollars a week. That meant quite a bit to me. I was able to afford a few extra luxuries with that."

"And?"

He saw my eyebrows raised with innuendo and had the most interesting reaction: a grace note of anger, which slurred into rakish pride. "Well, it wouldn't have been that odd if Maureen and I were more than just landlord and tenant. I was in my fairly youthful mid-forties at the time. I may not have been a lifeguard, but I was pretty trim, pretty spry."

I added a tinge of admiration to my voice. "I can see that even now. And I'll tell you, if it were me, a woman of my age in a strange city, fresh out of college and on my own for the first time, I'd certainly be grateful to have had someone smarter, hipper, to advise me, someone who knew their way around this town, knew all its high spots and high jinks." I think that may have been the first time in my life I'd said the words "high jinks," and for the life of me, I had no idea from where in my memory I'd retrieved them. "I'm sure any woman my age would have been grateful for some intelligent conversations, too."

He nodded. "Oh, we had those. Some nights we'd watch TV together before she went off to work. *Make Room for Daddy,* with Danny Thomas. We liked that a lot. But like you say, it was mainly talking with each other."

The waitress returned with my change and stepped away. As I fumbled through the bills, Ludlow said, "No, no, I'll leave the tip." He set down a five and snapped his fingers at the waitress. "The tip," he called to her. "From me."

I rose from the table. "I'm sure Maureen learned a lot from you."

"Writing, for example," he said with some considerable pride, not getting up. "Sure, she had courses at that Hunter College telling her how to be the next Shakespeare or Silas Marner." I didn't bother to point out that Silas Marner was not an author. "But she knew nothing about the real world of writing. That's where I was able to help her." He smiled. "I'm in the trade, you know. Here, I'll show you."

He downed the last of his lollipop-flavored vodka, stood up, and put his hand on the tabletop to steady himself. The four gimlets had obviously accumulated on only one side of his body, causing him to wobble just a little. He led me down an escalator to the entry level. We were in between the afternoon and evening sessions of racing and among the last matinee customers to leave. I followed him to a cigarette stand, where a chunky, sweaty-lipped fellow said, "Yes, Mr. Ludlow, what can I do you for?"

Ludlow pointed to a row of tip sheets that were hanging by clothespins from an overhead line. "Let me have the *Gazette,* Lester."

"No, that's yesterday's, Mr. Ludlow. It only covers last night and this afternoon."

Ludlow shook his head at the doubting Thomas. "Let me have it, Lester."

Lester looked sullen. "Well, if you really want it, I'll sell it to you for seventy cents. That's what I have to give the distributor if I don't send it back."

Ludlow tossed a dollar at Lester, waited for his change, and walked me over to a shoeshine stand, which, with the cigarette counter, flanked two rest-room doors marked BOWSERS and BITCHES. Sitting asleep in one of two shoeshine chairs was a Hispanic man in a colorful open shirt that revealed sleeveless underwear and a potbelly. A diagonal scar across his forehead bisected two furrows in his brow, making it look like Zorro had struck again.

Ludlow lightly slapped the side of the sleeping man's knee. "Shoeshine, Pancho," he said. I desperately hoped that Pancho was the man's real name, but I doubted it was. Pancho got down from his perch and Ludlow replaced him in his seat and motioned for me to sit alongside him. I stepped up into the adjoining chair. The hem of my outfit was high on the thigh, and I was sitting mighty pretty from Pancho's perspective. If a peep show charged a quarter for this kind of action, Pancho currently owed me six boots shined and we were well on our way to having the suede ones weatherized.

As Pancho rolled up my escort's trouser cuffs, Ludlow instructed him, "Pancho, roll my cuffs up above my knees, will you?" Pancho smiled back broadly, nodding to himself but not acting upon the request. Ludlow added, "Oh, and use peanut butter on my shoes, okay?"

Pancho said okay with the same broad smile.

Ludlow turned to me. "He doesn't speak English. So. You're a journalist, you honor the journalists' code. Someone tells you something off the record, you can't reveal it, correct?"

I looked him straight in his watery eyes. "I have never disclosed an anonymous source in my life, Mr. Ludlow. Not ever." As a matter of fact, none of my sources had ever been anonymous; I'd known each and every one of them, sometimes on a first-name basis. "Just check through those articles I showed you if you doubt me."

I saw the glint of gimlets in the shallow pools of his eyes. "Can you keep a secret?"

"My lips are sealed," I replied solemnly. Luckily, I don't write or type with my lips.

He opened the *Gazette* to the center of its eight pages (really just two sheets of pink paper folded in half and stapled in the middle). He pointed to a column that had a caricature of a turbaned Hindu above it. *"THE SWAMI SPEAKS!"* was its breathless banner.

As Pancho switched shoes, Ludlow pointed to the copy below the headline and explained, "The Swami picks the best bets at the dog races around Florida. Has a forty-seven-percent success rate so far this year."

"Is that good?"

"Ted Williams never batted four-seventy. Read the Swami's picks for this afternoon."

I read and saw that Ludlow had bet the Swami's recommendations to the letter, including winners like Bobby's Baby and losers like Proud Fella.

"You follow his suggestions meticulously," I said, trying to find some merit in his servitude.

"Whatever the Swami says to bet, I bet. I never deviate."

"But doesn't that take some fun out of it for you?"

He leaned closer to me. "Not a bit. Because the Swami is . . . me." He waited for my reaction, and I made sure he got his money's worth. I was dumbfounded to the point of speechlessness. He nodded slowly, savoring the bombshell he had dropped.

"Uh-huh. I told you I was 'in the trade.'" Pancho was done with Ludlow's shoes and started retying them. "Now you understand why I had to swear you to secrecy. If the Swami's identity became common knowledge, there'd be no end to the pressure on me to tailor my predictions so as to influence the odds. Bookies *and* the management here hate it when possible winners start to show long odds. If the Swami started touting these longshots, the pari-mutuel odds would go down, and the track and the bookies would be out of danger."

I thought of the paltry number of spectators at this afternoon's races, standing at the one- and two-dollar betting windows, and had to assume he was aggrandizing the amounts of filthy lucre actually at stake here. "It must be very tempting, Mr. Ludlow," I said. "I'm sure there are any number of shady operators out there who would pay all sorts of money to have you in their hip pocket."

He fixed me with a stare and brought his face very close to mine, breathing gimlet breath on me. "I am a man of integrity, Miss O'Connor. I've written a column for the *Gazette* for over twenty years now. It's never paid very much. Enough to defray some of the costs I incur when I put my own money where my mouth is, to mix a metaphor." I wasn't sure exactly what metaphor he'd mixed. No matter. "But it's been respectable work. The *Gazette* and other such tout sheets may look cheap, but that's the intent. They're actually all owned by the Tate-Donner Syndicate—they control the *Miami Sentinel* and the *Hollywood Financial Weekly*. They *want* the *Gazette* to look like it's 'under the counter.' That's its appeal." He paused melodramatically. "When I die, Miss O'Connor, perhaps you'd be kind enough to let the world know who 'the Swami' was?"

The world was probably not as keen to know the identity of a prognosticator of dog races at a fading venue in a suburb of Miami as, say, the identity of Woodward and Bernstein's Deep Throat, but I nodded solemnly at the immense responsibility I'd been handed.

He got down from the shoeshine chair, handed Pancho the going rate of fifty cents, and then gave him another quarter. "That's for *you,*" he said. He opened the exit door for me, and the heat hit us both in the face.

"Give you a lift back to your apartment?" I asked.

He said in a carelessly dashing manner, "Oh, I thought I might dine at the Embers this evening. It's only a few blocks from there, if you wouldn't mind . . ." I said that would be fine. He demurred, "I'd ask you to join me, but I'll be catching up with many friends, regulars there, whom I've not seen for quite some while." He patted his breast pocket, where he kept his wallet. "This has been an exceptionally good day for me."

We arrived at the parking lot across the street. An attendant fetched me my cool rental car. Ludlow got in the passenger seat and looked about with the expression of a man eager to be seen in a sporty car being driven by a young woman who is dressed in risqué fashion. I drove slowly, and he liked that.

"Mr. Ludlow, one last question about Maureen O'Flaherty? Why do you think she died?"

Ludlow looked at me with some resentment. He was enjoying his little run of luck today, and this topic was spoiling that. "She died because, if I believe the newspapers, she stopped breathing. I assume she drowned."

We turned onto I-95 and traveled for half a minute in silence.

"I hate that she died." I don't know if he even heard himself speak.

"You miss her company," I ventured diplomatically.

"I hate that she died because it was so *stupid* of her. Unless it's a health problem, it's stupid to die young. The rest of us who go on living, we're left to deal with it."

I reached over and placed my right hand over his left hand. It was cold and small and fixed, like a claw. He seemed to shiver at the warmth of human contact.

"You cared for her, didn't you?" I asked, and he moved his hand away. "Sorry if I seem too personal, but I just want to know if she had found a friend, a caring friend here before she died. It would make it easier to wrap up the article about her if I could say that someone here in Hollywood still missed her."

He reached into his side pocket and took out a very long pack of More cigarettes. Their brown paper made them look expensive, but they weren't. He asked in a sullen voice, "Have you ever been in love with someone who just didn't love you?"

"Yes," I answered truthfully.

"Not that they hated you, or didn't like you. They just didn't love you and there was no way they could even consider feeling that way."

I told him I had known both sides of that deal.

"You're pretty," he laughed flatly. "I think you've spent more time breaking the bad news to others than hearing it yourself."

He had trouble lighting his cigarette, which kept moving away from the flame of his lighter as if he were performing a carefully rehearsed burlesque routine. He finally gave up trying to be suave and held the cigarette still with his left hand while lighting it with his right. "In the end, the only way most people can deal with that kind of rejection—it's so much, and so hopeless—is to hate the other person. Out and out hate them. You invent reasons if there are none. Like the way you hate people who belong to country clubs that won't let you be a member. You hate those elite snobs, right up until the second they ask you to join. That's why I guess so many divorced couples end up hating each other. It isn't really that, suddenly, they don't like this person they'd planned to spend their life with. Each hates the other because the other just doesn't care about them anymore. Not one bit. You turn right into this circle here."

I turned into Young Circle, a grand rotary named after the fellow who'd decided there should be a Hollywood on the Atlantic. I slowed down because the engine threatened to drown out Ludlow's voice, which had grown softer.

"I wasn't a very happy man before I met her, but I had no way of knowing how unhappy I'd been until I had a little happiness. So now I have to hate her, for showing me that my life could have been different. I hate her because she couldn't care for me, and because she died. The dying part was just stupid, however it happened."

"And however it happened . . . where were you when it did?" I asked bluntly.

The water in his eyes froze over. "The papers didn't say exactly when she died, but it wouldn't make any difference. I was here in Hollywood, at the track, in my apartment, at the Embers one night and a lobster place the night before. She died in New Jersey, Miss O'Connor. I've never left the state of Florida in my entire life. It didn't matter where I was."

We had looped around three-quarters of the grand circle, and Ludlow had me make another right onto Hollywood Boulevard. As directed by Ludlow, I pulled up in front of the Embers. Neon flames flitted back and forth above its name.

He nodded at the building. "If you feed a man on nothing but red beans and rice his entire life, he'll only complain about the weather. But God forbid you treat him just one time to"—he read from a sign in the window—"*'our famous charbroiled strip sirloin steak, done just as you like it, served with shrimp cocktail, baked potato, creamed spinach, choice of soup or salad, coffee, and our famous key lime pie.'* God forbid you then tell him he has to go back to only red beans and rice for as long as he lives. That would be cruel and inhuman punishment." He opened the car door and readied himself to go inside. "Wonder if any of the gang are still here?" he pondered a bit nervously. I had the feeling "the gang" might never have really considered Ludlow a member.

He reached across to shake my hand. "Thank you for the drinks and the company. It was very interesting to have you to talk to." He hesitated and then said, "I assume I shouldn't be looking for any articles about dog-racing from you, Miss O'Connor?"

He smiled a thin smile. I watched him adjust the waistband of his pants and primp up the shoulders of his polo shirt before he entered the restaurant.

I made a right on Twentieth Avenue (where do they ever find these names!) and another on Tyler. I saw a sign for the airports of Miami and Fort Lauderdale and started to turn left, but impulsively hit another hard right and a right again. I pulled over to the curb in front of the Embers. Double-parked, I hopped out of the car and into the steak house.

It was really a glorified coffee shop. An old geezer worked a charcoal grill about the size of a beginner's jigsaw puzzle. All the other people in the place were geezers and geezettes. Ludlow was seated alone in a booth, trying with no success to get the attention of a waitress in her mid-fifties.

I strode over to him as noisily as I could and waited until the patrons were all eyes. I was easily the youngest in the place and definitely the dressiest (or perhaps undressiest might be more accurate), although in my healthy-looking Moon Drops demi-makeup and Geminesse eyelashes, I certainly didn't look like a hooker. "I just came back to thank you for the most *wonderful* time," I said in as lascivious a tone as I could muster. I bent down to him and kissed him. I didn't kiss him on the lips (that much of a Samaritan I am not), but by holding his alarmed face in both my hands, I ensured that no one would see that I caught him on the cheek instead. I made a second smacking sound with my lips to account for the lipstick on his cheek and pulled away from him. He was a darker crimson than my particular shade of Helena Rubenstein. "Kef, you are *such* a man," I said for public consumption, adding in a low whisper for his ears only, "Let's see how *this* plays with the old gang." I turned on my stacked heels and ambulated my way out of the Embers, with a knowing sway for whosoever had eyes to see.

I'm not all bad, right? It was stupid, but I'd been touched by him.

Back at the airport, while settling up the car-rental bill, I went into my purse for my wallet and noticed that the notepad with the hot-pink cover, the one with Maureen's address in it, was now missing. It was no loss; its lone entry had been the 1350 North Dixie address, entered for the sole purpose of displaying it to Ludlow. But now it was gone.

It might very well have fallen out of my bag in the bar or on the shoeshine stand or when I was doing my little lovey-dovey routine at the Embers.

Or Ludlow could have filched it from me, curious to see what else was written between the covers of my hot-pink book.

There was no way to take back the kiss I'd given him. But I promptly stopped at a Rexall pharmacy, bought a pack of Kleenex and some Albolene cream, and wiped off every trace of my lipstick, replacing it with Blistex, in case my lips might be burned by the harsh Florida sun.

TWENTY-FIVE

At the back of one of the bars at Miami airport, there was an unusual coin game called Pong. It was played on a black TV screen, the white outline of a rectangle representing a Ping-Pong table, two short vertical white lines representing two players' paddles, and a small white dot representing a Ping-Pong ball. I thought it was absurd to put a kid's game in a bar, but you couldn't keep adults away from this thing. Two players could square off against each other or, if you were alone, you'd play the computer that controlled the game and if you did, you were dead.

Next to the machine they'd put in another machine for the sole purpose of changing dollar bills into quarters. I ordered a greyhound (such a whimsical person I am) and asked the bartender if I could have the change in singles, which I then took to the change machine by the Pong game. It swallowed my first dollar bill and spat out four quarters just as nice as you please. By my sixteenth dollar, a false sense of elation had come over me. I felt like I was playing the slots and winning with every spin.

I drank half my greyhound to bolster my nerves, then gathered up my sixty-eight quarters and went to a pay phone in the loudest part of the terminal, near the public-address system.

My first call was to Connie Wechsler, my editor at Neuman and Newberry. I had to give her some explanation as to why I'd abandoned my interview schedule with Vince and flown to Florida, so that she could then relay this explanation to Greg Gavin.

The best version of the truth I could present to her was that I'd made a possibly stunning breakthrough regarding the girl found dead in Lanny and Vince's hotel suite in New Jersey, and that I'd had to fly to where Maureen O'Flaherty had lived in South Florida to get more background before I continued questioning Vince. This was, in a way, completely true. What I didn't tell her was that I'd been motivated to leave because I couldn't let Lanny Morris see me in any guise other than as Bonnie Trout, schoolteacher from New York, because I'd lied to Vince's ex-partner about my identity just prior to having immense sex with him at the Plaza hotel. No, were I to tell Connie that, she might feel she'd just possibly misplaced her trust in my professionalism and integrity. I did explain that, not wanting to delay the interview schedule any more than was necessary, I hadn't even bothered to book through N&N but had headed straight to LAX and purchased a ticket for the next available flight, and I wouldn't even think of requesting reimbursement (largely because they'd rightfully question why in God's name I'd routed myself from Los Angeles to New York to Miami). And that, not wanting to arouse Vince's suspicion, I'd improvised a cover story for his benefit.

"What was the cover story?" asked Connie, who'd been wonderfully understanding about all this.

"Just that my half brother was killed in an accident in New York and that I had to go to Florida for his funeral. His ashes were scattered over the Everglades. You see."

I heard silence on the other end of the connection.

The operator kicked in, asking for three dollars and seventy-five cents. I dropped in the appropriate amount of quarters and faced Connie's scorn.

"Boy, that's a pretty god-awful story," she said. "Remind me never to hire you to write fiction. Did Vince Collins buy it?"

"I'll know soon enough. He's my next phone call after this."

"You're back in L.A., I assume?" asked Connie.

I held the phone up so she could hear an announcement for Air Florida Flight 586 to Pensacola and Memphis, now boarding at Gate 4. "No, I'm at Miami airport."

Connie hissed into the phone, "Dammit, I just this second agreed you'd do an awards ceremony tomorrow afternoon! When will you be back in L.A.?"

I told her I'd be home that evening and heard her emit a small sigh of relief. She explained that the P.R. woman who handled the West Coast for Neuman and Newberry had called asking if I could hand out a Scotty award, named after F. Scott Fitzgerald in honor of the myriad number of fine writers of fiction who'd been seduced and stomped out by Hollywood. The awards leaned heavily toward books about motion pictures. The first three years they'd had to tell people in advance that they'd won in order to get them to come, but although that meant the losing nominees *didn't* come to the Event, it did in some instances guarantee that the winner would buy an entire table or, rather, that their publisher would. In a few scandalous cases, when a winner had told them in advance that they couldn't make it to the Event, a different winner was chosen.

"I hate the Scotties," I told Connie.

"So do we all, but when your book wins one, you'll hate them a whole lot less," Connie advised. "It will be a great way to serve notice about your book with Vince—they promise they'll mention it when they introduce you, and the people who are there are exactly the people we have to hype. They originally had Rona Barrett announcing the winner of the Best Critical Book on Cinema. Then they decided maybe Rona was a little too trashy all on her own, so they figured, have two people present the award, Rona from the gossip side and someone from the journalism side. Rona is Miss Dish and Dirt and you're Ms. Woodward and Bernstein. Do it, you owe me, you owe N&N."

I did owe them, especially considering my incredibly shady behavior, which might at any moment backfire not only on me but on them. "Fine," I said. "Just remember in the future that I was a team player. So who's winning the award?"

"They don't know. They're doing the Scotties 'legit' this year. They're a little worried that no one will show up, but they figure they have to go straight sometime or they'll never have credibility."

I sighed. "Okay, I'll be there."

She told me "there" was a luncheon at the Hollywood Roosevelt. I was secretly pleased to have been considered an acceptable presenter by the organizers of the Event. I was certainly not known to the public by any means. I could only imagine that if you interview enough celebrities, some of their notoriety begins to rub off on you, at least within the trade.

The next call I had planned to make was the one I most dreaded, because it involved sustaining more complex fabrications than the ones I'd inflicted on Connie, which were largely lies of omission. Procrastination being the one thing I rarely put off until tomorrow, I called Beejay instead. I needed to hear a friendly voice. More important, I had not had an extended conversation with anyone in the last twenty-four hours to whom I hadn't been lying: Vince, Adolfo, Tony the doorman, Kef Ludlow, Connie . . . I wondered what it would feel like to speak the truth.

Beejay didn't give me much of a chance to find out. She had a romantic triangle on her hands that, at the moment, was a lot more functional than my non-ménage with Lanny and Vince. Beejay had been seeing the vice principal of her school, who was married, and also seeing a New York actor who was not married to anything other than his mirror. Last Friday, she'd done the dirty deed, as Beejay so sensually put it, with the principal of vice in his office, and then gone home and bathed the scent of sex from her body so that she was virginal for Mr. Method's big entrance. The next afternoon she'd received a spectacular bouquet of flowers. But there was no card. She said the hippie delivery boy, whose blond pageboy haircut made him look like Illya Kuryakin on *The Man from U.N.C.L.E.,* hadn't a clue as to who had placed the order, or anything else for that matter. "So what do I do?" she fretted to me. "I want to keep both of them for a while, but they're both very jealous personalities. Do I thank them both for the flowers and see which one knows what I'm talking about?"

I told her that if she did and both of them said, "I'm glad you liked them," she could be certain that one of the two was definitely a creep. Always the detective, I suggested she call each and fake sneezing at the very start of the conversation. "Then explain you're highly allergic to flowers. The guy that sent you the flowers will immediately apologize." She said she didn't know if she could fake sneezing very believably. I told her that when we were roommates in college I'd heard her fake a lot more than sneezing while I stood waiting outside the bedroom we shared.

Finally we were allowed to get to my problems with *my* two men who didn't know about each other. I explained why I'd had her call me at Vince's home and what I'd done since.

My supply of quarters had now been halved, and I had no idea how long my next phone call, the most long-distance of the three, would take. I reluctantly signed off with Beejay, took several deep breaths, rolled my eyes heavenward in order to invoke an alpha state of relaxation, and dialed Vince's number.

He was home, and he said he'd answered the phone in the hope that it might be me. I was glad I hadn't gotten his service or office. I needed him to hear the airport behind me. Air Florida cooperated tremendously by announcing *"Last call for Flight 586 to Pensacola and Memphis at Gate 4"* just after I told him where I was.

"Miami? I thought your brother was in New York."

"He was. But the funeral ceremony was here."

There was silence on the line for a moment, during which Eastern Airlines announced that their 7:00 P.M. flight to Washington and Philadelphia would be delayed by a half hour.

"I'm very sorry," Vince said at last.

"That's all right. We weren't all that close. He was my half brother."

"Older or younger than you?"

"Older."

"So your mother was married twice?"

I didn't like that idea. My own mother was devoted to my father. "No, Clifford was my father's son from a previous marriage." That was better. "Actually, he was my father's stepson."

"So he wasn't even really your half brother," Vince observed.

"Mmm. As you say. But still, it felt— For example, he had a crush on me when I was a teenager, and there was nothing genetically stopping us from pursuing the relationship, yet I told him it just felt wrong." This was getting much too richly hued for my comfort. I'd meant to simply distance myself from "Clifford," to explain why I would resiliently be back to normal by tomorrow, but instead I was on the verge of scripting a Bergman film.

"The funeral was so soon," noted Vince.

"It wasn't a burial. It was a private ceremony. He had asked that he be cremated as soon as possible and that his ashes be scattered over the Everglades. He loved the Everglades. He grew up there."

"But when he had a crush on you, he was up north? Or were you—"

"He visited my family, to see my dad, who was his"—what was he again?—"his stepfather, in the summer months. He was cremated this morning, and I accompanied the ashes down here. Tomorrow a private airplane will distribute them." I was tired of saying "scatter." "There was a ceremony today for his mother and my father. His biological father is no longer alive."

"How did he die?" asked Vince.

"I have no idea, he passed away before I was born."

"No, I— Not how Clifford's biological father died. I meant Clifford."

This part I'd planned in advance. "He worked for the government. The project he was involved with is a classified matter. I was given very few details, but it was clearly an accident and, thankfully, he didn't suffer." I changed my tone to apologetic. "Vince, my feelings need time to sort themselves out, and I think it would help if I didn't talk about this for a while. Is that okay?"

"Sure, I understand," said Vince in a very reassuring tone.

"I think the best remedy for me is to focus on the book and our work together. Will you help me with that?"

He said he would and we scheduled to meet the next afternoon, after the Scotty Awards luncheon. Now I had to make a larger request. I had to ask him not to involve Lanny in any of our meetings. To broach this, I began, "By the way, before I hang up, it's been very much on my mind: can you tell me a little of what you felt seeing Lanny again, after so long? What was that like, Vince?"

"He didn't show up. I never saw him." He sounded disappointed, perhaps even hurt. "After all that buildup. So anticlimactic."

He told me that Lanny had called him about five minutes after I'd left to tell him he was unbelievably behind schedule doing a Morris the Cat commercial out at the Sunset-Gower Studios and wouldn't be done until early evening. Vince had told him about my brother and they'd both agreed to reschedule the meeting for another date.

I told Vince that, as per our contract, I was respectfully going to exercise my editorial jurisdiction over the project and stipulate that Lanny not be invited to any of our meetings again. He made some bewildered sounds and I explained: "Look, I've thought about it, and whenever I tell a story about something funny that happened to me and a friend, I always tell it differently when my friend is with me. She'll interrupt, saying, 'No, it was the other guy who wanted to dance,' or 'You left out why we went there in the first place.' And sometimes she's right, so I back up the story a bit, or I disagree with her and we get caught up in a mini-debate, or I adhere so strictly to the truth that it ruins the story. We end up with a flat, lame, compromised, confused rendition of what either one of us individually could recount in an extremely funny way. That's what I'm afraid will happen if you and Lanny jointly answer any of my questions. Even if he doesn't say a word, his presence alone would influence what you say. I don't want that. You're contractually obligated to answer my questions, but Lanny isn't. He can pull a 'no comment' and get away with telling me only what he wants me to hear. You can't. He can put something off the record, but for you and me, everything's been on the record since I first met you. It would be like a tennis game where one player observes all the boundaries and regulations—"

He cut my explanation short and said he understood. He apologized for having invited Lanny in the first place and said he looked forward to seeing me directly after the Scotties ceremony.

I hung up the phone and, scooping up my remaining quarters, went back to the bar, where I purchased myself another greyhound. I had an hour to kill before my flight to Los Angeles. I paid for my drink, tipping the bartender a generous eight quarters, and took the remaining change over to the Pong machine. The bar was pretty empty now, as there were only a few evening flights left. No one was playing the game. It looked remarkably simple and easy to beat. I popped in a quarter and squared off against the computer, which knew all the boundaries and regulations of the game. It gulped down my quarters like a ravenous slot machine and gave me a sound thrashing, beeping and blipping as it boffed me over and over again.

TWENTY-SIX

I had interviewed Richard Harris a few years after the success of his hit record "MacArthur Park," which was named after a real place in downtown Los Angeles and which, on the recording, Harris continually and mistakenly referred to as MacArthur's Park. During the course of the interview, he told me that his favorite place to stay in Hollywood was the Roosevelt Hotel, and I'd been puzzled by that until he explained that when he stole the towels in his room, they were correctly monogrammed for him. Much as he, Rita Hayworth, and Rex Harrison might have adored the Roosevelt for this specific reason, the hotel had clearly once seen better days, and its view of those better days was growing dimmer as they receded into memory. Like MacArthur Park (around which a Central American community was building but no real estate developers were), it was not that anyone was doing anything awful to the Roosevelt. It was simply that, when something broke, no one fixed it.

The Roosevelt Hotel—its address was 7000 Hollywood Boulevard—had been built in 1927, around the same time Joe Young built his Hollywood-by-the-Sea in Florida. It made a lot of sense as the place to hold the fourth annual Scotty Awards. At the Roosevelt's once-fashionable Cinegrill, F. Scott Fitzgerald used to be a social drinker who never stopped being social; he once went ten rounds with Ernest Hemingway (I'm not referring to boxing) and won on a technical blackout. I wondered if Lil Walker had any Cinegrill stories to share with me.

I stepped into the hotel's still-handsome two-story Spanish Mediterranean lobby, its tile floors bouncing the sound of my footsteps up to the hand-painted ceiling and back to my ears in a pleasant, precise ricochet. I walked by the staircase where Bojangles Robinson had purportedly shown Shirley Temple how they might perform a dance routine in *The Little Colonel.* Then on to the Daisy Room, where I found Nita Cowan, who was handling P.R. for Neuman and Newberry. I'd been told I would be able to spot her because she would have the darkest tan of anyone there, including Leslie Uggams. I went over to a woman with Caucasian features who was the same color as the balustrade I'd just held and introduced myself. She told me how thrilled she was that I could be part of the event. If she were about to be beheaded, she'd probably also have said this to the hooded man carrying the ax.

The room was smartly dressed, the tables in salmon-colored linen with a centerpiece of white flowers at each table. There was a dais, with a podium at center stage. Behind it was a transparent Lucite triangle upon which sat three clear shelves, the resting place for twenty-three Scotty awards, which were in the shape of Fitzgerald's profile. I asked if the winners' names were on them and was told no, that they would all be inscribed after the ceremony, if the recipient so wished it, for a very nominal fee. I asked if Rona Barrett was there yet (I had never met her, although like anyone who ever watched TV, I knew what she looked like). Nita said Rona had a taping conflict and that she would be arriving just before our particular presentation was to begin. I told Nita that my only concern was that I had a meeting with Vince Collins set for this afternoon, but she assured me the ceremony wasn't going to go over two hours.

She suggested I head up to the podium and get the feel of the stage. She handed me a file card on which there were some quips I was supposed to exchange with Rona.

"Really?" I said upon hearing this information. "I'm a writer—can't I just use my own words?"

She explained with not much patience that Rona would be working from the same script and that it would be unprofessional for me to depart from it, not to mention confusing for Rona. I walked up to the podium.

The microphone was placed a little high, and when I bent its gooseneck down, it gave off the same sort of feedback that had made Jimi Hendrix the star of Woodstock. Everyone working in the room looked annoyed with me. I reeled off a sentence and retreated from the stage.

Nita looked displeased. "You better speak up when you do it for real. I couldn't hear a word you said."

I looked down at the card in my hand. "Nita, I see that Rona is supposed to say to me, *'Well, I'd say you really knocked one out of the park with your book. Has to be the first time anyone hit a home run on ball four.'* What does that mean?"

Nita examined the card with mild curiosity. As she read it, I added, "See, I've written for magazines and newspapers. My first book isn't out yet." She looked the notes over again and handed the card back to me.

"I don't know, I guess it's a joke. It *is* sort of funny. Just go with it."

I stared accusingly at Nita. "Someone else was originally supposed to do this with Rona other than me—that's what this is, isn't it? Look, I don't mind, I'm not a celebrity or famous, I know that. But could Rona just talk to me as if I'm me? I don't know how to reply to what you have her saying."

Nita gave me a frosty smile. "Sure you do. You read what's on the card. Rona already has hers, she said she'd look it over on the way here." She looked at the card again. "I have no problem with this. Look, it's not like this is on TV or anything. And you must have interviewed someone in sports in your life."

She was obviously expecting me to answer. "The closest would be Paul Newman when he made a film about hockey."

Nita smiled. "There you go. I'll see if I can fix it. Just be nice, okay? Neuman and Newberry had to fork out a thousand dollars for the table we're at."

It was an otherwise empty table. Nita and I sat there watching the proceedings alongside the three steps up to the temporary stage. It was silly for me to be nervous, but anytime I have to speak before more than five people, I get the jitters. The luncheon wasn't exactly star-studded, but Richard Benjamin and Paula Prentiss as hosts were charming and sly. Shari Lewis presented the Best Children's Book award to a lavish Disney edition of *Lady and the Tramp,* which was accepted by Dean Jones. Roger Vadim presented Best Book on Foreign Film. He said that up until recently, he'd thought that California champagne was imported and his ex-wife Jane Fonda was a foreign film star. They'd divorced only a few months earlier, and he added that now she was foreign to him all over again.

I was getting anxious that Rona Barrett would be a no-show. We were only one category away from our presentation, which was for Best Critical Book on Cinema. But as a round of applause went up for Best Song Folio from a Motion Picture, Rona Barrett slid into the chair next to Nita. She had clearly just come from taping because she had on the heavy makeup required for TV. Or maybe she always looked that way. As she took note of any celebrities who might be in the room, I leaned over to her and extended my hand.

"Hello," I whispered. "I'm presenting the next award with you."

Rona looked at me. "You're not Jim Bouton."

I nodded my head glumly. "I know. I've tried to be throughout my life, but as you see . . . a dismal failure." Ah. So I'd been summoned in relief, as it were, for the pitcher-author of *Ball Four.*

Rona's reaction was reasonable, intelligent, and proved me not insane. She gestured to the file card in her hand. "Well, then, what they have us saying makes no sense."

"I know."

"No sense at all. Typical."

Richard Benjamin was introducing us. "Our next award will be presented by two women from parallel tracks of reportage. One is the first lady of TV gossip and the editor of three, count them, three magazines featuring all the showbiz news that's fit to ooze." Richard looked at the card in his hand with mild dismay. "Your turn, darling," he said to his wife, Paula, murmuring, "and not a moment too soon."

Paula took over. "And with her, a young woman whose questions of the famous have sometimes resulted in answers we never thought we'd hear. She also writes a lot about sports." This was news to me. I looked at Nita, who winked as if to say, "Told you I'd fix things." Oh thanks so much. Paula continued, "And her first book about, and written in collaboration with, Vince Collins will be published by Neuman and Newberry this spring."

She proclaimed our names. Rona and I stood and headed toward the podium. Rona stopped to talk to about three people on the way to the temporary stage, so I was left up there alone for a good ten seconds with nothing to do but wonder what I was going to say. Rona arrived at the mike. The first line was mine, and I decided to not read what was written. Instead, I somberly intoned: "Ladies and gentlemen, the lovely Ms. Barrett here was originally scheduled to present this next award with Jim Bouton, former major-league pitcher and author of the best-selling book *Ball Four.* She was, of course, surprised to be told that *I* would be presenting the award with her." I let mild anguish register on my face. "However, I'd like to make it clear to all of you . . ." (dramatic pause as I summoned the courage) "that I actually *am* Jim Bouton." I put this across with solemnity. There was a moment in which I wondered what had made me think that was funny, and then there came a good-sized laugh across the room. "I hope you appreciate how hard it was for me to come up here and let you see me for who I truly am, and how hard it has been for me to keep my proclivities a secret shared only by my very closest teammates . . ." By now there was quite a lot of laughter, including the encouraging howls of Rona. I added, "And if you thought my previous book contained some shocking revelations, wait till the next one." I looked down toward the general area of my crotch and looked back up. "Its title will be *Balls None.*"

Hilarity ensued. The great thing about this setup, which Rona instantly realized, was that we could then do the Barrett-Bouton repartee as written, me in a slightly butch voice, she as her usual self, and it played very humorously in this context. Oh, I was an old pro at this now. Yes, yes. Carson would no doubt be having me fill in for him on *The Tonight Show* one of these days, especially if he cut back to four nights a week, as was rumored.

Like every serious actress who's ever found herself in an out-and-out stage farce, I instantly, shamelessly became a slut for laughs, a camp follower for a guffaw. Yes, this was what I'd always wanted. How lonely it had been, never hearing the laughter of my readers. I'd finish up my silly book about Vince and then head straight into stand-up work. College concerts more than nightclubs, I thought.

But before I did that, there was the little matter of announcing the Scotty award. Ho hum. Well, we'd soon dispatch that assignment. I had the envelope with the nominees and Rona had the envelope with the winner. I read:

"In the category of Best Critical Book on Cinema, the nominees are: *Howard Hawks: The Vanishing Breed* by Karl Thompson; *Hitchcock and the*

Gaumont Studio by Robin Wood; *Lelouch on Lelouch* by Claude Lelouch; *The Shy Genius of Harry Langdon* by the late Arthur Conklin; and *Val Lewton at RKO* by Daniel Gerstein and Michael Croft."

I stepped back and relinquished the microphone to Rona. My chum. She might want me to cohost her gossip show with her. I went back to get a Scotty award from a five-foot-eleven waif whose job it was to take the awards from the shelf and give them to the presenters.

"And the Scotty goes to . . ." Rona tore open her envelope and announced, "*The Shy Genius of Harry Langdon* by the late Arthur Conklin!"

There was applause that hopefully Arthur could hear somewhere. Paula Prentiss stepped over to Rona and whispered something in her ear. Rona nodded eagerly and proclaimed into the microphone:

"Ladies and gentlemen, accepting the award is Mr. Lanny Morris!"

I heard this as I took the Scotty award from the model, heard the crowd start applauding at their loudest level of the afternoon, heard the sound of the Scotty hitting the Lucite base of the display shelves, where it had fallen after I'd let it pass through my hands.

The model picked it up and handed it to me again.

I had to run before he saw me—oh but of course he's seen me already, I'm on a goddamn stage, I was just prattling away thinking I was being funny. Funny!!! That's right, God, fuck *me.* Fuck *me*!!

More applause for Lanny.

Mom, please save me. I saw him moving quickly up the steps to the stage, looking dashing in a tuxedo.

Mom wasn't going to save me. And Rona was too busy applauding Lanny to save me from this man who had taken me to Shea Stadium, taken me for Chinese food, taken me to the Drive-In, taken me to the Plaza, taken me. Lanny was now on the stage. With a big smile on his face, he pointed a finger at Rona, who hugged him.

He never took his eyes from mine, not even for a second. And he never stopped smiling. It was a big painted circus poster of a smile that had no mirth. His television technique served him well. He had always been able to cheat his angles so that when he seemed to be talking with Vince or a stooge at his side, he was actually looking past their shoulder at the cue cards. He would read the cue cards, but millions of viewers would buy that he was looking straight at Vince. Suddenly, Rona was Vince and I was a cue card. He could read me like I was *Hop on Pop.*

I had made love with this strange man now wearing this immense, motionless smile. I had held my body against his, surrounded him with my mouth, and drawn him into me gladly, angling myself to help take him deeper, encouraging him to slam his body against and into me. Now he looked at me with his big smile of hatred. I was so afraid of him.

I walked the Scotty award over to Rona, to hand it to her, but he let go of Rona and took the award directly from my unsteady hands. I felt so ashamed, as if I were five years old and had wet myself while sitting at my parents' dinner party and now everyone getting up from the table would see the wet all over my pale yellow skirt.

I thought, Maybe there might be an earthquake. Oh God, if you ever did something for me, an earthquake now. Structural damage, yes, but no deaths. And if there have to be deaths, all right, but at least not children. Maybe I could just yell, "Earthquake!" But the audience wouldn't take my word for that; they'd have to feel the room moving beneath them, the way it was moving for me this very moment.

Maybe he doesn't quite recognize me. Maybe he's smiling at me because he's uncertain. It *is* possible for two people on two different coasts to look alike.

He plucked the award from me, took my left hand in his right hand, and spoke into my left ear: "Hello, Bonnie Trout, you cute little piece-of-shit liar." He raised his eyebrows and smiled even bigger at me, as if I should find this funny. "Laugh at what I just said, you fucking little fraud," he said, his back to the audience. I laughed out of fear, trying not to vomit at the same time.

Lanny stepped over to the podium mike, never relinquishing my hand. I had to walk there with him. I'm sure to the audience it was as if he'd simply forgotten to let go.

Lanny fell into the public style I'd not heard much when I'd been in his company, the voice he'd used to calm the woman on the airplane.

"Uhm, I thought it would be I should let you know I offered to accept this Scotty award for whomsoever because with it all being so very with the decorations and the nice ladies . . ." The audience laughed, just from recognition, and his voice got a little less nasal. "And I just want to say to Mr. Jim Bouton . . ." He nodded at me amid pleasant laughter. "And boy, she sure could have fooled me, huh? I thought she was somebody else entirely other."

He gave my hand a squeeze. It hurt. I remembered from the Plaza how strong he could be.

"And to Miss Rhonda-Rhoda-Rina-Rona Barrett of Wimpole Street." He beamed at her and she laughed good-naturedly. "You know I love you, sweetheart, and don't say anything too not nice about the Lanny-Man, okaaaay?" Rona nodded an okay.

He leaned his lithe body into the podium and intoned, "Folks, Harry Langdon was one of motion pictures' greatest comics. He possessed the sweetness of Laurel and Hardy, the stoicism of Buster Keaton, and the timing of Chaplin and Lloyd. I am overjoyed that this fine book by Artie Conklin has received the Scotty award, and I hope it will heighten awareness in the years to come of the profound contributions Harry Langdon made to American film comedy. I'm honored to accept this award for both Arthur and Harry. Thank you so much."

He gave Rona another hug, which was difficult since he still hadn't let go of my hand. I waved a good-bye to Rona the way my grandmother had waved good-bye to me as they'd wheeled her in for surgery that she did not survive. Lanny walked us off the stage, where Nita had six cameramen prepared to assault us. The flash guns fired and fired at us. (*"Lanny, look over here—What's your name, miss?—Lanny, you ever talk to Vince? Lanny, this way please—What's the spelling on that name, miss?"*) I was truly blinded by their flashbulbs. No wonder celebrities arriving at opening nights look harassed and terrified. I was relieved when Lanny said "That's it, fellas" and stepped us through the service doors into the kitchen—relieved until I realized I was alone with Lanny.

"We're going to have a little private talk, you devious bitch," he said. "That all right with you? Because if it isn't, I'll turn right around and tell your publicist from your precious Neuman and Newberry about the huge deception you put over on me. So you okay with a little private talk?"

Without waiting for an answer, gripping my arm, he hurried us down a service corridor and a flight of steps. "You know this hotel, 'Bonnie'? I know it real well."

Frightened as I was, I protested, "Listen, you can't just abduct me like this—"

"No complaints, Bonnie. I still haven't decided whether I blow the whistle on you. Be nice now."

We emerged into an enclosed cabana area attached to the hotel. "You like? Right in the middle of Hollywood Boulevard. Two stories of rooms surrounding all four sides of the pool. Very private." Still moving at a fast clip, he walked us up a flight of steps and unlocked a blue door on the second level of the cabanas. "My room. Marilyn liked to stay here." He gestured for me to enter. "She told me the first modeling job she had in Hollywood was lying on the diving board out there, wearing a terry-cloth swimsuit. She loved coming back years later, knowing she'd never have to pose for another cheesecake picture if she didn't want to, that she could just stay in her room and fuck whoever she felt like fucking or, even better, nobody at all. That was her idea of success. Fucking nobody at all." He drew the curtains in the room.

I sat on the bed, rubbing my arm. "You hurt me. You're not above the law."

"Sorry, but when you're famous, you actually *are* above some laws. And you get a better shake on others. You don't get executed if you're convicted of murder, for example. You get life. It's an understanding the courts have with the Screen Actors Guild." He pulled out the room's desk chair and sat, positioned opposite me. Behind him were color prints of Sacré-Coeur and Montparnasse. "And let me remind you that within the limits of our relationship, you are the lawbreaker, Bonnie Fucking Trout, falsely assuming another person's identity, representing *her* home as your home, all for the purpose of eliciting confidential information from a business competitor. That's what was going on, right?"

He got up restlessly, went to the small refrigerator, and got out a can of Pabst Blue Ribbon beer. "Mouth a little dry, Bonnie?" he asked.

"Yes."

"Yeah, I'd expect so." He shut the refrigerator door, pulled the tab on the beer, and drank.

"Now look, wait a second," I said in the strongest voice I could summon. "Obviously, I lied to you about who I was. I'm sorry. It was a huge untruth. It wasn't planned, I was freaked out by suddenly being on the plane with you, having read your memoirs, having tried to get you involved in my book and been rejected—and once I was in the lie, I couldn't get out. I know I would have told you eventually."

He laughed one short snort. "When? After a reporter said, 'Hey, Lanny, that girl whose hand you're holding isn't a schoolteacher named Trout like you're telling everyone, she's a journalist named O'Connor, I used to have drinks with her at the Old Town Bar, she's writing an exposé about you, didn't you know that?' Would you have probably told me then?" He threw the beer can at me, but it hit the wall instead. I think he meant it to.

I snapped back, "But what about you, you bastard—you screwed me and left my body to be discovered by a maid at the Plaza hotel!"

"Fuck you. Don't pull that 'a strong offense is the best defense' crap. You have no defense. Go take off your clothes." He nodded toward the bathroom door.

I guess I was not the first imbecilic young woman to have entertained the thought "If he rapes me, maybe I can convert it into a seduction, and I can pacify him." Usually these women die.

I felt guilty, I wanted him not to hate me . . . but he had also treated me horribly in New York and now he was saying hateful things to me. I invoked Marilyn's spirit. I didn't have to fuck anyone I didn't want to.

"No," I said. "If you touch me, I'll scream loud enough that the cabana boys will come in through the window, and then it won't matter whether I'm Trout or O'Connor or Bouton, you'll be Lanny Morris, America's Favorite Rapist."

I thought he was going to hit me, and I thought I'd better make my first scream as loud as I could because I might not get out a second one. Instead he brushed by me and slid open a mirrored closet door. "Don't flatter yourself. Put these on. We're leaving, fast."

On a hanger was a dove-gray shift in my size. From the shelf above the hangers he produced sunglasses and a blond wig. I turned to him and asked, "Do you always keep a woman's change of clothing in your hotel rooms?"

He sneered like an intellectual Elvis. "You think my being here today was a coincidence? You think *your* being here was either? I asked Jim Bouton to bow out as a favor to me yesterday morning, which he was more than glad to do. I told the committee if they could get you to present an award to the late Arthur Conklin, who was certain to be a no-show, I'd appear at the ceremony and accept it for him, as long as they kept my involvement totally secret from you, your publisher, and your publicist. They jumped at the chance."

I inwardly winced. So my star was not yet on the ascendant. Lanny had gotten me the invite, for purposes of his own.

"How did you find out who I was?" I wondered if Reuben had spilled the beans, but then realized that he knew me only as Bonnie Trout. And he was not the type to rush back to Lanny with the juicy news that I was in town. If anything, he'd have tried to spare me any further contact with his employer.

"A friend of yours told me," Lanny stated matter-of-factly as he examined the blond wig. Clearly, he was not going to elaborate. "Go change."

I was growing increasingly nervous about what Lanny had in mind once I'd donned the outfit he'd had ready and waiting for me. "I don't understand. Why do I have to disguise myself?" I asked.

"Because I don't want to be seen with you in public," he said airily. "You were just very visible at an awards luncheon, the press now knows who you are and about your current project, you did your little comedy turn, some of the same reporters may be staking themselves out where my limo is. If they spot the two of us, I'd rather they see me leave with a mysterious blonde than with a journalist who's writing a book about me with my ex-partner. It might look like I'm endorsing the book, or even helping you with it, or anything other than trying to convince you, as my lawyers and I have been trying to do for some time, *not to write the goddamn thing!*" He glared at me for a moment, then gave me a funny smile. "So go change."

A few minutes later he was hurrying us down the inside hallway of the ground-floor cabana area. Most guests on this level left their rooms via sliding glass doors that verged upon the pool's patio area, thick with foliage, from which they could walk to the hotel proper. It was a pleasant, sunny route. The alternative was to exit your room by the front door, which put you into a narrow hallway used primarily by the maids and room service. This was how Lanny led us away from the hotel and out a service entrance where laundry was delivered. We walked down a few steps and were in the rear parking lot of the Roosevelt. Above us I could see huge letters mounted on a grid atop the hotel's roof, proclaiming its name proudly, if backward. There was a limo lurking behind a dumpster. A driver with a hard face and big arms in a uniform that was too small for him was leaning against the car, waiting for us. He opened the rear door the instant he saw Lanny and looked around for possible paparazzi. There were no members of the press to be seen. It appeared that Lanny's attempt to disguise me had proven unnecessary.

"Okay, Mr. Morris?" asked the driver. "Home?" This was a much rougher-looking man than Michael Dougherty had been.

"We're taking the lady to her next appointment, Dominic. Bel Air." He looked at me. "You're going to see Vince, right? That's what Nita Cowan told me you told her. I was sitting with her at your table while you were up there pretending to be a comic."

So this was the end for me. Dominic closed the dividing window and partition and we moved along Highland toward Sunset.

Lanny stared out the tinted window. The last time I'd seen him look this way, he'd been recalling the time he got beat up by a gang in Brooklyn.

"How'd you manage to get the seat behind me on the plane?" he asked at last. "That must have taken some doing."

"It was pure coincidence," I said sullenly. Clearly everything I'd done or said was now going to be appraised in its most cynical interpretation. "Now I get to ask a question. How could you have just left me there that morning at the Plaza?"

"Stop trying to build it up. You were asleep, unconscious from the workout we had. So was I, but Reuben woke me, told me I had to be a substitute performer-conductor with the L.A. Philharmonic that evening, at the Hollywood Bowl. Charity comedy concert for Lanny's Club. It was supposed to be Sid Caesar but Sid, you know . . . I had to get the first flight out. I knew we'd be together again. And see? I was right."

He smiled coldly at me as we passed the igloo of the Cinerama Pacific Dome.

"But you could have left me a note or called me there."

"I didn't want to wake you, airplanes don't have telephones, by the time I got to L.A. you'd left the hotel, and I left you a note with my numbers," he said, looking away from me.

"Where?"

"I don't know, I think I left it on the pillow next to you. If not there, then in the living room. Maybe the maid threw it out."

Not even a clever lie. "And when you didn't hear from me, you didn't think, oh, maybe you should try calling me?"

"I did. Your— Bonnie Trout's number was disconnected."

"Really."

"Yeah, I got a dead line. I called it more than once."

There's nothing that annoys me as much as when a man thinks a woman is stupid enough (or smitten enough) that she will accept his lamest excuses. The fact that we don't always bother to challenge them is simply our prerogative. I'd called Bonnie myself almost every day since I'd left New York and always gotten through. And she'd called me from my apartment in L.A. with no difficulty whatsoever. I would soon have the phone bill to prove it. At worst, Lanny would have gotten the answering service. The number had never been disconnected.

"And you didn't try reaching me, Bonnie, at my school?"

"Look, why are we even *talking* about this?" he blared at me, obviously eager to get away from specifics. "Have you not understood me? I don't *like* you. I'm sorry we met. You put stuff over on me, I'm sure you probably *laughed* at me—I'm one of the great comedians of this era; no one is ever supposed to *laugh* at me until I cause them to do so!" He leaned forward and barked at Dominic, "Head up Stone Canyon Road."

We turned off West Sunset Boulevard, following the "sane" route to Vince's home that I'd figured out for myself after my first visit.

Lanny scoffed in a low voice, "Look, you're not going to get around this. You told me you were someone else. You took me to your—sorry, to Bonnie's—apartment and told me it was yours. You had *just read my manuscript* a few days earlier, something almost nobody on earth has seen, and you didn't think you should have mentioned that to me when we met? Or at the very, very least before we had sex?"

"I was going to tell you."

"When?"

The limo started to work its way up Tortuoso Way. "I don't know," I conceded.

It hadn't been enough to go through this with Lanny. Now I'd have to witness the *son et lumière* of Vince's shock, surprise, anger, resentment, and disdain. I'd partaken of recent sex with Vince's ex-partner and forgotten to mention it to Vince. I'd allowed Vince to think that our book was being done without Lanny's involvement when in fact I'd not only read fragments of Lanny's own reminiscences but heard them from Lanny's own two lips, pried and plied by me. I'd invented a half brother and flung his ashes across the Everglades. Duplicity, thy name is O'Connor.

"How did you find me out?" I couldn't help but ask.

Lanny leaned forward and said to the driver, "Stop here, Dom."

We pulled over and, with a slow crunch of gravel and dirt, stopped alongside a Cape Cod–style house with blue shutters. On our left was that same unmarked driveway with painted white stones on either side that led up to Vince's home. Lanny wore the satisfied expression of a detective revealing the murderer's identity to suspects assembled in the study. "I had to be in Washington last Friday making nice with some congressmen. Lanny's Club needs to keep its federal funding. Saturday I spoke at a Boosters' Breakfast for my Kids and had the rest of the day to myself. They've got this new train service to New York, the Metroliner. It arrives just across town from where you live—I remembered the apartment building real well. I thought instead of flying back to L.A. out of Dulles, I'd book myself out of JFK. I'd been thinking about you. I thought I might surprise you."

Translation: I was alone in Washington and horny.

"So I bought some flowers when I got there, put on my usual disguise, you know, that blond wig—"

"Illya Kuryakin," I realized aloud.

"What?"

I thought of Beejay's description of the hippie with the blond pageboy haircut. "You looked like Illya Kuryakin. The character David McCallum played on *The Man from U.N.C.L.E.*"

Lanny considered this. "Yeah, I guess the wig does make me look a bit like him. So now I buzz your buzzer. 'B. Trout,' it says. You ask, 'Who is it?' I say, 'Flowers for Bonnie Trout.' You buzz me up. I take the elevator. You open the door. It's not you."

Poor Beejay. Neither the vice principal nor the narcissistic actor had sent her the flowers. Worse, she had met Lanny Morris and not even known it.

"The woman who is *not* you says, 'Yes?' I say, 'Flowers for Bonnie Trout.' She says, 'That's me.' I feel like a jerk. I wanted to ask her, 'Well, who is that girl who says she is you?' But that might get you in some kind of trouble. I don't know what the play is. I just know I don't want this girl to recognize me. Lanny Morris is not supposed to go around ringing the doorbells of strange women living in the East Thirties. So I railroad myself back to Washington, completely confused. Sunday, I uncancel a speech I'd canceled at an Interfaith Luncheon. I fly back to L.A. that evening from Dulles."

He knocked on the smoked window divider, and the driver lowered it. Lanny asked him for a pen and something to write on. Dominic produced a pen from his shirt pocket and a copy of the day's *Hollywood Re-*

porter. Lanny wrote something on the back page, shielding it from my view. He handed the magazine and pen back to the driver. "Dom, give this number to the radio operator on the car phone after we're outside the car," he instructed. "Keep your voice down, it's a private number."

Well, since Lanny already knew the number and since he was giving the number to the driver, it was a safe bet the person he was keeping the number private from was me. Lanny opened the car door, stepped out, and motioned for me to step out as well. There was no dial on a car phone; you had to verbally request the number from an operator. I guess all this was simply to stop me from hearing what the number was. Frankly, at the moment, I felt better being out in the open than in the back of a limo driven by a thug named Dominic.

A car drove by, its driver not surprised to see a man in a custom-tailored tuxedo standing in the sunlight outside a limo in Bel Air. To while away the moments, Lanny continued his story as breezily as if he were pitching a movie to a cohort over drinks at the Polo Lounge. "I have a firm here in L.A. that handles security for me. Did you know that if you have the right people working for you, you can access anyone's phone records? So Monday, I give them Bonnie Trout's name and address. Tuesday afternoon, I was supposed to meet with Vince and a journalist named O'Connor, but as luck would have it, I'm doing this huge shoot that morning with Morris the Cat. The gag is Morris and Morris, like we're the new comedy team. And they've got us in a nightclub set and Morris is saying Vince's catchphrases and I'm saying, 'With those kinds of jokes, we'll need 9-Lives,' very distinguished stuff for a forty-two-year-old man. Only they've got the guy from the ASPCA, and apparently you can't have Morris under the lights for more than five minutes each half hour, and the director thinks he's Otto Preminger, only more Teutonic. I get out of makeup four hours later than planned and Vince tells me you've already left for New York. How's your brother, by the way?"

I didn't reply.

"By that evening, I have an accounting of Bonnie Trout's telephone calls in front of me. I was particularly interested in the night I left you in her apartment after we both had flown from L.A. together. After all, you had just spent the day with '*the* Lanny Morris.' Who would you want to share this big news with first?" He smiled, aware how this sounded coming from his own lips. "Well, there was only one long-distance call made that night, but it was for three hours, no less! A collect call to a phone in Los Angeles, a Studio City exchange. So I dial the number and get your answering service. They answer in your name. The same name as the journalist I was supposed to meet with Vince! I have my people try to get a photo of you, but they can't find one in any of the articles you've written, except once when you wore a mask. That's when I contacted the Scotties people and made a barter deal with them to get you up on stage at the Roosevelt. So I could take a good look at you. Looking good, Bonnie."

The front right window rolled down and Dominic said, "They're putting through your call, Mr. Morris."

Lanny reached into the car and pulled the phone just beyond the window, as far as its coiled cord would stretch. He said, "Hello, Vince? It's me."

"You don't have to tell Vince about this," I whispered. "It was between you and me, it was a private matter."

He looked at me as if I were truly demented. "Don't be ridiculous." He turned back to the phone. "Listen, Monsieur Collins, I wanted to pay upon you like a personal visit. Oh, say in three minutes, that okay?" He listened to Vince. "Has it been *that* long, really? My, how time flies when time flies. Yeah, I know. Uh-huh." Vince said something that caused Lanny to react. "Oh, she's coming by? You mean the one who's writing your book? What's her name, Bonnie Something? Oh. No, for some reason I thought her name was Bonnie, I have no idea why." He gave me a condescending glance, enjoying himself. "Yeah, well, I won't be staying. Just had something I wanted to drop off. Yeah, Captain Mysterious, that's me."

He handed the phone back to the driver and gestured for me to reenter the limo. Was there any way out of this? If I ran away, what would happen? Lanny would tell Vince anyway. Better I tell him my side of it before Lanny poisoned his mind completely. Another car slowly maneuvered its way around us, a convertible. It was driven by an elderly woman with a gaunt, unattractive face; she'd had plastic surgery around her mouth that had not gone right. How pleased she would be, I thought, if she knew quite how much I wished I were her right now. I wished I were anyone but me.

As we headed up between the white stacked rocks, Lanny looked as if he was debating with himself. Finally he spoke, in a very different tone than before.

"Listen, now I know you think you're smart, and you are, although not as smart as you think. That's okay. But in the unlikely event that you have any further dealings with our friend Vince, I want you to be very careful how smart you try to get with him. Because I'll tell you something now: Vince is not that swift. I realize he's intelligent, sensitive—I'm even told he's well read these days. But let me tell you, Vince doesn't always do what's best for him. He just wants problems taken care of with quick fixes without considering the consequences. And like you, he thinks he's a lot smarter than he really is."

It was a ridiculous statement coming from a jealous man. The limousine had reached Vince's gate. Dominic pushed the button on the intercom and gave Lanny's name. The gate opened and here we were, rested after a brief intermission and a short lecture, ready and eager for Act Two of *The Worst Day of My Life.*

Through the windshield I saw Vince step out from the sheltered courtyard. He was wearing a nice navy blue suit and club tie, the first time I'd seen him dressed that way. I thought it an odd outfit for a resumption of our interviews.

From the backseat, Lanny murmured to himself with not one drop of sarcasm, "Wow. Vince Collins. Looking pretty damn good there, pal." He turned to me. "Listen, you stay here for a minute. I haven't seen him in over a dozen years and I don't know if we'll ever see each other again, so I'd rather not start out with you as the primary topic of conversation." He didn't wait for my response but got out of the limo, saying to the driver, "See she stays put, Dom." Lanny slammed the door shut and I heard the locks in the doors click. I gently tried opening my door, but Dominic must have had an overriding power lock. I could do nothing but watch this historic meeting through tinted windows and try to read their lips.

They stood and looked at each other. Lanny mouthed, "Hello, Vince." Vince apparently replied, "Hi, Lanny." There they were, one in tuxedo, the other in dark suit and tie; they used to wear matching tuxes or suits when performing in nightclubs or replicating that mode of performance on TV. It was strange to see them stand this long together with neither doing anything funny.

So far this summit meeting wasn't exactly Stalin and F.D.R. at Yalta. It looked like Lanny may have said, "I'm glad you're doing so well." Vince offered something pleasant back. They both laughed. Then the discussion seemed to grow more serious. Lanny asked a question. Vince looked down at his shoes and replied, shaking his head.

I rapped on the divider window and Dom turned around. I called out, "Do you have any drinking water in the car?" I made a hacking coughing sound. He shook his head no and turned back around. What a sweetie.

I coughed three more times, and on the last long cough, I toggled the button for my window. It slid down one-third of the way before I stopped. Dom didn't seem to notice. I strained to hear the boys.

"I know, but I've got it covered." (This was Vince.)

"How's the drinking these days?"

"The drinking is doing great these days, it's the sobriety that isn't doing so well. No no, actually, it's very under control. Thanks for asking. But some of this other stuff that's out there—"

"Don't get stupid with that," advised Lanny. "You know, doing this book of yours is going to—"

"I know."

They stood there. The sun decided to throw a green filter over this master shot, so it ducked behind a big, polluted cloud.

Vince nodded at Lanny's tux. "Nice threads."

"Paolo designed it. I was accepting an award. For somebody else."

Vince laughed. "Awards. I haven't gotten an award in— You, you've got the whole humane-society thing going."

"Yeah, well, thank God for that. Can't get arrested for a movie, you know. Did you hear I was offered the title role in *The Picture of Dorian Gray*?"

"*You're* playing Dorian Gray?"

Lanny said in the official Lanny voice, "I'm playing the picture. Rim shot. Walk on ankles."

"I'd brain you if you weren't already brain-dead, you monkey," Vince intoned flatly.

They had fallen into their ritual exchanges automatically but spoke them through to the end, as if not completing the Litany would bring upon them horrendous misfortune.

There had been a general backwash of sound from the cars that traveled on the road far below this perch. The sound stopped for a moment, the way all conversation in a crowded restaurant can suddenly stop, by sheer coincidence. I heard more clearly:

Vince said, "*You* know. You do, don't you."

Lanny gestured with his open hands as if he were comparing the weights of two bags of gold. "Vince, I know by default. You understand? It's math. That's how I know."

Vince looked at Lanny as if his partner were a trick question. "But all it has to be is that you're lying, and then the math means nothing. It would be so easy for you to do that." His face went dead. "You know what, Lanny? I'm glad we broke up."

"No more than me, pal." They looked at each other as if they'd come to a new understanding. Lanny slapped his hands together once. "And now you're going to be even gladder we did. I am, Frère Collins, the Bearer of Evil Tidings."

Lanny walked toward the limo. Dominic hit the button that unlocked all the doors, and as it made its quadraphonic clicking noise, Lanny opened the door on my side and said, "Step out and meet Vince, sweetheart."

I had never been in this kind of situation before. I'd be damned if I was going to step out of the limo with my head bowed, biting the nail of my index finger with shame. On the other hand, I really was in no position to brazen it out and act like a proud Jezebel. I'd been caught and been inarguably wrong. But suddenly I knew that I was not going to let a prick like Lanny Morris extract his full measure of flesh from me.

I got out of the limo, bringing with me the laundry bag containing my dress from the awards luncheon. Vince was truly shocked to see me, that much I believed. (On the other hand, I'd believed his tears in *The Maginot Line* when Elke Sommer had died in his arms, and to the best of my knowledge, Elke was still very much alive.) Vince looked at me, at Lanny, back at me. "I don't understand."

I spoke in the even tone of an independent auditor at a stockholders' meeting. "Vince, a few days after we first met, I found myself seated behind Lanny on a flight to New York. Neuman and Newberry's travel agent booked my seat—I had nothing to do with it. You can check that if you like. Whether Lanny had something to do with sitting in front of *me* is an unanswered question."

"Oh, please—" Lanny groaned.

"Owing to the table-for-four seating in first class, I ended up having dinner with Lanny, his manager, and his valet. They asked me my name. Vince, I had just finished reading the first chapter of Lanny's autobiography, obviously a rival work. His lawyers had let me see it in the hope of discouraging our own project. As a reflex, since he probably viewed me as 'the enemy,' I gave Lanny not my real name but that of a friend of mine whose apartment I was going to stay at in Manhattan. In other words, I lied to him, and I'm responsible for what came out of that lie. I thought at the time I simply had to get through the awkwardness of the flight itself, but the trouble is that Mr. Morris, as you know, is quite the self-promoter. We went to a ball game the next day, where he'd arranged to sing for a sell-out crowd at Shea Stadium. Then he flew me by helicopter to a rooftop in Manhattan, bought out a room at a restaurant so we could sip immense martinis in total privacy, took me on the mandatory hansom-cab ride through Central Park, and Vince, by the time we were back at his hotel, I admit I was completely starstruck, suckered, and schnockered."

Vince nodded. "You slept with him."

Lanny spoke up. "I think her words, Vince, were *'Oh, take me, please!'*"

I shook my head. "I swear I never said that."

And I *could* swear, because what I'd said was "Oh . . . of course, yes, have me. By all means," which was, of course, very different by the Spiro Agnew Standard of Nondenial Denial. I added, "But honestly, I don't remember much of what happened after that." Immense lie. I remembered everything, vividly. I'd hoped and expected it would happen again and again, if only Lanny hadn't revealed himself to be the world's biggest bastard. But Lanny couldn't be inside my brain, wouldn't know how much the night had meant to me, how much I'd fallen asleep thinking I'd awaken to a new phase of my life, so there was no way he would know what a lie this was. "All I can tell you is the next morning, I found that Lanny had left town without explanation. He never contacted me again. Today is the first time I've seen him since that evening. And that, Vince, is the truth."

Lanny turned in a small circle. "Vince, she's so full of crap I can't even begin."

Vince nodded. "Okay. What did she lie about?"

Lanny sputtered. "It's the way she's presented it. She's one shrewd bitch, Vince. You can't give her your trust. Understand? That's the only reason I brought her here. To warn you."

Vince withdrew a pack of Viceroys from his pocket and lit one with his gold stick lighter. He exhaled and looked at me. "So. You slept with my ex-partner."

Oh God. What could I say? "Technically, yes."

"Doesn't sound like things were particularly technical." He half-smiled. "I don't suppose he forced you to do anything? I mean, it was all voluntary on your part."

Something about this seemed familiar. I noticed Vince's suave but wounded expression, the look of hurt when the world has let you down and you are not surprised. Where had I seen this before?

Then I realized where.

I'd seen it in my mind's eye, when I'd read the very first part of Lanny's first chapter, which recounted how Vince had "discovered" Lanny sleeping with Denise, the Florida P.R. woman whom Lanny helped Vince discard. Was this now a staged routine, was I seeing the grand reuniting of Collins and Morris? Did I detect a look passing between them, these two boys who on a nightclub stage had been able to read each other's minds?

I wasn't going to fold my cards like Denise had done and slink away, leaving the boys to find their next victim.

I spoke to Vince as if Lanny had evaporated. "When I came back here, I was never so glad to embrace this work we've been sharing. I made a terrible mistake in New York. I apologize to you more than I know how to say. If my bad judgment and stupidity have destroyed the wonderfully comfortable friendship we were having, or made repugnant to you how we planned to"—I searched for the word—"conclude our work, I will be so woefully sorry. But, Vince, the realization of your life's story shouldn't be threatened because I have failings, or because I can't handle two huge martinis, or because your ex-partner knows how to play to an audience of one. Please let me continue to work with you, Vince. I'll help you tell your story right. Give me the chance to earn your trust, your faith, and your friendship again."

Vince threw down his cigarette and put it out with his foot. He looked right at Lanny. "Nice seeing you, pally. We'll have to do this every thirteen years."

Lanny started to walk to the limousine, stopped after a step, and faced his ex-partner. "Just you be careful, Vince." He turned slowly toward me. "Oh, and great recovery, Bonnie. You bend in even more directions than I realized." Lanny headed back to his car and this time did not stop.

As the limo drove off, the sun decided to reappear. I stood looking at Vince's suit. I'd never seen navy blue so brightly lit. "Nice suit," I commented, not knowing at this point what else to say.

He looked at his outfit, seemingly embarrassed. "I made reservations for us for dinner. Somewhere special, requires conservative dress. You warned me on the phone yesterday that you'd still be wearing your Scotty-presenting outfit, so I thought it would work out fine."

He looked at the drab A-line dress Lanny had made me change into. I held up the laundry bag from the motel. "I still have my outfit. I can change back into it in a second."

He looked toward his house and up at the sky. "Oh, for God's sake, it's not as if I thought you were a virgin. Or that we're both in high school and Lanny and I are rivals on the track team. By show-business standards, you're a saint. For all I know, Lanny went out of his way to seduce you, just to get in a dig at me. Let's go inside."

We walked into his home. He had, with all good intentions, placed the tape recorder on the coffee table, near where I'd left it three days earlier. I looked up at this man who was taking off his jacket, loosening his tie. He was the remedy, the solution.

We went about our work, after a fashion. I asked him featherweight questions. Nothing today about the girl in New Jersey, whose name for the moment I couldn't remember. To his credit, Vince raised the topic. I told him that, under the circumstances, I didn't feel this was the day to embark on anything that serious. He understood. In my current state, I was not going to challenge Vince Collins, who I hoped still liked me and wanted me.

His answers to my powder-puff questions were as charming as ever. We laughed. I was just so happy to be laughing with him. Vince suddenly stood up. It seemed we were finished for the day.

"Hey. Come on, put on your fancy dress." He smiled impetuously. "Let's go get drunk in Disneyland."

I thought he was joking. But oh, he was not. He was not joking at all.

TWENTY-SEVEN

New Orleans Square had been laid out beautifully by its designers, who'd warrened the area with surprising little courtyards, serpentining galleries, and unexpected arcades, imparting to its abbreviated lanes the same sense of mystery and discovery as an aimless wander around Saint-Germain-des-Prés on a gray morning.

On such a wander in this New Orleans, built upon the former orange groves of Anaheim, you might easily walk right past a sedate sea-green-colored door recessed from the street and tightly flanked by two charming columns trimmed in warm gilt, handsomely fenestrated at the top with a subtle mosaic of stained glass. The only sign, demarcation, or explanation for this door is its address on Royal Street: the number 33, tastefully inscribed in an oval plaque to the right. To the left of the door (which you would find to be locked) is a small brass box behind whose hinged flap is a doorbell. If you were to ring it, a polite voice over a speaker in the box would ask how they might assist you. Were you to say anything but the right thing, you would be gently and respectfully encouraged to continue your walk with the expressed hope that you have a very pleasant day. And you would never know that you had come as close as you were ever likely to come to entering the most secret place in all of the Magic Kingdom.

Club 33. The place, as Vince had promised, where we could get drunk in Disneyland.

He had wanted to take me there on our first visit, but he'd been told it was closed for the installation of some new ventilation. Today was the first date since then for which he'd been able to reserve a table. You had to be a member of the club to dine (and wine) there, for which you paid a sizable membership fee; it also didn't hurt if you happened to be, say, the ambassador from Luxembourg, or the head of General Motors, or Vince Collins.

We were dressed more than appropriately for our seven P.M. dinner reservation. We had entered the park through Guest Services once again, and had drawn some stares for our elegant clothing amid a sea of T-shirts, madras shorts, and Goofy hats, but, luckily, people were lining up for the staged parade down Main Street; most visitors were more concerned with finding a place where little Tommy could see Mickey than watching a sunglassed Vince and me slither along the shortest route to Royal Street.

There was the buzz of an electronic lock, and the door of number 33 was opened by a uniformed attendant who might have been plucked from the first-class dining room of the *QE2.* Electric candles and a chandelier brought out the rosy hue of the paneled foyer. Seated at a concierge's desk, an attractive young woman had picked up a French-style phone and, we would learn, was speaking to the maître d' upstairs, advising him of our arrival.

She welcomed us, asking if we'd like to ascend via the stairs or the lift (the technically more accurate name for the style of Victorian wrought-iron cage elevator that rested snugly within the wide spiral of the staircase before us). I wondered if anyone had ever opted for the stairs.

The young man who'd let us in also operated the elevator, which let us out into Lounge Alley. Seated at a smaller writing desk was the maître d', whose name was William. This room, too, was beautifully paneled and had original artwork on its walls from the Disney studio, mainly landscapes. Nowhere was there a sign of Donald, Goofy, or Mickey. We might as well have been in an anteroom of an elegant hotel in Oslo. We passed by a Victorian phone box and were told by William that it had been used in the movie *The Happiest Millionaire.* Vince leaned over to me and murmured, "When we finish our book, *I'll* be the happiest millionaire." It was just a silly joke, but it meant more to me at that moment than anything else he might have said. *Our* book. Finish. Together. We were back on track. Things were nearing normal.

Since it was my first visit, William suggested we take a look around the different rooms before the sun set. I didn't realize it, but the restaurant crossed over Royal Street, so that one could look down (literally) upon those guests on their way to Pirates or the Haunted Mansion or standing in line in hopes of a table at the Blue Bayou, where they served a Bloody Mary without the booze, which I had called a Bloody Shame.

From other windows could be seen the Rivers of America and Tom Sawyer Island over the tops of Frontierland's buildings. The fabulous thing was that, when seated, you couldn't see the crowd at all. The forced perspective made the waterway and its island seem as if we were in a Michelin five-star hotel that had been improbably erected in some vast wilderness above the mighty Mississippi.

We were shown into the main dining room, which had all the starched prettiness of the Grill Room at the Connaught. The room was lined with pairs of French doors, each pair containing twelve paned squares of glass and spanned by a wide transom in an elliptical design of the Edwardian style. Each set of doors seemed to lead to a tiny terrace overlooking the park. We were seated at what seemed to be the best table for two in the room. From my seat, I could view only the more rustic parts of the park, for which I was grateful. I didn't want to see any Rocket Rides or Flying Dumbos from this elegant room. I'd see the Flying Dumbos later.

"Well: your first cocktail while seated in the heart of Disneyland!" Vince smiled. "Better make it something special. You won't be able to get one next time you're at the Sunkist Citrus House." His comment, while sweet, added a tinge of unhappiness to the moment. It was a terrible curse of mine that I would pine for things even while they were happening. During my youth, I'd spent more time thinking how someday I would yearn for my lost youth than I'd spent *having* my youth. Vince's comment reminded me that someday this place might be off limits to me (as well might Vince himself). I needed to shake this out of my head. Enjoy *now.* There is only ever *now.*

"What do you recommend?" I asked Vince. I was going to go wherever Vince went tonight. I was the self-appointed recording secretary of Vince's Club. No feisty modern woman me. I was his *date* and I'd be a great date, I would, for this guy. If we hadn't previously made a pact to the contrary, he could have had me that night on a silver platter and you wouldn't have heard a word of complaint from me.

He ordered a vesper for me, an invention of Ian Fleming's, named after one of James Bond's first recorded romances. Vince's modification was that it be made with Tanqueray's Malacca gin, which was silkier and contained citrus. He had them garnish it with lemon peel instead of a slice of orange. Vince asked for his usual, a Jack Daniel's on the rocks, and our waiter knew without being asked to bring him his usual side of club soda and a straw.

My vesper arrived just as evensong might have been sung at a nearby church and as the evening star of Venus appeared in the soft magenta sky. It was smooth and warm, a martini without the steely edge. Vince smiled as I voiced my approval. We ordered from the refreshingly short menu and had another round each. Venus was beginning to glow.

Would it have mattered if the food was any good? It was traditional French but perfectly rendered. And the wines. With our *potage Saint-Germain,* Vince had chosen a 1969 Puligny-Montrachet that was absolutely spry and, like all really fine wines, intoxicated me far more quickly than usual.

With the rack of lamb that we shared, Vince told the waiter to dispatch the remaining third of our Montrachet to the chef with our compliments and asked the sommelier for a bottle of the 1959 Château Haut-Brion. He asked the sommelier if he would mind decanting it for us, and the sommelier said he would have recommended exactly that had Vince not requested it first.

The sommelier extracted the cork, offered it to Vince to sniff, and set a candle upon the table about a foot away from a graceful crystal decanter he'd brought for the task at hand. Lighting its wick, he then slowly poured the Haut-Brion into the decanter while the candlelight glowed behind the neck of the bottle. He eyed the illuminated ruby liquid carefully, like a diagnostician of X rays, and when the first dregs showed in the neck of the bottle, he stopped pouring, so that the wine in the decanter was now both well oxygenated and free from sediment.

Vince indicated that the sommelier should pour a trickle of the liquid into my glass for my sampling and our verdict. It was a continent of its own. It had met with the approval of Samuel Pepys in the 1600s, and it was now meeting with mine. No wine had ever been so complex on my tongue as this, and I must have moaned a bit.

"Anything the matter?" asked the sommelier, concerned.

"No . . . no, nothing. Heaven." I looked at Vince. "Thank you, it's wonderful."

The sommelier nodded. "I suspect there will never be a year in this century as special as 1959. Do you agree, Mr. Collins?"

Vince frowned. "Yes, 1959 was a great year for French wines," he concurred. I wondered if he was thinking that 1959 had not been a very great year for Maureen O'Flaherty, or for her mother.

But the wine fueled and infused my happiness, which grew to be delight, which by my third glass had become bliss on the outskirts of rapture. The food was sensual and reassuring, as was our conversation. I was out of the woods and I was in love. It had taken nearly losing Vince to make me realize how warm and strong he was within me.

For dessert, I had ordered a chocolate raspberry soufflé an hour earlier and Vince a simple crème caramel. To go with it (yes, the decanter of Haut-Brion was empty and the wine was singing to me from deep within my bloodstream), he ordered a half bottle of a dessert wine, Château d'Yquem, perhaps the most famous dessert wine in the world. I needed only a glass.

While they were making us *café diable* (by trickling flaming cognac down the skin of an orange that had been peeled in one long coil until the cognac's blue flames dripped slowly into a waiting cup of French espresso), Vince told our waiter we just wanted to step out onto the terrace off the Trophy Room for a few minutes and would it be all right if we took our wineglasses with us? The waiter said he was sure that would be quite all right and understood why we'd like to take in the view.

Vince took my arm and we walked out of the main dining room. When we got to the lobby lounge, he put his arm around my waist. I felt as comforted by this as a little girl who, after being in trouble with her father all day, is reminded by him that he loves her more than anything on earth. My Freudian slip was at the moment spun from clingy, diaphanous silk, thigh-high and slit nearly to the waist.

He stepped us out onto a small balcony. The Haunted Mansion glowed merrily in the night, as did I, I was sure. I sighed, "You deliver on your promises, don't you? I'm drunk in Disneyland, Vince. Only I wish there were a different word for the state I'm in other than *drunk*. I'm not giddy; I feel calm. I'm not slurring my speech or saying foolish things, am I?" He reassured me I was not. "I'm not pickled, or plastered. I'm not dizzy. What can I call it? Heady?"

"Under the influence?" he suggested.

I shook my head. "Too many negatives attached. We'll have to work on this, Vince. Tell me we can still go on some rides tonight?"

Vince nodded. "What would be the point of achieving this divine state and not going on some rides?"

I was worried all of a sudden. "How long before this buzz wears off, do you think?" I was doing it again, dammit, living in the "it's over" while the thing was still happening. "I mean, once we leave the club, we can't come back later, right?"

"Right, you're not allowed to come here and just have drinks. But I think I have a way we can stretch the buzz right up to when the park closes. Look." He unfolded his beautiful hand. He held two small capsules. They looked like little bumblebees in their yellow-and-black jackets. He popped one in his mouth in a flash, hiding his face so no one would see, and swallowed it with a sip of the flinty but luscious Château d'Yquem.

"Want to join me?" he asked good-naturedly. He still had one capsule left.

Wherever he was, I wanted to join him. "What are they?"

He shrugged. "They're like very, very mild-mannered quaaludes. You must have done a few 'ludes in your time, right?"

Right, I had. These days people were getting busted for *not* doing drugs. Health fanatics in San Francisco would show you the device they had to deionize the air, they'd drink nothing but water melted from subterranean ice caverns, they'd serve you a meal consisting solely of steamed desert-grown kale, and finish off with this really superior cocaine studded with little yellow dots. An active, healthy lifestyle included vigorous exercise, consistent meditation, and amphetamines. Heroin was gauche, booze was an embarrassment, but whatever came out of a pharmaceutical lab *had* to be okay—I mean, that's why we have the Food and Drug Administration, right? Girls in their twenties who weighed no more than ninety-one pounds easily convinced physicians to prescribe them black beauties to help them get their weight down. And a quaalude was merely an entire bottle of codeine cough syrup in convenient tablet form.

What I'd enjoyed about them was the way they affected time. If you were feeling good, they made you seem to feel good a lot longer. Like if you love a hit record played at 45 RPM, imagine how much you'll love it at 33! Oh, and what do you know! We're here *at* Club 33. An omen. I never needed much more than an omen when it came to Vince.

"You're sure they're okay with alcohol?" I asked.

"They work even *better* with alcohol. I would know, believe me." His face was creased with the most inviting smile. "Hey, come on in, honey, the water's fine."

If he had suggested we get tattooed together, I would have been having *Widowmaker* inscribed on my left buttock in a flash. To drop one little 'lude on an evening that I wanted to last forever . . . this was not what you would call the Great Debate. I smiled, popped the pill in my mouth, drank from his cup of sweet wine as if this were part of a wedding ceremony, and looked up to him for approval.

As soon as I swallowed, I saw fireworks in clean, phosphorescent golds and reds and blues. Not because of the pill. There actually were fireworks, a mid-evening display over the Rivers of America. We stood on our little terrace and toasted the Chinese, who had been so civilized as to have invented fireworks without once considering using explosives as weaponry.

Vince wasn't given a check (it went onto his club account, and God knows with the wines he'd ordered the meal was easily into four figures), but he distributed cash tips subtly and no doubt generously. Oh, how I hated leaving. At least outside the club it was dark now, and no one could see that the man I was with was Vince Collins. I got to hold his arm and press my head against his shoulder. I hadn't been this wobbly-kneed-smitten with a guy since I'd given myself up to my high school boyfriend Todd. And one of the moody romantic albums we'd played in the background (to cover our immense embarrassment) had been a classic LP, lushly arranged by Nelson Riddle, called *Torch Songs for When the Lights Are Low . . . Sung by Vince Collins.*

"Hey. Partner," he murmured. I loved him calling me that. "Do you want to go on Adventures thru Inner Space?"

A shiver went through me. Did he understand that the closest thing to a Tunnel of Love in Disneyland was "Adventures thru Inner Space"?

"I would if you would," I answered huskily.

We stepped quickly down the path that led directly to Tomorrowland.

Vince was no longer afraid of tomorrow, it seemed, just as I was suddenly enamored with the *now.*

The attraction bannered "Monsanto presents Adventures thru Inner Space" was never crowded, for which I had always been grateful, because I liked the ride a lot. Its main problem was that it was absolutely free, not even an A coupon. I suppose guests assumed that something free would be simply a commercial for Monsanto, but it was in fact a very cool ride. It was the first to feature Omnimovers, an endless conveyor belt of two-seater cars, each of which wrapped around its passengers on all sides but one, creating a nifty eggshell that limited what you could see of the ride, and others, and—more significantly—what others could see of you. In Adventures thru Inner Space your car was called an Atommobile. In the Haunted Mansion, the same cars were called Doom Buggies.

The conceit of the ride was that the "train" of Atommobiles entered the Mighty Microscope. Disney had devised this so that, from the outside of the ride, one saw the real cars with their real passengers entering a "real" giant microscope and then saw a miniaturized train of Atommobiles with miniature people seated in the cars coming out the other end of the microscope. (In reality, the moment your car entered the Mighty Microscope, the conveyor belt hung a hard left turn and you were carried through a series of dark tunnels for the remainder of the ride.)

Once embarked, you sat back snugly in your car, walled in and surrounded by stereophonic sound, as you were purportedly shrunk first to the size of crystals, then molecules, and finally atoms. You were truly surrounded by projections on the curved walls around you, and since you were limited to the peripheral vision of the car you were in, the effect was encompassing and hypnotic: floating in the middle of a drop of water, or entering a galaxy of electrons that circled aimlessly around you, or, with a loud heartbeat pounding in your ears as if it were the first moment of your life, entering the heart of an atom. It was quite a journey. But far more pragmatically, from the point of view of hormonal adolescents, two people could do almost anything they wanted in that snug little cupola, from the time they entered the good old Mighty Microscope until the time they emerged from the nucleus of that atom.

Disney rides tended to feature "gags" at their conclusion, as if to wink and say, "It's not real." In Adventures thru Inner Space, the gag was seeing the single eyeball of a scientist looking at little you through the other end of the Mighty Microscope. This was also the warning cue for couples to make themselves presentable to the world.

And this was the first ride Vince, *my* Vince, wanted to take with me? I was so ready. We walked into the pavilion (none too steadily, for we were magnificently buzzed) and there were some lonely Disneyland interns virtually ecstatic to see us.

Giggling, Vince and I ducked into the cocoon of the car. Paul Frees—the voice of half of the Disneyland rides, from the Haunted Mansion to Pirates of the Caribbean—began in his ersatz–Orson Welles voice to tremulously describe the awe and wonder of being reduced to the size of a single snowflake.

Vince put his arm around me as if we were in the last row of the Bijou Theatre in Pittsburgh, Pennsylvania, and with nobody twenty cars ahead of us or behind us, we entered the Mighty Microscope.

And the pill I'd taken kicked in.

Oh, Lordy me. My guess was that I felt the effects before Vince, being lesser in weight and size than my wonderfully tall fellow. I think the slightly psychedelic effect of the ride may also have helped the chemicals take hold, the way hypnotic music can amplify and augment the effects of a joint. We were entering the tunnel as part of this giant, endless caterpillar, snug as a bug in a Monsanto rug, and as the darkness of the tunnel surrounded us, that's when I first felt it. The pulsations started in my groin, not my head. They rose up through me like a warm fountain of shameful feelings, up into my breasts, my shoulders, my neck. And then they gently rushed into my brain and I had never understood but now I did. I might once have been scared by these feelings, but I'd been readied for them by the nectareous wine I had drunk, and now the wine was drinking me. And Vince was with me, so I had nothing to fear. "Do you feel it?" I asked him softly. He told me it was just beginning.

The tunnel promised warm, glowing light ahead. *This* was the true Alice in Wonderland ride. Oh yes. I was definitely crawling along the dark rabbit hole, and now I was falling gracefully with Vince into a vast and expanding space. Straight and sober and unstoned, the ride would still have been somewhat hallucinatory, so imagine experiencing it from within my current sensory state. Vince and I drifted through a light field light-years away from everything. "Do you feel it?" I asked him. He kissed me. He kissed me and held my head in his hands and kissed me again. Our faces were illuminated by a billion water crystals whirling their lyric dance around us. I was happy. Could I please be this happy always?

His hands groped for me. They were strong and big. I wanted him to have everything of me. I wanted my breasts to nurture him and my legs to coil tightly around him and pull him to me as if I were some alluring creature of the sea drawing him toward a glorious death in my arms and then we both would live. I needed him to have more hands, to touch me more places at once. "Oh Vince," I said so cleverly, my higher education coming into play. "Vince." It was such a beautiful word and the molecules agreed with me, swirling as they talked to me. We, the molecules and I, noticed the *V* at the beginning of his name, so valiant and victorious, and the modest *i,* and by the time we had reached the *nnnnnnnnnnn,* it was me making that sound as he was pressing the strong heel of his hand against my *c* in such wonderful ways that I thought— But then I forgot what I'd been thinking. Apparently the long assembly line of cars (we had become all humanity; this was Heaven's escalator and we were rising to be with Our Maker) had gently pierced the wall of the tunnel and was now emerging into the larger universe that lay outside Disneyland where we were in the endless rhapsodic daylight of the stars. And then the giant eye of the good scientist who had helped us find this world could be seen, and Vince, who was always so much wiser and stronger than I, was helping me adjust my clothing back to respectability and we emerged, miraculously, once again in the pavilion in Disneyland. Vince's strong arm helped me get up out of the car. "Must I leave?" I asked, somewhat wrenched out of my happiness.

"You okay, miss?" asked a Disney intern as I made a slightly shaky transition onto the moving walkway that ran alongside the disembarking area of the ride. He was just the most wonderful fellow—short of Vince, that is.

"That's so like you to be concerned," I said graciously. He gave me a goofy smile. "He's very nice, isn't he, Vince?" I asked Vince, who assured me the Disney fellow was very nice, indeed. We were walking now and I asked Vince if we could go on another ride. He said he wanted to sit still for a while, but I pointed out to him that the Haunted Mansion was another slow cozy ride and we could sit in that. I just wanted to be in the dark with him some more, I wanted him to have his hands on me again; he hadn't even touched my nipples—how hard he would find them. "Haunted Mansion, Vince," I said, my choice of words inarguable. "Haunted Mansion." We were passing by a ticket booth and he put down a ten. He was so very smart. He knew how to handle money and talk to people. I could only watch in awe. "E," I said. It was the kind of ticket we needed to get on the ride and also the letter I had never reached in the name "Vince." That was good, that I had now finished his name. Now he could finish me. "Haunted Mansion, Vince," I said, eager for him.

We spent several lovely years together in the Haunted Mansion that evening. We got into our Doom Buggies and moved along the shadowy corridors of the handsome Victorian manor. On prior visits, I had enjoyed the ominous promise of the hallways past which the ride drifted but did not explore. Now we explored them, Vince and I. We got off the ride (I was very sure we had) and walked the corridors. I wasn't frightened, not I. I have always been a part of this house, I'd sensed that when I first arrived here. The tormented Lord of the Manor needed me more than he knew. Others might find the ghostly apparitions troubling, but I knew that they were, like Vince, merely seeking rest and release. And I was there to help them and him. He had his hands on me again and it was not what we had vowed, it was wrong in the eyes of the church, but— We had found our way back into our car somehow and we were outdoors, in the graveyard, a million ghosts (or protons and neutrons) whirligigging around us again. There was not as much privacy on this ride; others could see us, the townspeople—they had always disapproved but I had known. Outdoors, in front of his mansion, Vince held me. The estate was ours now. I felt another upward rush of the warmth inside me and the light went wilder in my brain.

"Vince. I need you," I told him. Did he understand? He would have to.

"I need you, too," he said.

"Oh, Vince-voice," I teased him wittily.

He walked us (but of course we didn't need to walk because our feet had been turned into Omnimovers) in the direction of the Monsanto ride, but when I got all sentimental about it, he told me no, we were going on a better ride. "How long have we been here?" I asked. "Is this our—is this still the same night?" He assured me this was still the same night. He knew everything. Now we went up an inclined walkway and a giant snake hissed up to us. It was the Monorail. "Oh, Vince, everyone will see us," I complained. I knew the Monorail was lit and there were no private compartments. We would not be able to neck the way we had on the other rides. He reassured me that the ride would get better soon.

The Monorail stopped at the Disneyland Hotel, and we got off there. We passed the Monorail Bar and I said I wanted a drink, a vesper or maybe a ginger ale. Suddenly I was dying for a ginger ale. He said he'd have them bring me a ginger ale.

Then we went from Bar Land to Elevator Land. We were alone at last. "Vince, stop the elevator," I asked him. He said he had a better stop in mind. We were now in Hall Land. There was an elderly couple, and they watched us with curiosity. We would be that couple someday.

"Weren't we in Disneyland a while ago?" I asked. "Or was that the other day?" Vince assured me that we had been in Disneyland just five minutes earlier. Now we were in Door Land. Vince produced a key and opened it. And there it was. Room Land. "Oh, for us?" I asked. He said yes. I started to sing ecstatically, *"This room is your land, this room is my land, from the New York forests, to the red tree waters . . ."* and I grabbed him. Vince was so wonderful. We kissed. Then he sat me down on the bed. "Have to get you that ginger ale," he said, picking up the phone. I was busy taking off the clothes I'd been wearing for, oh, I guess several years now. Before Vince and I were a married couple and had lived in England. When we went . . . I wanted him to see my breasts. They weren't huge, but they were very nicely shaped and my nipples . . . I pinched them to primp them up. "Five minutes?" said Vince to what I assumed was room service. He turned and saw me naked from the waist up and laughed sweetly. His hands went instantly to my breasts. "Everywhere," I said. "Put them everywhere." He pulled back the bedspread, pulled back the sheets. I watched him take off his jacket. (He had long ago tucked his tie into his jacket pocket.) Now he took off his shirt. He was as I had imagined. I loved him. I didn't ever want to lose him.

He took out his pack of cigarettes and, searching inside it, pulled out a joint. I had never seen him smoke pot before. He used that lustrous gold lighter to give it a glow and took a good hit on it. He winced as he held in the smoke and handed me the J. I hadn't done grass in a while, but I'd do whatever he was doing. It was toasty and strong. Vince was a star. His grass would be really good, would it not?

The joint inspired the drug I'd taken to explode a couple more of its time-release capsules. I felt the surge again, but this time from the center of everything that was sexual in me, rushing up to cannonade within my brain. *Pow-pow-pow.* I needed Vince to start doing things to me, right away. Then I remembered all the mistakes I had been making lately, all the very good advice I had never followed. "Vince, what about our promise?"

His hands slid my dress off the slopes of my body. Why had I worn panties to the luncheon? Foolish me, they were all in the way now. Vince explained, "We agreed that we would sleep together when we finished the book, but not before. And I think we both knew that 'sleeping together' meant 'intercourse.' But there's lots we can do other than that."

I yielded to the drug again, allowing it to take control of time in a way that would have pleased Einstein to no end. There were more electrons in my brain than stars in a planetarium, and each was pulsing its own ecstatic message semaphorically. I wasn't sure what Vince had in mind or where he was going to draw the line and if he had the self-control to resist being drawn into me when my hands pulled at him. It was hard to think specifics as another wave of the drug swept over me. I couldn't take just kissing, necking—I was far too aroused, it would demolish me to stop at that.

We were on the bed now. I pulled him onto me, I ground my hips slowly into his groin like the most obscene of strippers, trying to put pressure against myself and against him, and this went on for months and yet his pants were not even off yet. I was about to beg him please, out of compassion if nothing else, to just bend me across the end of the bed and fill me when there was a light knocking sound at the door.

I couldn't remember whose house we were in. I remembered I had a vibrator in my house. I wanted to get it now, because if I didn't find some release I was going to die. Vince could be so mean sometimes. Oh, there he was, getting up off our bed. I remembered we were still at the Disneyland Hotel. We had come here after we'd been to that stately English home in the mountains of Mississippi. "Is that the ginger ale?" I asked. I think I was almost ready for room service to do me if Vince would at least hold me while it happened. I was naked across the bed, my hair disheveled, my face and breasts and belly beaded with sweat. I would have to let room service see me this way because I'd forgotten how to move. Vince gently pulled a sheet to cover me from the shoulders down, kissing me tenderly and stroking my face. He could be so thoughtful sometimes, except when he wouldn't put his cock in me.

Vince opened the door. A young woman stepped into the room. Was she from room service? They had very strange uniforms. A shiny white plastic raincoat down to her knees. She stepped over to the side of the bed.

"Oh, I remember you," she said. "We met in Disneyland."

Everything I do takes place in Disneyland. She was lovely. Her hair was long and fine and blond.

Vince asked her, "Are you wearing it?" The girl nodded and unfastened the raincoat, tossing it onto a chair. I remembered her now. She was Alice in Wonderland, in the blue dress and white pinafore and white stockings.

"You like?" she asked Vince. "It wasn't hard sneaking it out, because they didn't know I'm not coming back."

"Lie down," said Vince to her. She lay down beside me. Her face was exquisite.

Vince lit another joint and offered it to her. She laughed. "I don't know. I'm really a little stoned out of my head already. Is it good?" She took a hit. "Oh Jesus, wow." She offered me the joint, but I wasn't sure I would be able to hold it and I certainly didn't want to set fire to the bed. "You're really attractive," she said to me. She drew a line with her finger along my face. "I love faces with character." She took another hit on the joint and giggled. "Oh, this is like monster grass, Vince, do you get this all the time?"

Vince just smiled. He could be very modest. *Bing-bing-bing* went the medicine in my brain. I wished Vince would explain more to me, but for the moment I was willing to let the afternoon slip by, keeping such pleasant company. I knew it was the afternoon because her hair was so golden.

"You're Alice," I said.

She nodded and looked slyly at Vince. "Want to see what every guy in Fantasyland wants to see? It's an F coupon."

She slowly raised the hem of her blue dress, riding it up along her slender, white-stockinged legs. She revealed white thighs, of a slimness she would have for only another year or two. And then she revealed a golden mound, curved like the gentlest slope of a riverbank, covered in a small, soft coat of golden down as strokable as the fur of a white rabbit. The lightest and palest of pink lips were sweetly puckered as if for a kiss.

She wriggled out of the rest of the outfit and started to peel off her stockings.

"She's so beautiful, Vince," I said.

"She's ours, honey," said Vince. "Isn't that so, Alice?"

Alice nodded slowly, her blue eyes wide and honest and true. "I'm yours," she said to me. She looked at Vince for approval. He nodded and she assured him, "I'm mainly straight, you know, but I love doing scenes."

Vince slowly pulled the sheet that covered me away from my body. It felt like a cool, huge hand stroking me. I was shy of my nudity. "Vince, no, I'm naked."

Alice soothed, "Oh, it's okay, I'm a girl."

I took note of this and Vince reassured me, "It's all right, honey, she's over eighteen—aren't you, Alice?"

Alice nodded. "Twenty last month. Oh, I like your body," she said to me, now that I was totally uncovered.

"Thank you," I said. Pinpoint explosions in my brain this time.

Vince slowly rubbed my thighs and my stomach and he teased a little, brushing the back of his hand against me. As long as his hand was somewhere on my body, I guess I wasn't completely uncovered.

Alice said admiringly, "I like your breasts." She looked at Vince. "Let's have fun."

Vince took me in his arms. "Oh, Vince," I whimpered, and his mouth and tongue met my mouth and stayed there, as simultaneously there transpired a searing explosion of spring at the epicenter of my grateful groin. Vince ravaged my lips as a second tongue, playful and industrious, made gleeful pirouettes against my clitoris, while girlish fingers entered me, swirling busy circles within. But surely Vince had only one mouth and one tongue and they were still pressed warmly against my lips. He was staring into my eyes, watching me react. He seemed to be richly enjoying this, especially as he could see my realization that it was Alice's mouth and tongue that were having their mad little tea party with me . . . but Vince approved, and this was all for him, wasn't it? I could give this to him and that would be loving of me. As long as I kept my eyes fixed only on his face. This was Vince making me feel this, and I was feeling this for him. For him.

I was building to the strangest orgasm. I raced up and down the corridors of our haunted mansion, trying to avoid the wave of water that was sweeping toward me. If I could get to the tunnel, if I could get smaller, if I could— The tunnel was blocked. I turned and saw the tidal wave coming at me, blue as Alice's dress, foamed with froth as white as her pinafore, the same blue and white as her eyes, but then I saw Vince's eyes, brown and dark and immense. My orgasm was going to be so powerful that I now laughed at the drug I'd taken, scoffed at its pallid euphorias as I approached the outskirts of cataclysm.

And then the feeling stopped. Vince had pulled Alice away from me. I screamed in torment.

"Not yet, honey," he said. There was no way to measure my desolation.

Alice laid her head down on the pillow beside me. Her face was glossy but still angelic. "Hi," she said to me. "I like you."

"Let's kiss her, honey," Vince said to me. He kissed Alice's cheek tenderly.

Alice scrunched her face close to mine. "You're so pretty."

"No, you're the beauty," I said.

"Show me how you love him," Alice said. "Show me what you can do to him."

Vince had backed into the shadows, away from the bed. "Show her," he counseled. "Show her what you'll do to me."

I'd never been with a girl in my life, other than silly sex games at slumber parties and in college.

But it wasn't hard at all. She was fair and downy and pink and pretty.

"It's okay," said Vince, now behind me. His hands were on my shoulders, massaging me warmly but also moving me closer into her. "Show me," he urged.

I touched Alice lightly with my tongue where I knew I liked to be touched. She gasped a light, girlish gasp, instantly responsive.

"Yes," said Vince as I felt his hands leave me. It was so very important that I show him how I would make him feel, so I gave her more of the same, tenderly, steadily. If I did well for her, maybe Vince would hold me again and make me feel the same way, too.

I heard her breathing deeper, in that way I've heard in myself, when things are changing, when I've reached a new plateau from which I know my orgasm will inexorably launch.

I heard Vince behind me saying, "Good. That's good." I kept hearing a repeated clicking and whirring noise behind me, and there were flashes of light in the room that weren't emanating from my brain, but I was focused on my work.

Alice in Wonderland was speaking only to me now, encouraging me.

"Eat me," she urged in a whisper that lay somewhere between a sob and a sigh. "Drink me."

TWENTY-EIGHT

When I woke late the next morning in a room at the Disneyland Hotel, I regretted to discover that, unlike Lanny, Vince had *not* abandoned me.

The girl was gone. But Vince was seated comfortably in a corner of the room, a tray at his side upon which was a thermos of coffee, the remnants of scrambled eggs and bacon, a few rounds of cinnamon toast, and pink grapefruit juice. He was smoking a cigarette and enjoying his coffee.

"Morning," he said brightly enough.

I looked at him hatefully. "That was never a quaalude you gave me. I've *had* quaaludes."

He smiled. "I said it was *like* a quaalude."

"And you didn't take one yourself. You palmed the fucking pill."

He shrugged. "Somebody had to drive. What's the matter, morning-after recriminations? Don't worry, you won't get pregnant. Not from Alice. And certainly not from me. I never took off my pants, as you may or may not remember."

My head hurt terribly. The slightest movement sent pain all around my brain like a steel skullcap two sizes too small. I got up out of bed and realized I was naked. "Look the other way," I snapped.

He obliged and commented, "That's okay. From now on, whenever I want to see you naked, I can."

I got into my stupid dress from the Scotty luncheon. I would buy myself a Daisy Duck sweatshirt and Goofy sweatpants in the lobby of the hotel and burn the frigging dress in the parking lot. "There are laws against drugging people."

"Oh, please. You took it voluntarily. I didn't slip it into your drink. You chased it with a glass of the most expensive dessert wine in the world. You're just all in a dither because you discovered you can swing both ways."

I had no problem with anyone's sexual persuasion, including my own. "I've been straight until now, Vince, but if I keep meeting a few more men like you and Lanny, I may go over to the other side full-time. What galls me—" I paused. I thought I might throw up from the migrainelike pain, but I overrode the feeling.

I saw another tray of food on the dresser. He had thoughtfully ordered me something, but I wanted none of it. I did pour myself some coffee. "What angers me and frightens me is not the girl. It's you. You planned all this. You already had the room, you had the girl waiting to join us, you got me susceptibly drunk and tricked me into taking whatever the hell that pill was. You're a devious little prick."

He smiled. "I think I resent the word 'little.' Especially since you haven't seen me with my pants off. Have some cinnamon toast." He offered me a plate from my own breakfast tray.

I waved the toast away. "What is this all about, Vince?" I asked. "It can't just have been about the scene we had here last night. You don't need me for that. There must be a thousand would-be starlets who would gladly make it with you, a llama, and the front four of the Oakland Raiders. Did you even have an orgasm last night?"

He said in a shy way, "The girl—her name's Jennifer, by the way—she was kind enough to give me head. You had passed out, so I didn't think you'd object. I like getting it from young women, especially if they're relatively new to the experience. Jennifer is a little more knowledgeable than I prefer, but watching you on her aroused me to the extreme."

I wanted to attack him, and I definitely planned to, but first I needed information. "Vince, are you crazy? We had work to do together."

"Yes, well, as it happens, last night was largely about the work. Sit down. I need to explain."

I did so. He waxed expansive: "Look, I admit I enjoyed the 'scene,' as Jennifer would put it. I especially liked that, stoned or not, you went along with it, not because you were into it or because you thought it would advance your career but because you cared for me. I thought that was really charming. You remained sweet in my eyes, and you were meanwhile doing all these nasty things and having them done to you. All for my sake. I felt like I had been captured by an ancient Oriental army, and you were my adoring betrothed, and the only way my life would be spared was if you gave yourself sexually to the beautiful daughter of the enemy's leader. And in chains, I was forced to watch this. Pretty hot stuff."

I went to the window and opened the curtains. I needed sunlight and reality to be let into the room. This was what you got when a self-absorbed performer had been catered to all his life and thought there was nothing odd about that.

He went on, "But the other reason for the scene was: I wanted to get something on you. Of course, I hadn't known about your behavior with Lanny when I planned this. The stuff with Lanny, that's even better. But I'd gone to so much trouble setting things up with Jennifer and the restaurant . . . I thought, what the hell, I can always use the extra ammunition. Plus I was dying to see the two of you together."

He took out a cigarette and lit it with pleasure. "Your behavior on this project has been really shocking, Miss O'Connor. You offer to sleep with me if I complete the book with you. My ex-partner refuses to be a part of our work, so you introduce yourself to him, lying about who and what you are, and sleep with him." He was warming to the subject. "And to top off your misconduct, you come with me on a pleasant social evening to an innocuous place like Disneyland and pop pills in the ladies' room until you're nearly incoherent. You're such a mess that I decide to let you sleep it off in the room of my new singing discovery, Jennifer Howell, whom I've put up at this very hotel. This room is registered in her name. There are two beds and she's fine about letting you have one of them. After I've left the two of you, you offer Jenn a mild sedative, since she's such a light sleeper and you snore. Turns out the pill is a powerful variation on MDMA with additional hallucinogenic properties. You take advantage of Jennifer and have sex with her, because you're that way. You have a friend come by and photograph the two of you. The next day I get a letter in the mail saying that the career of a promising young singer who I plan to manage will be ruined if I don't cooperate . . . in essence, extortion. Because in the envelope are a few Polaroids of you and poor, innocent Jenn."

He lifted a silver cover on the room-service tray, revealing two Polaroid photos. He tossed one over to me. I saw what I expected to see.

I asked, "Do you have one where I don't look this heavy?"

Vince nodded and tossed me the other one. My essence had not been captured by Bob Guccione, but my butt looked cute enough and the angle flattered my breasts. He said, "That's the best of the outtakes. Jenn took the camera and the rest of the snapshots with her. I'm meeting her in a little while. Some of the photos came out pretty nice, if I do say so myself."

I tore up the one where I looked heavy and walked over to the door. "If I step into the hall and invite anyone to look in, they'll see Vince Collins, in person, sitting in this hotel room. In your scenario, what would you be doing here now?"

He retrieved the pieces of the torn Polaroid, put them in an ashtray bearing the outline of Sleeping Beauty's castle, and ignited them with his handsome lighter. "I got a hysterical call early this morning from Jenn saying you'd drugged and raped her. I told her to clear out as fast as she could. I came over to confront you."

I hesitated, my hand still on the doorknob. "Yes, but you're wearing the same suit as last night. The waiters at the restaurant could verify that."

"Obviously, I was in a hurry to get here—I just put on the clothing I'd draped over a chair in my bedroom last night."

I pointed at the empty trays. "Ah. And in your anger you ordered room service?"

"No, in reality, Jenn phoned down the order before she left. She told them she was a Miss O'Connor who was staying in Miss Howell's room. She asked room service to leave the trays outside the door at nine A.M. It will seem like *you* ordered a cozy breakfast for the two of you, not realizing how hysterical Jenn would be when she woke in the morning."

I let go of the door handle and walked back over to him.

"Jenn is going to have to do a lot of lying."

He got up from his chair. "My management company is going to see that Jenn has a great recording and performing career, if she plays her cards right with me. And as you know, she actually has talent beyond the skills she demonstrated so vividly last night. The two of us spent a very nice day together while you were in Florida. Jenn'll say whatever she has to. She's a pretty good little actress, too."

"Yes, but if this sordid story got out, it would really tarnish her name."

"No, the only one it'll discredit will be you. You're a grown-up journalist playing loose with the rules. She's a young vulnerable singer you drugged and molested. Actually, it would be amazing publicity for her. Beautiful, victimized blondes are very big these days, or didn't you know? I guess you don't listen to pop music much. What, did you think she was going to record children's songs?"

I sat back down on the bed. So far, Lanny had been wrong. Vince wasn't any less clever than he thought he was. But I thought I was smarter. Now we'd see.

I asked him for one of his cigarettes. I hadn't had my own at the Scotty Awards luncheon and I'd been bumming his yesterday up through dinner. He put one in his mouth and lit it, then offered it to me.

I shook my head. "No. Not one you've had in your mouth."

He shrugged and handed me a new one.

I said, "Tell me: in this storyboard of lies you've come up with, exactly *why* am I trying to extort you?"

"I haven't made up my mind yet. Maybe it's because you want the sole royalty on the book. Or half of my million dollars. It really doesn't matter, honey, because no one's ever going to know about *any* of this. Because you're going to cooperate and then we're going to get along fine. When we finish the book, I'll even sleep with you if you want. Just the two of us this time."

He said it very amicably, as if it were foolish for us to be quarreling this way.

I folded my arms. "What's the deal?"

"We're going to continue working on the book. You're going to do a great job. I'll continue to tell you all kinds of juicy, funny, heart-tugging stories. But you're not going to ask me any questions about what happened to your 'Girl in New Jersey.' Dorothy Kilgallen covered it, Jack O'Brien covered it, Moe Cohn put the story to bed. I'll give you my account of what I know, and you're not going to ask me a single follow-up question. I suggest you tell your publisher that you tried every angle and could find nothing odd or suspicious in what I told you. I'll even try to make my story more interesting than what's been reported, so it won't look like you completely failed. Spice it up with stuff such as how I'd wanted to sleep like a babe the night before the telethon, so to cover my bets I kept a few babes on hand." He leered a bit. "Well, not exactly on my *hand*. That's not my preference, as you may have gathered by now."

He was sounding more like his ex-partner every minute. "And?" I asked.

"And that'll be the deal." He slapped his hands like a Vegas blackjack dealer relinquishing a table. "See? Not so terrible. You'll get your best-seller, I'll get my million, Jenn will get her hit record, and everybody goes home happy."

"And if I don't accept the deal?"

He frowned. "Then I'll just have to go to Neuman and Newberry and lay out for them the incredible pattern of duplicity, immorality, and near-criminal behavior you've displayed toward this project, myself, and even Lanny. I'll demand they pull you off the book and replace you with someone who's more compatible and trustworthy."

"Meaning someone who'll write a puff piece."

"Exactly."

I shook my head. "I don't understand, Vince. Since Day One you've dreaded talking about Maureen O'Flaherty. If it was something you so wanted to avoid . . . why, why, why, Vince, did you ever agree to do this book?"

He looked sad, and his answer was even more pathetic. "Because I need the money."

He raised his shirt collar, wrapped his tie around his neck, and became intent on making a Windsor knot. I wanted to kick him in the balls, but he had over half a foot and sixty pounds on me.

So I kicked him the best way I could. "Listen, Vince, despite my behavior this last month, you should be nervously aware that I actually do have some guiding principles. For example, I believe it's the solemn obligation of a writer not to mind if something he or she reveals in the course of telling a story is personally embarrassing or humiliating."

He was dismayed by the tie's length and began the arduous process from the beginning again. "So?"

"Check your contract, Vince."

The statement hung in the air. My invoking a legal document caused him to listen more attentively. He let the two ends of the tie dangle for a moment. "What about it?"

"Anything you say in my presence is mine to use. For example, for the last fifteen minutes I've been asking you questions and you've been answering. And since I am also allowed to include 'contextual background'—where we were when you said things, how we got there, what you were doing at the time, who we were with—I can write everything, absolutely everything, about last night and this morning. How you set me up. Jenn's involvement. How you tried to blackmail me into not asking you about the Girl in New Jersey. Hell, I'll even put the Polaroids in the photo section." I patted the remaining photo. "All photographs taken during an interview are the property of the publisher."

He tied the tie perfectly this time and put on his jacket. "Neuman and Newberry are a respected outfit. They wouldn't want to go near something this tainted. You'd be laughed out of the business. No one would ever take you seriously again."

"I think they would take me seriously if I owned up to everything. Not excused myself in any way but admitted to all the colossal mistakes I've made, some with your able assistance, since we met. Owned up to my sheer stupidity, thinking I could play games with either of you devious little boys. I'll tell it all, no matter how awful I look in the recounting, or in the Polaroids." I grabbed his arm. "Listen, it could be the bravest thing I've ever done, Vince. If a journalist destroys her own career in order to tell her reader the truth, then she's at least served the truth. I would have that, even as I was being laughed at. In my own destruction, I could at least gain something. And you'll have nothing."

He walked toward the door, ready to conclude this conversation. "It would be your word against mine," he said and waved his hand, dismissing me.

"A person who makes a full and detailed confession to a crime and then names their accomplice has a hell of a lot more credibility than a person who says, 'I didn't do it but she did.' "

Suddenly, he wasn't looking so masterful.

I pressed my point. "Real life generates its own details, Vince. A lie generates only the lie. If I walk down the fire stairs to the lobby, somewhere along the way there's liable to be a bucket of sand. What color is the bucket? What floor is it on? If you lie and say you took the fire stairs, you don't have that information. You just have the lie. I've got the details, Vince. You don't."

Vince stepped into the bathroom, pulled a few Kleenex out of the dispenser, and blotted some sweat that had beaded on his neck. He checked in the mirror to make sure he was fit for public consumption. He smiled. "I've never said anything to you that could be used against me."

I shook my head sadly. "That's subject to debate. But there are people who know things, Vince, and they're talking to me, especially since there's money in it for them. And remember: there's nothing in your contract that limits how loaded my questions can be or how many loaded guns I can have up my sleeve."

He stopped by the door, looking puzzled. "What do you mean by that?"

"I mean, contractually, there's nothing stopping me from putting any information I want *into* a question I ask you . . . information that I'd like to make public or that the police might want to look into. Just so long as it's in the form of a question. Kind of like *Jeopardy!* Would you like me to fire one of my loaded guns . . . sort of as a free sample?"

"Sure thing," said Vince.

In fact, I only had the one gun up my sleeve, but I was going to shoot it now, when I needed it most. I took dead aim at his gut.

"Vince: in your suite at the Versailles Hotel in Miami, was it your idea or Lanny's to put Maureen O'Flaherty's dead body into the metal locker containing shellfish and ice and then have it shipped to New Jersey . . . or did the idea originate with the both of you?"

Oh, it did my heart good to see him turn the color of a corpse. What a shame Jenn had taken the Polaroid camera away with her. I would have loved to have shown that picture to Maureen's mother. I raised my eyebrows. "No answer, Mr. Collins? So noted. Oh, incidentally, by not answering, you're in violation of your contract. What a shame. I understood that you needed the money."

Lanny was right about one thing: neither Vince nor I was as clever as we thought we were. Vince was stupid because, in trying to push me off a cliff, he hadn't noticed that he'd gone beyond the edge himself. And I was stupid because I'd said all this without calculating that Vince might at that moment try to kill me.

He lunged and pushed me down onto the bed. In movies, when a man tries to strangle a woman, I had always thought, "But if her life's at stake, surely she can summon the strength to fight back?" The answer is ultimately no, not if the man is stronger than you. He was choking me and it was working. I couldn't get air into my lungs. I reached to grab the lamp or vase that's always available in movies for women to hit their attacker with. There was no lamp or vase to grab. I clutched for the famous scissors, but there were no famous scissors. I was just going to die. I waited for the Great White Light and for the Caring Voices to ask me if I was ready, but all I heard was the ghastly sound of me trying to breathe, and Vince's grunts as he tried to stop that from happening.

And then he simply abandoned the struggle. Apparently, he couldn't bring himself to kill me.

I had froth and mucus all over my face. I sucked air painfully into my lungs, and I was making noises I had never heard myself make. Through my wrenching gasps, I asked him (because I had been hired to ask him questions), "Was that how you murdered Maureen O'Flaherty?"

He looked at me with the expression of a man who realizes there is no way out of his dilemma. His face was bleeding where I had scratched it with my nails. He croaked, "Ask Lanny that. He seems to be the one who knows."

There was a rapping at the door of metal against wood. It might have been Alice, eager to pose for more photos, or perhaps Lanny, here to assist his ex-partner, or—*"Housekeeping?"* said a woman's voice. A louder rap of a metal key against the door. *"Housekeeping?"*

The door opened and Saint Rina of Anaheim entered with her novitiate sidekick, Sister Esmerelda. I coughed out in my terrible Spanish: *"¿Usted conoce a Vince Collins, la estrella famosa del cantante y de cine?"* I pointed at Vince, famous star of singing and cinema.

They made excited sounds and moved forward to greet Vince.

I stepped past them and stumbled to the fire stairs, needing to get away from that room, not wanting to wait for an elevator. On the third floor, I saw a metal bucket of sand. It was red. There were two cigarette butts in it. Also a chewing-gum wrapper. I observed these little details as I fell to my knees and retched into the bucket, over and over again.

TWENTY-NINE

It had not been hard for him to get the suite he wanted. The Versailles was still one of the fanciest of the hotels along the beach, but now, well into the 1970s, its era had passed. The beach had become "the Catskills with Cubans and melanoma." The joke went, Take all that's lovely in Bermuda out of Bermuda and you have Miami. Lenny Bruce said Miami was where neon went to die.

They'd thought it was odd, him wanting a two-bedroom suite when he'd arrived alone. Maybe he was planning to have company later that evening. He certainly had never lacked for it in the past.

He didn't go into either bedroom at first. After the bellman had left, he had stood in the middle of the living room. The TV was different, a color model. All of the furniture was new. Well, after all, it had been nearly fifteen years. But the floor plan was still the same. Right in that spot. That was where the truth had come out. And that had been the end of everything.

That was why the girl had had to die.

She had stayed the night—a night that for her would never end—here in the living room, in its convertible couch. Imagine that: a Castro in Miami. (Joke.)

The boys had retired to their respective bedrooms, either of which could be reached by a door on either side of the living room or its own door in the hall. There was a lot to sleep off. It had not been a good evening.

How had the end begun?

He picked up the phone and dialed room service. "Hello, Room Service? I'm holding a service here in my room and I don't have enough to make up a minyan. What? A minyan. It's a Jewish prayer service, we're doing a Kaddish tonight. I'm in Shul Twenty-five-oh-one, oh-two, oh-three, oh-by-the-way, what's your name, sweetheart? 'Robertson,' yeah, no wonder you don't understand me. Listen, I need three able-bodied men to fill out my minyan, but if you can find me three able-bodied *women,* the hell with the minyan, we can have us a party. Joke. Forget it, listen, this is Lanny Morris in 2501. Yes, *that* Lanny Morris. Well, I'm a big fan of yours, too. No, I really mean that. Mr. Collins? Saw him quite recently, as it happens. He was looking really good, but then again, when does he not I should say, huuuh? Now look, can you send up three filet mignons done rare, rare, and rare, with béarnaise sauce, the usual stuff on the side. Great, and look, I don't want you to take this the whole entirely way other, but you have a very sweet attendant down there, very lovely young lady, and she's just terrific, you know who I mean? That's her, could you do a favor for a tired entertainer and make sure she's who brings the order up? Even if you have to pull her off some other room. For the Lanny-Man, okay? No, we got all the booze we need here but, say, have her bring up three bottles of Moët on ice, okay? She can wheel it all into 2502, that's the living room. Thanks, sweetheart."

He hung up the phone. That's how it had begun. Vince was no longer with him now, which was a blessed relief. But it was kind of unnatural staying in three empty rooms like this. He thought of having a word with Reuben, who had his own smaller room down the hall, but then he remembered Reuben wasn't on this trip either. So he sat in the dark.

Room service had become woefully understaffed at the Versailles. It wasn't until almost an hour later that he awoke to a knocking at the living room door.

"Who is it?"

"Room service," said a lilting female voice.

Still dozy, he opened the door.

She noticed the dark. "Oh, can you turn on a light?"

He fumbled around the room for a switch. Turning it on, he went back to sit on the couch.

The young woman was at most five feet tall, very slender. Her Versailles outfit fit her as if she were Lucille Ball farcically donning a bellman's uniform for comic effect. She had rolled up her sleeves and cuffs and looked adorable. Her hair was long and gleaming black. She had almond eyes. She was not Maureen O'Flaherty.

"Three steaks with the trimmings. You want me to set up the table?"

He indicated that that would be very nice, even though he had no intention of eating a single bite. It was all for old times' sake.

She busied herself, dressing a circular dining table by windows that overlooked the ocean, except that at night, of course, the ocean couldn't be seen. She took out a folded tablecloth and flapped it into place, then started transferring covered dishes from the Sterno-heated box within the room-service cart.

"Are you Japanese or Chinese?" he asked.

"Korean." She smiled. "The kitchen told me you're a famous person. Why are you famous?"

"Beats me," he replied. "What's your name?"

"Mei Ling. Chinese name, but I'm Korean. Your name?"

"Lanny Morris. Jewish name, but I'm a nebbish. Joke. How long have you been in this country, Mei Ling?"

"One year, ten months. You ordered three bottles of champagne and they gave me three ice buckets, because we didn't know if it's one for each room or— You want me to open one now or do you want to wait until company comes?"

He smiled. "You can open all three, Mei Ling. You have a check for me to sign?"

She handed a billfold to him. "I do. Maybe I should get you to autograph something else too, because the kitchen said it would be worth something. You know, when you die."

He was overtaken by laughter.

"Don't forget a tip for Mei Ling," she instructed him.

He alternated between adding an extravagant sum to the check and glancing at her face. "You know what, Mei Ling? You don't look Korean."

She checked the tip he'd left her and was very satisfied. "I'm Vietnamese, originally from the North, but who wants to get into that? The guests don't, and I sure as hell don't. I do a lot better with tips as Madame Butterfly than I would as Trinh Le Truong. Pour you some champagne now?"

He nodded that that would be all right. She took a champagne goblet from the cart and filled it to the brim. He asked if she'd like a glass herself, but she explained that she was on duty. He smiled as she handed him the goblet. She was definitely not Maureen O'Flaherty.

At the door, she said, "Listen, could I get that autograph from you? They won't let me keep the one on the check."

He nodded and went over to an end table. There was a notepad and Versailles pen there. He scribbled, "Thanks for servicing me (JOKE) . . . Lanny Morris."

She looked at it with curiosity and tucked it into a pocket. "Are you really famous, Mr. Morris?"

"In my day. Before your time, I guess."

She explained they'd had no TV, and American movies had been banned where she grew up. "What did you do, Mr. Morris?"

He thought. "I made Vince Collins's life very difficult."

She didn't understand, but her policy was not to linger in the room of a solitary gentleman one second longer than was necessary. She wished him a good evening.

He went over to a shelf by the bar, took down a water tumbler, and tossed the contents of his champagne goblet into it. Then he took the first champagne bottle out of its nest of ice cubes and filled the tumbler to the brim. And drank the entire tumbler down.

He took his glass toward the room he'd slept in that night and headed for its bathroom. He turned on the single tap in the combination tub and shower. Water started spraying from the showerhead and he flipped the mechanism that diverted it to the tub, setting the water to "hot."

While the tub was filling, he went to the desk in his bedroom and took out a sheet of Versailles stationery. Sipping now and then from his tumbler of champagne, he wrote a few lines so no one would misunderstand. For moral support, he placed a small bottle of pills before him on the desk while he was writing.

When he was done, he fetched the three champagne buckets from the living room and carried them into the bathroom, neatly setting them alongside the tub.

He then shed his clothes, turned off the water, and tested its temperature. Damn. It was scalding hot and he didn't want to wait. Then he had a stroke of genius. He took the champagne bottles out of their respective ice buckets and dumped the ice into the tub. Then he nestled himself down into this cocktail of hot water on the rocks. There was poetry in it. Poetry that he was lying in a tub of water and ice.

He didn't think he had the courage to kill himself, not just yet. But his plan, his clever plan, was to drink enough champagne, perhaps all three bottles, and to accompany the champagne with ample medication, so that eventually "ending things" would become a very acceptable, even a nice, idea. He thought he just might be able to manage that. He knew for certain he could no longer manage anything else. So the choice really wasn't his.

He opened the bottle of pills and took one, downing it with a fresh tumbler of champagne. Things were so much better already.

Based on the contents of his note, his conversation with Ms. Truong, and my conversations with the Miami police investigators, this is my best effort at reconstructing his last evening.

A call came in early that afternoon to the Beverly Hills office of Irv Fleischmann, Lanny Morris's business manager, from the operations chief at the Versailles in Miami.

Fleischmann took in the news. A maid had come to clean the hotel room. She almost passed out when she discovered the body floating in the cool water.

Fleischmann turned to the man who was seated comfortably across the desk, wearing tennis shorts. Fleischmann told him as gently as he could that Vince Collins was dead. He'd died of a drug overdose while lying in a tub at their old suite at the Versailles. There'd been a note, signed by Vince. There was no question but that it was suicide.

Lanny buried his face in his hands and sobbed for almost five minutes. Irv Fleischmann wasn't a hugging person, and he felt Lanny wouldn't have wanted that. He instead tried to be useful. He went out to his secretary's desk, told her the news, calmed her down, said he would be taking no phone calls. Mr. Morris would release a statement later that afternoon, but he would not be talking to any press, at least not for the moment.

He phoned Reuben at Lanny's home and told him to bring a change of clothing, including a dark suit and tie, over to the office. Lanny had been dressed for tennis. Reuben himself was almost as upset as Lanny, but he said he would come over with Dominic and his limousine, in case Lanny needed it. Irv thanked Reuben, took a box of Kleenex off his secretary's desk, returned to his office, and closed the door behind him.

Lanny was doing better. He shook his head. "God, Irving. Why now? If now, why not fifteen years ago?"

Irving had no idea what to say to this bewildering statement. He knew that often people said strange things under such circumstances. He offered, "Maybe he went off his rocker. The fellow from the hotel said he told room service his name was Lanny Morris. Even signed an autograph that way. Maybe he just went crazy."

Lanny shook his head. "No. That's not it, Irv." Lanny took a cigarette from a circular holder on Irv's desk and lit it. "He just hated being Vince Collins."

THIRTY

I did almost nothing for the first week after Vince's death.

I'd wanted to write a book that dealt with Maureen's death, and Vince really hadn't wanted me to, but he couldn't resist the money. A million dollars was a great deal of cash to earn for simply talking about oneself, more than Vince could have gotten for making a couple of movies.

I didn't think it had been wrong for me to want to write the book. Vince knew that for the sum he was being offered, a puff-piece biography wouldn't suffice. From the outset, I had told him we would have to grapple with the question of the Girl in New Jersey.

Connie called as soon as the news of Vince's death came over the radio. She was very Connie about it. She didn't waste time on sentiment or "what might have been." She wanted to know if the material I had already accumulated was enough to fill out a book. I said that anything can fill out a book; Rod McKuen had proved that. But if we went only with the interview material, it would have to have a ton of nice pictures and the story would end before Vince met Lanny. She groaned and said Bernard Besser and Jay Drelitch were poring over the contracts, trying to figure out what their obligation was. They were grateful, she said without a wisp of shame, that Vince had killed himself rather than, say, been run over by a truck. By voluntarily "absenting himself" from the deal, it was likely he'd defaulted on the monies that were to be paid him.

She then broached a different notion: What if the book became *my* book, about meeting Vince, investigating Vince? What of that breakthrough I'd mentioned when I'd called her from Miami? Would that be enough, combined with the interviews, to make a real book, something juicy? I said I'd have to review what I had and report back to her.

What I had, as Connie was in no way aware, were tidbits of information, my sordid Lanny story, one huge theory about where Maureen was murdered—about which Vince would now never comment—and my infatuation, partial seduction, initiation into the sapphic arts, victimization, and physical confrontation with and/or by Vince. If the book were to be about me, I suppose there might be enough there. But was that a book I would ever want to write?

It had been Vince's complaint when he first met me. "You were *in* the interview a lot. All over the place, almost every sentence. They were as much about you as about them." I had told him it was the current style, but then, so were bell-bottoms.

It was early afternoon and a large gray envelope was tucked between my door and the four-gallon container of Arrowhead spring water that was delivered to me every two weeks. It bore no postal marks.

I picked up the envelope and, while I was at it, also retrieved my mail. One letter stood out amid the humdrum. It had been sent special delivery from the post office in Anaheim, postmarked the last day I'd seen Vince. There was Scotch tape around its seams.

I needed a pair of scissors to open it. I cut the side rather than the top, and out spilled a dozen Polaroids of me and Jenn. On the back of the most erotic one (God, that Jenn *was* beautiful) was written in a ragged hand "I'm sorry. Vince."

Before I had a chance to rethink my decision, I had turned on the gas beneath the ceramic logs in my little fireplace and set the photographs ablaze.

Then I sat on the couch with the larger package. Perhaps granting the opposition too much credit, but too curious to wait, I assumed the envelope would be clean of fingerprints and tore it open.

It was a sheaf of pages, clearly Xeroxes. There was an accompanying letter, from Lanny. But the letter had not been written to me.

John Hillman, Esquire
Weisner, Hillman and Dumont, P.C.
7760 Sunset Boulevard
16th Floor

Note: This letter and enclosed contents are a private communication from a client, Lanny Morris, to his attorney, John Hillman, Esquire. All rights to privacy in a communication between client and attorney are to be strictly observed. The enclosed document is only to be unsealed by John Hillman, Esq., or his legal representative (who is bound by the same laws of privileged and private communications between client and attorney) and only after the death of Lanny Morris.

FOR THE EYES OF JOHN HILLMAN, ESQ., ONLY

Dear John,

First, if you're reading this letter, I'm gone. So I really hope you aren't reading this letter, my friend. But if you are, thank you for all your help over the decades.

John, as you are already aware: for a variety of personal reasons, reasons which I believe justified the effort involved, I have in the last year written several chapters for what might have someday been memoirs of my times with Vince Collins. I purposely wrote them in the style of delivery that the public knew me for back in the fifties, because the times were brash and vulgar, we were brash and vulgar, and this was the way we spoke privately and (with some censorship) publicly as well. It was the way things tasted, and I wanted to invoke those flavors for the reader, raw and sour as they might seem now.

Although I was writing specific chapters for specific

purposes, I knew when I began that there was only a slim chance I might complete the work. If I misled you into thinking otherwise, I apologize. Sometimes people are deceptive for what they hope are good reasons. The white lie is, for me, one of the things that keeps society from turning into anarchy.

John, one of the chapters I wrote is already on file in your office and will hopefully serve one of the purposes for which it was intended. A copy of it and two additional chapters are enclosed in this envelope. They might be of passing interest to anyone writing about show business in the late 1950s. The first chapter certainly depicts, in a fairly unflattering way, two rakes having their way with the world and women. I don't back away from this. The second chapter, which covers a period later in the same year, continues that depiction and also clearly lays out a timetable showing the absolute impossibility of our involvement in the death of Maureen O'Flaherty.

John, the third chapter enclosed here is sealed. It contains my brief, frank, and honest account, voiced again in my language of that period, of certain events that occurred one evening in Miami that ultimately ended my working relationship with Vince Collins. I've intentionally made its tone compatible with the first two chapters, so that anyone reading all three (God forbid) will hear the same "Lanny" speaking. Even writers of comedy material for crass showbiz duos have their artistic ego, you know.

John, I have worried that, after my demise, things might someday be said (perhaps even by Vince) that I would not be able to contradict, and it's been of grave concern to me that only two people now living know the truth. Therefore, without trying to make this more important than it is, I am going to burden you with this knowledge as well. My hope and guess is that you will never need to cite any of it. I leave that to your good judgment, with the request that you err on the side of discretion.

Thank you, John, for your assistance and your friendship.

Warmest regards,

Lanny Morris

I skipped past the second chapter, which seemed to be identical to the one Bonnie had brought to me from Los Angeles, and looked at the third. It was typed with the same Selectric ball that had typed the two chapters I'd already read from Lanny's autobiography (which apparently was not as far down the road to completion as I'd been led to believe). That manuscript follows.

We knew we wanted to make an early night of it, with the telethon coming up, so Vince suggested we dine in, ask Maureen to join the two of us, and have her maybe *really* join the two of us for dessert. I told him Maureen thought that, the way we sometimes boffed the same girls, we might be joined at the hip, and Vince said we'd give her the chance to discover otherwise. I said she'd be hip to that (joke).

I picked up the phone and Vince, always my best audience, listened to me order. I said, "Hello, Room Service? I'm holding a service here in my room and I don't have enough to make up a minyan. Yeah, we're doing a Kaddish tonight. I'm in Shul Twenty-five-oh-one, oh-two, oh-three, yeah, it's the Lanny-Man, who else? Now look, can you send me and my pally here three filet mignons done rare, rare, and rare, with béarnaise sauce, the usual stuff on the side. Great, and look, I don't want you to take this the whole entirely way other, but you have a very sweet girl down there, very lovely young lady named Maureen, and she's just terrific. Could you do a favor for a tired entertainer and have her bring the order up? Even if you have to pull her off some other room. For the Lanny-Man, okay? No, we got booze but, say, have her bring up three bottles of Moët on ice, okay? She can wheel it all into 2502, that's the living room. Thanks, sweetheart."

I knew it would be Maureen's last call of the night. She got dinner up to us pretty quick. God, was she beautiful. We sat around the table, she sat between us, and she knew where we were going with this. To help us get in the mood I did a Tuinal, and she did one, and Vince, he did two 'cause he was *always* doing one. (No joke.) We got into the second of the three bottles of Moët we'd ordered, Vince switched over to his Jack Daniel's, and Maureen started unfolding the convertible couch in the living room (we thought it would be fairer to keep the action in neutral territory). She also chain-locked the front door to the living room, to make sure that someone from housekeeping, eager to turn down our beds, didn't walk in on a Versailles employee having a ménage à trois with the hotel's headliners.

When I got out of the shower, I was going to bring her my robe, in case she felt a little bashful, since she'd only slept with me before, not Vince. I look through the door of my bedroom and see she's already stark naked and on top of Vince. So much for bashful! I threw the robe on the bed and ran into the room, half-worried they'd finish without me. But she said we had plenty of time and we all popped another Tuinal to make sure of that.

Listen, she was a beautiful, beautiful little shiksa lay. She had that terrific Irish thing, the hair all downy and auburn. If a pubis could have freckles, she'd have had them. The lips weren't prominent at all, and like lots of Irish girls, her vagina was placed real high and small. A secret pocket. To enter her was a mysterious privilege.

Vince realized he'd been hogging the action, so he stepped aside for a minute and I was on top of her fast. I know a lot of people like it other ways, but I've always preferred the missionary position. I like, maybe I even *need,* to see the girl's face, to watch the Jekyll-Hyde thing happen. That really turns me into a lead pipe, I'm telling you. I have to see her face, look into her eyes. Unless she's acting (I like to think I can tell the difference), there comes that moment when a woman totally accepts that she's going to be fucked, that now it's being done to her, and in that moment, if a guy takes the trouble to really look at her, he'll see exactly who she is. I'll be balling some sophisticated woman with her wiseass manner and a closet full of Dior dresses and she's in charge of everything, she thinks. Then I'll look down as I'm going long and steady into her and right there I'll see a girl who's lost her mommy at the supermarket, or a little brat who wants punishment from Mr. Man, or a choir girl, or an upper-class junkie who smiles as a Park Avenue doctor injects her with an impeccable fix, or a wild animal who just wants to snarl and bite.

Maureen was just beautiful. We were blurry together, steamy but not sweaty . . . steamy like from a vaporizer in the corner of the room, soothing. Our movements felt steady and certain. All the teamwork and telepathy that Vince and I shared was coming into play now, and for the moment, I was the main beneficiary. We had only done a threesome once or twice before, with mixed results. But now he was gently primping her nipples into their own small erections and moving her breasts against my chest as if they had a life of their own. It must have felt good to her, because she sighed as it was happening.

Jesus, I felt good. Some of it may have been the pills, but I had that "harem" feeling I'd sometimes had. I was resting on a huge bed with satin covers, veils hung like curtains around me, making everything secret and hidden, the girls' bodies dressed in pale blues and pinks that you could see through, their faces veiled as well, but you could see their smiles, the sweet, amused smiles of Irish lips, and all their hands were stroking me. It felt *too* good, hands everywhere, my back, my ass, my thighs, my balls—

I had been losing track of Maureen's hands. They were everywhere, magical, like one of those Hindu goddesses. Vince and I had done a routine in *From Brooklyn to Bali* where four dancers crouched one behind the other and the camera angle made it look like it was one dancing girl with eight arms. I felt like I was making love with *that* goddess. Maureen's hands were slow and skilled. She was stroking me at angles it didn't seem humanly possible she could reach. I looked over my shoulder and saw that two of the four hands moving against and around me were Vince's.

I said, "Hey, *compadre,* watch it, will you?"

Vince smiled his bleary smile. "Oops. It's a little hard to tell who's who down here."

"I'm the one with the tan, you dumb dago," I cracked without losing a stroke of my hips.

He nodded. "Gotcha, pal. And you remember I'm the only one of us who has a foreskin."

I laughed. Maureen muttered with some urgency, "Shut up, I'm really close. Come on. Fuck me harder."

Then Vince did the coolest thing. He reached his arms past my hips and slid his hands smoothly under Maureen's ass, elevating it as if a pillow had been placed beneath her, pulling her into me as I went into her. That did something crazy-wild to her, yeah, and to me. I saw this look of release on her face, like she knew she was now a part of something bigger and stronger and there was nothing she could do but let the team of Collins and Morris perform their routine. Who could argue with the two of us? We *were* bigger, stronger. We were fast on the uptake. We had the best suite in the hotel. We got paid the best. For me, it was as if we were achieving in bed with Maureen what we achieved every night on the stage.

I was completely owned by the moment. Vince's arms pulled Maureen into me over and over again, and I saw the tendons in his wrists flexing like those of the captain on a rowing team. He was strong. Our breathing, his and mine, was also that of a team, synchronized and overpowering Maureen's gasps. She couldn't keep up with us. She couldn't match us.

I felt Vince shift, as if to get an even harder grasp on Maureen, and suddenly I felt something hard between the two of us. I thought, half amazed, half exultant, "He's going to try to fuck her at the same time," and with the pressure building everywhere in my groin, I thought it was almost a hot idea. I wondered in a half second if Maureen could take the both of us, and then reassured myself that if she could be expected to accommodate the delivery of a seven-pound baby, she could probably handle the double thickness of me and Vince. I wasn't sure how I felt about rubbing up against Vince's—

I felt a sudden pressure against my ass, as if a clumsy doctor was about to examine my prostate.

"Watch it," I warned. "You got the end zone, Vince."

I felt Vince's strong chest on top of me and his breath damp around my right ear. "C'mon, you'll love it, pally," he assured me. "You never felt anything like it." I could feel him trying to burrow into me. I tried to squirm away but he had Maureen's body and his own arms pulled up around me like a cage. I was sandwiched between all this hot breathing and panting. Maureen wouldn't stop; she had her own climax she was going for. Vince said, "Believe me, it's like from another planet. I'd never hurt you, baby." I looked over my shoulder as he whispered these things that were in no way sweet nothings into my ear and suddenly I realized how he felt about me.

"Get the fuck off me!" I cursed, but he had me pinned. Maureen grunted beneath us, my weight and his strength pressing her into the mattress.

He crooned, "No, no, no, trust me, baby, it's like double the sex. If you don't like it you never have to do it again, don't say you never thought about this." He prodded himself further into me, still soothing me, crazy with his Tuinals and Jack Daniel's, telling me what a good idea this was. "I didn't think I'd like it the first time either but wait till you feel it, pally, it's like you never came before."

In trying to push him off me, I hit Maureen in the face with my elbow. This sort of ended the magic. I was off the bed like I'd found a live eel tucked between the sheets.

"We don't FUCK, Vince!" I screamed, with the worst kind of scorn and horror and rage in my voice.

Vince had made a huge miscalculation, and he must have been terrified to see the contorted fury in my face. I screamed at him, "We're buddies, we're pals, we're partners, a duo, a twosome. We adore each other, I worship you, you're my big brother, we hug, we kiss, we love each other, but *we don't FUCK!!*"

He stared at me, unable to speak.

I cried out to him: "Oh man, Vince . . . when you say you love me . . . you don't *love* me, do you?" I waved my arms to the heavens. "Oh God, don't tell me this is, this is— We don't fuck, Vince. Shit! Don't put *that* into it, not, not when we're beating the world! We aren't British or in ballet. We're not flamenco dancers or figure skaters or chorus boys, Vince. We're stars! We live together, travel together, go out together—we're like firemen, we *can't* be *queers*! People would laugh at us and it wouldn't be funny!"

I looked at Maureen. Her nose was bleeding, and she was sopping the blood off her face with the end of a bedsheet.

Vince had moved into the bathroom, where he got a towel and wore it back into the room. He sat in a shiny gold tufted armchair in the corner and busied himself with the lighting of a cigarette.

I looked back at Maureen, but I didn't know what to say, never having been in this situation before. "I'm sorry."

"About what?" she inquired.

"Well, for the bloody nose. It's not broken, is it?"

"No, I don't think so." She tucked a corner of the bedsheet into her right nostril and wadded it in so it plugged up her nose. Obviously, she looked pretty goofy with this sheet like the train of a gown attached to her nostril, but I guess making a sexy impression on us was no longer the number one thing on her mind.

She snapped a finger at Vince. "Got a butt?" she asked. Then she looked back at me with a flat expression. "No offense intended."

Vince tossed her his pack. If he was feeling something unusual, he was keeping it to himself. She caught the cigarettes, extracted one, and lit it thoughtfully. She took a very short drag on it.

"I guess the question," she said, her low tone pushing smoke out of her mouth nice and slow, "is who pays me."

So she was a hooker.

I hadn't thought about it before, but it made so much sense to me that I was almost filled with admiration. What a fabulous setup, I thought. Work for room service in a hotel, tons of horny guys, even a few horny couples. Everybody's on vacation, fun in the sun, she brings booze or champagne into the room, tight uniform, looking good, there's a bed right over there and next to it a bathroom to wash up and gargle in afterward. What a clean, perfect package. And if you're a married man, the hotel even lets her have a room of her own for a few hours. Hubby can say he's having a couple of drinks with the fellas, and off he goes for a quickie in Room 308 with a view of a ventilator shaft just above (joke coming) the Ballroom.

Give the head of room service and the house detective a piece of your action and you're set. No cops. *"I was just delivering his eggs Benedict, Officer."* Clean sheets, fourteen hundred bedrooms to flop in . . . sure.

Vince and I had a lot to talk about, a whole fucking lot, but we sure as hell weren't going to do it in front of some Irish whore. I felt awkward being naked in front of him, if not her. I walked over to my bedroom door and told her, "In here." She got the tote bag she'd brought with her and followed me into the room. I shut the door behind us. My wallet was on the dresser atop my silk robe, and I withdrew three one-hundred-dollar bills and tossed them onto my bed, which is how you're supposed to pay whores.

She looked at me with an amused expression. I suddenly felt as bothered by my nakedness in front of her as in front of Vince. I unfurled the folds from my robe and wrapped it around me quickly, tying its sash in a huff. She was laughing at me.

"What's the big joke?" I asked.

"You're flouncing," she said, putting a lisp on the *c*. "I guess I'm seeing you in a whole new light."

"Yeah, same here," I snapped. "Take your money."

"No thanks," she smiled.

"That's good money, considering you didn't get anybody off," I pointed out.

"I'm not a prostitute," she said. "I use sex in my work to the minimal extent necessary. Sometimes, when I'm not working, I also enjoy sex, to the maximum. This evening was a case of a happy overlap. And it seems I've just found a skeleton that you two boys would probably prefer to keep in the closet. You wouldn't want it to come *out* of the closet, I'm sure."

She was worse than a whore.

She said, "Lanny, I went to Hunter College—"

"That's no excuse," I sneered.

"And I want to do things. Things as big as what you've done. To do so, I sure could use a lot of money, and to get it, I sure could use this information I've acquired. All that matters is who pays me, and how much. If it's you, it's going to cost a lot. But it'll only cost you once. If someone else pays me for the information . . . it'll cost you forever."

She walked back into the living room. Vince was over by the bar, hitting the Jack Daniel's. God knows how much he had drunk while we were out of the room. He looked hurt, and resentful.

Maureen picked a bottle of champagne out of the ice bucket and poured herself a glass. "You guys sleep on it. Think about what it'll be worth to you. I'm so fucking tired, I'm not even going home. It's those Tuinals." She dropped her tote bag by the couch and got under the sheets of the bed we'd been in.

She gave me a sweet, sleepy smile. "Hey, Lanny, nothing personal. The other times, you were a wonderful lover and you've got the sweetest little butt." She smiled at Vince. "Guess you noticed that about him too, Vince."

Vince snapped off the light by the bar, took his bottle of

Jack Daniel's, and looked back at her from the doorway of his bedroom. The living room was dark.

"Anyone can say anything about anyone, Maureen," I snapped.

"You know I'm not stupid, Lanny. I can make it stick. If we don't come to terms, the world's going to hear the dulcet tones of Vince Collins crooning his swan song." She yawned. "We'll do business over breakfast. Order me French toast, will you? And think big, guys. Think very big."

The bitch pulled the sheets over her head. I looked across at Vince, who'd ruined everything. He was too wasted to waste my words on. He gave me an attempt at a smile but fell against the door frame to keep himself standing.

I would never be able to love him like I had.

I closed the door connecting my bedroom to the living room. I put a DO NOT DISTURB sign on the door and fastened the chain lock in case the maid didn't believe in signs. I left a wake-up call for eight and went to sleep, knowing that the telethon was the least of the ordeals I was going to have to face in the morning.

The Tuinals had really conked me out, and I slept through my wake-up call. The operator called Reuben in his room down the hall to see if he could wake me, but he couldn't get in with the key he had because I'd chain-locked the door. He had to pound for two straight minutes to get me out of my stupor. I staggered to the door, unfastened the chain, and let him in.

I went into the living room and saw Maureen in the bed. I knew from across the room that she was dead. There was a mashed pillow over her face, and her body was lying at a funny angle. All the same, I shook her and tried to see if she had a pulse. I wondered if someone could have broken in, but no, I looked at the living-room door and it was still chained. I yelled for Reuben to get Vince while I worked on Maureen. Reuben ran out from my room, saw Maureen, almost fainted, and ran into Vince's room. Next thing I know he's calling me, saying he thinks Vince is dead, too, but Vince is just unconscious;

I've seen him that way a dozen times. One too many Tuinals and eight too many whiskeys. I looked at Vince's door and it was chained as well.

John, my friend, I have no idea when you will read this, but I'm not now reliving that night in 1959. In all the ensuing years since what I've described took place, here's the thing I am stuck with: Maureen's autopsy in New Jersey showed no indications of poisoning. She'd been alive when I went to bed. All three doors to the suite were chain-locked from the inside when I awoke and found her dead. Whoever killed her had to still be in the suite. Which left me with nothing better than this:

She didn't kill herself.

I know I didn't kill her.

And Vince couldn't remember anything that happened after I left the two of them, she in the living-room bed, he framed in the doorway of his room.

So that, John, is how I've known for many years that my former partner and friend Vince Collins murdered Maureen O'Flaherty. I know this simply by default. It's mathematics. Two possibilities minus me equals him. I don't like those numbers, but that's how they add up.

The one other possibility I've thought about over the years, John, is that somehow I did it, that *I* was the one who had the blackout and that Vince, out of affection or loyalty, let me think it was *he* who had committed the murder. This would have been a noble sacrifice, but there were so many bitter words between us when we split up shortly after this terrible event that I think something would have slipped out or been said in anger.

I think Vince can be forgiven for two reasons. The first is, I honestly don't think he knew what he was doing. I don't think he's pretending not to remember. I think he was so far out of it that night that he truly doesn't know what happened. That must be some kind of hell to live in.

The second reason to forgive Vince is that he was justifiably terrified that his incident with me (and whatever feelings may have been attached to it) would become public knowledge. In the fifties and early sixties, the slightest rumor of homosexuality could destroy a show-business career in an absolute instant. At that time, there were many arranged marriages for leading men with "tendencies." One successful TV actor, playing the part of a man in your profession, John, even created a story of a wife killed in a tragic plane crash when no such wife had existed or crash had occurred. In the climate of those times, I can understand Vince's totally appropriate fears.

Obviously I'm no babe in the woods here. You must have guessed by now that Vince and I together covered up his crime and found a way to relocate Maureen's body to a hotel in New Jersey. I cannot explain how we accomplished this, for reasons that I'd prefer to keep to myself. This is the one criminal act that *both* of us committed, but if you're reading this, then I'm beyond the reach of the American judicial system and will have to plead my case in a higher court.

For Maureen, I feel the least amount of sympathy I can feel for a victim of murder. I have never fully understood what game she planned to play with us. But upon witnessing Vince's indiscretion, she clearly intended to gain the maximum benefit for herself or inflict the maximum damage on Vince and myself. I now believe that, from the outset, she got close to me with the sole intent of trawling for whatever she could turn up in our lives that might profit her.

I do feel terrible pain for her parents and I'm glad that by protecting Vince all these years, I've also protected them from learning more about their daughter than they should ever be told.

Finally, there is the obvious fact that I've known of Vince's guilt and have never reported what I know to the police. Part of the reason for this is that I can't prove anything. Not to the police, not to you, not to anyone but myself. The only reason I know that Vince killed her is simply because I know that I didn't. He could make the same claim for himself.

There are a number of times when he's said to me, "But what if you're lying, Lanny?" It's a valid point.

Without our supposedly ironclad alibi, if the police knew anything of what I've just told you, they could probably pin the murder on both of us, since we both had so much to lose and were both locked up in the same suite with her the night she died. Florida's electric chair has taken the life of more than one innocent man. If the police knew what I've told you here, I might be added to that list. Certainly it would be the end of my career as someone who makes people laugh. You can surely understand why I kept this matter secret until my life was over.

John, that's the truth as best I know it and as best I can convey it.

I sat in my sunny little apartment, the smell of freshly burnt Polaroids adding its own wicked spice to the scent of Jungle Gardenia that usually inhabited the premises.

The document was extremely revealing, to say the least.

Or extremely self-serving.

Really, while all breathless revelation, it was just the "truth" as Lanny was choosing to depict it. And conveniently, it pointed all the blame at Vince.

The entire document really meant nothing. It hadn't been notarized or witnessed in any way. The fact that it was purportedly addressed to John Hillman gave it no legal authority. I could write the same letter and mail it to him myself. Anyone could.

For that matter, there was nothing saying this had ever been sent to Hillman or to anyone other than me. And suppose one were to ask John Hillman to verify that he'd received this letter, what could he possibly say? After all, he wasn't supposed to read it unless Lanny Morris was dead. Even if he had, all he could say to anyone about it (including the police or a judge in a courtroom) was that it was a privileged communication between attorney and client and that he could not reveal or comment upon its contents without his client's permission.

On the absurd notion that Lanny Morris might have died last night, I turned on my TV. The local ABC affiliate had an afternoon news show that would be on in a couple of minutes. If Lanny Morris was dead, it would definitely be mentioned. Ah, there was my good friend Rona Barrett with her five-minute update on Hollwood. An informed public is a nation's greatest asset. Funny, she hadn't called me yet to co-host. Show business is so fickle. One day you're someone's best friend . . .

But what if this document *was* what it claimed to be? What could I glean from it, and, by the way, why in God's name had Lanny sent it to me?

If this was the truth as best Lanny knew it . . . then I at last had my answer to the question of why Maureen O'Flaherty had died. She'd known too much and had intended to profit from it.

ABC was running a commercial for a special that night about the Watergate scandal. There was a shot of Haldeman and Ehrlichman, and a clip of John Dean testifying. Behind him was his wife, Maureen, who had sat behind him every day, her blond hair pinned tight around her head like a halo. She'd been a stewardess, of the "Coffee, tea, or me?" variety, according to John Dean. That's how he'd met her. I was willing to bet that, like Maureen O'Flaherty, she wasn't quite as angelic as she was making herself appear for the benefit of Congress. Probably she—

A thought occurred to me. I went to the big legal portfolio in my bedroom, where I kept Xeroxes of clippings and articles written about Collins and Morris in the fifties. Kilgallen, O'Brien, Earl Wilson . . . Moe Cohn. There he was.

The scandal columnist out of Miami whose columns had, surprisingly, chosen not to speculate about the Girl in New Jersey. Cohn had faded from the scene fairly quickly, but he'd certainly raked up the local dirt in his brief prime. The byline photo showed a bald man in big sunglasses with a cold-blooded smile in the shadow of an oversized nose. . . .

Quickly, I grabbed a pencil and filled in his bald head with black lead. I was generous with it. And I tried to imagine rheumy, watery eyes behind the sunglasses.

I recalled that Maureen's mother had been related to a more famous denizen of New Rochelle: the great George M., whose last name had also been *her* family name. Cohan. And a standard diminutive of Maureen (as John Dean would tell you) is . . . Mo.

Yes. Of course.

Maureen O'Flaherty was Moe Cohn.

And her front man, delivering the dirt she'd acquired in her various jobs and liaisons, had been Kef Ludlow, who used to leave the apartment at eight A.M. wearing sunglasses and a broad-brimmed hat that hid the fact that he was venturing out without his toupee. He made his morning deliveries on Sundays through Thursdays because Moe Cohen's column ran on Mondays through Fridays. No wonder he was whistling as he left the apartment. His betting tips as "the Swami" might have been written for a humble racing form, but he'd bragged to me that it was published by the majors; he'd had the connection to the *Miami Sentinel* that Maureen had lacked. When he'd shown his superiors the dirt he'd written in a wry and scathing voice (penned by the talented Maureen, who'd told Lanny she planned to go places), they'd given the column a shot . . . not realizing that this forty-six-year-old male hack was merely the front for Moe Cohn, the pen name of a promising if promiscuous young woman. She'd gained access to (and the confidence of) celebrities, financial players, and assorted hotshots, chatting with them across a table or a pillow, and what they didn't tell her, she could overhear or see as she wheeled her way into their rooms with food and drink. After all, no one knows who's been sleeping with whom in a hotel better than the person who brings them their breakfast in bed.

But after Maureen died, Kef Ludlow had nothing to report. His blind items became bland items, echoing local press handouts. His column was dropped by the end of the year. Losing whatever his cut was of the income that Moe Cohn had been generating, Kef had no choice but to bid a wrenching good-bye to his secondhand Buick LeSabre and dinner at the Embers. Painfully, he'd had to revert to the spare lifestyle that "the Swami" could afford, living off the meager salary from his dog-racing column, supplemented by the occasional winning streak at the track. And, of course, he'd lost Maureen. It was easy to imagine how she might have led him on in the beginning . . . and how she had really felt about Kef Ludlow.

My discovery gave the ring of truth to the entire document Lanny had sent me. I read it through carefully again, as if it were all Gospel, as if Lanny's recountings were as accurate as he claimed, as accurate as the memory that had allowed him to remember intricate dialogue for comedy routines on live TV, to remember ninety-minute monologues for the one-man show he'd done on Broadway.

And I saw it. One fact after another tumbled in place . . . like four or five little patches of jigsaw puzzle, those mini-assemblages that you've kept sitting outside the rectangular frame of the Big Picture (because you believe they can't be from *this* puzzle, that they must have been included by accident). Then suddenly you find a place for one—and look, this goes with this, and that's part of the farmer's tractor, and this is just the top of the haystack . . . and a huge section of the puzzle is suddenly complete.

The police love a suspect who's a good talker. They'll order him doughnuts and a BLT on white toast and send out for cigarettes and bring in fresh coffee and fresh cops to shoot the breeze with, anything to keep him talking. Because no one can talk forever without telling some bit of the truth, even if they have no idea they're doing it.

Why Lanny would send this document to me now, I couldn't begin to grasp.

But if I were to believe what he'd written, then he'd revealed much more to me than he'd realized when he'd floated these pages onto my lap.

Like Vince and me, maybe Lanny wasn't quite as clever as he thought.

The ABC afternoon news concluded without mentioning Lanny's demise. Vince's funeral had been in the news several days earlier, though. Lanny had spoken, it was reported, both eloquently and affectionately.

Sally Santoro had attended the ceremony as well and afterward was seen to be openly weeping. Through his sobs, he announced that he would open the Salvatore Santoro Wing of a Pittsburgh hospital "in Vince's honor." When asked which hospital, he said he'd be announcing further details once he was inconsolable. *Sic.*

I wondered who had spoken at Maureen's funeral. And as I thought of Maureen's burial, I felt a cool bristling of the hair on my neck as it dawned on me that now, like Maureen, I knew far more than was healthy for a growing girl to know, especially if I hoped to grow older. I knew what was in this third "memoir" of Lanny's. I had also divined how poor Maureen had been transported to New Jersey, a promiscuous princess lying in state on a bed of ice, surrounded by a court of condemned crustaceans. The knowledge stored in my brain was very dangerous to the liberty of Lanny Morris, and unfortunately, it is generally assumed that human brains do not retain their stored knowledge once death has occurred. If Lanny Morris was to get any inkling of how much I knew, I assumed he would be delighted to hear of (or arrange for) my immediate demise.

So in that great tradition of idiocy that was rapidly becoming my permanent *modus operandi,* I tried to figure out how I could speak with Lanny as soon as possible.

I had no phone number for him. All my dealings had been through his attorney's office. The message I had for Lanny, concerning what I now knew and why he might want me dead, was not one I was likely to leave with a third party. I had to contact him in person. Luckily, being a seasoned journalist, I knew how to obtain such clandestine information as his home address. I drove to the Sunset Strip, where there's always this guy standing in traffic, from whom I bought a Map of the Homes of the Stars.

Off North Beverly Glen Boulevard, there is actually a street called Scenario Lane. The end of the lane overlooks the Stone Canyon Reservoir, and Lanny lived there in a brick Gothic manor patterned after Toad Hall from Walt Disney's *Wind in the Willows* (a book that at one time had been written by Kenneth Grahame). I pulled up to its black iron gates and pushed the button on an intercom similar to the one at Vince's home.

A woman's voice answered. "Yes?"

"Delivery for Mr. Morris," I informed her.

"You can leave it in the mailbox."

"Sorry, it's too big," I countered. "And it requires his signature."

"Mr. Morris left for New York City an hour ago. He won't be back until Monday. I can sign for it if you want, I'm his housekeeper. But if it has to be his signature, he won't be back until Monday."

"Can you tell me where in New York he's staying? Maybe we can forward it to him."

"I'm sorry, I can't give out that information," she told me.

That was all right. I was certain I knew where to find him.

THIRTY-ONE

I knocked on the door to 2302 at the Plaza hotel.

You can rest assured I'd confirmed that Lanny was at his usual suite at the Plaza before I made another transcontinental flight for no good reason. Yesterday, I'd hung up as soon as the operator had rung Mr. Merwin's room and I'd heard Reuben's voice answering the phone.

Now Reuben opened the door to Lanny's suite. He was dressed in one of his white houseboy jackets. The golden glow of his face beamed a little brighter when he saw me.

"Oh, Miss Trout!" His pleasant greeting faded as a concerned look came over him and he signaled to me with his eyes, indicating that Lanny was seated at a table, having breakfast with a woman. I could only see the back of her head, but her suit was trimly fitted and well made.

"Hello," said Lanny, looking up from a cup of coffee. "How are you?"

I was a bit disappointed that he didn't act surprised to see me. In the taxi on the way up from Beejay's, I had somewhat savored the mini-melodrama of my reappearance at the scene of his crime of passion.

I set my portfolio down on a coffee table as if I'd been invited to stay. "Well, I have a publisher ready to kill me for not getting more on tape from Vince Collins than I did, and the same publisher equally ready to pay any price under the sun for anything that might salvage my book about him . . . but no amount of money is going to bring him back, right?"

I moved to get a better look at this woman, his latest Plaza Sweet. Good luck to you, sugar, I thought. I took a few more steps and felt foolish (and, foolishly, relieved) when I saw that his breakfast companion was old enough to be his mother. Very nicely groomed, with expensive jewelry, but unless Lanny was into a level of kinkiness he'd not displayed with me, this septuagenarian was probably not his latest playmate. Although who knew with the boys. Then I remembered that the plural didn't fit anymore. Now there was only "the boy." Lanny asked if I wanted some breakfast.

"No thanks. I'm not a big breakfast person," I said. "I just like to wake up, stretch a little, remember where I am, and be told by the maid that I have to leave."

Lanny's companion gave me a bewildered smile. Reuben had been moving the breakfast things onto the cart from room service, and he cast me a sympathetic glance.

Lanny said, "Do me a favor, Reuben, would you move the cart to the service room by the elevators? I hate dirty dishes sitting outside my door and I have people coming in later. And then I'm going to need some privacy for a little while, okay?"

"Certainly," said Reuben. He spoke to Lanny but looked at me as he said, "I'll be just down the hall in 2307 if you need me."

The door closed behind him. Lanny did the honors. "This lovely lady is Dorothy Vanderheuvel, she does an absolutely incredible job raising funds for my charity. Dorothy, this is . . ." He looked bewildered. "I'm sorry, what name are you using today?"

I introduced myself with my real name. Dorothy Vanderheuvel, sensing all was not serene, said she had to be at the Gulf and Western building by ten. Lanny nodded. "Go get 'em, Tiger," he laughed as he showed her to the door.

We were alone. But I'd made sure to tell Beejay where I was going, and asked her to ring Lanny's room and demand to speak to me if I hadn't called her at the vice principal's office by noon. I thought it would be a good idea to let Lanny know this in advance, so I told him what I'd done. I also pointed out that Mickey the elevator operator had seen me walk in, and Reuben knew I was there. "And Bob down at the front desk remembered me from last time, which astounded me since there must be so many women going in and out of this place," I commented tartly. "Is that why you rent a two-bedroom suite? Four beds, no waiting?"

I had meant to get to business with him but found myself unable to stay off the topic of my past humiliation. I walked over to the bedroom that we hadn't visited on my previous visit and opened the door. It was clearly unused, although there was quite a bit of luggage about the room.

Lanny shrugged. "I don't like the room where I sleep to be cluttered with bags and files and work. I use the second bedroom as a storage room. And—look, I'm no psychiatrist, but for a number of years, Vince and I always shared a two-bedroom suite. I think if I were in a one-bedroom setup, I'd feel lonely." He grimaced a bit and went to shut the door to the second bedroom. "As for the traffic in and out of here, I think you flatter me a little. Let's get this straight. I got laid all I needed to get laid in the fifties. But I'm not the person I was then. Oh sure, I can put on 'Lanny' . . ."

Remarkably, he did just that; without him even speaking, "Lanny" flickered on and off his face.

". . . but that's just a character I play. Over the years, the character and I have grown farther and farther apart, just as Vince and I did. One of these days, not too long from now, I look forward to breaking up the team of Lanny and Lanny."

He went to the window. Outside, you could see all of Central Park. How it hadn't been sold off and made into apartments and parking lots over the centuries was one of the great miracles of modern times.

"So," he said, taking in the view, "here you are again. What can I do for you? I assume it has something to do with Vince's death. You're pretty much up a creek there, aren't you?"

I stared at him, but he said no more. He was waiting for me.

I began, "I have some wonderful material that I was able to draw out of Vince, about his early years, almost up to the time he met you. It's not really enough to make a book out of, but it would be nice if this warm, funny side of Vince could reach the reading public, especially in light of the way he died."

He came back over to me. "That's swell that you care so much how Vince is remembered. Seeing as it was your project that turned the screws on his psyche. You remember the day when I was going to see you and him—when your 'brother' died? He'd called me after years of not talking, simply because he was scared out of his mind. Scared he'd say the wrong thing."

"What was he scared of saying, Lanny?"

Lanny glared at me. "I don't know. That's the answer I'm giving you and anyone else who asks me why he killed himself. I don't know."

I thought, Ah but you do, Lanny. I said, "Fine. But why I came here, with the full approval of Neuman and Newberry, is to propose that the material I have on Vince, along with all my extensive research and notes, be joined up with your own book. Clearly, Neuman and Newberry would love to publish the result, but if you don't wish that, some sort of co-publishing structure could be arranged. I think these chapters on Vince would make a marvelous preamble to your own story."

Lanny looked at me suspiciously.

I added, "Obviously, I wouldn't be looking to take any share of the writing credit for any of your story, Lanny. A secondary, smaller credit on the title page would be appropriate. My name wouldn't be on the spine. Basically, I just hate the thought of this material not having a life. Can I ask how much of your own book you've written?"

"Not a lot," he said, still watching me as if I might be carrying a concealed weapon.

"How much is not a lot? Assuming that the chapter I read at John Hillman's offices was a chapter—which was very entertaining, by the way—how many chapters? Eight, twelve . . . ?"

"No, not that many."

"Well, do you have a sense of when you might be finishing it?" I asked in the most casual of tones. "Just so that we could—"

"It's not going to be finished. I've abandoned it."

"Of course you have," I said. "Of course you've abandoned it."

He looked down at me. "What does that mean?" he asked.

"Oh, Lanny, you never were writing any book. You were simply doing what you'd done for years."

"What was that?"

I took a cigarette from my bag and enjoyed making him wait while I lit it and exhaled. "You were writing for Vince Collins."

He sat back down on the couch.

"You'd always written the material for the act, hadn't you? And now

Vince needed you to write him a new act. And because you loved him, and feared for him, and feared for yourself, you did. But as an opening act, kind of a warm-up, you did something that makes me want to lower my eyes and blush."

He nodded, deeply interested. "And that was?"

"You wrote a chapter for me. Me and anyone else who might ever try to write a book about the two of you. You wanted to nip any such project in the bud before a seed was even planted. So the purpose of your first chapter—the one you instructed your lawyer to have me read—was to accomplish just that. And, Lanny, the way you wrote it was ingenious. You purposely depicted two ravenously heterosexual men who went through the opposite sex as if an orgasm was a sneeze and every woman was a Kleenex."

Lanny grimaced. "Hate to tell you, but that was pretty much how we were."

"Well, maybe you two were a little like that back then. But you, the man you are today, you would never write *now* about those days in the incredibly callow voice you chose, as if a rooster had been given the power of speech. That voice was an invention, a combination of your 'Lanny-Man' and a libidinous Lothario without an ounce of shame. You may be a lot of different things, Lanny, but you know how to behave in public. If you'd really been writing your memoirs for posterity, you'd never have presented that side of yourself for mass consumption. You'd tone it down and dress it up and try to rationalize your behavior. The chapter was all for effect, the effect being that your mythical book would give the reader such a sordid, unvarnished, and explicit depiction of you and Vince that anyone else's effort to do the same would seem as bland and watered down as a press release. You could afford to write as unflatteringly about yourself as you did because you knew the pages were never going to leave the confines of your lawyer's office! And their second but equal purpose, of course, was to make sure that anyone who might read them in the course of writing about you guys would hear all about the women, the women, the *women* you and Vince slept with."

I was pushing it, but I had to see his reaction. His face clouded over, and I could detect the ever-increasing chance of gale-force winds. "I understand the first part of what you're saying, but I don't get the last thing."

"You will soon enough, Lanny." I got up and removed the jacket I was wearing. "The only thing that undercut your very excellent creation was that you never knew that I, the writer for whom you wrote the chapter, was going to meet you and get to really know you. My love." I said these last two words without irony. "If you had known who I was when you met me, you would have behaved much more like the 'Lanny-Man' character you wear in public. I even noted to myself the incredible disparity between the man talking on the pages I read and the man who talked with me on that plane trip and that drive into Manhattan. It might have been understandable if the pages you had written were penned fifteen years ago. But they weren't! They were written in the last year. It would be like Shirley Temple writing her autobiography in baby talk!"

He smiled at this. "Okay. But why do you say I was writing for Vince Collins?"

I reached into the portfolio I'd brought with me, produced the second chapter of Lanny's memoirs, and tossed it onto his lap. "Because of this."

He picked up the manuscript that had been delivered to my home when Beejay was staying there. He flipped the pages and looked up at me angrily. "How did you get this?"

"It was delivered to my home."

"Bullshit. You stole it."

"From whom?" I asked. Lanny just glared at me. I added, "At first I thought your lawyer's office sent it to me. Maybe by accident."

Lanny said, "My lawyer never had a copy of this."

"I know. And then I thought that *you* might have sent it to me, though I couldn't imagine why. Tell me that you did, Lanny."

"I didn't. There'd have been no reason for me to do that. Why would I keep the first chapter under lock and key at my lawyer's office but hand over a second chapter to a *journalist,* no less! If I wanted you to read it badly enough, I'd have had you go back to my lawyer's office."

I nodded. "I agree with your logic." I stretched, if only to remind him of the breasts he hadn't had a chance to fondle lately. "So if you didn't send it to me, then I can tell you exactly who did. It was Vince."

I noticed he was not disagreeing with me.

I said, "Vince was the only person other than you who had a copy, because he was the only person who *needed* a copy." I took the manuscript back and started thumbing through the pages. "These were Vince's crib notes. His cheat sheet. The script he had to study. This was your way of making sure that you and he agreed on every detail of what happened the night Maureen O'Flaherty died. How you spent that night, why you did the telethon, why you were obligated to fly directly to Sally Santoro's hotel, how you had an alibi for every minute prior to the discovery of Maureen's body. You wrote it in the same style as the first chapter in case you ever felt it was necessary to show it to me, or anyone else, in order to give the official, certified, Good Housekeeping Seal of Approval, annotated, and unexpurgated 'white paper' of the events surrounding that night. You even invented a couple of extra babes for Vince to sleep with that evening, and made a little joke about it."

I held the sheaf open to the page I'd located:

" 'Vince and I had both popped a couple of Tuinals to ensure that we'd sleep like babes, and Vince bought insurance on his bet by having a few babes on hand. Well, not exactly on his hand.'

"Imagine my surprise when Vince, as he had a couple of times before, quoted *exactly* your own words from a manuscript supposedly no one had seen . . . or asked me if I expected him to have paintings on black velvet of matadors, nude women, and clowns . . . the same three images in the same order as described twice by you in your memoirs. As if he'd memorized a brand-new Lanny Morris routine, despite the fact that you hadn't seen each other in almost fifteen years."

I tossed the manuscript onto the couch next to Lanny. "It was Vince who sent me his copy of the chapter you gave him. As soon as he'd agreed to do the book with me, he got so panicked that he decided, 'Hey, let's make sure *she* has the Monarch Notes too, so that when I say the same thing, she'll know it's the truth.' I think in the end he'd hoped I'd just paraphrase *your* version as an undisclosed source. That's also why he wanted you there with him when I was going to question him: he knew you'd serve as his guardrail if he got off the track that you'd paved for him."

"The big jerk," said Lanny reflexively. He instantly looked back at me, realizing that this simple response confirmed everything. But I wasn't done with him yet.

"Listen, Lanny, you're a wicked little tyke. Because look what you did throughout this chapter: you put in just enough of the truth, of the sinister, scary stuff, to remind Vince of what it was you *weren't* saying: you talked about the case full of lobsters and ice, the reference to sending

Maureen 'packing,' that you slept the 'sleep of the dead' that night, just to remind him that you had even more beans to spill than he did, and that if he were to reveal to me his own rendition of the truth—setting you up in the process—Lanny Morris was the master at delivering the killer punch line. No joke. Even as you were showing him what to say, you were warning him that he'd better say his lines as written." I smiled. "Will you excuse me for a moment?"

While he tried to absorb all this, I picked up the jacket I'd shed and my portfolio and walked into the bathroom of his bedroom.

I knew I'd said too much, but I'd done so intentionally. I had work to do, and fast, while he calculated the implication of what I'd just said and what I therefore knew.

To him, I was surely at this moment the most dangerous person in his world.

It took only a few moments before he knocked lightly on the door. I instructed him to come in.

What he saw was a young woman in her mid-twenties with a figure that a number of men (and one younger woman) had found pleasurable to partake of, snuggled invitingly against the length of an empty bathtub, naked. I was facing him, my weight resting against my left buttock and the length of my left leg. The room and the tub's porcelain were cool; that and the fact that I was very frightened caused my skin to be goose-bumped and my nipples to be their most erect. His eyes roamed the length of my body, starting with my toenails, which were French-tipped in shades of coral. Along the way, he may have noticed that I had shaved for the occasion, everywhere. If one is to be nude, one might as well stop at nothing. When he reached my fingernails, similarly coral, it would have been very hard for him not to notice that my left hand was handcuffed to the old-fashioned faucet of the Plaza tub. Although I hoped I was pretty damn fetching (I have an ego, you know), my intent was not aimed so much at seduction as at self-protection.

He said softly, "What is this?" His eyes darted around the bathroom. "Where are your clothes?"

"My clothes are out the bathroom window, honey, floating down the Plaza's air shaft, unless a benevolent wind has wafted them over to the Central Park Zoo." I indicated the seat cover of the toilet. "Sit down. We're going to have ourselves a little chat."

He sat down slowly. "You're fucking crazy," he muttered.

"We'll see. The way I figure it, for the next hour you and I are going to have a little heart-to-heart. You're going to tell me all the truths that you know, and I'm going to tell you all the truths that I know. We're going to make a clean breast of things," I smiled, looking down at my own immaculately cleansed and moisturized pair. "It dawned on me that in the course of our discussion, you might entertain the idea of killing me. And I thought, 'Well, what will get him to rule out *that* idea?' Then a voice popped up in my head saying, 'Lanny could ill afford to have another dead, nude young woman's body found in a bathroom in his hotel suite, could he?' One might perhaps innocently have one such body in one's lifetime, but *two*?"

I looked to see if he was getting it, and he was.

"I mean, it would be kind of hard to say that I'd had a nasty accident that had removed all of my clothing from the premises and handcuffed me to a faucet, wouldn't it? And if you broke the faucet, they'd notice the damage. And if you threw me out the window . . ."

I turned, revealing my back. The vain part of me wanted to think that Lanny's eyes went first for my rear end, which had earned the approval of Mickey the elevator operator, but I knew eventually Lanny would notice that across my shoulder blades in red laundry marker was emblazoned PLAZA HOTEL—RM 2302. I'd had Beejay write it on my back before she went to school that morning, after assuring her that it would fade away in a few months.

"Your friend Dorothy Vanderheuvel and Reuben both saw me here, fully dressed, by the way. So in case you get any bright ideas, Lanny, rule them out. When we're done, I'll tell you where in this suite I've hidden the key, you'll uncuff me, loan me that nice Burberry's trench coat of yours hanging up in the other bedroom, and I'll call Beejay from a pay phone on the street. Of course, if she doesn't hear from me in an hour, she'll send in the police. You may be able to think of some way to counter this gambit of mine, but I don't think you can get a six-foot metal crate of lobsters and ice up here in under an hour."

Lanny looked at me with stunned surprise, grudging respect, and cool contempt. "Always so smart," he said.

I hadn't told him that I was so smart that I had a second key to the handcuffs hidden on my person. I'd prefer not to tell you where; suffice it to say that a handcuff key is quite small and there are many uses for Playtex tampons even when it's *not* that difficult time of the month.

I just shook my head and admitted, "I haven't been smart at all, Lanny. But this seems kind of a fitting conclusion, don't you think? Maureen and I? Two women in our twenties, both eager to make our mark in the print media, not too careful about our morals, all means serving our ends, both of us involved with you and Vince . . . and here I am, just like the late Mo Cohan O'Flaherty . . . lying naked in a bathtub in your suite in a hotel near the Hudson River. The only difference is, I'm still alive."

Lanny stared at me ominously as I looked around the room. I nodded toward a wall phone near the toilet, a sinful luxury of the Plaza.

"Call Bonnie Trout's apartment," I instructed him.

He looked puzzled. "You said she was at her school."

I nodded. "Uh-huh, she is. But I've got a surprise waiting for you at her apartment. Go ahead. Make the call."

Lanny took out a folded sheet of paper from his pocket. It was a list of frequently dialed numbers, most of the page typed, but with some new numbers added in ink at the bottom. Lanny scanned down for a number and jabbed the digits into the buttons of the touch-tone phone.

I watched him do this, and knew that in a matter of seconds I'd discover virtually everything that was left to know of the truth . . . except perhaps whether, as has been said, the truth can sometimes hurt. Hurt enough to kill you.

THIRTY-TWO

Whether it was because the jet lag hit me on a delay (as it often does) or because I was totally exhausted from the physical and emotional marathon of the last few hours, I had—perhaps understandably—fallen asleep late in that same afternoon. I was wrapped tight in darkness, as if oblivion were an Ace bandage, both supportive yet constricting.

I heard the melodic ringing of a phone. Voices urged me to answer it, saying it might be important. But I didn't want to work for the phone company. Why would I spend each day of my life answering their phones? What were they paying me?

Of course, the moment I awoke, the phone stopped ringing. Luckily, it started again. I sat up straight and cracked my forehead yet another time against the ceiling above Beejay's loft bed. I ignored my pain and jumped down to the floor and under the elevated bed to find Beejay's Princess phone. I answered, and it was Reuben. This was fabulous. I had wondered how I might find a credible way to get him into a private setting where I could speak with him. I hadn't been relishing the idea of languishing in the produce section of my local Safeway back in L.A., waiting for the day he'd buy more tomatoes, and now here he was, calling from a pay phone literally across the street, only a few hours after I'd seen him at the Plaza. I told him I was alone and to buzz apartment 4D and I'd let him in.

It had been raining on and off, with thunder grumbling intermittently. The sun was nowhere to be seen. Reuben's golden face lit Beejay's dark New York apartment, where, on the brightest of days, sunlight could come streaming in the window if you simply moved to a different apartment across the hall. I apologized for the dinginess, advised him to duck his head, and we sat ourselves in the space beneath Beejay's bed. He eyed her beanbag chair warily and opted for the small, straight seat.

"This is wonderful that you were able to come by," I said after he'd passed on my offer of Beejay's tap water, which was so brown I could have palmed it off as iced tea. "Where does our Mr. Morris think you are?"

He told me Mr. Morris had a meeting at CBS. They were interested in a sitcom that would star him as the widowed veterinarian father to a headstrong daughter and two monkeys who had become like members of the family. They would be in negotiations until dinnertime. Lanny had instructed Reuben to "mind the store" (I pictured Reuben selling fresh produce out of his Plaza hotel room) until three, after which he had the rest of the day off. Reuben had taken a subway from Lexington and Fifty-ninth and arrived at Thirty-third Street only a few minutes later.

He asked me how my meeting with Mr. Morris had gone. I told him I'd uncovered a few things. He kept calling me Miss Trout, and I thought it was time to set him straight. He said he'd been confused because the last time we had talked, I was looking for a new job in Los Angeles, but it seemed like I had found work here in New York. He had been particularly thrown to hear me speak about my publisher being willing to pay anything to complete my book about Vince. He had known me to be a schoolteacher, and yet now I was working on something related to the late Mr. Collins . . . ?

I told him I had a confession to make and that I hoped he would still be willing to talk to me once I had told him the truth. I then related, as honestly as I could and without trying to make excuses for myself, a thumbnail history of my professional involvement with his employer and Vince Collins. (There was, of course, no need to tell him of my *personal* involvement, because he had packed Lanny's bags around my unconscious body as I'd lain in Lanny's bed at the Plaza.) To confirm that I was not some groupie who had delusions of being a writer someday, I showed him the permanent residents of my pocketbook: the letter addressed to me from Connie Wechsler on N&N stationery confirming that I'd been commissioned to write about Lanny and Vince, and my plastic sleeve of past articles and interviews. The one part of my story that sounded slightly suspect, even to me, was that my being seated near Lanny (and directly next to old Reuben himself) was pure coincidence. I pointed out that if you had been flying first-class to New York that particular day on American Airlines, the chances were not one in a million but one in four (American had four nonstops to JFK) that you'd be seated somewhere near Lanny. But Reuben seemed to accept my word at face value.

When I was done, and he had with some initial hesitancy started calling me Miss O'Connor, a mildly stricken look overtook his face. He took a deep breath and then said he had a confession of his own to make, one far more serious than the one I'd made to him. He asked me if it was true that things he said to me "off the record" could not be repeated by me. I had sometimes danced around this concept, but I felt I owed Reuben an honest answer. I told him that every journalist was their own police force as far as confidentiality was concerned, but that courts had ruled differently at different times on how much that confidentiality was protected by the First Amendment. I said that if there was anything he didn't want anyone else to know, the only way to absolutely guarantee that was to tell no one, including myself. I added truthfully that in my experience, when more than one person knew the same secret, eventually many others would.

He hesitated and then said he instinctively felt he could trust his confession with me, and that he had always tried to go with his instincts in his life, as they had rarely failed him, whereas sound logic sometimes had. Then he made a statement that would have shocked anyone who knew this reliable and gentle man. "I have consulted with two different criminal attorneys, whom I hired on my own, and without giving them any details that would implicate any other parties, they have advised me that my own actions are now legally past the statute of limitations for prosecution."

Although I already knew from reading Lanny's letter to John Hillman that Reuben was aware of Maureen O'Flaherty's murder that night, it was still eerie to hear him own up to that. I'm sure for him it was very strange to be letting light fall upon this secret that he, Lanny, and Vince had hidden away all these years. I thought it wise not to turn up the lights in Beejay's shadowy apartment, as there are some things that can only be spoken of in low tones and in the dark.

Most of what he told me was identical to Lanny's account. He'd been called by the hotel operator in his room at about ten after eight in the morning because Lanny hadn't answered his eight A.M. wake-up call. He had a key to Lanny's room, but there was a chain across the door. He banged on the door and called to Lanny, who took more than a few moments to get to the door and unchain it. While Reuben started to collect things from his employer's bathroom that Lanny might need at the telethon, Lanny called to him from the living room. He rushed in and saw Lanny trying to revive Maureen, although Reuben knew enough from his war experiences in the Philippines to assume she was already dead. Wondering if someone had broken into the suite, he looked and saw that the door to the living room was chained. He raced to Vince's room and found Vince, seemingly as dead as Maureen, passed out on the floor. The door there was chained as well.

He called for Lanny, who came in, and the two of them revived Vince. Lanny insisted that the last time he'd seen Maureen she'd been going to sleep in the living room and Vince was looking at her from the doorway of his own room. Vince himself couldn't recall anything that had happened beyond that moment. He became hysterical, and Reuben and Lanny had to literally slap him silent. They made Vince lie down, and then the two more levelheaded men decided that they had to get Maureen's body out of the suite and far away from the hotel. If either of the two performers were suspected of murder, that would be the end of the world for Reuben as well. "If one cannot be a rich man, Miss O'Connor, then the next best thing is to be a domestic servant for a rich man. You eat much the same food, you often drink the same wine, you stay in smaller rooms in the most luxurious hotels, you travel in limousines. . . . My life in the Philippines . . . you here in the United States cannot imagine what some levels of poverty are like. I could never go back to that. I would sooner die. But my only skill, my trade, is to do"—Reuben held his hands out—"what I do. I would have helped Mr. Morris and Mr. Collins out of loyalty alone. But I had a second motive that made it even more urgent for me to assist them: my own security and comfort."

I interrupted Reuben and asked him if they had thought of turning to Sally Santoro, who owned the Versailles, for help.

He shook his head gravely. "To ask for that kind of assistance from a man like Mr. Santoro, that would have been like the leader of an African tribe going to the Deep South before the Civil War and asking a plantation owner if he would employ him." He almost laughed at the image. "As it was, Mr. Morris and Mr. Collins always tried to be ahead of Mr. Santoro when it came to favors. That's why they were willing to fly up to New Jersey without taking time to rest after the telethon. What had seemed like a burden now seemed like an opportunity from heaven for both of them to establish an alibi."

It had been Reuben who had thought of using the metal locker of lobsters, crabs, and ice as a hideous coffin for Maureen's body. It was always to have been under his supervision when he moved Vince and Lanny's things from the Versailles to the Casino del Mar Hotel. It seemed incredibly providential. Reuben's wartime experience with battlefield corpses when he was a medic for the Philippine Scouts made him well aware how extreme heat or cold could confuse any efforts to establish a time of death, at least by the standards of the late fifties, and much to the advantage of the men's alibi. They hid Maureen's body under the covers of the pullout bed (which was easy to do, since it wasn't as if she was moving around) and had two bellmen bring the metal locker back up from the meat freezer, purportedly for Lanny and Vince to show to some friends. Vince being completely useless at this point, the grisly task of loading Maureen into the metal locker had fallen to Reuben and Lanny, who said that he could never eat lobster or crab again. Vince raced off to the TV studio, eager to put the suite and the Versailles and the memories he couldn't remember behind him. Lanny and Reuben resealed the locker and had it taken away to be flown up, along with Sally Santoro's other boxed gifts, to New Jersey, under the watchful eye of Reuben.

All went well up to a certain point. Reuben saw that all the men's luggage and crates were taken up to their Casino del Mar suite. They had discussed what they would do with the body once it was in New Jersey. The main thing for them was that it be found *there* rather than at the Versailles, where the boys were. It had been Reuben's hope to get Maureen's body into one of the wooden crates once they'd been emptied, and to get his brother-in-law, who lived in Park Slope and had a pickup truck that he used for his lawn-maintenance company, to help him move the crate out of the area. However, the hotel manager, one of Sally Santoro's lieutenants and eager to be of help, said that he would have some men bring the lobsters and stone crabs down to the Blue Grotto, where they could be stored in water tanks reserved just for Lanny and Vince. Reuben had only a few minutes alone in which to move Maureen and the ice into the bathroom. He then watched as the metal locker, now containing only a little ice but still bearing its fruits of the sea, was carried out of the suite. Reuben, who'd been unable to reach his brother-in-law by phone (it turned out Reuben's sister had gone into labor with a third child), found himself in the vulnerable situation of potentially being in an empty hotel room with an unexplained corpse, so he made a great show of leaving with the men, turned the keys to the suite over to the desk clerk, and rushed to Park Slope, trying to locate his brother-in-law and waiting for the shoe to drop once Vince and Lanny appeared. Since he figured the time of death would be moved to within hours of Vince and Lanny's arrival, he knew that he would be free from suspicion as long as he was seen nowhere near the hotel but rather at the hospital in Brooklyn, where he made sure his alibi was established as solidly as that of Collins and Morris.

With some shame, he told me that since he had merely helped to conceal a murder (he would not legally qualify as an accomplice, since the deed was done before his involvement), the statute of limitations on the potential charges he might have faced for his crime had long ago passed.

"Well, obviously," I said at last, in the murk of apartment 4D, "this is stunning information, Reuben, and I understand your reticence in relating it. So tell me: why *are* you telling me?"

As an answer, he leaned forward (as if there could be anyone other than the two of us in this cramped studio apartment who might hear him) and asked me how my meeting with Lanny had gone.

I told him, with complete honesty but in strict confidence, that I didn't think Mr. Morris would be in a position to employ Reuben very much longer and that I hoped Reuben had made plans for such a circumstance . . . that I suspected Mr. Morris was actually *not* at a meeting at CBS but already in hiding . . . and that my guess was Reuben should not expect to see him at the Plaza that evening or possibly ever again. And that was as true a statement as I've ever made to anyone.

He nodded and said he was not altogether surprised. He said that since Mr. Collins had decided to tell me about his life, Mr. Morris had been very concerned that some of the awful truth we'd been discussing would be uncovered—that at best both their careers would be ruined and at worst both of them might be indicted for murder. And he would no doubt have to give testimony that would verify those charges.

"I've already told you that I have some serious objections to certain aspects of my employer's personality, Miss Tr—" He corrected himself: "Miss O'Connor. Is it terrible of me to be worried not only for Mr. Morris but also for myself? If his world collapses, so will mine."

I said that his concern was only human.

I knew there was more, and it was difficult for him. At last he fumbled, "I . . . I heard you say at the hotel today that your publisher is looking for some way to add to the book you were writing. That they would pay a great deal for something that could achieve this."

I said that he had heard correctly.

"Miss O'Connor . . . I have a tape recording of the night Miss O'Flaherty was murdered."

He'd found it after Vince and Lanny had left for the telethon, in her tote bag, which she'd brought with her to their suite. It had been a little battery-powered Grundig reel-to-reel, the reels being three and a half inches wide. It had been in a tight case that kept its operation silent, and there had been a small omnidirectional mike stitched into the top of the tote bag itself. At its snail-pace slowest speed (unsuitable for music but acceptable for speech), it could get an hour's worth of conversation onto a reel.

I quickly explained to Reuben why such a tape recorder would have been standard kit for Maureen in her dual identity as Moe Cohn. He understood better. "I don't think the tape will tell you whether it was Mr. Morris or Mr. Collins who murdered her, but I've heard the tape and it will definitely tell you *why*. It will amaze you, I think. And it will also make a book that contains a transcript of the tape very, very successful." He explained that he had personally transferred the tape to the new medium of cassette but would make both versions available for Neuman and Newberry. There would have to be arrangements, of course. He couldn't just "loan" them the tape. His golden skin flushed orange at the embarrassment of discussing such things.

"Reuben," I said gently, "you were very consoling, very thoughtful to me when we met at the Safeway back in Los Angeles. Let me help you around your squeamishness by saying it for you. You quite logically think to yourself, *'Once they have the tape, what if they don't give it back, or turn it over to the police, or to a radio station that plays it and it goes into the public domain?'* Then this thing that you've saved for nearly fifteen years—for a rainy day, as it were—would be worthless to you. Understand, I can't speak for Neuman and Newberry yet, but how would something like this sound to you: we set a price for the tape. You get half up front, whereupon you give it to us. We listen to it, with you present. If it's as represented, you receive the second half then and there."

He nodded gratefully. I could have sworn there were almost tears of relief in his amber eyes. I asked him if he had any kind of ballpark figure in mind. He leaned forward modestly and asked, "Would you think . . . would you think a million dollars would be too much?"

I coughed a little. "Reuben, Reuben, listen. Vince was being paid a million dollars for his entire life. You're asking the same for an hour of it?"

Reuben nodded slowly. "The most interesting hour of his life. I've heard the tape. I assure you, this is explosive material."

I sputtered, "Well, I can try, I mean, I guess I can see . . . I mean, they're only going to have to pay Vince's estate the initial advance to use the material we *did* record, so maybe if you were to lower your price—Hey. Wait a second. There might be a way . . . Reuben, you have this tape, right?"

"Yes."

"Well, I have a transcript. At least I think I do," I said, moving to my portfolio with considerable excitement. I produced Lanny's third chapter and showed it to him. "You put all *your* cards on the table, I can return the favor. Look, your boss left this for me outside my apartment. It's his version of what happened that night. It would be amazing to put this side by side with a transcription of your tape. You understand, Reuben? On their own, these pages are absolutely useless to me. I could have typed them myself, I can't quote from them . . . *but* if they closely match what's recorded on your tape, it would make them very credible. That makes your tape even more valuable. And guess what? If the tape were to differ greatly, then that would tell us that Lanny is trying to shift the blame onto Vince. Either way, I think suddenly your tape *could* be worth a million dollars." He beamed. I added, "That makes *two* amazing things that have transpired between us today!"

"What's the other?" he asked, excited.

"You called me!" I said, elated.

He laughed back. "Yes? And?"

I looked at him. "You called me. *That's* the amazing thing. You called me from a pay phone to tell me you were across the street."

He looked mildly puzzled. "Yes?"

"But since you and Lanny left me high and dry that morning at the Plaza, Lanny has said that every time he tried to call me, this phone was disconnected. Of course, I knew it hadn't been, so I just figured he was a liar."

Reuben nodded. "I've told you about him."

"Yes, you have. But today, when I was at the hotel, I had him call Bonnie Trout. He got out a number written on a list you update for him now and then, and dialed it, and you know what? It *was* disconnected. Because it was the wrong number."

Reuben shrugged. "Then I wrote it down incorrectly. I'm very sorry."

I reached into my portfolio. "But he says you've given him the phone number several times on other pieces of paper. He told me you're his human Rolodex. Sometimes, if he doesn't have his list with him, you write the number out for him on a small piece of paper. He found this one in his wallet for me today." I showed him a folded yellow square of paper with a number in his handwriting. "Again, the wrong number."

Reuben said, "I guess I got the number wrong when I first took it down. Very bad of me."

I shook my head. "But you called me this afternoon and you got the number right."

Reuben smiled. "I'm afraid I foolishly didn't have any of my phone lists with me. I had to call Information."

"The number is unlisted, Reuben. You'd know that if you'd ever bothered to check the number, as Lanny did when he found that it was disconnected. Lanny was going to have his security people try to figure out what was wrong with Bonnie's phone, but before he got around to it, he found out I'd lied to him about my identity, and he didn't plan to speak to me ever again."

Reuben sat placidly.

I said, "You had the right number. You gave him the wrong number repeatedly. You never checked with Information to see if you had gotten the number wrong because you *wanted* the number to be wrong. The one you gave Lanny was identical to Bonnie's, except you flipped the fifth and sixth digits; that's why Lanny didn't notice the difference when he got hold of Bonnie Trout's phone records. He was only interested in *who* she had called, and when he found out it was me, he wasn't interested in calling her or me ever again. You must have dialed variations on the correct number until you found one that was nearly the same but out of service. Now, why would you have done that?"

He looked at me kindly. "Perhaps, Miss O'Connor, I just was trying to spare you some hurt and rejection. I told you how he deals with women."

"I know, and oh, how I agreed with you about how loathsome he is. But why do I have this opinion? First, because of how he depicted his behavior fifteen years ago in his mock memoirs, which I believe was for calculated effect; second, because he never called me after checking out of the Plaza, which is hardly despicable if you kept giving him a disconnected number; third, because he left me no note. Of course, Lanny said he did leave me a note explaining why he'd left and where I could reach him, either by the bed or in the living room. But in the exhausted, blissfully unconscious state I was in, it would have been the simplest thing in the world for you to take Lanny's note and pocket it while you were packing or doing a last-minute check of all the rooms before you and he left."

Reuben shook his head. "But why would I do that?"

I smiled. "Why would you give him the wrong number so he couldn't contact me? Because you were afraid of what he'd do to me? Or because you were afraid of what I might do to him . . . and you?"

Reuben got up in dismay. He walked as big a circle as a circumnavigation of the room would allow. "Oh, for goodness sake. Is this what being a journalist does to people? Makes them see conspiracies in simple mistakes or honest concern? Why would I have been afraid of a public-school teacher by the name of Trout?"

"You weren't. You were afraid of a snoopy journalist by the name of O'Connor."

He stopped dead. "*Now* you're being a foolish girl. I only learned your true name and profession just now, when I read that letter written by your publisher about you."

I got up and walked to the kitchen for a glass of brown water that I didn't want. I needed him to be on that side of the room, where there were overhead fluorescents, which I now switched on.

"No, you learned that at the Plaza when you read that letter written by my publisher about me. It was in my pocketbook there, it's always in my pocketbook, and when I woke up, my clothes and pocketbook had been lined up on the dresser for my departure, the way they line up your luggage outside the boardinghouse door when you're evicted. That's when you went through my bag. That's how you learned I was the one who was going to write about the one thing you didn't want anyone writing about: Collins and Morris. And since the letter was addressed by Connie Wechsler to me at my home address, you then knew where I lived. Which is how you were able to follow me that day to the Safeway supermarket."

Reuben laughed richly as I drew myself a nice thick glass of water. "No, *you* followed *me*!"

I raised my eyebrows at him and took a much-needed sip from my glass.

"Now, that was a very odd response, Reuben. The correct reply would have been 'We met by accident!' or 'That was sheer coincidence!' But not 'No, *you* followed *me*!' "

For the first time, he let the dark brew of his anger show. As he joined me in the kitchen area, his golden face was turning to dull copper, tarnished.

I said, "Sure, you let me think I'd spotted you. Who knows how long you followed me around the store, giving me the chance to believe I was Nancy Drew. How you must have been laughing at me! You let yourself discover me at the checkout when I'd made it humanly impossible for you to credibly ignore me any longer. But if I hadn't spotted you, I'm sure you would have bumped into my cart in the parking lot. And once I'd 'found' you, you conveyed to me your profound mortification at the treatment Lanny had given me, and *all* women . . . and I bought the big depiction of heartless Lanny, when all I really had to base it on was your word and a rejection you engineered. You made me abandon any thought of trying to contact Lanny again or of telling him who I was, you made me feel I was less than nothing to him, because you were playing your own complex game with both men, and the more I was in the picture, the more I might open up lines of communication between the two of them, talking to Vince during the day and Lanny during the night. You needed me controlled and contained."

Reuben started idly opening and closing a drawer, casting a curious eye into it. If he wanted to attack me with Beejay's boxes of Saran Wrap and aluminum foil, I'd accept that challenge. He asked slowly, "What was this complex game I was playing?"

I thought that it would be a wise idea to make a little noise, so I reached for a skillet and placed it on one of the electric burners atop Beejay's combination demi-fridge and electric stove. I turned on the burner to "high."

"You don't mind if I cook dinner while we talk, do you?" I asked. "I haven't eaten all day."

I opened a drawer and took out some oven mitts. There was a half-full bottle of Wesson oil, which Beejay had told me she had used to facilitate a variety of enterprises (the least interesting of them being frying), and I poured the remainder of the bottle into the skillet.

I turned to face Reuben. "Oh, right, you asked me what the complicated game was." The pan quickly began to crackle amid the subtle hum of undisturbed oil reaching a boil. "You were blackmailing Vince Collins with the tape you're now offering to Neuman and Newberry. You wanted a million dollars. That's why Vince needed the money."

I opened the fridge below the electric burner and rummaged around the shelves for something to fry, rejecting three Spanish olives in a jar full of brine and a souring half-full container of Light n' Lively plum yogurt.

"It would be interesting to know which Vince feared more: his sexual secret on the tape being made public, or the fact that this would have given him a motive to murder Maureen. Or the secret that *you* carried around in your head, Reuben: that both of the boys had the *opportunity* as well as the motive to kill her. And that Vince couldn't remember what he did that night. So many different secrets. With so many diverse ways to blackmail Vince, it's a wonder he didn't try to kill you."

Reuben, still trying to stay within striking distance of his public persona, and very much within striking distance of me, said, "Mr. Collins was a tragic man." He casually opened the next drawer. It held silverware, plastic knives and spoons, some short birthday-cake candles, and a few long ones in case of a blackout.

I found a box of frozen peas in the tiny freezer area of the fridge and straightened up. "Yes, he punished himself more than anyone. He tried to kill me once and couldn't do it. Did you suggest to him that he try blackmailing me into writing a puff piece?"

Reuben simply stared sullenly.

"That would have been perfect for you. He would have had the money, but the book would have been harmless, leaving you and your tape to still be the only threat. The odd thing, Reuben, is that I was both your greatest ally and enemy. My book was supplying the million that Vince would pass on to you, but if it unearthed the truth about Maureen O'Flaherty, you'd have lost your hold over him. And then, when I told him I wasn't going to knuckle under, that he'd either talk to me about that night or go home without his million—in which case you'd squeeze your million out of what money he already had, which wasn't much more than that—he could only see one certain way out of his nightmare."

I dumped the frozen peas into the fat, and the green ice pellets sizzled madly, emitting a huge cloud of blue steam. "Of course, once Vince died, you were really screwed, weren't you? You had a very tough choice to make. You weren't prepared to quit your 'day job' as valet to Lanny Morris. That was your safety net between the poverty you'd known and the luxuries you enjoyed, being in Lanny's company. You'd never overtly blackmailed Lanny about covering up Vince's crime. You'd let the rewards come voluntarily from him. First-class travel, staying in the same accommodations, dining at the same restaurants. As long as you showed loyalty, it was hard to know who had the better life: lord or master. If you tried to blackmail Lanny, that could all end, and yet the tape wasn't as damning to him as it had been to Vince.

"And then you realized there was one other player who might cough up the same kind of money you were trying to squeeze out of poor Vince Collins. Myself, funded by Neuman and Newberry. How foolish you'd been to try to get the money from Vince when it was N&N's money you were after all along. When you heard me say today, as I meant you to hear, that my publisher would pay anything for something like your tape—oh, Lordy, what music that must have been to your ears."

The french-fried peas had settled down into a slow, spattering sizzle. My hand was very near the pan's handle, just in case.

Reuben said, "So you knew I had this tape when you were at the Plaza this morning?"

"I thought Maureen's confident statement that she could make a private incident—one that both Vince and Lanny would certainly deny—'stick' meant that she must have had some form of proof. The fact that she took her tote bag into Lanny's room when she had no need for it there made me wonder what might be in it. And her threat that the world would *hear* the dulcet tones of Vince Collins crooning his swan song sounded suspiciously like she was referring to a recording. But all these ideas coalesced in my mind when I made the most fascinating discovery of them all."

I walked back to the area by the loft bed and picked up Lanny's third chapter. To mollify Reuben, I assured him, "If you detect any hostility in my tone, please don't let that discourage you. I still think your tape will be very valuable, and I've never let my personal feelings stand in the way of a good story."

Reuben took this as reassuring news and joined me. "I think you have misunderstood many things, but hopefully, in time, you'll find you were wrong about me."

I thumbed through the pages. "Look, you may have caused my life a little misery, and you caused Vince enough that he killed himself . . . but here's where I realized you were a true Renaissance man." Reuben was not altogether displeased with this characterization. "Now, if we assume, as your first glance at this document seemed to verify, that Lanny's account of what happened that night is pretty accurate—" I looked at him for verification.

Reuben nodded. "From a quick look, they're consistent."

I said, "Okay, Lanny has just come out of the shower and he's going to offer Maureen his robe in case she's a little bashful, and he says, *'I look through the door of my bedroom and see she's already stark naked and on top of Vince. So much for bashful! I threw the robe on the bed and ran into the room, half-worried they'd finish without me.'* Eager little fellow."

Reuben chuckled.

I continued, "Now, after the fiasco in the living room, Lanny is going to go back into his bedroom to give Maureen her three hundred dollars. He wrote:

"'I walked over to my bedroom door and told her, "In here." She got the tote bag she'd brought with her and followed me into the room. I shut the door behind us. My wallet was on the dresser atop my silk robe, and I withdrew three one-hundred-dollar bills and tossed them onto my bed, which is how you're supposed to pay whores.

"'She looked at me with an amused expression. I suddenly felt as bothered by my nakedness in front of her as in front of Vince. I unfurled the folds from my robe and wrapped it around me quickly, tying its sash in a huff. She was laughing at me.'"

I stopped reading and looked at Reuben, who shrugged and said, "So?"

I closed the portfolio. "Pretty cool robe Lanny had there. Throws it on his bed, and when he comes back into the room fifteen minutes later, it's folded on the dresser and his wallet is on top of it."

Reuben moved toward me. "Let me see that for myself," he said, looking puzzled. I retrieved the document and handed it to him. He stepped to the kitchen to see it in the light. Suddenly he produced his lighter, as he always did so smoothly for Lanny, lit the corner of the pages, and tossed them into the french-fried peas. The crazed oil ignited itself and billowed high and white, engulfing the pages in a flare-up that smelled like nothing I'd ever encountered before. It's a good thing the landlord had been smart enough never to install smoke detectors or the whole building would have been on alert. After a moment, the document had turned to fatty ash and Reuben transferred the pan to the sink, turning on the faucet so the pan smoked itself out. He didn't seem to mind the momentary heat of the handle.

I sighed. "A shame that you would burn that letter, Reuben, when you went to the risk of stealing it from your employer's files and making a copy for yourself. Those dramatic words at the start of the letter—'only after the death of Lanny Morris'—must have made it tempting reading. And then you were thoughtful enough to get a copy to me, because it made your tape a much easier sell if I was already aware of the secret it contained. I bet Lanny's letter spells out what happened much more clearly than the muffled sound on that old tape. But equipped with the former, one could easily understand the significance of the latter. By the way, the copy you burned is a Xerox of a Xerox."

Reuben now headed toward me, making no illusion of his attitude. I backed up a bit and found my head against the edge of the loft bed. I moved around in the opposite direction. I needed him facing me this way.

"So this is how I have it figured, Reuben, and you tell me if I'm wrong. You had let yourself into Lanny's room, as you always did, to clean up and make his room ready for when he turned in. You had just folded his robe and put his wallet on top of it when you heard the fascinating activity in the living room, so you monitored the drama through the open door. When you heard Lanny coming toward the bedroom, you hid in the bathroom and overheard what serious danger the team of Collins and

Morris was in. You stayed in the bathroom while Lanny put the chain across his door and fell into bed.

"Sleep came fast and heavy to Vince, Maureen, and Lanny. You sat there in the dark of the bathroom and realized that this could be the end of everything. Either Maureen would bleed the team dry or she'd go public with what she knew, spiraling them into oblivion. Either way, Collins and Morris were on the verge of ruin . . . and if *they* were ruined, where would that leave you?"

I stared at him coldly. Now there were no illusions on either side. "The only question in my mind, Reuben, is whether you found the tape recorder before or after you killed Maureen. Any hints?"

Reuben just glared at me as if I were a plump priest saying grace at a cannibal luau.

"No? Well, my guess is that you found it first. With the amount of drugs in the three of them, you could have held a Led Zeppelin concert in that living room and not awakened them. We already have a working postulate that you search women's handbags as a reflex. Your first concern may have been protecting your world by silencing Maureen, but when you saw that tape recorder and realized what must be on it, the late Miss O'Flaherty was as good as consigned to the angels, may she rest in peace. For you realized that while she might have the upper hand at that moment, once she was dead *you* would be the one with the tape, *you* would be the one with the upper hand.

"Surely no murder could have been easier to commit. Your victim was in a deep sleep, bordering on a stupor. There was a pillow right there. You held it over her face. She may not have even struggled. And she was gone. There went her ambition, and Moe Cohn's very existence, and Kef Ludlow's dreams, and her mother's heart, and her father's mind. And ultimately, Vince's life. Not bad, Reuben. Six with one blow."

Reuben was tensing himself now. It would happen any second. He asked, "How could I have killed her if all three doors were chained? You'll have to tell me that."

I moved closer to him. If he tried to kill me, it would confirm for me everything I was saying. A signed confession to the police would have been nicer, but it was never going to come to that.

"After you murdered Maureen, you left the suite by Vince's room, knowing that Lanny's door and the living-room door were already chained.

You knew when you left that the boys weren't going to wake up at eight A.M. without your help. In the morning, you banged on Lanny's door, telling him you couldn't let yourself in with your duplicate key because his bedroom door was chained from the inside. When you followed him into the living room, again, you made sure he'd seen that the door there was chained as well. While Lanny tried to revive Maureen, you ran into Vince's room alone. Vince was still lying unconscious on the floor, where you'd walked over him to leave only a few hours earlier. The first thing you did when you entered the room was to fasten the chain. Then you called for Lanny, who found you bent over Vince's body, and who saw that Vince's door was also chained from the inside."

"Now you had the tape, which you'd taken with you after you'd murdered Maureen. You had the goods on Lanny and Vince in many different ways. And so then you merely lived the not-very-unpleasant life of Lanny's valet as you let the years tick by, taking you past the statute of limitations for the help you 'loyally' gave Vince and Lanny to cover up the murder that *you* committed. You let both of those men believe for all those years that one or the other had killed Maureen O'Flaherty. Vince Collins lay in that tub, slipping toward a lonely, stupefied death, believing into oblivion that he had committed murder. May you rot in Hell, Reuben."

"Why don't you get there ahead of me and do my unpacking?" he suggested. He drew himself up to his full height and oh, I was sore afraid. "So you were lying to me when you said Mr. Morris wouldn't be in a position to employ me, that I wouldn't see him at the Plaza ever again, and that you thought he might already be in hiding. You said that to make me drop my guard?"

"No, I was being very honest with you. He won't be in a position to employ you because you won't be free to work for a living. You won't see him at the Plaza ever again because you're not going back there again. As for him being in hiding—" Reuben grabbed my throat with both hands. Although not as strong as Vince, he was not as conflicted about his intentions.

But it had been foolish of him to interrupt me, because I'd just been about to tell him that Lanny Morris was *already* in hiding, under a sheet in the shadows at the back of Beejay's loft bed, where we had only just finished making spectacular love twenty minutes before Reuben woke us from the contented sleep we'd been sharing. Although Lanny's legs had gone to sleep from lying still for so long (I'd tried to make some noise at the stove to let him stir a bit, as well as to draw Reuben's attention away from the loft bed), Lanny was able to hit Reuben hard (though not as hard as Lanny would have liked) with the steel bar that Beejay kept in her bed.

When Reuben came to, he found himself tied up in the bathtub with wet "rope" made from torn bedsheets. He could barely breathe through the gag in his mouth and, you know, we really weren't all that worried about it. Neither Reuben, Lanny, nor I were one hundred percent clean. The difference was, neither Lanny nor I had ever killed anyone. We thought that was enough of a difference.

We could discern from Reuben's cries that he wanted a lawyer.

Lanny said, "Why would you need a lawyer, Reuben? It's not like you're going to be arrested or tried or convicted or paroled. Relax. You don't need a lawyer."

Lanny then dialed a number he hadn't called in many years. It was a New Jersey area code, and it must have been an extremely private number because Sally Santoro answered himself. Lanny made sure Reuben could hear him clearly.

"Sally. It's Lanny Morris. Can we talk on this line? Okay, look, you know fifteen years now, I don't think I've ever come to you and asked for a favor. Thank you. Well, I'm in Manhattan, and I have a package that I could use the Lattanzi Brothers' help with. What? Good question, hold on." Lanny called out to Reuben, "Hey, Reuben, Sally wants to know if this is temporary storage or final disposal. What do you think?"

Reuben, who'd heard about the trucks at the Casino del Mar that used to take passengers on two-way and one-way excursions to the Lattanzis' landfill, screamed a terrible "Noooooooooooooo!" from behind the gag.

Lanny looked at me for my opinion. I had no idea what to tell him. I was busy trying to clean up Beejay's sink before she got home. I felt just awful about the mess.

Lanny got back on the line with Sally. "Well, I'll tell you, Sally, it's a tough call. You see, this package blackmailed my partner, Vince. Yeah, your Vince, our Vince. That's the reason Vince felt he had to end things." Lanny listened to Sally for a moment. He had to strain to hear him, and my research had told me that the more softly Sally spoke, the more dangerous he was. "Well, yes, I understand," Lanny responded to the almost inaudible voice. "And this is also the package that murdered Maureen

O'Flaherty at the Versailles. Yes, that redhead. Well, the package brought her body up to New Jersey, which, as you'll remember, ruined the grand opening of your new hotel. For which you and I and Vince worked so hard. Yes, Sally, I'm sorry, what?"

He looked at me. "The connection must be bad, I can barely hear him." Lanny put the phone back to his ear but stared at Reuben as he continued: "What's that? I don't know, Sally, you've always been a fair man. Why don't I just leave it up to you?"

THIRTY-THREE

She and I sat peacefully in the backyard together, with unhurried silences between our spoken thoughts. The peach tree was empty, but its leaves were still green. Her long, pointless harvest was over for the year. The fruits were all resting in comfort near the tree that had given them life. The summer was almost over.

I had told her, "Your daughter learned something about Vince Collins that he didn't want anyone to know. Because of that, she was killed. If it's of any small comfort, she probably didn't suffer at all."

"Except in that she didn't get to live the rest of her life," said her mother softly.

I nodded, corrected.

She went on, granite entering her voice: "I want the person who killed her to be punished."

I paused, allowing the hesitation to assist me in a deception. "Vince Collins is dead. He committed suicide." I looked at her meaningfully and permitted her to misunderstand me.

"Then he was the one who killed her?"

Again I paused. "He could outrun what happened that night for only so long. If you want someone to suffer for your daughter's death, it might help you to think of him these last fifteen years as a man on death row who fights his execution every way he knows how, delaying it without there being any real hope of a retrial or reversal. A stay of sentence is not the same thing as being free."

She rose from her chair. "I want people to know about this man. I want them to know what he did."

I didn't rise with her but took her hand and gently pulled her back down into her seat. I continued to hold her hand. "Do you trust me?" I asked. She foolishly nodded assent. "There is someone in all this who is totally innocent of any involvement in the events of that night but whose life will be made infinitely worse if I tell the truth at this time. I want to protect this person from any further pain. They've suffered so greatly already. I promise you I will write down now the truth that I've learned, but I have to let matters lie until this person has died and the truth can no longer touch them." I saw no indication in her face that she knew I was talking about her.

"But you promise that someday you'll let people know what happened?"

I stood. "Yes. Once no one else who's innocent can be hurt any further. Can you understand my wanting it that way, having felt so much pain in your own life? When I was a girl, I was told, 'The truth never hurt anyone.' But I don't think that's the way it is, Mrs. O'Flaherty. I think a lot of the time the truth can hurt everyone."

She opened the side gate for me and looked at me almost fearfully. "Did my daughter . . . did she do anything— I guess what I'm asking is, did she deserve what happened to her?"

I looked back at her with what I hoped was the reassuring conviction of a successful, sinful evangelist. "Your daughter was a wonderful, moral girl who did no one any harm, any harm in the world. You have my word on that, Mrs. O'Flaherty, and you can believe it. You can sleep well tonight in the knowledge that your daughter is with the angels."

Her face had life in it for the first time since I had met her. "You swear that to me, Miss O'Connor?"

I placed my hands on her shoulders. "I swear that to you on my mother's grave." I didn't think my mother would mind my saying this. She wasn't dead yet.

The mother of Maureen Beatrice Margaret Cohan O'Flaherty

searched every corner of my face. I let her do so like a Victorian virgin allowing her husband to touch every inch of her on their wedding night. I was confident she would find no lie anywhere. I had now learned not to care one flying fuck about the truth.

She drew back, satisfied, looking as close to contented as she was ever likely to be. "You've been very good to me. And my daughter. Thank you."

"You're welcome, Mrs. O'Flaherty."

I stepped away from her house and, reaching the sidewalk, turned as if to walk into town.

After two blocks, I made a right and found Lanny where I had left him, parked in the car that had been driven up to the steps of the Plaza for us after we'd had eggs Benedict as appetizer to a multiorgasmic Boff Royale. He had managed (he could manage anything, I suppose) to rent a 1960 Corvette, not the trendy new Stingray but the original *Route 66* red convertible with cream-white top, those rakish side scoops with three vents for deep breathing, black interior, ballsy tube radio, 283 dual quad, and two hundred and seventy of the nicest horsepowers you'd ever want to know.

Lanny was half-dozing, a small straw hat covering his face. The car radio was playing classical music, something stormy and full of hot air—Richard Strauss was my guess. Strauss would have been insulted to hear his grand finale played at such a low volume. I got in the car.

Lanny straightened up and started the engine. "How did it go?" he asked.

"It went well, considering," I said. I pushed a button on the radio, which slid the tuner's upright pointer to an oldies station. We joined "Come Softly to Me" (and if ever there was an oxymoronic sexual command, surely it was that) by the Fleetwoods, already in progress. It was smooth and dreamy, as was our comfort with each other.

"Where to now?" he asked me.

"Anywhere."

He thought. "South Carolina?"

"What's in South Carolina?" I asked him.

"I have absolutely no idea."

I nodded. "Sounds great to me," and before the words were out of my mouth, he had *pow-pow-pow*ed our car away from the sidewalk.

Now. Of the others. You will either half-forgive me or half-damn me when I tell you that, through Lanny's intervention and my own, Reuben was not killed by Sally Santoro. Yes, he was taken by truck to the landfill, and he was forced to experience the deaths of his victims in ways even an unfeeling man could feel, but he was not killed. Reuben now lives (and he has no choice about this) back home. The Philippines have seven thousand islands and Reuben is on one of them, not even remotely close to Manila or his family. Our last report was that he is working as the lead buff-and-shine man at a carwash outside of Calbayog. We can only hope this is true.

A Lanny's Club for the treatment of young burn victims now exists in New Rochelle. Not that this in any way compensates, but it bears the name "The Maureen Cohan O'Flaherty Wing" of New Rochelle Central Hospital. Maureen's mother lived to be at its dedication and worked there as a volunteer six days out of seven virtually every week.

Perhaps the greatest tragedy is that the very secrets that led Vince Collins to commit suicide would, in our slightly more enlightened times, now be completely irrelevant. The duo might even have been able to incorporate Vince's bisexuality into the text of their humor. It would be as if Lanny had killed himself simply because someone found out that he was Jewish. Though no consolation to our tortured friend, Vince's recordings are as popular as ever on CD, and his voice is heard as source music in many a period motion picture. The movies of Collins and Morris have been rediscovered by a lucky generation that is getting to see them fresh, for the first time.

In addition to Mrs. O'Flaherty, Lanny was the other person I didn't want to be harmed by the truth, and thus my second reason for not wanting this story to be told until after someone's death. It wasn't that he had done anything in this accounting that he would have disclaimed or been ashamed of. It was simply that he had many more years left in him of amusing and diverting people, even after his work in film, as both an actor and director, became somewhat more serious. I didn't want the sordid aspects of this story to in any way confuse or cloud anyone's perception of his work, which continued productively for many years.

It's vital to our survival that there be people capable of amusing us and diverting us from the truth now and then. Lanny continued to have that ability virtually until the day of his death, an event that saddened the world almost as much as it devastated me.

Work being the best antidote to sorrow—as Sherlock Holmes once advised his Watson—I quickly set about organizing all that I've shared with you here.

It was, of course, particularly easy for me to access the chapters from Lanny's intentionally incomplete autobiography, as the court had appointed me the sole and undisputed administrator of his estate, as is generally the case for an author's widow.

ACKNOWLEDGMENTS

This book exists because of my editor, Jon Karp.

He inspired, encouraged, cajoled, guided, honed, and "homed" these pages into whatever life they now live. He's also a wonderful writer and a glorious librettist, which has made his compliments only more meaningful to me. I don't know what I ever did to deserve such a noble ally, but he owns deed and title to my lifelong (and clearly inexpressible) thanks.

I'm deeply grateful to all at Random House for their patience, support, and enthusiasm while I stretched out the writing of this book over many years. Benjamin Dreyer, my production editor, and Bonnie Thompson, my copy editor, did their jobs not only adroitly but cleverly as well. I'm immensely thankful for (and in awe of) the craft they ply.

Working with Heather Schroder, my literary agent at ICM, has never been anything less than an absolute pleasure. Interacting with her astute mind and vivacious personality has been not only invaluable, but a true delight all along the way.

Before anyone sees or hears anything I create, it's first auditioned, screened, sent back to the shop, cautioned, trimmed, aided, abetted, advised, and amended by my closest associate and beloved friend Teressa Esposito, whose memorable voice has been heard, both figuratively and literally, in virtually all of my work for the last ten years. I could not have written this book, nor much of anything else, without her. Thank you ever and always, Teressa.

Charles Dickens once said that he had in his heart of hearts a favorite child whose name was David Copperfield. I, too, have favorite children. Their names are Wendy, Nick, and Tim.

My daughter, Wendy, died at the age of ten. I miss her every day of my life, and the enduring memory of her goodness and grace has become what passes for my conscience. She was a beautiful, brilliant, gentle girl who was entitled to a lifetime.

My younger son, Tim, carries the weight of autism with literally unspeakable courage. I live and long for the day when he can talk to me and tell me what he has been feeling all these years. Until then, I treasure his smiles, I hold him, I wait.

My older son, Nick, was born after Wendy died, and did nothing less than save his parents' lives. He gave us hope. He is a very funny and feeling and strong young man. I'm incredibly lucky and proud to be his father. Every page in this book represents an hour I couldn't spend with him, for which I can only ask his understanding and forgiveness.

This book is dedicated to these children whom I so love, and particularly to the woman who is their mother and my wife, whom I've loved since and until forever.

About the Author

For his Broadway musical *The Mystery of Edwin Drood,* RUPERT HOLMES became the first person in theatrical history to solely receive Tony Awards for Best Book, Best Music, and Best Lyrics, while *Drood* itself won the Tony Award for Best Musical. The Mystery Writers of America gave Holmes their coveted Edgar Award for his Broadway comedy-thriller *Accomplice,* the second time he received their highest honor. He created and wrote all four seasons of the critically acclaimed Emmy Award–winning series *Remember WENN,* and most recently authored the Broadway play *Say Goodnight, Gracie,* based on the life of George Burns. Holmes began his career in the seventies as the writer and composer of story songs, some so intricate they've been included in several hardcover and softcover mystery collections from Ellery Queen. *Where the Truth Lies* is his first novel.